*Naima,
Enjoy!
Roslyn*

ENDSONG

by

Roslyn Renwick

First published in Great Britain as a softback original in 2017

Copyright © Roslyn Renwick

The moral right of this author has been asserted.

All characters and events in this publication, other than those clearly in the public domain, are fictitious and any resemblance to real persons, living or dead, is purely coincidental.

All rights reserved.

No part of this publication may be reproduced, stored in a retrieval system, or transmitted, in any form or by any means, without the prior permission in writing of the author, nor be otherwise circulated in any form of binding or cover other than that in which it is published and without a similar condition including this condition being imposed on the subsequent purchaser.

Typeset in Garamond

Editing and typesetting by UK Book Publishing

www.ukbookpublishing.com

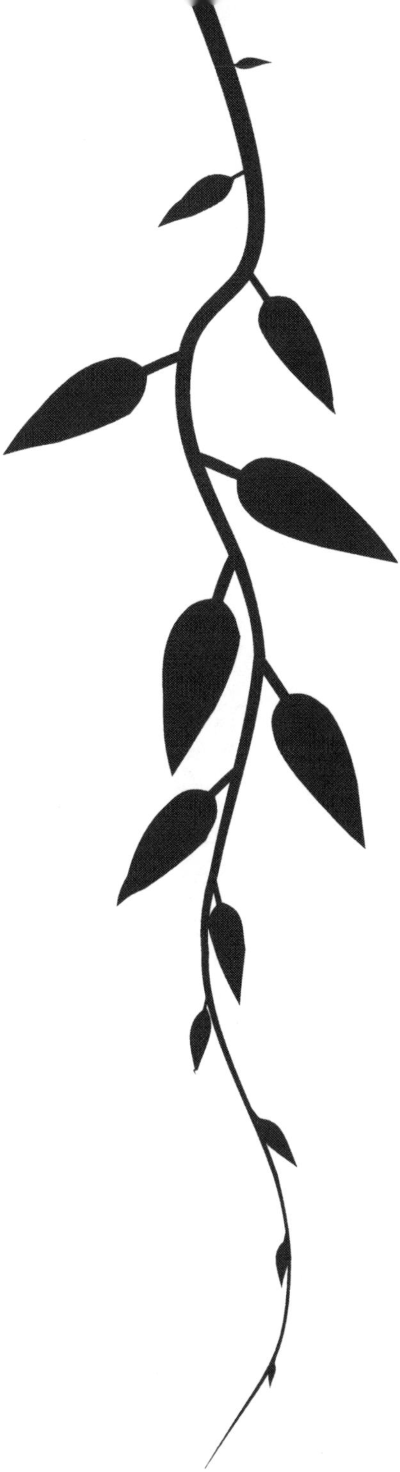

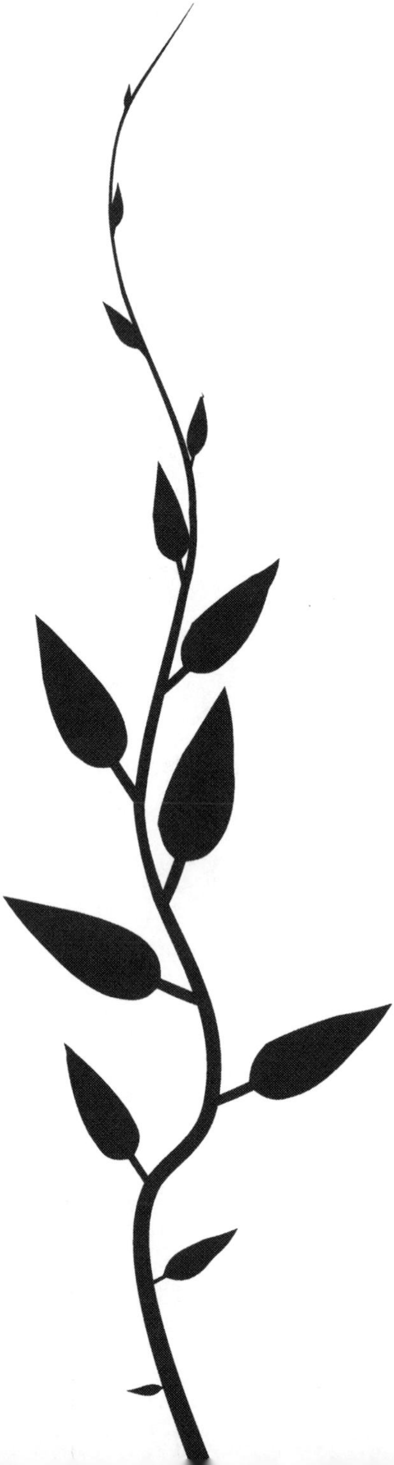

CHAPTER 1

Rhea woke up with a start. It was dark. The silence was only broken by the sound of her own breathing.

She couldn't move. She tried, but her body just didn't want to respond. She wasn't in pain, yet somewhere in her woozy mind she aware she should be, was aware that she was injured.

She was in a bed. Even without moving or looking, she knew it wasn't a hospital bed. If she wasn't in hospital, then where was she and how had she got here? More to the point, who had brought her here and why? She could make no sense of it, but she had to, or panic would take over.

'Start at the beginning,' The thought jolted through her like a defibrillator, leaving her no other option but to obey.

Just a few days ago, life had been safe, ordinary, and the only problem she'd had was trying to explain to her friend Laura why she was following up her innocent and perfectly harmless aspiration.

"You know when you walk down the same street you've always done, but you suddenly notice all this stuff that's always been there that you'd never noticed?" Rhea said, struggling to justify her latest wildlife interest to her baffled friend.

She searched Laura's face for an understanding that never came. Instead, she saw Laura Watson sitting on her bargain leather sofa (just paid off) in the tiny living room of her housing association flat (which she hoped some day to buy a share of) in front of her latest acquisition of which she was hugely proud (a large smart T.V.), and felt maybe just a little crazy for not doing the same.

"Naah, that's you all over. Notice nowt me…too busy workin and keepin this place goin for me an little Colin," Laura said cheerily, getting up to usher Rhea out. "Anyway, I thought bird watchin was for blokes."

Rhea laughed, now more at ease.

"It's not just birds, its…well… a conservation club. You know? Nature study things. Anyway, Jack likes all this stuff, so it means she doesn't think her mum is a complete dunce."

Laura opened the door, her face as kindly as ever.

"Yeah, okay. See you at the school gates tomorrow, but save some energy for Saturday night. There's goin to be a good crowd in and that George likes you," she said, giving Rhea an affectionate nudge.

Rhea just managed to grin in semblance of delight, covering both the sinking feeling she'd got at the prospect of the night, especially with the handsome, but as only she had seemed to notice, slurring George, and the surprise she'd felt at her own reaction.

As she hurried down the road towards the conservation site, wondering what was wrong with her for not finding these perfectly normal, ordinary delights appealing, she took no notice of the heaviness in the air that caused the birds to chitter nervously. She took no notice of the be-suited young men with their identical old fashioned haircuts, and demurely dressed young women, all with their frighteningly identical shiny-eyed smiles, filing into the evening service of the building that served as their church. She took no notice of the fiery-eyed young men dressed in the tribal garb of a foreign land that they saw as their future, but which she thought of as "in the long gone prehistoric past." She took no notice as they huddled together at the door of their meeting hall, and, like their shiny eyed counterparts, talked earnestly of a disturbingly archaic tribal version of righteousness that would put right the ills of the world. She took no notice of the news headlines flickering on the new public information screen by the shops, declaring "Climate Change a Myth?" "No to Terrorism." and, "Increase In Illness Despite wealth. New Pandemic Feared This Winter."

She wasn't blind. She knew they were there. It was simply that she never took any notice. No one did. It was none of their business, unless they were specialists such as: celebrities, politicians, journalists or police officers. These things were for the news, to be tutted at of an evening as a kind of entertainment after the realities of normal, ordinary life, like: breadwinning, shopping, cleaning, sorting out the kids, and maybe a little lovemaking with the significant other. In short, the headlines were simply what made up the backdrop to life in the suburbs of a modern city.

What she did notice with relief, was that it wasn't raining. Then she continued her current preoccupation of trying to see things from her friend's point of view.

'Okay, it's true, George is sort of a catch, as Laura keeps reminding me,' she thought grudgingly. He was good looking and there was no harm in him, well, no intentional harm. But he wasn't for

her. Anyway, she'd already learned what devastation the likes of George could do.

A flashback of her short and damaging marriage made her shudder.

Dave, her ex husband, was a bright, happy-go-lucky chap with a good job, who loved company. However, she had soon discovered he liked a pint or five just as much.

And yes, he had an open handed generosity to all and sundry. He'd even bring mates home to supper but, as she found out all too painfully, she wasn't included in all and sundry. He just expected she would provide on demand, like she'd become his stand-in mother, while her dreams were dismissed as unrealistic and childish.

That pain was long gone, but she was damned if she was going to be caught out like that again. Certainly not by the likes of George. *'A catch?'* she thought bitterly. *'Well it's not for me.'*

She'd once tried to make friends with George, more for Laura's sake than anything else, talked to him about how she felt there was a whole world out there and she wanted to know about it. But he'd simply dismissed this, and let slip his true miserable self, telling her there was nothing you could do about it, so you might as well ignore it, enjoy yourself and have another drink.

'You do that George, I'm off,' she thought, as she anticipated her evening's eccentric solitary pleasure.

She smiled up at the still light, clear blue evening sky, and felt that same thrill of excitement she'd felt when she had played truant from school in order to go daydreaming in Mrs Johnson's overgrown garden. It was a beautiful evening and it was all hers.

She had been due to team up with someone else to do a survey of wildlife on the derelict land around the old lorry park

CHAPTER 1

by the railway. The conservation club had a rule about going around in pairs for safety's sake, especially in the evening. She'd been teamed with nerdy shy Paul, the one person she'd have felt relatively at ease with, but he hadn't come to pick her up. She'd left messages, then gave up on him rather quickly. She was glad. She hadn't fancied sharing her secret garden with anyone. It would have put paid to any chance of a daydreaming fantasy adventure.

She did like them, the conservation club folk. Admired them really, but she knew she wasn't one of them. They were all confident middle class types, bright as buttons, and right on with their green politics.

She would listen with awe as they discussed, eyes shining with zeal, the coming end of the world as they knew it, and how the blame had to be laid at the door of their own society's misguided ways as it used up and polluted this green paradise to support their profligate lifestyle.

They were more than ready to spread the word, change the world, but first they had to collect the data and save the innocent bats, badgers and foxes. Although Rhea didn't enquire too closely about what they did privately to the rats, mice, spiders or beetles which attempted to invade their homes. She did, however, wonder what the moral thing to do was, concerning the above.

The club members were kind to her, especially when they discovered how good she was at keeping the paperwork straight.

Rhea sat on a log in her little would-be wood, letting out a sigh of contentment. She sank gratefully into contemplation of her surroundings in the gathering dusk of an early summer's evening. She knew it wasn't a place of orthodox beauty. It was just a piece of rough ground really. Once, it had been an optimistic scheme of workshops and factories, but the buildings had been abandoned years ago and finally collapsed, exhausted from holding their stiff straight lines. She smiled appreciatively. The bushes and trees had taken their exuberant dance of life through the broken fences and tumbled walls, till all artifice, all signs of human activity were hidden, taken back into this tiny patch of would-be ancient woodland, *her* ancient woodland. For nature, it was that easy.

She riffled delightedly through her bag, laying out pens, clipboard and notes. This was now a secret sanctuary for birds, beetles, bright fairy like butterflies, mice, bats, a hedgehog, maybe a rabbit or two, and even a fox. It was a little island of the wild joined to the causeway of green verge fringing the road side that reached out through a treacherous sea of concrete and tarmac, to the real land, the countryside beyond. Rhea wanted to believe it would always be here for all those ordinary city people of the future, who wanted to daydream in green leafy surroundings just like she did. Still, she'd wished she'd had someone to share it with.

As she gazed about, she noticed a tall, vaguely man-shaped shadow had formed from the shade of a young sycamore. She studied it for a moment. Laura would have immediately thought it a sinister ghost but since she couldn't have the real thing, her imagination lighted enthusiastically upon the possibility of shaping it into a sympathetic fantasy companion.

"Hi. You're not from around here are you?" she said amicably. "Nice evening for studying the wildlife though."

A slight breeze moved the branches, making the shadow appear to tip his head in acknowledgement, delighting her.

'*Well, you're a lot more forthcoming than the silent Paul, and a lot less irritating than the handsome George,*' she thought wryly, so glad to be relieved of the pressure to entertain unsuitable companions. Then she smiled at herself, musing on her supposed childish inclination to daydream.

Images of her daughter Jack and her friends, acting out fairy tales in the long grass, glowed warmly in her thoughts. Children were like that. They could escape into the worlds of the imagination and then come back to the everyday, to land as deftly as one of those fairy folk they were so fond of. Adults didn't find it so easy. She grinned mischievously. Why should you stop when you reached a certain age? There was nothing wrong with a little bit of harmless escapism.

She looked about her patch of scrub and sighed happily. Tonight, it would be her magical wood, and this shadow would be the sprite who looked after it.

"Are you doing a survey of human activity?"

She gave a chuckle at her own joke and watched the shadow tip his head again in seemingly friendly response.

"Go on then, catalogue me. Homo sapiens, female, studying her environment. Activity category? Excuse for sheer pleasure. And what's wrong with that?" she chirped, before sighing sadly as the anxious, guilt ridden chatter of the conservation club came back to her. "Yeah, but don't tell the club members though."

She stuck her chin out in defiance.

"That's what's wrong with our world. All this guilt over enjoying ourselves. That's how we mess things up. If we could all relax, take time to really appreciate, enjoy, then the world would be a kinder, safer place for all the creatures in it."

She shrugged her acknowledgement of her own shortcomings.

"But... this is the nearest I get at the moment," she pointed out, and picked up her clipboard.

After happily ticking a few boxes, she watched in delight as a solitary bat flittered by in jagged chevrons above her, and found the urge to drift back into daydream mode impossible to resist. Unable to keep her mind on the job in hand, she abandoned the clipboard.

The earthy air eased off the overcoat of Rhea's everyday rationality, and ushered her into a timeless meeting ground of the imagination where, dressed in starlight, she was greeted by the spirit of the trees.

She dreamed of timeless inhabitants of timeless woods, dancing with the pure joy of being, spiralling up into the air on velvet wings. She smiled. Jack would be proud of her fantasising abilities. She looked up at the shadow, which now, since the fading of the light, was no more than a thickening of air. In her mind's eye, it grew denser and began to take a more defined shape

She smiled as her imaginary wood sprite gazed down on her with strange but friendly eyes set in a fearsome, darkly ruddy face, framed by a mop of black curls. He shifted, sinewy and strong as a wild animal, and as graceful as a cat.

"You're kind and playful. You understand and love these little green spaces don't you?" she murmured to herself.

"You're my wood sprite, okay? Even if I know you're just a shadow. Still, I wish you could keep an eye on these little wild things," she murmured sadly.

"They don't have much of a life on this side do they?"

Did the shadow move in acknowledgement? She was almost certain it did, despite the still air.

Reluctantly, she roused herself and, looking at her watch, she murmured her farewells to the bats, beetles and moths.

CHAPTER 1

Quietly, she slipped away into the darkness to emerge onto the street, unlooked at and unseen as an anoraked housewife coming home from the club.

As she came within reach of her door, she fussed in her bag for her key before noticing the bin on the corner of the building.

'Can't remember moving that,' she thought briefly as she clattered into her hall. Her dreamy mood came to an abrupt halt and she shrank back.

The expected welcome wasn't there. She switched on the light. Something in the hallway had niggled at her senses, slipping out of her line of perception. Every hair on her body tickled with alarm. Her nerves screamed.

All was neat and clean, but the whole house seemed to be holding its breath, awaiting noisy revelations.

Silently, she eased open the hall cupboard and slid out her broom, gripping it like a quarter staff, ready to defend herself. She stood still, unable even to take a breath, listening for voices, soft creeping footsteps, any sound signifying intruders. Everything was still, silent.

She stepped forward boldly, against the resistance of her screaming intuition, and opened the door of her living room, surveying it minutely. It was tidy, not the upended wreck burglars would have left. The pressure built up unbearably, preventing her from stepping into the room, preventing her looking behind the door. She steeled herself, and stared into the room again. No, something did not look right. Suddenly, she obeyed her screaming nerves, and fled, slamming the door. Terrified of being followed, she scooted silently off down between bins and shadows, all the way to the safety of her friend Laura's, a few streets away.

"I'm sorry to wake you, I..."

"whatssamatter? Oh my god, you look awful, what's happened?" Laura interrupted, blinking at her sleepily, anxiety beginning to rouse her.

Rhea was in, closed the door, and was halfway towards the phone before she answered.

"Dunno yet, but I think I've disturbed burglars. Can I use your phone?"

In dumb shock, Laura indicated the telephone, trying to get her sleepy brain into gear.

Rhea pounced on it, ringing the police.

"...No, I'm at a neighbour's house. 25, Woodland road, that's right. Yes, I think they're still there. Just now, a few minutes ago. Look, I'm really frightened. We're two women alone and we've got kids. Can you get someone to come out now and check? ten minutes? Okay."

Laura was rooted to the spot in fright.

"Burglars? Really?"

Rhea sat down, hugging herself.

"The police won't be long,"

The sight of Rhea looking so pathetic galvanised Laura, and she hurried forward to give her a hug.

"I'll put the kettle on," she said, as much to calm her own nerves as Rhea's.

Two police officers arrived within minutes and took Rhea home to check her house out. PC James McCardle took Rhea's keys from her trembling hands, while his partner treated her to a professional smile of assurance.

"Its alright, we'll check the house inside before we go, but we found nothing outside," the other PC said in that smooth, routine manner that police officers hope will reassure and satisfy the unnecessarily anxious.

PC James McCardle strode into Rhea's house, scanning the scene with a cool, expert eye. As he walked through the hall, a faint incongruous smell slipped past him like a guilty shadow. He turned his head trying to locate it but it was gone, so he made for the living room.

"Hmm, tidy, no one here. Caron?" he queried, "Upstairs?"

His colleague nodded, giving him a knowing smile, then scanned the rooms upstairs in seconds flat before she clattered back downstairs.

"Dunno how this one got past the control room," she muttered conspiratorially to him before turning and beaming at Rhea, who had just crept nervously into the hall.

"All clear Madam. You were right to call. Better safe than sorry..." she began, going into her leaving speech as she strode toward the front door, but James McCardle, his policeman's sixth sense tingling and unsatisfied, interrupted her.

Smiling reassuringly, he asked Rhea, "Would you like to examine the house? See that nothing's missing?"

His now irritated partner scowled at him behind Rhea's back, signalling for him to get on and get out. He ignored her, steering Rhea into her sitting room. Rhea stared at the television.

"Well that's still there," the female officer remarked rather sharply, making Rhea start. "Telly and computers are the first things to go in a burglary. So you see? You've nothing to worry about."

Rhea was frowning.

"But someone has been in," she pleaded.

The female officer huffed, clearly ready to reject this, but PC James McCardle cut in smoothly,

"What makes you think that Mrs Forrester?"

Rhea was looking at her living room. "Too tidy... I left out some magazines. And the chair, it's been moved..."

The female officer rolled her eyes in exasperation, which Rhea couldn't help but see, and her heart sank. Desperately, she turned to PC McCardle.

"It's a heavy chair. Look!" she said, frantically pointing to the side of the chair, "That's the dents in the carpet where it usually is. I know this sounds stupid."

James McCardle shot his partner a warning look, before turning his reassuring smile back on Rhea.

"Let's check the rest of the house more thoroughly, shall we?" he said brightly.

Just then, there was a furious rustling and scratching from the kitchen causing his partner to whirl around in alarm.

Rhea shrugged, unable to stop feeling gratified for the insensitive female officer's discomfort.

"Oh, that's just Vincent. He'll be wondering what all the fuss is about."

"Who?" the female officer spluttered.

In answer, Rhea led the way to the kitchen and switched on the light. She opened a large cupboard, where a very big black bird was perched in a rather small cage, which was balanced on the edge of a shelf and a stool, leaving the base open. The bird extricated himself deftly from the bottom of the cage, then hopped up onto a kitchen chair back.

"He roosts in that for the night when he comes to visit. Don't you?" Rhea said fondly, turning to the menacing looking bird.

"What is he? A vulture?" the female officer. grumbled aghast.

Rhea scratched his head gently, oblivious to the vicious

looking beak the female officer was eyeing nervously.

"He's a crow. My daughter found him. He was exhausted and had a hurt wing. He's alright now, but he just comes to visit from time to time, and sometimes stays over."

The crow was scanning everything with an anxious eye, his crown feathers still raised a little in alarm.

"You look upset old son," Rhea said to the anxious bird, then made commiserating noises to him.

James McCardle's face creased into an affable smile.

"Yeah, I remember going through that as a kid. Our house was a wildlife hospital, though nothing quite so ambitious," he said, as Vincent stared at him lopsidedly.

"Do you always put him in the cupboard?"

Rhea nodded as the bird, reassured all was well, began to settle and obligingly scuffled back onto his perch in his tiny cage.

"Want the lights out Vinnie?" Rhea cooed.

The bird cawed softly, fluffing out his feathers comfortably, and she closed the door, turning to P.C. McCardle.

"Yes, birds like a bit of dark to settle them down. I couldn't cover his cage. He'd suffocate. But something disturbed him. He's not happy. He'd never normally wake up until morning."

The female officer made faces at James McCardle, indicating her belief in Rhea's insanity, but much to her exasperation, got no response

"I'll look upstairs," Rhea said, feeling a little calmer now that she knew PC James Mc Cardle was sympathetic. But she still hung back at the doorway to her bedroom until he urged her in.

"Anyone got a house key?" the female officer asked as Rhea opened her wardrobe.

"No," she answered, preoccupied with her task.

"That's odd, my boots are gone...my jeans!"

She rummaged through her clothes in mounting panic. There were socks and underwear, nightwear, tops and jumpers and a jacket gone. Rhea stared at her wardrobe, bewildered and frightened.

"What's going on?" she whined.

"In a relationship at the moment?" the female officer continued doggedly.

"No." Rhea answered mechanically, too lost in bewilderment and shock to give anything but cursory attention to this wearisome woman.

"You sure they're gone?" James McCardle asked, looking into the neat, sparse wardrobe.

"Yes," she answered absently as she tried to extract some sense out of the revelation.

"Even my travel bag! They've packed it and took it." she said, as the implication that they must be coming back for her reignited her alarm.

She scrabbled through a dressing table drawer.

"My passport! It's gone too," she whimpered.

The female officer calmly ignored this problematic information and persisted with her line of questioning

"Anyone in your past still got a key? Ex-husband? Boyfriend? Girlfriend?"

Rhea was looking at her tiny computer desk.

"No, no one, I've just recently changed the locks."

The PC pounced on this bit of information, mouthing,

"woman with relationship troubles," at James.

"Yeah? Because someone wouldn't give back a key?" she asked, the contempt in her voice barely hidden.

Rhea only half heard her. "Nahh, lock was knackered and I got insurance. They insisted on upgrades. This is really weird. Someone's been at my computer as well."

The officer frowned in obvious exasperation.

"Wouldn't that be your daughter?" she said, her tone all too sweet reason.

Finally picking up the female officer's condescension, Rhea gave an exasperated laugh.

"Its obvious you haven't got children. Look! All the flash drives and discs are still packed away. I left the box open. If Jack had been in, they'd be all out. Hey! There's one missing? That's odd. Why would anyone want my club accounts?"

PC James McCardle caught Rhea's eye, attempting to comfort her, attempting to make up for the anxiety his colleague had caused. "What accounts? Can you think of any reason why anyone should want them?"

Rhea sat down in a heap, ready to cry. She should have kept her head down like George said. Her lovely little escape, doing something worthwhile, had made her a target for crime.

"No, they're the accounts for the conservation club. You know, the wildlife sanctuary? I've been doing some admin for them. We've got about 10 regular members and a few occasionals. It's hardly worthy of robbery," she said miserably.

James sighed. Motive was for others to consider. He just had to show that a crime had been committed.

"Okay, it seems we've established someone has been in and taken some of your things without permission. Now all we need to know is how they got in?"

His partner was signalling again above Rhea's bowed head. "No way! She mouthed. "She's just a lonely nutter!"

He leaned toward Rhea waiting for her answer, and she looked up with bright frightened eyes.

"I don't know. I don't know."

"Its okay," James McCardle said consolingly, "Let's go downstairs. Could you stay with your friend for tonight?"

Rhea nodded.

"Okay, collect some things and we'll take you," he said, as he considered his notebook.

Obediently, she gathered up her remaining nightie, some clean clothes, and hurried downstairs to the hall.

"It'll all look different in the morning. You'll remember who had your key," the other officer purred insistently.

Rhea finally snapped. "No one had my key!"

"Then how did they get in?" she reasoned sweetly.

Rhea stared at her, finally needled enough to take her to task, but as she drew breath, she stopped. She'd noticed a smudge on the wall above the officer's head. She looked at the window above.

"In there." She pointed to a high hall window. "And there's a fingerprint," she said triumphantly.

James McCardle could see, even from where he was standing, that the print was no more than a smudge, but he kept silent. Unfortunately his partner noticed something about the window.

"But it doesn't open," she wheedled smugly.

Rhea was already up on a chair.

"Fresh silicon. Look! This window has just been renewed. That's what I smelt. That's what was different. I told you I sensed something at the door. I just didn't know what was giving me the creeps." she said as she got down, her eyes shining with relief, now that she had proof, now that the problem was concrete, manageable.

James tapped his notebook, mentally assessing whether they had a workable situation.

"Mrs Forrester, you were at work today, where do you work?" he asked.

"Oh, at Snow Street Wings Couriers office, why?"

"I'm just trying to establish who might want to break in. Could it be anything to do with work?" he asked.

"No, no. It's a happy workplace," she insisted, hysterically batting away any thought of further invasion into her self-contained little life.

"I was supposed to go out with them tonight as it happens, but I did my conservation work instead."

James nodded. "What about customers? Any know where you live?"

She shrugged, "Don't think so...Topic's never been brought up."

James wrote down 'customers'.

"Notice any who have more interest than they should? Any who seemed, you know, a bit nosy?"

Rhea reeled through her memory with a defensive compulsion. Was there any sneaky creep she hadn't noticed, angling for private information?

"No," she said decisively.

He smiled

"Don't worry, probably means that there wasn't anyone."

He looked around.

"Well, that's everything, let's take you back to your friend. And when we've done that, I'll have another look outside, see if I can find the glass from your hall window."

Rhea cast a surreptitious glance towards his colleague. "So you believe me? There's been a break in?"

He nodded, "Clothes, passport and, computer disc's been taken without your permission. There's been a crime, but it's all very odd, that's for sure. I'll have to report all this back and someone will speak to you tomorrow. Now, let's get you back to your friend."

CHAPTER 2

The next day did not usher in any relief for Rhea. The break-in didn't make sense, didn't point accusing fingers in any direction, didn't allow her to name the danger let alone plot a way to avoid it.

So as she hurried to the bus stop on her way to work, she was jumping at shadows, revving engines, pushing and shoving children, and even the little grey dog which greeted her every morning with its wet-nosed kiss on her ankles.

Then something jerked at her attention, gave it focus. It was the sight of two anonymous, large, sleek, dark windowed, high-powered saloon cars swishing by in the never ending line of boring, dusty commuter cars. This was the sort of car careful, tidy, kidnappers used. She dodged into the only cover her frantic mind could see: a group of scurrying commuters. Head down and in step with her fellow pedestrians, she watched under her eyelids as the cars passed by, ready to run should they turn out to be the faceless ones who, she was now certain, had come to abduct her the night before. Her heart rate slowed in relief as they were swallowed up by the morning rush hour, but her mind still churned.

The ominous nature of the break-in had been bad enough, but now she was beginning to realise it had shown up the fatal cracks in her friendship with Laura.

When the police had taken her back to her friend, Rhea had trustingly spilled out her thoughts and fears as Laura had often done with her, fully expecting a sympathetic ear and a few kind words of encouragement. But on hearing that "nothing much" had been taken, and that the house wasn't trashed, Laura had proceeded to comfort Rhea by telling her everything was okay now, it wasn't a big deal. Thus she had conveniently ignored the alarming implications of Rhea's missing passport, travel bag and clothes. She then "reassured" Rhea that she was always oversensitive, so no wonder she was upset. Laura had finally kindly suggested Rhea "get some pills" for "her nerves" from the doctor, and everything would be all right again. Well it would be, for Laura.

Rhea was angry and hurt all at once. But she also knew, was becoming resigned to the fact, that it wasn't Laura's fault. She was only being the same Laura she'd always been, always would be. It's just that they really didn't have much in common any more. She, Rhea, was growing, going places Laura couldn't follow. She sighed, feeling so lonely.

She reached the couriers' office where she worked, too exhausted to think about it any more. So, forcing the events of the night before to the back of her mind, she pasted on a smile and gratefully threw herself into the steadying mundane rhythms of the tiny office routine. And it worked. At least while it was busy, while things went on as normal, and office chat bubbled along on the surface of the work of the three colleagues.

"A big storm drain thing burst on the road out by the

immigration offices this morning," Kevin muttered as he clattered away on his keyboard, busy with his latest flush of deliveries.

Linda winced. "Eargh! Sewerage!"

Kevin snickered.

"Na, it's a little river that was conduited, put into a pipe," Rhea corrected, and sighed, "Nature fighting back I suppose."

"Well, does she have to take it out on me? Traffic's still snarled up for miles around and I'm still having to divert bikes," Kevin grumbled, giving her a glance of surprise, "Bloody loads of police around."

Rhea grimaced. "There's probably hordes of spies and gangsters running off with armfuls of passports, ready to bring down our civilisation before tea time," she muttered with sardonic flippancy.

This time, Kevin blinked in theatrical astonishment, his fingers stopping mid clatter. "Eh? Spies? Wow! Linda! Our once sweet dreamy Rhea is now into conspiracies and spies!" he said, with mocking admiration. But before he could say any more, his screen flashed and a call came in.

"Humph! Incoming from grumbly Gerrard," he said, his heart sinking as he focussed his attention back on the work in hand.

All too soon, the rush slowed down. Rhea looked hopefully to her co-workers for distraction. Kevin was rattling manically at his keyboard, and Linda had disappeared into their boss's office. So Rhea was left to the mercy of her painful thoughts. The clamour in her head became a disabling roar, so she slunk off, climbed into the stationery cupboard, and buried her face in her handkerchief. The same question, "why me?" that had turned and twisted its vicious blade into her mind all last night, flashed its torture implement before her again, wheedling that it would be better for her if she only confessed an answer.

'What would they want with me? I haven't got anything.'

She couldn't think of anything, she couldn't even imagine anything.

She pleaded that she was just too ordinary to be causing anyone any bother, but the question twisted again and she clutched her head, imagining all sorts of terrifying possibilities. *'Maybe it was mistaken identity. Maybe it wasn't criminals. Maybe they thought the passport was false, maybe it was...'*

The door to her sanctuary opened, interrupting her churning thoughts.

"What the!?" a startled voice exclaimed. "I wondered where you were."

Linda's surprised smile froze with concern as she caught sight of Rhea's anxious face.

"Rhea? What is it?"

Rhea looked up ready to tell all like it were just a bit of juicy gossip, but she just couldn't pull it off. Mutely, she shook her head. She made a weak attempt to get up, threatened to fall back into the shelves, but Linda caught her.

"Come on out of there. It's obvious something awful has happened, but we can't have you crying all over the envelopes. Let's find somewhere a bit more comfortable and private so you can tell me all about it," she said, in a brisk motherly sort of way. "It's quiet. Nothing expected for at least an hour. Kevin will hold the fort for now, so you've got plenty of time."

Linda led Rhea to the cubby hole they used as a staff canteen, and closed the door

"Come on, sit down in the comfy chair and you can tell me all," she soothed. "Tell you what, I've got some of that lovely hot chocolate drink."

Rhea gave a pained smile and just sat for a moment, gathering her wits as Linda rinsed mugs and filled the kettle.

"Got burgled last night. Just it's unnerved me," she blurted out, then wincing, she bit her lip, waiting for the same lecture Laura had given, already feeling the demoralisation that would come.

Linda gasped. "Well! It would! What happened? Have they taken much? Was there a mess?"

Rhea looked up miserably.

"Not much. I wish they had. Taking the telly and things and leaving a mess I could understand, but this is weird."

Then the tale tumbled out, every detail, as she tried, once again, to make sense of what had happened.

"I think someone is after me but I don't know who or why. They took my passport. I know it's silly, but I can't help feeling that if I'd walked into that room, that's the last anyone would have seen of me, and you'd all just have thought I'd done a bunk." she said, then wished she hadn't, waiting for that glazed look of wary incomprehension, but it didn't come. Linda listened.

"No wonder you're in a state. I just can't make head or tail..." Linda began.

Just then, there was a yell, and scuffling and crashing from the front office. They both ran to find Kevin sprawled on the floor among upturned chairs and scattered papers. He sat for a moment, still too stunned to get up. "I'm sorry, it all happened so quick. I didn't see the other geezer. They got it," he muttered distractedly.

Linda and Rhea took an arm each and helped him onto a chair.

"They got what? Are you alright?" Linda queried.

Kevin dusted himself off.

"Yes thanks," he said before turning to Rhea. "They got your bag. I tried to stop him but the other bloke sneaked up. Was so quick. They asked if you'd brought your bag in."

He rubbed his head. There was definitely a lump forming.

"I turned around to check, and he jumped the counter."

Linda slid a quick assessing glance toward Rhea whose face was draining of all colour.

"Hey! Catch that before it all blows away can you please?" Linda said to Rhea, who dazedly chased the scattered papers to the far side of the room.

Linda muttered urgently in Kevin's ear, "C'mon, phone the police and whatever you do, look cool calm and capable. This is all Rhea needs. She was burgled last night and she's hysterical already."

Rhea stood there, clutching the papers she had picked up, the relentlessly advancing freezing fog of fear swamping her initial burst of adrenaline fuelled energy.

"Did you catch what they looked like?" she half whispered.

Kevin shrugged

"Was all so quick. But he was a tough character. didn't look like your average bag snatcher...Too well dressed. Was really cool..."

"They're trying to frighten me. But I don't know why. I don't know who they are!" Rhea protested, trembling and about to cry.

Linda hurried over and hugged her. "Stop that! Stop!" she ordered. "They are a bunch of stupid thieves that's all," she insisted, smoothing back Rhea's hair and leading her towards the back room. "Come on, we'll sort it out," she soothed, then threw out a string of orders over her shoulder for Kevin.

"Get the police over here now! And shut up shop for the time being. Set up the calls to transfer to Belford Road office. I'll phone Don and explain."

She turned her capable attention swiftly back to Rhea, regarding her with a cool, assessing eye.

"You're in no fit state to do any work. Where's Jack?" Linda finally said, as she chewed over the problem.

"Jack? She's safe, she's safe. Laura's picking her up from school."

Rhea looked up in alarmed realisation, her eyes pleading. "They wouldn't know Laura's mother. They're going to her mother's for the night. I didn't want Jack panicking too. What am I going to do? I don't want to go home. I'm too scared. They might follow me. Oh god what about Jack?" she said, her mind swirling with all manner of fears.

"C'mon, sit down. You're all shaken up. I'll sort something out."

As Linda closed the door, the strain became too much for Rhea, who still feared a repeat of the encounter she'd had with Laura. "It's the same ones, it's got to be! And they'll be back. They'll be back!" she said in desperate protest, frantically trying to persuade Linda that she was still in danger, and therefore also a danger to Jack.

Linda shushed her. "Its alright, it's alright. Yes, I know. I believe you. Look at me. Come on. You know I believe you," she said, trying to hold Rhea's gaze as she attempted to reassure her.

Rhea relaxed a little, soothed by the calm acceptance in

Linda's grey eyes.

"That's better," she crooned. "Now, here's what we'll do. I'll talk to the police. You don't have to. You definitely need time to rest, calm down, let someone else make sense of what's going on."

She considered what to do for a moment.

"I'll tell you what. You can stay at my place. I'll give you my spare keys. If anyone *has* been watching you, they won't expect that! And if they've been watching me, well, they'll have no joy either."

Rhea nodded uncertainly. Linda gave her a wink.

"Even I have forgotten where I live since I've been living with Richard. I had a policeman as a tenant until just a couple of weeks ago, so no one is going to look me up in the phone book," she added with a flourish, whilst carefully observing Rhea for reactions. "I'll even send the police round to your house to check it out again."

Rhea didn't run away or even protest; she just stood there clutching her purse.

"Keys. I had them in my purse. I left it in the tea room this morning." Rhea said, holding out her purse to Linda, realising through her daze, that she had snatched one small triumph from this onslaught, even if it was unknowingly.

Linda gave her a kindly smile of acknowledgement.

"Weeuph! That's one small miracle in your favour then!" she said, glad to find something to be upbeat about. "Give them here and have mine. I'll have some clothes picked up for you while we're on. Now, that only leaves Jack. Leave me Laura's mother's phone number and I'll pick her up okay? I haven't seen that young lady for some time. It'll be nice."

Rhea nodded dumbly, then looked at the keys she'd just been given as Linda bustled out. She had no further opportunity to ponder as Linda returned full of instructions.

"I've rung a taxi, it's the usual one. I know the driver. She's coming round the back now to collect some stuff for the boss if anyone asks. Her name's Carmel."

A sound of sirens interrupted her.

"Oh, that sounds like the police. Don't worry. No mugger wants to hang around while the police are here. Now just go to my place, have a hot bath, then put the telly on and relax. I'll be with you as soon as I've got sorted out here. We'll have a curry and watch a silly film alright? Now go! I can hear the Taxi."

Rhea stumbled out into the rear courtyard, and climbed into the taxi.

"Brunton Terrace?" the taxi driver chirped.

"What?" Rhea said absently.

"You going to Brunton Terrace?"

Her mouth went dry and her heart rate rose. Brunton Terrace? Stay on her own in a strange house? A strange neighbourhood? She was being hunted. It wouldn't feel safe until Linda got back, and she was likely to be a few hours. A wave of sheer panic blanked out all ability to think, leaving her overtaken by the animal need to get to safety, to run.

"I want to go to the seaside," she said, wanting to escape into the safety of memories.

The taxi driver laughed. "Well, I've got all day, but it'll cost a bit. Tell you what; I'll take you to the station. Trains run every half hour, and take an hour and a half. You'll get through the station security checks really quickly at this time of day."

A while later, Rhea stood on the promenade and took a deep

breath. The smell of salt, seaweed, and fish and chips soothed away her stiffness and fear, as happy childhood memories of days out at the seaside came dancing back to weave a temporary barrier between her and her troubles.

She didn't notice the highly polished, dark windowed, smart saloon car discreetly parked in the shady side of the seafront car park. If she had, she would have remembered it, and her premonitions from that morning. As it was, the fearful, suspicious frame of mind she'd been in, was left behind.

She trailed dreamily along the beach, watching seagulls chasing each other and squabbling over what one or the other of them had just caught. She was glad to see there weren't many people about today. She smiled. It was the start of the season. The sun was cheerful, even if the breeze was cool. She was grateful for that coolness on her face, soothing away the tension headache she had developed.

She hadn't particularly noticed how far she'd walked, until she realised that the only sounds were complaining seagulls and little waves lapping and swishing.

She turned around, walking backwards for a few steps, as she took in the scene down the beach.

In the distance, people busied themselves entertaining a variety of pooches. One or two sat contentedly fishing. There were even two hefty looking fellas, dressed in city clothes, ambling along towards her

'I suppose even bouncers like to take the air,' she thought, watching them for a moment before turning to continue her walk.

As the *scrunch scrunch* sound of their footsteps fell in step with her own, her fearful suspiciousness returned, and a terrible realisation finally broke through her nostalgia.

CHAPTER 2

'They aren't bouncers, and I've led them to a lonely part of the beach! How stupid can you get?' she thought. But she didn't run or scream. Something in her mind broke off, separated, and began to assess the situation. It was as if she was watching someone else.

She looked up into a pugnacious, pale, freckled face, framed by an aura of close cropped, red hair, noticing that, surprisingly, he smelled of a rather subtle, upmarket aftershave.

"Ahh. Our elusive lady. Just hold on a moment. We have a message for you," he said in an unexpectedly soft, well spoken voice.

'We?' she thought questioningly, and gazed from side to side uncomprehendingly, then her slow motion memory caught up. Where had his mate gone? A cold chill ran up her spine as she felt, rather than heard, him behind her.

An incongruous huff of relief left her lips. The amorphous terror that had been stalking her since the night before, had shrunk into the form of two rather overweight men in dark suits. Anger pulled her scattered mind back to reality, but it was a cool, calculating anger. After all they had put her through, she was not going to give them the satisfaction of seeing her fall apart or panic. They'd enjoy that. No, she would give them nothing. Now, her fear would serve only to sharpen her wits, keep her alert.

She smiled, determined to act out the innocent, to give herself as much chance as possible to make an escape.

"It's a beautiful fresh day for walking. I'm sorry, I don't know your names."

She waited, hand outstretched, and was rewarded with a little pantomime as Ginger blinked in bewilderment, his threatening train of action momentarily stalled.

"Er...Rod, and this is Giles," he said shaking her hand.

"Deborah, Debby." she said pleasantly.

She watched as he shuffled around from foot to foot, flapping the hand he had just given her, attempting to regain his aggressive flow.

"Our friend Tim believes your name is Rhea," he said, in a too pleasant voice for menace, still hitching about uncomfortably, and she could plainly see he was wondering for a moment if they'd got the wrong woman.

"Does he? she said, making a performance of looking around for Tim, giving herself a cover to check for helpful passers by. But she already knew there was no one else within reach. "That's probably because he's so far away he mistook me for her," she continued diplomatically as she struck out once more along the beach. They followed her, walking awkwardly sideways.

"Still, it is a nice name. Who is Tim?" she asked innocently.

Rod regained his composure and laughed nastily.

"Tim's the man you..." he leaned into her face to emphasise the menace, "Borrowed some goods from, and he wants them back."

Her expression remained mild, unintimidated, a trick she had learned as a barmaid when dealing with furious drunks.

"I'm sure he does," she agreed. "It all sounds so serious. Just what did this woman borrow?"

She watched them surreptitiously from under her lowered eyelids, as Giles rolled his eyes, mouthing to Rod over her head.

"It *is* the wrong bird!" Rod lowered his face for a moment, determined to threaten her now, even if she was the "wrong bird", mouthing, "What's the matter with her? Why isn't she screaming abuse at us and trying to run off?"

She gave Rod a sidelong glance. 'You're beginning to doubt

yourselves. I'll not stop looking for a way out. I might just have a chance. If I'm very lucky, you'll both just fade away,' she thought grimly.

Giles pulled something out of his pocket and gazed at it out of her line of sight. It was a photograph. Then he turned to her.

"Look, we don't want to spoil such a nice day. Just give us the goods and we'll be on our way," he said in a mellow, but emotionless voice.

Up until now, everything that happened to her could be dismissed as burglary, vandalism, or spite. Real faces, descriptions of real people asking for "Goods" would induce someone to start asking questions, and they'd not want that, not want any witnesses. But hadn't they already attempted to set her up as having fled? Taken her passport to prove this? She looked into those perfect cornflower blue eyes, and saw only coldness, finally understanding that, whether she could give them what they wanted or not, they'd kill her.

"You're mistaken. What makes you think I've got your goods?"

Giles' face set into that hard, rather comical caricature of a gangster. "You've got it," he said harshly. "We will get it back."

She sighed sadly. She knew the game was up. There was no way out. It was curious, she noted, she was more resigned than frightened,

"How did you find me?" she asked absently, trying to gain a few last moments.

"Oh, Luck. We were taking a breather. Then you came walking past," Rod purred nastily.

She shuddered at the possibility they might try to torture the whereabouts of whatever it was they were looking for out of her.

They certainly looked like they'd stop at nothing.

'*And I can't let them use Jack,*' she thought.

There was only one thing she could do to stop them.

She flicked a quick look ahead. There was a little rocky outcrop that went almost to the water's edge. The low line of rocks would give her some cover to get to the sea, and she could make the short run and slither in before they realised what had happened. The beach shelved away steeply here, and there was a telltale line of a rip tide running out to sea, so she doubted they'd risk their own necks to follow her. '*I suppose out here, on this beautiful beach, is as good a place as any to find eternal rest,*' she thought wistfully, gazing out at this, her last view of the seaside with its innocent sparkling waves. "Alright. I haven't got it with me. I'll have to show you, but... give me a moment. I'll just nip behind those rocks if you don't mind."

They both gave her a hard stare of denial.

"Oh come on, be gentlemen. Call of nature," she said briskly.

The one called Rod scanned their lonely section of beach and shrugged at his mate.

"There isn't anything but beach here, no one to hear or help her, and anyway, I don't fancy piss on the car seats," he grumbled.

She sauntered off to the rocks in as dignified a fashion as she could muster, then crouched down, hidden from them, free of their grasp. She felt light, unreal. Her body might be here, but her mind was retreating into the safety of another dimension. Giles and Rod were facing the way they'd come, their backs to her.

She heard the raucous, familiar call of a crow, and glanced up the little gully of rocks towards the cliff for one last look at land, at life. A little way up from the base, a shadow moved. '*A shadow? Am I that far gone? Am I hallucinating? Is that all I have?*' She shivered, struggling not to fall to pieces and cry, as her protective shell of shock cracked in the warmth of the hope of a friendly presence.

"Jack," she murmured, trying to steel herself and get on with it, and attempted to move towards the water once more. But she was paralysed, her whole being crying out for this one last crazy hope. A tear of anguish dripped down her face, as the memory of her peaceful evening meditation floated unbidden into her mind. She couldn't do it. She couldn't kill herself. She silently snaked her way to the base of the cliff and looked up. Hallucination or no, it was all she had.

"If I look with different eyes, I can see your forest," she whispered, desperate to escape into this flashback of a happier time. Sure enough, the shadow thickened as it had done that night, but this time, eyes, strange, but friendly smiling eyes, clearly swirled into view.

'If I just reach up, I can climb up beside you,' she thought, finding herself looking up to a ledge, where minutes before, she had seen only the tumbled base of the cliff. As she reached up, she felt a big strong hand grip hers, pulling her up to the ledge.

She watched, as Giles shuffled in impatience.

"She must be finished by now," he grumbled, and walked over to look.

She watched as Rod ran this way and that.

"She can't have gone! Where could she go? That cliff's sheer. She'd have to fly. She can't just have vanished into thin air!" he hissed.

Giles groaned, scanning the innocent waves.

"Nothing. That's the bloody second time she's given us the slip. This one is a real operator! C'mon, she's been well and truly tipped off now. Get back to Tim and find out what he wants. Oh this is getting a bit too messy, we're gonna become too visible for my liking."

Next minute, Rhea was lifted, higher, higher.

A few minutes later, she stood, stupefied, in front of a pretty little pub, wondering where she was and how she'd got there, but only for a moment. She had to get off the street to safety. Where was she? Which way was it to the train station? She had to get back to Linda's and to Jack. She was shaky, too shaky to walk more than a few steps. She'd be safe in the pub among other people, and she could rest, find out where she was, and phone Linda.

After she'd used the bar phone, she ordered a large glass of lemonade and a brandy to steady her nerves. "Am I far from the station?" she asked the barman.

Amazingly, she discovered she was only two minutes away and, she remembered, the trains were every half hour.

She sat down in a corner, away from the bar and other customers, trying to shake the hazy, unreal feeling of shock. The pub cat strolled across to greet her. Gratefully she stroked it, glad of the attention and the homely comfort of his purr. He jumped onto a chair and gazed up at her with kindly golden eyes.

Those eyes stirred something, a recognition, seeming to rise and settle at a considerable height from the floor. She blinked in astonishment as this fragment of memory refused to be anchored to any logical explanation. As she stared into this space in her jangled mind, a face formed around the eyes, and a body gathered out of the shadow. "Oh!" she said aloud, realising that this was whom she had seen on the ledge, this was who had reached out and taken her arm, yanking her to safety.

She puzzled over this strange vision for a minute or two, then gave up. She could ponder these things later, when she was safely away, away from the two thugs whose hunt for her must surely soon spread from the beach to the town.

She finished her brandy. The glow of it sedated her nerves and relaxed her knotted muscles. In this cocoon like haze, she slipped out of the pub and slunk to the station, still fearfully glancing frequently at the reflections in shop windows to check who was behind her, or watching her from across the street.

Soon, she was on the train and relieved to find herself among a noisy gaggle of teenagers. She reasoned no one wanted to be among them, so her would-be attackers wouldn't expect her to be here either.

She smiled. One of her young fellow travellers had propped up his placard on the table. It proclaimed. "Say no to Pharming Frankenstein Foods." She felt a flush of pleasure at the thought of being among young people standing up for nature.

They were happy, these young folk, yelling, nudging and teasing each other, singing some pop anthem, with no care or thought for the consequences, feeling utterly invincible and free from fear. She started to hum quietly along with them. Each mile the train took through the countryside was a mile further from her fears into that numb state of the overwhelmed.

CHAPTER 3

"Hi Linda," Rhea said into the borrowed phone, then ran out of words as she wondered what to do next. She couldn't bring herself to leave her hiding place in this crowd of laughing youngsters. She'd been buoyed along in their midst, off the train, all the way out of the station, and along the road down a tiny side street to this cafe´. At the door, she'd suddenly woken out of her protective daze and frantically looked up and down the little side street. She could see there was no one lurking menacingly, no one watching her, but her fear simply displaced to beyond, to the streets between this sanctuary and Linda's flat. One of the band of youngsters had obliged her by phoning Linda for her, before handing over her phone.

"Where are you? I'll have some tea ready when you get in," Linda said in a motherly tone.

"The Blue Mermaid Cafe´. By the train station," Rhea answered, relieved of the effort of thinking.

"Okay. Get a taxi..." Linda started, but was interrupted by an alarmed gargle from Rhea.

"I can't. frightened. I can't...someone might follow!" The thought of getting into a stranger's car just left her terrified.

"Yeah, taxi's will take far too long," Linda responded sympathetically, attempting to soothe the panicky Rhea. "Tell you what; our Gerry will be only too glad to pick you up. I'm calling him now. Okay?"

Rhea blinked as a picture of the large, intimidating, grumbly Gerrard flashed comfortingly through her mind, and she relaxed enough to contemplate getting home, although not enough to stop worrying about being followed.

Gerrard, far from being grumpy, was a perfect, but silent knight of the road. His incongruously warm, knowing smile convinced her she was safe in his care, and would reach Linda's unseen, hidden behind her helmet's visor, an anonymous pillion on just another large bike.

Linda was rattling around in the kitchen when Rhea arrived. The smell of curry reminded her that she hadn't eaten since breakfast. Suddenly, hunger cut through all the confusion and fear of the past two days, bringing her back to a fleeting normality. "Wow, that smells good! Looks like I'm just in time," she chirped.

"Where's Jack? Is she here yet?"

Linda looked around, her hands full of plates and cutlery.

"Jack's had her tea. She was up late last night, so she's already asleep. We can eat in peace. C'mon, help me serve it up. We'll talk later," she said, making an effort to keep any anxiety out of her voice.

"Grab the chutney and we're set," Linda said brightly, then bustled into the living room.

As she organised the meal and settled Rhea in front of it, gossiping about the familiar safe topics of their boss's colds, and Kevin's two girlfriends, she inserted mention of her mate

Rowena's caravan in the country into the conversation. Happily, it seemed to be Rhea's sort of thing.

Rhea sighed wistfully,

"I could do with a nice country break to get myself together a bit."

Linda gave a satisfied grin.

"Good. I was hoping you'd say that. It's a nice place and we could have you there by late afternoon tomorrow."

Rhea felt a wash of nervousness at the thought of leaving her current sanctuary but, at the same time, was only too ready to flee the city and her problems.

"Um, yes, um, good idea. We'll talk after we've eaten," she said, giving herself some breathing space in which to settle her nerves.

Linda nodded. It could wait an hour or two.

Rhea let the mundane chattiness wash over her, smoothing down her spiky nerves and soothing her digestion, allowing her to relax enough to finish her meal and even feel a little sleepy.

Linda looked on at her handiwork and gave a self-satisfied smile, thinking, 'That worked like a charm. Magic doesn't have to be mysterious does it?'

Then, as Rhea's eyes drooped a little, she took the opportunity to clear the plates and crept into the kitchen to make tea, giving Rhea a few minutes to doze. Even so, she did notice that there was an odd and ominous blank in the conversation. Rhea had carefully avoided any mention of her afternoon's seaside jaunt.

As Linda reappeared with the cups, Rhea looked up with a grateful smile.

"Thanks. I feel much better now."

Linda sat down. "You did look pretty frazzled," she said

carefully.

Rhea gave a rueful smile.

"Totally. I thought an hour or two at the seaside would help."

Her smile faded, her face tightened and she seemed to shrink.

"Wasn't a good idea at all," she said, in a distant, almost childish voice.

Linda nodded warily, wondering how much worse things could get.

"I assume something else happened."

Rhea cocked her head, blinking through a haze of fatigue at a strange rewind of memories.

"It's as if it happened to someone else," she said, as she edged towards the memories, to the shock which had earlier engulfed her.

Linda nodded, throwing out a lifebelt of a smile.

Rhea clung on desperately.

"I went for a walk on the beach," she said tentatively, waiting for the slap of a wave of confusion. When it didn't come, she allowed the list of events at the seaside to stutter out, that as yet, didn't make a story, even for her.

"I wanted to be alone and was miles from anyone, when these two heavies caught up with me. They wanted something, I haven't a clue what. I can only guess its information. I mean, somebody's been on my computer, someone's going to an awful lot of trouble to get whatever it is. I haven't taken anything of anyone's. I knew they were going to kill me. Even if I had known, even if I had what they wanted, I'm sure they'd have killed me."

Rhea looked around. The fear of "Them" ebbed and flowed less and less as she let these disjointed fragments of thoughts and memories tumble out, finally dissipating into a manageable confession. "S'funny, I was angry."

Linda snorted with outrage "Course you were angry! Bloody hell woman! They were threatening to kill you!"

Bit by bit, with her acceptance, Linda was drawing Rhea back to the shore of the safe, known world she craved, where things would make sense and she'd know what to do.

"Can you remember what they looked like?" Linda prompted, "It would help the police, give them something to work on."

Rhea gave another of those eerie distant smiles, as she re entered her memories.

"Yes...They were sort of ...blank...no feeling. Just greedy mouths."

"Ohh c'mere, you need a hug. Greedy mouths sucking the life out of an innocent woman is exactly what they sound like, but this isn't the sort of description the police can work on... It's alright, lets just leave it," Linda cooed soothingly, making a mental note to write down anything useful Rhea might say.

Rhea took a deep, strengthening breath.

"No! I want to tell you. I was angry because I didn't want to die in a back alley, and I didn't want them to get to Jack!" she said sharply, her eyes glittering with remembered defiance. The light died and she looked into Linda's eyes, her voice almost a whisper. "So I thought I'd cheat them. I'd choose where I would die." She sighed wistfully.

"It was a beautiful day and the sea had little white horses."

Linda blinked away threatening tears. "You poor love, they just about frightened you to death." she murmured.

"Hold on... what did you tell these goons?"

Rhea's eyes flitted about guiltily.

"I never said anything that could bring them back here. I

gave them a false name."

"It's okay. I've got back up. Anyway, I'm involved girl, I wouldn't just let you go like this. We have to look out for each other the way things are these days."

'The way things are these days?' Rhea wondered fleetingly. Then instantly rationalised she meant the trouble she had got into.

"I wouldn't forgive myself if I didn't. What goes around comes around eh?" Linda said, trying to be reassuring.

Rhea shook her head. "I can't bring this down on your head. What about Richard? I'm so sorry."

Linda put an arm around her shoulders. "You didn't do anything. They're the ones making things hard. Anyway, my Richard said he's glad to help."

She gave Rhea a knowing grin. "He's already warned the lads to keep an eye."

"Lads? Who?" Rhea said in confusion.

"Gerrard might be grumbly, but that's because he's so picky. He's got a sharp eye, sees all the little details. And he's really handy if you know what I mean. Him and the others will keep us all safe I promise."

Rhea smiled at the mention of Gerrard, remembering how safe she'd felt on that big old bike of his. *'So Richard knew the bike crew from work?'* She nodded her acceptance.

Linda gave her a little squeeze. "See? So what happened?"

"I just thought I might manage to put them off, convince them I was just a fluff head taking a walk on the beach."

Linda smiled approvingly. "Well, you don't sound like a fluff head to me. Nice try eh?"

Linda was looking into Rhea's eyes with some admiration. She might be a mess now, but she'd obviously put up some kind of a fight.

Rhea sighed, feeling just a little less helpless.

"If they hadn't had that photograph... I didn't have a chance until...I really don't know how I got away," she said, her voice becoming noticeably more hesitant.

"Anyway, I said I needed a pee and ducked behind some rocks. I was waiting for them to turn their backs, then I was going to rush into the sea..."

She paused, puzzled, trying to make sense of it again, tried to line up the events, "...But this crow started making a racket up on the cliff, and I looked up. Something happened. They turned their heads and..."

She shook her head feeling a faint flush of embarrassment flit across her face.

"I'm not sure what happened. I woke up a mile away. I was in a dream. It all feels like a dream," she protested, more to herself than Linda, then saw the anxiety on Linda's face.

"Did they drug you?"

Rhea stiffened, anxious that explaining something she didn't understand herself was going to look crazy and lose her Linda's support.

"No, they didn't have time."

She was exhausted, and no matter how much she wanted and needed to make it fit reality, she just couldn't.

"Ohh this is really difficult. Someone helped me, and not in the normal run of things," she said, letting the last phrase hang in the air between them.

"I can remember looking up at the crow, then suddenly seeing this space that wasn't there before. I can't really explain. We were looking down from above, laughing as they ran around looking for me. That's all I can really make sense of."

She looked up to meet Linda's eyes, terrified Linda would dismiss it all and throw her mind back into chaos.

Linda gave Rhea a kindly sympathetic smile.

"So, you imagined another place and someone in that place carried you off to safety?" Linda prompted.

Rhea frowned, struggling to make her mind give her some clear pictures to work on. "Well, yes. It's hard, nuts."

Rhea was confused by Linda's calm interest, and looked away nervously.

Linda shook her head. "It's all right," she soothed, "Don't worry about making sense. We can try to sort that out later. Just tell it like you saw it. Have you ever seen this person before?"

Rhea closed her eyes to concentrate.

"Not exactly, in a way, I sort of made him up, imagined him. He was part of a daydream."

She fidgeted nervously, waiting for an alarmed reaction, but Linda just continued to smile

"Shh, it's okay. I think I'm beginning to understand," she said, and Rhea was dumbfounded to see Linda was decidedly relieved. "Though I hadn't expected to find you, of all people, telling me about it."

Then she urged Rhea to continue her story.

"Think about when you first imagined him. Can you remember anything about him?"

Rhea relaxed a little as she thought about the friendly presence.

"He looked fierce but kind, bit like a kindly panther."

Linda looked at her askance.

"He looked like a cat?" she queried.

Rhea gave a nervous little giggle.

"No, not that way. Just sort of... like some strong wild thing. He had a fierce face but kind. He was dark, though not normal dark, sort of reddish brown like mahogany. You know? Like he lived outdoors, and he was very tall and wore some sort of tunic thing. Then there were his eyes. They were sort of dark gold, yellow. They glowed. Yeah, bit like a cats, and..."

She frowned with the effort, there was something shadowy behind him, but her mind just wouldn't give it up.

The sound of her own description finally shook her out of the remnants of her cosy trance and she began to panic.

"All this has got to me! maybe it was the strain. I might have gone into some kind of shock. Do you think? You think I'm mad." she said in fearful embarrassment.

Linda took her hands, anchoring her sanity.

"You're not going mad. You have had a very nasty experience, and somehow or another, you've managed to conjure up a protective spirit. That sounds like a particularly sane thing to do, wouldn't you say?"

Rhea's feelings see-sawed in seconds, from absolute certainty of her sanity, to fear that she was losing it. She hadn't expected such a matter of fact acceptance from the down to earth, practical Linda of all people.

"Okay, let's see if I've got this right," she said, gathering her courage to see if Linda would continue to be supportive. "I am somehow conjuring up a man with my imagination, and he rescued me."

Linda nodded

"Further, he isn't human," she heard herself say in a small but precise voice, his image before her mind's eye.

Linda gave a strange smile

"No, he wouldn't be. I don't know many men with golden cat's eyes. He's a protective spirit," she repeated reassuringly.

And to Rhea's surprise, she underlined that acceptance with a beaming smile. Rhea let a small puzzled frown flash across her face as she tried to adjust to this development, becoming aware that Linda appeared to be weighing up what to say next.

"Well! Even in these times, with books on aura reading and clairvoyance to be found in common book stores, beliefs in wood sprites and protective spirits is still likely to stir up a guffaw or two, or a call for an appointment to the doctor, so I suppose you've got a right to be worried."

She cocked her head on one side, surveying Rhea closely. Rhea winced.

"But I'd say you've been honoured and have the best bodyguard ever," she said softly, looking down at her hands. "I believe in such spirits. I'm a little jealous."

'I've hardly given a description of an angel. Or maybe I have. Have I?' Rhea considered this new Linda, as the last shreds of the old, solid Linda disappeared in a herbal scented puff of new age smoke. Then pennies not only dropped, they started to shower down like change from a drunk's pocket.

She stared at Linda, then around the room, seeing things she hadn't noticed before. A broom stood in the corner. There was a small table spread with a few pebbles, a pine cone, a pretty crystal, some leaves, a little pot of something white that might be salt, and an arty wooden cup. A bunch of some kind of home made incense was burning in a little tray. The smell had soothed her until she had seen, or rather noticed these things.

It was a bit much to take in all at once, and made her feel

slightly dizzy.

"You always had a lot to say about all things green and eco. You're some kind of New Ager or something aren't you?"

Linda sighed good humouredly. "New Age? Well, it'll do for now. What's important is that you believe you have a guardian. Something got you away from those thugs. They didn't follow you did they?"

Rhea struggled to remember, now not so afraid of what she saw in her mind. Pictures jumped up, voices, and laughter, hers and... Whose? "No, I was well hidden. They didn't know what had happened. We sat there, right above their heads, as they ran back and forwards. Eventually, they went away and he took me, I can't remember how, to the town."

Tears suddenly sprang to Rhea's eyes.

"I don't care about being mad but I'm frightened. I'm trouble now. I've got to get away, they're bound to come looking for me and you'll be next."

Linda hugged her again. She had her own guardian spirits who looked out for her. She had already called on their help. "Its okay. Look, there's no way anyone could trace you back to here. I told you, I've got a policeman friend down as a tenant. I'll have a word with him about all this and we'll work out a cover."

She'd already arranged for her friend and ex tenant PC James McCardle to go meet Rhea at the caravan in two days time, by which time she hoped everything would be sorted out. "Have a good sleep. In the morning, we're going to send you off to the country to hole up and have a rest."

Rhea looked at her wildly. "I couldn't stay in a guest house. I'd be too scared of the strangers."

Linda nodded "I know, but we, my cov...err group have a

caravan we use for meets. Remember? Rowena's caravan? It's more the size of a cottage. It's in a secluded spot and nobody knows about it except the local farmer. The family is lovely, and very discreet."

Rhea frowned. It did sound suitably hidden.

"We'll sort out a car in the morning. I'll make you some herb tea to help you sleep. Now go on, get yourself ready for bed," Linda ordered.

But Linda was not so sure of Rhea's security. Whatever they thought she had taken, whoever they were, they were obviously very thorough, and it would only be a matter of time before they found Rhea and Jack if she did not move very quickly.

The next day, Linda waved Jack and Rhea off, relieved that all was going according to plan.

As Rhea got ready that morning, she had felt excited, as if she really were going on holiday. But once in the car, anxiety and fear had hissed and worried at her once more. She had driven through the city in a state of intense alert, watching for recognition, a gun, or weapon, from every pedestrian, every car. But nothing happened. After all, how could they know where she was? She reasoned with herself.

Once they were out of the city, Rhea let her tense body sink into the car seat, allowing herself to enjoy the brightening day, and the road unrolling before her, over gentle green hills.

"I think we've got away Mam," Jack confided.

Rhea was startled, "Got away? Who from?" she asked, as nonchalantly as she could muster.

"The gangsters who are chasing us," she said, as she stared into the rear-view mirror.

Rhea's heart started to thump, but her face was a calm mask.

"Jack! What are you on about?" she said with a strained smile.

Jack squirmed around to face her with a look of earnest excitement.

"You know, the gangsters who came in our house. Do you think it's because we are eco terrorists?"

Rhea burst out laughing, with anxiety more than anything.

"What? Who said we were eco terrorists?"

Jack looked embarrassed.

"Oh y'know, Colin's cousin. But we do care about the eco... the...the world, don't we?"

Rhea smiled.

"We care about the Earth, that's right, and I help with the wildlife garden, protect the frogs, bats, butterflies and moths, but that doesn't make us eco terrorists. Terrorists are people who attack other people, fight them with bombs and guns and things."

Jack nodded wisely. "Yeah, like those crazy people on the news."

Rhea gave her a sidelong look, feeling a stab of guilt for not protecting her from such stupid stuff. She might take no notice of the antics of these idiots, but kids would. Everything is so real to them. Rhea nodded, knowing it was better to ignore what she wanted to play down, or else Jack would launch into a torrent of excited questions.

"That's right. We just look after wild things and write to the news and the M.P.s."

Jack was satisfied with this and resumed her humming for a moment or two. Then, much to Rhea's relief, as the noise was becoming irritating, she began to fiddle with pencil and paper.

They were heading into a leafy wooded area, and Rhea knew

Jack would be coming to the end of her patience. She would begin to demand food, drink, and a place to pee.

"Mam? Can we stop and have a picnic?"

Rhea nodded, '*Right on cue,*' she thought, then answered "Soon."

Jack looked longingly at the woods, hoping to go on a berry picking expedition. "What about that little road down there?" she asked excitedly, spotting a lane with lush hedgerows and paths into a wooded area.

Rhea sighed. '*Why not?*' she thought, and headed off down the pretty country lane that seemed straight out of one of Jack's fairytale books. Soon, there were no cars in sight, nothing but the birds and the trees for company.

She pulled up in a lay by, and let Jack out. "Don't run off! Wait for me. I'll bring out the picnic."

Jack scooted behind a bush after a butterfly "Yes Mam," she called over her shoulder.

Rhea looked up at a happy blue sky, watching a large crow idly surfing the light breeze, and relaxed, wondering fondly if it might be one of Vincent's cousins. The scene was pretty, and more to the point, no one had followed them. In the distance, she could hear the comforting industrious chugging of farm machinery, which flattened, with its everyday practicality, any threatening atmospheric imaginings that might make an attempt on her. With a light heart, she gathered up their provisions, and set out back into the wood. "Right then madam, let's find a nice place to have this picnic," she called.

Jack skittered out from the undergrowth she'd been truffling about in, and skipped merrily along beside Rhea.

"Are we really staying in a caravan?"

Rhea laughed. "How many times do I have to tell you before you believe me? Yes, we are staying in a caravan, in a wood, in the country. Will this spot do?"

Jack stopped, solemnly surveyed the clearing by the brook, gave a gentle experimental scuff with her foot at a hummock or two of grass, then nodded. "This is perfect," she said wisely, and started to unpack the bag almost before Rhea had put it down. "Will there be a cauldron at the caravan?" she asked, as she found her favourite juice.

Rhea's jaw dropped "What?"

Jack was happily attacking the bottle of juice. "She's a witch. A nice witch. She told me about her broom and things. Can I be a witch mam?"

Rhea blinked in astonished amusement. "Er, why not?" she said, shaking her head.

"Yeay!" Jack exclaimed, solemnly laid a pie on the box lid she was using as a plate, and made a few mysterious passes over it with her hand, then ran off with it to go watch a squirrel in a tree nearby.

"Stay within sight and earshot!" Rhea called, watching her affectionately.

After a few bites of pie and an apple, Rhea allowed herself the luxury of stretching out and just gazing into the trees, emptying her mind, dozing in the mottled summer sunlight under the trees. Jack dabbled in the brook, and pattered about the clearing, prodding at interesting seeds and twigs.

The farm machinery had stopped. Rhea slowly became aware of the ensuing lack of the comforting sound. She twitched nervously like a mouse listening for a cat, then eventually managed to persuade herself to ignore her nerves. 'Well, I'm sure

CHAPTER 3

even farmers stop for dinner too,' she thought.

She settled back again with her carton of pineapple juice, and looked up at a large pine tree, strong, straight and dark against the golden dapple of beech trees. Shadows danced lazily for a moment, as a breath of wind rustled by, drawing her eye to their shapes. She allowed her imagination free play. A shadow deepened, condensed, took shape. Rhea smiled, comforted. "Oh hi" she whispered. "I could do with a friend right now, especially one who can protect me from those gangsters."

"Mam! Look what we've found!"

Rhea was jolted from her reverie as Jack came running up to her with a handful of wild strawberries, her face smeared with the juice. She laughed, happily accepting her daughter's sticky gift of a strawberry, but didn't have time to question her use of "we"

A car was purring slowly down the road, setting her nerves on alert again. She drew Jack close, easing silently behind a tree. The car stopped. Her heart pounded. She signalled to Jack to be quiet, straining her ears to hear something, anything that would give her an advantage, a chance to get away.

There was a distant sound of scuffling footsteps. *One person? Two maybe? Yes, at least two. Was that a murmur of words?* It was tantalisingly too far away to be deciphered. *What was that faint creak?* A car door slammed, another door clattered shut. An engine burst into life and purred off into the distance.

She slumped. *'Silly girl, it was probably someone stopping for a pee,'* she thought, admonishing herself, then gave Jack a hug.

"Your Mam has ragged nerves hasn't she?" she said, giving an anxious chuckle and turned to collect her bag before heading back to the car. Jack danced around ahead, miming peeping around trees.

She'd climbed into the car, but Jack was fussing about.

"I didn't say goodbye," Jack said.

Rhea was too busy looking at the map to question who it was she should say goodbye to, and assumed it was some little mouse or bird Jack had been watching. "C'mon, fasten your belt. I'm sure he'll understand."

Jack suddenly jumped up "I've forgotten my strawberries!"

Rhea groaned. "Okay, hurry up."

Jack was up and out before she'd finished speaking.

Rhea started the engine and a white flash wiped out her world.

Jal had burst out of the trees just as Jack was thrown towards him "No!" he yelled, sweeping up the child, who grabbed onto him like a little monkey. He turned round in one very swift movement, handing her to his horrified son, who had just caught up.

"Take her home, quickly, look after her," he ordered, hardly slowing on his trajectory toward the flames.

The child screamed, the meaning of her strange language transparent in her desperate little face. "My Mam! My Mam! Help me!" Her fear had tugged at his heart, but he had already dived into the burning car, and with lightning speed, was dragging out the pathetic little bundle that was her mother.

Jack heard him yelp, and the boy who held her, shuddered.

"Father!" he cried fearfully, as he watched him scramble out, trails of smoke issuing from his hair and clothes. Jal kept his back turned to his son as he examined the battered little body he held. "I'm alright, just go. I'll follow as soon as I've helped her."

The boy, now reassured, obeyed, and sped away into the trees, Jack clinging to him, sobbing with shock.

Jal wrapped Rhea up, then he hid her under a bush before looking across at the burning car.

"Luckily for you it didn't blow up. I think they wanted it to look like a fault, an accident," he murmured to her unconscious form, as he scanned the scene and considered his next move.

"Someone will try to find evidence of your bodies. You would be safer if they believe you both dead."

Covering his tracks was wired into his genetic make-up, so it took him only seconds to see the fuel tank waiting to be collected by the farmer, plus a dead lamb. Soon, the car had exploded into a superheated fireball that would consume every little bit of evidence of its occupants, leaving nothing but ash. There would be traces of organic carbon amongst those ashes, but not so much as a bone splinter to help identify the cremated remains it came from.

He toed the bag that had been thrown out, turning it over. It opened. He took the notebook, the cards, things that made up a recognisable sketch of her identity, and dropped them on the ground where they would eventually be found. The rest he took with him.

Now, he was free to focus on the considerable task of helping the poor battered creature he'd rescued. He looked down at the burned body, ignoring the nauseating smell and horrifying injuries, searching only for signs of life. *'Yes! There's a spark!'* he thought with relief, *'I can work with that!'*

"You are going to live," he murmured softly, as he worked to stabilise her wounds. It was all too clear though, that keeping her alive was not going to be easy.

He had done his best, but there was no way she would survive long enough to get her to a town and a hospital. Even if he managed, her chances of survival would be slim. There was only one other option; he would do the job himself. He fastened his wrap around her like a baby sling, and then followed his son's path back to his home.

CHAPTER 4

Rhea woke up with a start. It was dark. Some part of her woozy mind knew she was injured. She was in a bed. She knew it wasn't a hospital bed. If she wasn't in hospital, then how had she got here? More to the point, who had brought her here? Yes, it must have been him, but she couldn't remember. He was there the night of her conservation study. He'd been there on the ledge when she was on the beach. He'd lifted her onto the ledge beside him, lifted her to safety. It was true, this didn't make any sense, but that wasn't important right now. She needed to know why she was here.

A jumble of intense emotions and images slunk in the shadows of her memory, like dreams sliding out of the mind's grasp as the sleeper wakes. She forced her mind back to her last clear memory. She'd turned the key in the car engine. The world had gone white and then...Nothing.

She lay for a moment, shocked anew to relive that inexplicable nightmare. She'd been right. They wanted her dead. The car. An explosion. Fire. That's when she'd been injured.

Pain? Was she in pain? She didn't know, maybe. She had been badly injured. Suddenly she knew. She felt as if she were hovering on the brink of some swirling horror. It was a noise and it grew closer and more insistent. It was a scream, her scream, and it swallowed her up in its jagged whirling agony.

She was desperate to be free from the loneliness of pain, to fly into the bright, blank light of oblivion, before the pain dragged her down into the isolation of madness. Shadows hovered. Lights, colours, flickered. Sounds, like pure singing, hummed through her, holding her back from that enticing white oblivion.

Was she dreaming? She was struggling, slowly losing the fight against a deep soul exhaustion. She yearned just to slip away into that soft eternal whiteness, and edged gratefully closer. Then something happened, made her hesitate.

"Stay! Don't let go."

The voice seemed to come from everywhere at once.

"I can't. Just let me go," she answered in her thoughts.

"No! Stay! Try!" that now familiar voice pleaded. It was her imagination. Wasn't it?

She couldn't move towards the light, couldn't fade. Something was stopping her. How?

"Don't go, fight!" she heard him urge again.

Was it her imagination? Maybe not, but if not, where was he? It was a he. She could sense that much. But sense what? Was it a scent? The scent of skin? Did he have a voice? He must have. She'd heard him. She knew the voice. He was the one who had rescued her from the beach.

'No,' she decided. It was in her head. It had to be. She must be dreaming. Besides, she couldn't do as he urged. She was fading, dissipating like a cloud of steam. She hadn't the energy to even hold her molecules together, let alone have the energy to reach out. Briefly, she wondered if this was what dying was like, and realised she wasn't afraid. In fact she longed to just fade on the breeze.

"I have to go. So tired. Can't hold on. Hurts," she whispered towards the dream voice, reality and imagination now so blurred, she didn't care. Then a shuddering storm of pain shrieked through her.

"Hold onto me!" he urged. "The pain will lessen. Please, don't let go!"

There was a jolt like a bolt of lightning, and a rush of energy fizzed through her. She felt, or heard, a groan of pain from somewhere near, and then the voice again.

"Don't fight me. Let me help. Stay with me."

Strange images from somewhere else, someone else, floated into her mind. They were of a terrible accident, flames. A child, not Jack, was screaming. Someone was yelling in terror and despair. She stopped drifting, reaching out in her thoughts to comfort him. *'It's alright, I'll stay. I'll stay.'*

Her pain subsided, but she was so very tired. "I won't let go," she said softly, reassuring the voice.

But where was he? She puzzled, and as she had the thought, her body felt stronger, sharper. Was it her body? There was something, not exactly a smell or taste, maybe it was a feeling, but familiar from somewhere. These arms and legs felt big, long, longer than she could ever imagine hers to be. And there was so much more which was so very strange. *'No,'* she decided, these arms and legs weren't hers, and yet she was aware of them as if they were hers, as if she could use them.

'I don't want to hurt you,' she suddenly thought, fearful that she might, that somehow, her disembodied spirit had settled in this man.

She then realised she was also aware of her own, small, shattered body. And it wasn't lifeless. She could feel activity, just the pain was suspended. Each battered little cell, no matter how torn, was fizzing with hope, plans for the future, as they repaired themselves.

'*Yes!*' she thought triumphantly, fascinated by this wonder, this magic of being aware of her body healing. A deep gratitude welled up in her, and she turned her attention toward the presence who was making it happen.

A dark face murmured something to her in the shadows. Even though her vision was extremely blurry, she could see it was a very strange face. She reached out towards him in a gesture of comfort, and touched his hair. She felt him smile, then he gently returned her hand under the cover and she drifted off into a deep sleep.

She opened her eyes very carefully. Blink. Blank. She tried each eye, realising with a shock that one did not work at all. She remembered she was badly injured, her legs wouldn't move. In a rush of panic, she nearly squeezed tears out, but self preservation made her stop, take stock.

Despite all evidence to the contrary, her reason was still desperately clamouring for her to believe she was in hospital.

She searched her memory to see if she could work out what had happened. Once more, she returned to that memory of sitting in the car. She turned the key in the ignition, then the whole world disappeared in a blinding flash.

"Jack! Jack! Where's Jack?" she gasped out, returning frantically to that terrible memory.

'*I've forgotten my strawberries!*'

Her daughter's voice echoed soothingly around her memory.

CHAPTER 4

Jack had not been in the car. Relief flooded through her.

'You were collecting our supper,' she thought fondly, 'and it saved you.'

She relaxed a little. She looked around. Her one working eye only allowed very fuzzy images. She was crippled and almost blind.

A flash of outrage made her want to scream her revenge. The explosion was deliberate. It was them. They had followed her. Course they had! They were relentless, they wouldn't stop. They wanted to kill her. What could she do? Panic and self pity ripped up any shreds of sanity, and she let out a howl of anguish as she tried to move, get away.

"Help me! Help me!" She yelled frantically for the one person she felt could and would protect her from the gangsters, the nightmare.

Someone responded. There was no expected scent of disinfectant or other hospital smells. He did smell fresh, but as if he'd washed in rain dripping from the leaves of forest trees. She could feel his hands and arms, warm and alive in this nightmare of death. She could even hear him. But when she looked at him, all she could make out was a huge dark shadow. And yet she recognised him

"It's you! It really is you!" she said incredulously.

"Yes. Try not to move around. Let yourself heal," he murmured reassuringly in his strange, but soft purring voice.

"Jack, me, help us hide!" she muttered feverishly, momentarily lost in her terror.

"You're safe, you and your child. You're in my home, they won't find you here. Lie still, just rest, let yourself recover. That's it," he soothed .

She looked up. "Did you see them? Did you see what happened?"

"Shh, gently. Yes, and your child is unhurt. You need to take it easy. You'll have plenty of time for questions later when you've recovered. Breathe deeply and relax. That's it. Close your eyes," he continued, attempting to settle her back into a healing sleep. But she was not going to succumb to sleep without making some sense of her situation.

"Are you a doctor?" she asked, her sensibilities still attempting to insist on normality, but her reason knowing he wasn't.

"I'm a healer," he reassured.

A little thrill of triumph and a flash of embarrassed ridiculousness flushed her face.

"I knew that," she muttered, wondering why she had asked such a silly question against all the evidence in front of her.

She screwed up her eye trying to focus.

"Where's my daughter?"

He patted her hand in reassurance then left, returning seconds later, but it seemed like an age.

"Mam! You're awake! Oh wow! You look a right mess. Does it hurt?" Jack asked, bounding into the room and carefully laying her head next to her mother's.

Rhea jumped, startled by the avalanche of words and energy, then dumbstruck, gazed at Jack with astounded relief. Finally, when she had satisfied herself that Jack seemed well, she gave a cheery wave.

"No, it doesn't hurt. And hello to you too Miss!" she said, managing to reach out a shaky hand to pat her.

Jack stroked her mother's cheek in an attempt to reassure her all was well.

"You'll get better, but it's going to take a long time," she said solemnly, trusting implicitly the kindly reassurance her strange guardian had given her.

Rhea felt her heart swell with tenderness at this little show of bravery by Jack. "Yes, I'll get better," she said softly, for her daughter, but she was not so sure for herself.

Jack grinned.

"Then you'll be able to see the rest of the house and the village! It's great here! We're the only humans," she chattered on excitedly.

Rhea's jaw dropped.

"What?" she asked stunned. But Jack was moving away.

"Come on sprout, let her rest," a now familiar voice purred, and Jack was swept up away from her.

She struggled to focus, and saw Jack, tiny against the chest of the shadow, her arms affectionately around his neck as she hugged him. He set her on her feet.

"Oh alright. Bye Mam! See you later," she said, and was gone.

Rhea realised the shadow was still there. She heard him stir and knew he was smiling.

"Thank you for taking care of her," she said towards the dark blur.

"You're welcome, but now you really must rest," he ordered, and began to stroke her head and face, soothing her back into a healing calm.

She sighed sadly.

"I'm very badly hurt. I'm going to be crippled aren't I?" she moaned, as a wave of self pity took her.

"You are badly hurt, but no, you won't be crippled. You will heal," he insisted. "Remember, you felt the healing happening."

To Rhea, he was just speaking soothingly, yet the effect was profound. She was floating on a bed of trust. She believed him totally, even had an image of herself, whole, happy and healthy, in her mind's eye. She tried a squint of a smile.

"Can you see me?" he queried, watching her making desperate efforts to look at him.

"Just a shadow," she answered, searching for hope. She saw his head tilt in a gesture of satisfaction.

"Your eyes will recover too, given time," he reassured.

A whole lot of protests rose to her lips then faded without her speaking one word.

"No more questions. Now, you must sleep," he said firmly, and she found herself once more sliding into sleep.

The next time she woke, it was lighter than before, and the music was very quiet, just audible. It was like being on that delicious, edge of dreaming state, and she revelled in it. After a while, she looked around. Shadow was right. Her sight was clearing. She could now make out the contours of the room she lay in. The soft colours of the lights chased across the rounded walls and the supporting ribs of the domed ceiling. It looked as if it had been grown rather than built.

Something made her turn her head and rise out of her comfortable half sleep. She smiled in anticipation. Shadow appeared silently beside her. She drew a shocked breath and gasped, as an image finally forced its way out of the recesses of her battered memory.

"Jal," she managed to murmur dazedly, as she gazed into now familiar, dark gold, rather cat-like, eyes. His face, that dark gargoyle like face, was all harsh straight angles. Even his up slanted eyebrows were straight. Everything was harsh except his mouth, which was oddly full and sensuously curved, with the gleaming white tips of two fangs just showing. He wasn't human. She knew he wasn't human. She'd always known. But now, he wasn't a shadow any more.

For a full minute, her heart thudded with shock

He sat down near her and waited, folding his hands in his lap that showed he meant no harm.

This was her wood sprite, the person who had rescued her, nursed her back to life. He was the one she had called out to in her fear, in her nightmare.

For a few minutes, she just stared, dumbstruck, examining the frightening gargoyle like apparition in front of her, checking and double-checking what she saw, against her memories of his kindness.

"I'm awake now," she finally pronounced.

"Yes, you're awake," he agreed.

"But," she protested, and managed to reach out and touch his arm, "You're real."

"I'm real," he agreed, kindly sparks of amusement dancing in his amber eyes.

She checked his face again. Here was her Guardian of the woods, not imagination, spirit or sprite, but a flesh and blood creature. And yet he could have walked straight out of one of the old folk tales she had read. She began to laugh.

"You were out wildlife watching. And I'm wildlife."

He tipped his head in acknowledgement.

People weren't necessarily kind to wildlife, she thought, then felt a flash of fear.

"I expect you're really hungry now. How about some soup? I've just made some mixed vegetable," he said, her stampeding thoughts forced to a halt against such an ordinary offer.

The tension made her giggle. "You can't be vegetarian!" she blurted out incredulously, staring at this distinctly non human, demonic looking vision before her.

He tipped his head, smiling again, flashing those fine white vampire-like fangs, a sight which produced an automatic shudder in Rhea.

She shook her head against the contradictions she saw. This was so absurd it was funny. "I'd love some soup," she said gratefully. Her tummy rumbled in anticipation. "And have you got any bread? I'd love a hunk of bread too please."

He inclined his head in what she began to realise was his version of a nod, then left silently.

Someone came in and Rhea looked up, expecting Jal. But what she saw was a smaller, younger version of him, only with bright green eyes and something disturbing on his back. She blinked, trying to work out if this was dream or no, but he stayed. With his mop of black shiny curls over his sharp features, he looked like a young woodland faun. Did he have horns? She strained to check. No, but he should have.

"Marn!" Jack called out, breaking Rhea's trance. "Is she awake?"

The young faun eyed Rhea uncertainly.

"Yes Jack, but don't tire her," he purred, with a consideration she didn't expect, but which left her well disposed towards him.

At least she thought it was a him. It mightn't be. She couldn't be too sure of anything right now, except that she was safe. Jal would keep her safe.

Jack rushed in and kissed her cheek lightly. Rhea whispered conspiratorially into her ear. "Has he got wings?

Jack slid a glance at Marn and giggled. "Yeh."

He looked a little embarrassed.

Jack grinned affectionately at her playmate.

"It's alright. Mam's just noticed your wings. That's all," she said, much to Rhea's amazement.

Marn brightened, absently easing the other pinion from its tight, triple fold.

"Oh, um that's good. You can see," he said, trying to say something helpful.

Rhea gazed at him, feeling just a little disorientated. Course she knew he had wings. Jal had flown her from the seafront to the pub. Rhea blinked, stunned by this memory. *'That's right. Jal had unfurled velvet black wings, then wrapped her in his wrap, and tied her tightly to him like a parcel, before leaping into the air. Jal, that's his name.'*

Jack slid back down to the floor and the nervous Marn visibly relaxed, making Rhea wonder if he was looking after Jack.

"Is there something we can get you?" he asked brightly. Rhea smiled, warming to this kindly young being. Just then, Jal reappeared with her soup and bread.

"You have guests," he noted smilingly, as he set down the tray. "Marn, go serve yourself and Jack while the soup is hot. I'll be along in a little while," he said, as he affectionately patted his son's shoulder and ruffled Jack's hair.

He placed the tray in front of her.

"Now, let's see, are you going to try this, or let me help you?" he asked brightly.

She squinted at the bowl and attempted to hold the spoon. It wobbled dangerously, and she let it plop back into the bowl. "I think I need help," she muttered, sighing with disappointment.

Very carefully, he held her hand, helping her move it.

"The activity will strengthen your hand," he explained in response to her quizzical look.

After her meal, Rhea settled back, full and content. "Very tasty. Thank you."

"You're welcome. I'm pleased with your progress," he said, as he helped her settle back on her pillows. "I think you could be out of bed very soon."

She looked up at him, imagining walking out of the house to see a whole village of these giant wood sprites, and her head began to swim again.

"I think I need to take my time," she said, her voice wavering with anxiety.

"Are you in pain?" he asked, checking she was lying comfortably.

Rhea shook her head, trying to settle her dizzying thoughts. She looked up at her rescuer, this strange, fierce looking being.

"Why are you helping me?" she asked piteously. A guardian spirit taking care of her she could accept, but why should a… what had he said he was?

"You helped Vincent the crow. Why did you do that?"

She gave a surprised smile.

"Because he was hurt and needed help, and I could and felt I should. Anyway, I liked him and he seemed to like me…" she answered, as her mind struggled to grasp the implications of what he had said.

He tipped his head in agreement.

"Me too. When I was watching you sitting studying on your log, and realised you were beginning to see me, you caught my curiosity. Humans don't usually sense us. I liked you," he said good naturedly, watching her carefully for any signs of distress.

The world seemed to twitch, tip with her struggling thoughts, and she put out her hand to steady herself.

"Woa! Vincent, the crow? You've been watching me for some time. Course you were! I was the wildlife. And you're not human!" she half whispered, nervously allowing herself to meet his eyes, his strange, alien eyes.

"I'm not human," he agreed, sparks of amusement lighting his strange, non human, amber eyes, pleased to find her dealing with her situation so easily.

"Aazaar Kind, you're Aazaar Kind, means children of hope," she murmured, as another fragment of memory surfaced.

He smiled, obviously pleased by this utterance, and inclined his head in his version of a nod.

"That's right," he said encouragingly. "We introduced ourselves on the cliff ledge."

She shook her head. This was so weird. She liked him, this man who rescued injured animals. She trusted him, but couldn't look at him without a flash of fear at his strangeness, the massive implications of what he was, and suddenly, she had a lot more admiration for Vincent the crow, who, she now realised, had obviously made such a huge effort to appreciate and befriend her. "And you're not from Earth," she said.

He sighed, and she was surprised to sense something wistful in him.

"My race is not, no, though some of us in this community were born on this fragment of Earth."

This left her dumbstruck. Jack had said there was a village, but she hadn't thought, hadn't taken it in. Aliens visiting, or just recently arrived, seemed acceptable somehow. But the thought that they had been going about everyday life long enough to be born here, whilst she, and the whole human race, were oblivious to their presence, was too much.

"I imagined you," she muttered defiantly.

He inclined his head to one side. "Yes," he agreed, then took her hand.

She felt his large, firm, long fingered hand. It was solid, all too real.

She closed her eyes, the reason of her old life furiously protesting, protecting a reality that did not include him.

"You're impossible. How could you fly?" she muttered incredulously, feeling hot with the effort, almost convincing herself she was simply delirious. But his hand still held hers.

"It's difficult, realising I didn't imagine you," she insisted bravely.

He inclined his head again, pausing to find the gentlest way to explain.

"But you did. I was there, and because you imagined me, you could sense me, see me," he said softly.

"But you don't make sense!" she protested.

Unable to claim some sort of delirium any more, she could see the careful construction of her whole life, a fine erection, woven of the sturdy girders of whispers, conversations, demands, expectations from family, friends, teachers, employers, lovers, bus drivers, doctors, M.P.'s, shop assistants, everyone she shared her world with. The tower trembled and shook, and she felt sick, waiting for it to come crashing down on her. Then she realised, far from looking at the world from her tower, she was looking at the whole tower of her everyday world from the outside, and Jal was sitting outside it with her.

Her head swam, and she let out a nervous laugh, gripping

his hand, this anchor of reality. She closed her eyes, fighting the oddness she saw.

She finally opened her eyes, knowing she would never see anything the same way again, knowing she had to find a way to construct this new world. *'Well, he might be from out there amongst the stars, but he's a man. Might as well start with familiar questions,'* she thought.

"So where are you from?" she asked boldly, as if she'd just been introduced to him on a Saturday night at the pub.

He smiled, but Rhea noticed that wistfulness again.

"My people are travellers. We've been travelling the stars for so long, we only have legends of the world of our origin," he said, and this time, she was certain that she sensed a touch of poignancy in his remark. Tactfully, she decided to drop that subject, at least for now. Still, it amused her to think of the existence of some rather gentle intergalactic gypsies.

He shifted, absent mindedly half opening his curiously triple folded wings into an untidy sprawl, just as his son had done.

Rhea found this oddly touching.

"Marn, he looks a lot like you." she said hopefully.

He smiled warmly, fiery flecks once more lighting up his curious amber eyes.

"My son reminds me of myself at that age, just as your daughter must remind you of yourself."

Rhea felt some of the strangeness recede, now she had something everyday that they shared, something she could empathise with, feel at ease with.

"So what does his mother think?" she asked brightly, then instantly regretted it.

"My lover died some years ago," he said simply.

She was embarrassed. "I'm sorry." she said in confusion, nervously checking his face for signs of offence,

His eyes were no longer sparkling, but they were calm.

"You have no need to be. It was an innocent question. You haven't offended me. Where is your..." he hesitated over the term, "lover?"

If he'd been studying her world for some time, he probably knew humans had various arrangements for their love relationships. And there was Jack. She could have told him everything.

Rhea smiled wistfully at the quaintness of his words. Lover? Love? From the frenetic Dave? Chance would have been a fine thing.

"I live alone with my daughter. My ex husband," she paused, realising he might not know what husband meant, "officially recognised male lover, left some time ago. I'm not sure where he is."

Jal surveyed her with the disinterested concern and discretion of a healer, looking for signs of emotional rawness.

"Is that sad for you?"

"Once upon a time, but not any more," she admitted, an echo of regret taking her by surprise. "It didn't work out. Last I heard of him he had another wife."

It was true, she held no yearnings for Dave, but she did feel cheated of a mate, a happy relationship. She looked up at Jal guiltily. She hadn't meant to say so much. She just felt so vulnerable. Then she forgave herself, putting it down to the strange situation.

"I've assumed you're like us humans. I mean...you have children obviously, but... and relationships..."

He tipped his head in amusement. "Similar."

"Do you marry? I mean, have one partner to live with?" she asked, wanting to place these strange beings, work him out.

He chuckled,

"A good question from a diligent observer of living things. Yes, Aazaar Kind people choose a lover in the hope of staying together for life."

She looked up, now so full of trusting curiosity, as he surveyed her face.

"It's OK, there's no one waiting in the nest for me," she said with a wry smile.

"At least we know we both believe in long term relationships."

"Love." he corrected calmly.

She looked again into the distinctly demonic face with its sharp angles, a face that stirred up unconscious fears of all things alien, satanic even, of anything but love. Yet, however strange, those dark gold eyes shone with kindness and honesty.

"Yes, I believe in love," she admitted wistfully, as she thought of a happy ever after in a little place in the city, "Of finding someone to love and share life with."

Then the absurdity of their conversation hit her. *'So much for something familiar. All this love is definitely alien,'* she thought wryly, then laughed.

He raised questioning eyebrows. "What amuses you?"

She looked up into the calm kindly face and realised she was feeling comfortable with him.

"I meet a being from another world and what do I discuss? Technology? The universe? When are you going to take over our world? No, love."

Jal settled back in his chair smiling good-humouredly.

"It is good to realise we have something so basic in common."

She couldn't help but agree. The distance between them had shrunk.

She had just accepted that she had come face to face with an alien, and now she found herself beginning the journey to accepting he was a being with the same hopes as herself.

"And we have no intention of taking over your world."

She smiled, gazing up at this strange kindly gargoyle. If she had not been so imaginative, so dreamy, she would never have seen him. And by now, she and Jack would be dead. She had a lot to be thankful for. "What do you call your settlement, your home?"

Jal was making moves to leave her again. "This is your last question. I think you should rest now. I can see you are tiring."

She put out her hand. "Please."

He smiled. "Our lands are called Dream Hills. When you're well, I'll show you. Now you must rest," he said, as he set up the room for healing.

She turned the word around in her mind, allowing the light and music to soothe her. "Dream Hills…fairyland. What else would it be?" she murmured to herself in amusement before sleep once more took over.

CHAPTER 5

Rhea heard the outer door of the house open. Instincts from her old life still called a faint alarm at what they considered an ominous ensuing silence, but now, new ones got ready to give a pleased greeting.

Rhea called out a cheerful hello to Jal, and staggered to meet him in the main room. It had been some months since he'd first brought her to his home, and she was reconciled to her status as rescued wildlife. She hadn't really thought about it. She'd been too busy managing from day to day, and concentrating on recovering. Anyway, her life with Jal was safe, warm.

"Well met, Rhea," he called back brightly, watching her make her laboured way into the room.

"Look what I've been doing all day," she said proudly, and did a wobbly lap of honour of the sunlit room.

She could see Jal watching her with a keen, appraising eye. She knew she looked such a sorry state, with her patchwork peeling skin, and her all but bald head, but he smiled encouragingly.

"Wonderful! Your progress is very good," he answered, noticing the way she absently scratched and rubbed at her face and arms. "I must admit, there was a time I wasn't sure you'd have the will to survive, but you're a determined little thing aren't you? Keep still and let me see what I can do to relieve some of this discomfort."

He tilted her face to the light, scanning it with an expert healer's eye, murmuring, "You're peeling so profusely, no wonder it's uncomfortable. We'll see how much we can scrub off."

Then he settled among a comfortable pile of cushions, gesturing for her to sit beside him.

"Thanks," she said, delighted at the thought of sloughing off the tormenting flakes, but she had other things on her mind. She could see, walk (after a fashion), and she'd got her hands and arm moving nicely. So now, she was wondering about how she was going to return home to her life, wondering how she was going to work out when it was safe to do so.

"Have you seen the children?" she asked, straining to hear any signs of them.

"They're on the lower ridge, foraging something nice for tea, and then they're planning to catch up with my brother Issn to find out about his music plans for tomorrow. I think they'll be away for quite a while," he said, unaware she was about to ambush him.

"I'm glad you think I'm doing well. So you'll agree I can cope with having that talk about what happened? I want to know if you have any idea what those thugs were after. You know, the property I was supposed to have?"

Jal gave a soft laugh of amused resignation, "That sounds briskly efficient of you. Yes, I suppose you are well enough. And no, I know nothing more about that. I wish I did. I've spent..."

Rhea slumped, cutting him short.

"Oh. I thought I'd get a start on solving my little problem," she mumbled in disappointment. Since her recovery had taken some time, it had never occurred to her that Jal wouldn't have found a lead by now.

Jal smiled reassuringly.

"I'll make sure you are safe," he said.

"I know you will. But will you help me track down the mystery property I was supposed to have?" she asked, then she added a playful prod to his presumption, "Not only might it give us a lead about who's involved, It could be fascinating for your studies of human behaviour."

His mouth twitched in amused surprise.

"Yes it could. Am I having a lesson in the consequences of being condescending to my subjects of study?" he asked, with an ironic lift of eyebrows.

She cocked her head on one side in sham coyness, her eyes lit with a friendly mischief.

"Just a little. I suppose I'm getting to understand what my furry and feathered friends felt like." she said, giving away a strong underlying waft of vulnerability, even hurt in her remark, despite her attempt at teasing him.

"I might have studied you, but you're my guest, my friend." he said with a warm smile

"As for your request, I had always intended to encourage you to start investigations into your own situation, when you were fit enough of course. I thought it would help you ease your way back into your world."

She gave a delighted huff, and reached out to give him a hug of thanks.

"You're welcome. I had been hoping to find the mysterious property myself. It'll help my current study." he said, as she settled back again.

"Oo yes!" she began, her eyes shining with a sudden deep interest. "I'd love to hear what you make of us, and why I was attacked. What was it all about?" Realisation of her improvement, and that she would continue to heal, had given her mind a new energy she just had to use.

Jal gave a hesitant, wary smile. "Ah, apart from saying there's an efficient organisation behind it, there's not a lot I can say right now, nor wish to. I've got lots of bits of information, but no satisfactory story line yet to draw it together. I need that something, that one piece, which will make sense of the rest," he said.

"Look, give me a chance. I want to know what's going on, and it's bound to help you."

"You're a determined little creature that's for sure," he remarked, and was rewarded with a glint of acknowledgement in her eyes that let him know she wasn't done with her petition.

"No Aazaar Kind would just leave you to sort things out on your own once they'd meddled in your affairs," he assured her.

She nodded. She knew, however obliquely, this was agreement indeed from the sometimes infuriatingly evasive Jal.

"I wouldn't call saving me meddling," she said appreciatively, "But how about we make plans, start working on what I know, to see if I'm holding a clue."

He smiled his surrender.

"Yes, that sounds like a very good idea, but not today."

She grinned with relief, hearing in his agreement, his thoughts changing, his view of her changing from helpless object to… well, if not a partner, on the way to a person he had to consult.

"Great!" she said, content for the moment with such progress.

CHAPTER 5

"You haven't even seen Dream Hills, and yet you're already planning your escape," he said with an amused chuckle.

"I was planning on taking you to…"

A chatter of young voices suddenly exploded into the room, as Marn and Jack clattered in with their bounty from their afternoon harvesting trip.

Marn was first, greeting his father with a hug, and Rhea with a gentle pat on the shoulder, as Jack scrambled in behind him.

"We're going to cook tonight!" Jack announced.

Jal inclined his head, his eyes alight with what Rhea now knew where affectionate sparkles.

"Sounds good. So, how long will supper be?"

"Oh, an hour." Marn said, then glancing protectively toward his human ward, then added as soberly as his young years would allow. "Come along Jack." And Jack adoringly trotted off after him.

Jal smiled.

"It seems we have an hour. That gives us more time to chat about what happened," he said briskly.

She was a little surprised at him taking up her challenge so quickly, but happily agreed.

"Okay," she said, but was unprepared for his next question.

"Do you remember anything about your initial healing?" he asked.

She knew he wasn't talking about his curious light and sound technology. He'd explained how that worked, how different frequencies had been focussed on her to bring about optimum healing outcomes, even keep her in a healing sleep. She frowned. A flashback, to that strange protective trance like state she'd been in when he'd first brought her to his home, washed over her.

"Yes," she said distantly.

Deep in her heart, she knew what had happened. She looked up into those strange golden eyes, reliving her initial confusion when she'd first really seen him, and she gave a shudder.

As she came back to the present, she was still looking into his eyes. To her surprise, she caught a hint of something. Regret? No, maybe it was something a little sad or even lonely. She immediately dismissed it as imagination.

"It's all a bit overwhelming for me to think about. I need to sort of nibble at it a teeny bit at a time. But not yet," she said, with a self-effacing lowering of her chin.

There it was again! Just a faint hint of loneliness, but this time, she knew it wasn't imagination. Before she realised what she was doing, she was reaching out to his hand in a gesture of comfort, then stopped, unable to work out what was happening, a faint flash of bewilderment flitting across her face.

"Sounds like a very good and sensible way to deal with it," Jal said with obvious relief.

"When you're ready to nibble, I'm willing to provide the snack," he purred, his voice, his whole manner, once more so familiarly confident and reassuring.

She nodded, relieved of the anxiety of discussing what was presently unfathomable. Then she smiled, unable to help searching his eyes again for that incongruous feeling, but it was gone.

He cocked an ear kitchen-ward, and sniffed the air appreciatively.

"Mm, supper won't be long now. Galer will be dropping by just in time," he said, happily looking forward to his friend's visit, now he was certain nothing awkward was likely to be discussed.

She flinched, looking up worriedly.

"Er… well, you'll want to enjoy supper with your friend."

She had always hidden when people came visiting Jal.

"But I want him to meet you," he insisted.

She went red under her peeling skin, and visibly cowered, leaving him concerned and puzzled.

"What is it?" he enquired gently.

She frowned, taken aback that after so much sensitivity, he could be so dense.

"What do I know about Aazaar etiquette? I'll feel like a performing monkey!" she yelped, suddenly feeling acutely aware and ashamed of her status as rescued animal. "Anyway, I'm a mess." she wailed. "I can't face new people like this." Then she lowered her eyes, embarrassed at her ungrateful outrage, attempting to placate him. "I'm alright with you because I'm used to you, but… Oh! I'll be fine here, you just go and enjoy."

He patted her hand as if comforting a child.

"Galer is my oldest friend. He won't mind. He just wants to meet you himself, see how you are. As the community guardian, he has to check on…"

Rhea saw the hesitation and smiled wryly.

"Injured wildlife?" she interjected rather miserably.

"… visitors," he corrected.

"But he won't expect anything of you except to be yourself. Besides, I think you'll impress him."

Rhea looked dubious, still amazed he didn't get it.

"I mind! I thought you'd just agreed, I'm not just a dumb rescue animal or something. I've got feelings on the matter. Can't it wait until I look less like a… a medical illustration? I would never have sent poor Vincent out with half his feathers missing.

Poor bird would have been so embarrassed."

Jal frowned, studying her,

"Sorry, I can see that now. You were comfortable with Marn and me, so I hadn't considered there'd be a problem."

She rolled her eyes, ready to accept his apology, but she couldn't help noticing he was preoccupied, scanning her from top to toe, and she knew he had something in mind.

"I can't stop him now, but I can do something about your looks," he murmured apologetically, then beamed an irresistibly imploring smile. "Please. Help me out with the old policeman."

After all he'd done for her, how could she refuse him so small a favour? She nodded uncertainly, realising there was no way he was going to allow her to back out.

He had obviously read her thoughts in the expressions on her face, and was on his feet in a flash.

"Good! I'll give you a quick sanding down. That tunic is a touch dandruffy, as you would say, so let's see if we can't find you a nice fresh outfit," he said, offering her his hand.

Jal polished her face carefully before giving the rest of her body a quick rub down, freeing her from the worst of the itchy flakes, and then he applied some soothing, sweet smelling oil. He pulled out various bits of cloth, and some of Marn's old tunics, which he'd obviously been altering, from his needlework box, but in the end, she scrambled into a long sleeved T shirt and trousers that Jal had salvaged from the car wreck.

She frowned, examining herself. "Something's happened. These trousers are shorter."

Jal viewed the ensemble, remarking simply, "No, you're growing."

She laughed, assuming he was joking.

"I'm growing, yeah right. I suppose your high tech way of cleaning clothes can't possibly shrink them."

Jal's mouth twitched a silent dissent.

"I know these clothes are fitted." she said, pulling at her sleeves which hid the awful mess that was her skin,

"But that oil is so soothing, I'm sure they won't irritate for at least a couple of hours. I almost look presentable, apart from my patchwork head of course." She grinned up at him with a vulnerable playfulness.

He held up a jewel green strip of cloth.

"How about a hat?" he asked, as he deftly wrapped it around her head, turban style.

She turned this way and that, admiring her almost acceptable reflection, finally emitting a "hmm," of agreement.

Jal inclined his head approvingly.

"It looks good. You could wear those tomorrow for the Aazaar Spring celebration."

"The what?" she gasped in astonishment.

He smiled, "I was going to tell you before the children interrupted. I'm taking you to the celebration. I thought you'd like to get to understand us a little better. I'll take you to a spot on the hillside where you can watch."

She flushed, quaking at the prospect of not one, but two social engagements. "Ohh thank you but I'm not ready."

He smiled reassuringly.

"We're going with a picnic to a secluded spot where you can listen to the music and watch the dancing over the lake. You'll like it. You'll see."

Before she could protest again, the door alert sounded. He held out his hand.

"Come on, your audience awaits. Galer has been looking forward to meeting you," he said brightly, and she made her wobbly way, her blotchy scarred face a picture of determination.

She gave him a friendly nudge,

"Ahh, its okay, I won't sulk. I'll be well behaved and answer all his questions!"

Jal raised amused eyebrows, showing no shadow of the flash of concern he felt at this possibility.

"Mmm, that's understanding of you. But Galer can be energetic in following up lines of conversation. I know it's only enthusiastic curiosity, but I don't want you to feel obliged and get tired."

She nodded, grateful for the warning, now ready to accept any help Jal would offer.

"Well you'll understand won't you? Explain if I get tired..." She sighed, "...or mess it up." *'After all,'* she thought, *'he had studied humans and me for long enough to explain their foibles'*

Jal smiled his agreement and satisfaction. Rhea had willingly given him permission to control the conversation between her and Galer, allowing him to keep his secrets safe.

She took a deep breath. She was about to take the first steps out of the long hibernation of healing, into a strange new life.

"Okay," she muttered, as she steeled herself to meet Jal's oldest friend, the enthusiastic Aazaar policeman.

The children had set out places around the low table, and Galer already lounged on the cushions, rumbling pleasantries in his soft purring voice.

Rhea couldn't help shrinking into Jal's side at the sight of Galer, this huge, powerful looking creature, rising to his feet and bearing down to greet them both. "Er umph! Hello," she muttered in a flash of terror, as Galer reached down, engulfing her in a polite Aazaar Kind hug. She steadied her turban and herself, then smiled politely as she felt his bright, crystal green eyes, discreetly, but thoroughly, scanning her.

"It's good to see you looking so well in such a short time," Galer purred pleasantly, taking her arm and ushering her to the table before she could even think to decline.

"Thank you, I'm trying my best," she said sweetly. *'Smooth operator,'* she thought with wry wariness.

She watched Galer happily chatting with Jal and the children about the upcoming festival. Jal's brother was a musician of note, and had been helping the children of the community to ready their own musical performances for their Spring celebration. This predilection of the Aazaar to celebrate the changing of the seasons had, to her mind, made them sympathetic fellow beings, rather than some cold, fearsome creatures from the unknown.

She settled into her comfortable obscurity. She was too nervous to ask questions, so kept to diplomatic little smiles planning to wait until she felt confident enough to speak. However, she soon discovered Galer was unlikely to allow that.

"Your daughter here told me all about the injured animals and birds you looked after. Not an easy thing to get right is it?" he said agreeably, giving her a conversation opening.

Rhea nodded. She was painfully aware he had that deceivingly mild manner of someone at complete ease with his authority, and he was checking her out.

"Thank you. No, I don't suppose it is, but Jal has managed it very well with my daughter and myself," she said, flicking a gracious smile Jal's way, before settling a shy gaze on Galer, her mind now an anxious blank.

He chuckled, acknowledging her endorsement of his friend's integrity.

"Yes, so I see," he agreed with a good natured smile, and then tactfully allowed the children to catch his attention, freeing Rhea from her obvious discomfort.

Although grateful for this momentary reprieve, his consideration fuelled her determination to overcome her anxieties, and at least be polite. But she hadn't a clue how to make small talk with a policeman, an Aazaar Kind one at that.

In her head, whole massed teams of questions jostled and jockeyed for position to be asked. Did they have reckless or drunk flying problems? What did they know about their home planet? Did they have problems with noisy teenagers congregating on rooftops and treetops? Had Aazaar Kind ever had problems with humans? What did they and what could they do about it? She thought, an anxious little suspicion niggling at her. She dismissed them. 'No. Not suitable for the supper table,' she thought, desperately wondering what she could say, wondering how she could ask the questions about their intentions towards humans that her most basic gut reactions were now beginning to prompt her to ask.

She tuned back into the conversation just in time to hear Marn mention the celebrations, and make some remark about how it was in honour of their creator.

"You have stories of a creator? Like us?" she queried innocently, her heart leaping in hope of something they shared, something that put them on the same side.

Marn looked at her in confusion.

"Not like humans," he mumbled uncertainly.

Galer smiled benignly, explaining his people's deepest truth in an incongruously simple sentence.

"Your species evolved here, from the energy and matter of your world. We were created fully developed. Our creatrix was a real flesh and blood woman, not a metaphor or myth."

Rhea blinked.

"Oh!" she said, stunned.

Not a myth? She knew of others who believed that their ancient stories of creation were the literal truth, the only truth, and who were determined that all other explanations be stamped out. Something deep, primeval, reacted in her gut, now definitely warning of their difference, of danger. "So these are your religious stories?"

Jack shook her head. "No Mam. It's their history."

She turned to Galer. "Religion is a human thing, usually really old, from times when people lived in tribes. Each tribe had it's own god." she informed him with solemn pride.

Jal tipped his head giving her a fond smile of confirmation, flashing Rhea one of those reassuring glances that are passed between the adults in mixed adult child company. But Rhea was far from reassured. She wondered, did she teach Jack that? She couldn't remember doing so. There again, maybe she did, with all the stories she'd read to her. But what if someone else, some Aazaar, had been teaching her things? Telling her what to think? Telling her some crazy impossible religious thing for reasons of their own? Her gut instinct throbbed again and she felt dizzy. If they believed they were created, or even worse, really were, how do you find common ground with them? These strange, created-perfect-straight-off creatures would have no link, no sympathy with her, or with messy, natural life. She was just an accident. She looked across the table at that alien face as if she'd just noticed what he looked like, seeing how his fine fang like teeth gleamed white against that sharp, mahogany, gargoyle like face, that fierce face. That reassuring smile was out of place. Before she knew what had happened, she'd flinched.

Her head reasoned he was as kindly as ever, and anyway, she was in no position to be questioning her situation, but she couldn't stop the rush of questions her gut demanded as proof of the Aazaars' benign intentions and motivations.

"Who made you? What did she make you for? Are you androids or something?" she blurted out as she met Jal's eyes, then embarrassment and self preservation hit. She bit her lip, lowering her eyes from Jal's and Galer's kindly, but amused gaze.

"Oh, it's all a bit much to take in," she offered appeasingly, wondering if she could just make a rush for the door and hide from them all, from the whole whirl of unsettling emotions.

Jack giggled. Seeing her mother's awkwardness, she came to her rescue. "They're not androids Mam. They're real people, and it really is their history. It's like in the story of Atlantis where the Atlanteans made different creatures to do their work and things, only it's true. And anyway, the Aazaar Kind weren't made as slaves."

Rhea couldn't help but blink in dumbfounded amusement at her daughter's cleverness, allowing it to carry her away from her confusion and fear, at least for now.

"Atlantis?" she asked, and berated herself.

Of course no one was telling Jack what to think. After all, she'd been the one who had read Jack tales of Atlantis at bedtime. And now, Jack was using them to help her understand their situation.

Marn nodded with encouraging enthusiasm.

"Jack told us the story at the learning centre, so we found a copy. It's a bit like the story of the Brynewiln."

As she watched Jack grin with pride under Marn's encouragement, Rhea couldn't help remembering how touched she'd been to see how Marn had looked after her daughter.

"Yeah and the Aazaar Kind were made specially..." Jack struggled to explain.

Jal inclined his head, encouraging Jack with what Rhea could see, despite her fear, was a kindly avuncular smile.

"To help the people of the three worlds learn to live in peace," she said triumphantly.

'Jack knows more about them than me. She's tried to know more,' Rhea thought guiltily, feeling a twinge of embarrassment about her fears. She'd been lying around Jal's house all this time, accepting his help and hospitality, without any reason to suspect any harm from him. Furthermore, she had never really considered what reasons he had to help her. Of course he'd told her why; He said he wanted to, and that it was his belief that he should. She'd been too happy to accept this at the time. But, why did he believe he should? Why should he want to? She scolded herself for her silliness, with the thought that he was just being human... Human? But he wasn't human, and she wondered if he could even be considered living, if he, his species, hadn't evolved. They were made, manufactured, like machines.

She banished the grumbling fear of her gut to the depths of her mind, reminding herself she was so lucky to be having this momentous experience. People all over the world had spent years, and huge amounts of money, just asking if other intelligent life existed. And yet here she was, living in a whole village of them without ever even trying to find out about them or their way of life, let alone checking out their motives. She resolved she would make an effort.

She had been invited to one of the biggest celebrations of the Aazaar Kind. She would go, and she would open her eyes. She would watch and listen. After all, she knew how. She had learnt by watching those bats and birds.

She looked from her daughter to Jal, getting out her mental clipboard.

"Three worlds?" she echoed carefully.

Jal tipped his head.

"Yes, there were three inhabited planets in our home system. And on one, there was an aggressive race who had rejected their own origins as children of their home world. They were the Brynewiln.

Their elites couldn't accept that the other two worlds weren't already inhabited by species as advanced as themselves. Worse, they refused to be eradicated or enslaved, insisting on equality. And that was the beginning of the interplanetary wars."

"But wasn't there any trade? Intermarriage? I don't know. Maybe that wasn't possible, but surely some kind of cooperation was," Rhea protested incredulously. "I just thought that the cleverer people became, the less likely they would be to go to war, you know? Be destructive."

Jal tipped his head. "That depends on what their cleverness is based on, what they start from. They gave up their connection with their world at an early stage. They believed, rather than being part of it, that their world was there for them to exploit. So they got cleverer in a dangerously arrogant and unbalanced way, and saw themselves at the centre of the universe, at the pinnacle of development. In order to keep their view of the universe, they cleared away anything that did not fit. They even modified their own biology to fit their ideology, their beliefs. They did this by constant monitoring and life engineering of their population's development. Sadly, those beliefs led to the destruction of the ecosystem of their home planet. They'd made themselves into a cancer of their own environment. This was their vice and their tragedy."

"The plague of the Brynewiln. They made a plague and became it," she agreed, her green education at the hands of her conservation club members shaping her horror into informed revulsion.

"And this woman of the Brynewiln? She made you?" she asked with a wary awe. Her heart, which was searching for comforting evidence that they were on the same side, still wrestled to keep her fearful gut under control.

"Why did she make you? What made her different?" she asked, trying to imagine a woman who'd got so fed up with all her people's dark, death dealing beliefs and their terrible wars, that she decided to go out to work one Monday morning, wipe their slate clean, and create a whole new species, a whole new people.

Jal smiled indulgently, if a little wistfully.

"Maybe she was always different, maybe she was looking for something different. We don't know. We do know that she was a great observer of living things. She was what you might call a bio engineer, working for the organisation which kept her species, what they called, clean. On one of her observation trips to the smallest world, a place the Brynewiln weren't too keen on, she got lost in the wastelands and was injured. She was found by the people who had fled there. She had expected to be killed, but they nursed her back to health. She'd always felt there had to be other ways of understanding the universe, so with this ragged band of insightful refugees, she found an alternative way of thinking that led to her finally breaking free from the constraints of her upbringing."

Rhea nodded, reassured to realise she could identify with his explanation. "Sounds like human explorers. Travel broadens the mind. Especially when you're desperate to change it."

Jack shook her head.

" Oh Mam! That's not the end of it. She made the Aazaar to stop the war. And had a really hard time when she got back home. She hung onto her job for a while, but people stopped speaking to her, then she was arrested. She had all these different ideas no one liked. They called her the Night Bird. It was a spirit of their forests, a story from when they were like cavemen. They didn't have forests any more, and by then, they said the Night Bird was a demon who had brought nothing but disease and illness. So they were being nasty to her by calling her that. But she knew they were in the wrong, so she didn't give up."

A mother's pride in her child's intelligence swelled in her breast. Looking into her daughter's shining eyes, Rhea couldn't help but side with this amazing, brave woman of Jack's story.

Jal looked on, only too aware of Jack's effect on Rhea's doubts, and smiled contentedly.

"We see her name differently, as a symbol of freedom and hope. She made us as a synthesis of her hopes for life, hope for her own people, and the people of the two other worlds. She made us to find peace," he emphasised.

Admiration and excitement finally overtook Rhea.

"I just can't take in that you were made, manufactured? Wow!

So, is she still, you know, creating?"

Galer shook his head in amusement.

"No. We're not just freshly made. It was a very long time ago. In fact, it was a great many generations ago."

She glanced at Jack and Marn. "Oh" she said, giving him an indulgent knowing smile, feeling foolish for believing they were actually created, foolish and embarrassed for her fears. It was like human beliefs after all, sounding soothingly like some lovely old legend. She knew the ways of legends, and anticipated a charming story of this wonderful woman leading these ancient peoples into peaceful integration. Intermarriage, that's what the tale really meant. It was a happy ever after story, a story that would hopefully silence her fearful gut once and for all.

"So the Aazaar Kind were made up of all the peoples of the three worlds, is that how she hoped to do it?"

"No Mam. It wasn't that simple," Jack said, really getting into her retelling. "They were her children. She made them then she got them the best teachers she could find from the other two worlds. She also found a way to copy the vast libraries of the Brynewiln for them."

"So what happened? Where is Night Bird's world?" she asked eagerly, only to see the eyes of Galer and Jal grow curiously shadowed with sadness.

It was Jal who finally answered.

"Gone. Blown apart. We don't even know where it was. We've been travelling from the third generation of our people. Our communities are scattered across the stars. As Galer said, there have been very many generations since then."

Rhea sighed, finding herself moved to pity for the whole Aazaar race, and a little sad for the disappointment of being robbed of her happy ending.

As she imagined flotillas of lost and homeless Aazaar Kind wandering through space, her sympathy for them triggered a pang of longing for her own little backstreet house.

"But where do you call home? You've got to have a home," she insisted, as much to herself as to Galer and Jal.

Galer heaved a deep sorrowful sigh.

"We weren't born of a planet. We didn't evolve, so we never had a home. To have a world of our own to call home, a planet who will accept us as her children, is our greatest aspiration. That aspiration was what Night Bird gave us. That was her hope."

It was so poignant, her heart ached in sympathy for them. It wasn't just an old tale. At the same time, she knew now, in her gut, they really were created. She gave the tiniest of shudders.

"Mam, the planet means the creatures on it. They've got to accept them, live with them in harmony, or else it just doesn't work for them. That's why they're here in hiding. Humans don't look ready to accept them, but humans don't live here in Dream Hills."

Rhea nodded. She might not know their whole tale yet, might not really understand, but she already understood the moral. A whole species was created to follow a happy-ever-after ecological lifestyle such as she had dreamed of.

"In the meantime, you do have Dream Hills. I mean, I can understand why you like it here. You've got your own little place and are bothering no one, so there's no one to bother you," she said, as much to convince herself.

Galer inclined his head in agreement.

"Exactly," he said, then turned to Jal.

"I'm pleased to see your guest understands us."

CHAPTER 5

As she looked up into the face of the Aazaar Kind community policeman, she wondered if she did, if she could.

Next day, Rhea woke to a beautiful magical day, the sound of music a low insistent thrumming like huge didgeridoos, and lighter sounds, right up to fairy like tinkles that soared above it, washing through her, washing away all shadows. She limped her way to the main room, and found that every door and window had been flung open. Jal stood by the main door listening.

"My brother Issn has opened the chorus. Listen. You'll hear people all over the hillside join in," he said, his eyes sparkling with pleasure. "It will pass from this hillside to the next, until the whole settlement is playing and singing," he explained.

She stared out in delight, listening to waves of sound washing back and forth.

She thought she heard pipes, harps, violins and strange tinkling sounds she couldn't put an instrument to, and even sounds like huge church organs, and yet everything was in perfect harmony. Violin like phrases danced with didgeridoos, then soared away to a tinkle, before harps sounded their haunting melody and began the rounds again.

Jal sat down cross-legged, and began to stroke an instrument she hadn't seen before. It was vaguely harp shaped, but made of crystals. He sent curlicues of joyful soaring notes off in answer to the calls from his neighbours, holding a rhythmic thrum steady at the same time. The sound danced through her, a call of pure happiness and hope, until she felt she could lift off and fly with it above the trees.

"It's wonderful," she breathed in amazement, as Jal finally left off. "What is it? It makes you feel so alive!"

Jal smiled "Aazaar, hope. We celebrate what made us Aazaar

Kind and what keeps us Aazaar Kind. The music tells our story, though not in words."

She listened, wondering if she could make it out. "It feels, like...you want to grow with it, it's talking to every cell in your body. Like it's wonderful to be alive and you're connected to every other living thing."

Jal smiled his agreement "Yes," he murmured as he listened.

She found herself wondering if she dare venture out into this magical land of music.

Jal was watching her closely. He had known, had hoped she wouldn't be able to resist the music. "Come on, let's take breakfast with us. Get yourself ready and bring a wrap," he said, watching her standing on the threshold, her eyes shining with excitement and curiosity.

She needed no more prompting, and soon, she was limping out of his door for the first time, into a wooded wonderland that once, she had only dreamed of. Jal scooped her up, and in a flash, tied her in his wrap and flew off to a clearing higher on the hillside.

She sat with her eyes closed for some minutes after he freed her, waiting for her heart to stop battering her ribcage.

"Eer...That was a bit of a shock. I wish you'd warned me," she said breathlessly, patting the ground with both hands for reassurance. Then she gazed out across a beautiful wooded valley that held a shimmering lake, and sighed in delight.

She frowned, puzzled.

"Hang on, where are your farms? It is a spring festival isn't it?"

Jal smiled. "Farms?"

"Yes, you know? Where you grow your food," she said.

He gestured to the hillside and the woods. She blinked, still bewildered.

"Oh!"

"We encourage the optimum growth patterns of communities of plants, so there's always something to eat. At this season, that's these toadstools and shoots, some early flowers, and a few roots," he explained. "It's one way to feel part of the habitat."

She gave a delighted chuckle.

"Intergalactic Greenies!" she exclaimed, including them in her visions of a virtuous world before turning back to the scene before her.

Music was swirling around the trees, and dancers with velvet black wings spiralled in drifts up from the valley and above the surface of the lake below. Everywhere, there was the sight, sound and scent of exuberance and joy.

"It's like this is what you were meant to be," she said gleefully, suddenly feeling she was among real life fairies.

Jal's eyes twinkled, happy to find she could share it. "Yes it is. There'll be communities celebrating, just like this, right across the stars."

She sighed wistfully. "It's such a beautiful thing to do. I can't imagine a celebration in my world, simply about being human."

He inclined his head. "Maybe, but this is something we need to do. You evolved from the dust of Earth, one decision at a time, over thousands of years. What made you human, keeps you human. You know what you are. Even if you never think of it, you feel it in every part of you. We can't do that. We were created. So we have to recreate that moment of hope and joy. The music is our way of remembering what made us Aazaar Kind and what keeps us Aazaar Kind."

She smiled. Right now, in this swirl of sound, she understood, but she knew she would have to think about this mysterious pronouncement for a very long time to fully grasp it.

"Mind you, that means you get to choose your home," she said brightly, "So did you choose Earth or did you just happen by?"

Jal sighed with incongruous wistfulness. "We found her by good fortune."

'*Her?*' she thought, charmed by this description.

"You make the planet sound like a goddess," she said, remembering Linda's Pagan revelations. Until the Linda episode, she hadn't had a reason to take it seriously. Now? Well, she was in fairyland.

Jal gave her an indulgent smile.

"She gave birth to you humans, all the creatures and plants you share her with, and she is everything that defines and supports your life. Isn't that a goddess?"

Earlier, she would have thought it an oddly emotional statement to come from this carefully rational Aazaar, Jal. But now, in the midst of this intensely emotional celebration, it resonated with something buried deep in her very cells, something so old it was beyond words. She smiled, a momentary pang of understanding lighting a pathway from her heart towards these strange wanderers of the stars. '*You just need to feel you belong,*' she thought, giving him a smile of warm affection.

Her little spot, there on the hillside, became a camp for the day. Rhea was the mainstay, presiding over the picnic snacks and blankets, as the children and other visitors, came and went, joining her to rest and chat, before rejoining the music and dancing.

CHAPTER 5

When Issn crept silently into her sanctuary to take a rest between musical exertions, she found herself breathless and excited. She'd been chosen to be host for a big music celebrity. But far from imposing, despite his size, she found Issn gentle and quiet, his movements flowing, as if he were floating on the music, his dreamy green eyes seeming to see things no one else was aware of. But gentle as he seemed, she could appreciate his power. He had moved the whole community to action.

"You're a magician!" she said delightedly.

He tipped his head agreeably.

"A magician?" he repeated, examining the music of the word in his mouth.

"I like this word," he murmured affably.

She smiled.

"And this place is like a fairyland to me."

A thought struck her. *'Only those invited in get to see fairyland.'*

"How come you keep it hidden from humans?"

Issn studied her face for a moment, then gave her one of his dreamy smiles. "Did Jal not tell you?"

She shrugged.

"Only that I was in your village. I just accepted it. I never thought to ask where your village is."

He tipped his head, giving out a soft knowing chuckle.

"Oh," was all he said.

She smiled.

"Aren't you going to tell me?"

He tipped his head in agreement.

"We have a different way of seeing," he answered amiably.

'A musician is a musician, human or not. All clever remarks you can't understand,' she thought wryly, then looked up at him. He did have

kindly eyes though.

"Okay, so what's that got to do with it?" she asked.

He lazily chewed on the stalk of a feathery, aniseed smelling plant, making her wonder if he would ever answer her.

"It means we were able to see this place, but humans couldn't. Can't."

Rhea shook her head, bemused.

"But I'm human and I can see it, so can Jack," she countered.

He gazed at her knowingly, making her feel there was a whole lot he was seeing that he was not telling and maybe would never tell.

"Yes, you can. You saw Jal, then he brought you here," he explained airily.

She knew she would have to ponder that too for some time, and even then, she might never get hold of his meaning.

"Whatever, it is beautiful," she said admiringly, giving Issn a companionable smile before gazing out towards the lake. She liked him, even if she hadn't a clue what he was talking about. She felt comfortable in his presence.

"It's not a complete world. It's like a little bubble, a fragment of a parallel existence that is attached to your world, but it goes on unseen," he murmured, gazing up at the impossibly deep blue sky.

"And up to now, only we have the secret of passing between here and your world. So humans can never find us. Unless we invite them of course."

She started, having thought the conversation was finished, then gave a chuckle. *'Musicians, always on another planet, even when they're from another planet!'*

"Fairyland," she pronounced dreamily, flushed with

embarrassment, then was glad to see her remark had satisfied Issn.

That evening, Rhea watched in delight as the hillsides and the sky filled with twinkling lights from the jewellery of the dancers. Jal clicked on his own crystalline bracelets, and they gave off a soft rosy glow, lighting up the quizzical expression on her face.

"You look full of questions."

She flushed, embarrassed a little.

"Just thoughtful. Today's given me plenty to think about. I had a conversation with Issn."

He gave a soft chuckle of sympathy.

"Ah, he would have been at his most mystical, not exactly clear and concise, I fear."

She nodded, the ease of true friendship quietly moving in with them.

"But not all the time. I got some of it. It's that healing thing my friend Linda talked about. At least I think it is. He's one of what I call real musicians. He hears music in all the tones of everyday life, and plays our hearts' secrets back to us. "

She felt a little blush of embarrassment for getting so poetic. "Like a human musician."

He smiled. "So we're not so different from humans?"

'I hope you are.' she suddenly thought, ducking her head to hide her blush. When all was said and done, she had to admit, Humans weren't very nice, not even to each other.

She couldn't help it, she gazed at him under her lashes, following the lines of his strange looks, everything about him that didn't make sense in her world. They'd obviously known how to protect themselves if they'd survived a concerted attempt to wipe them out, let alone successfully wandering the universe.

"Humans don't have wings," she parried, knowing he would be expecting more.

He smiled a curious knowing smile, making her feel he had seen her fear, but said nothing on the matter.

"Our Creatrix not only wanted to give us any advantage she could, she wanted us to enjoy our lives. And despite your reservations, flying is so enjoyable I assure you," he said with a teasing grin.

"I believe you," Rhea answered with a laugh. "I just need to get used to leaving the ground so suddenly."

She smiled wistfully. "But it's really lovely too that she thought having wings would help you enjoy your lives. It makes her sound quirky, real."

The music had died away, leaving only the low rhythmic thrumming, when a haunting melody began and built up, slowly being picked up across the hillside. "This is the song of the Night Bird," Jal said dreamily.

Rhea was completely taken up by the whole spirit of the event, the music and the sight of the dark shapes and twinkling lights, gracefully spiralling in formation in the clear evening sky.

"I think she must have been a romantic creature," she sighed entranced.

"Romantic is not something you would normally associate with the Brynewiln, but maybe that was her secret," Jal agreed.

She smiled, wanting to know more, wanting to like this woman, but feeling apprehensive all the same. It was a bit like getting ready to meet your friend's grandmother.

"I know they were making war on unsuspecting natives of other worlds, but, I mean… were they that bad?"

Jal sucked in air through his teeth.

"Cruel, vicious, rapacious. Think of bad and they were worse. Still are."

"Still are?" Rhea repeated in astonishment.

"But I thought you said their world was blown apart," she protested. "I thought they'd have gone down with their world. I just assumed…"

He shook his head sadly.

She had one last protest in defence of her happy ever after story.

"Alright, but you said she made you to stop the war. Surely when your people stepped in and the war stopped…"

She was puzzled to see that shadow in Jal's eyes again, that shadow of an ancient sorrow.

"They didn't find a way to stop the war. They never got their chance to be accepted. Our Night Bird creator was killed protecting the whereabouts of her children, our ancestors. She was dismissed as mentally defective. We were declared an industrial accident, a threat to the germ line, health and ecology of the three worlds empire of the Brynewyln, and scheduled for clean up. We were to be wiped out, destroyed. And we've been hunted down ever since."

Rhea shuddered. Not only was there no happy ending to the tale of the Night Bird, in fact, there wasn't even an ending.

She gazed out at the dancers, revelling so innocently in this happy celebration of gratitude for their current home and who they were. They weren't footloose travellers, they were desperate refugees fleeing demonic monsters, demons whose inheritance they might well share.

"Oh! But…they could follow you here?" she said, realising that the Aazaar might be a threat to Earth after all.

"No, we are very good at staying hidden from them. They are far away." She nodded, still alarmed. "Okay, but...might they, you know? Spread? To here?"

Jal gazed up at the star studded sky, with a curious look of contentment. "No, they're contracting, turning in on themselves. Besides, the chances of them finding Earth, let alone arriving, are very small."

Maybe it was his manner, his words, and her wish not to feel such fear, but her discomfort simply dissipated, and she moved on to gentler considerations. "So what did she look like? I mean, do you know? What do the Brynewiln look like?" she asked. As she waited for him to answer, she suddenly felt strangely alone.

Jal was looking her way, but seeing something beyond her, something in his mind's eye. "You," he said quietly.

CHAPTER 6

"Jal, do you think this was what the terrorists were looking for?" Jack said piteously, as he passed the doorway of her little den.

An ominous thrill stopped him dead. It had been some time since Rhea had asked him to help her find the mysterious "It" that had caused her catastrophes and led to the attack. Could Jack have had it all along?

Jack was sitting on the floor looking decidedly small and lost in the middle of her few belongings, those he'd managed to save from the explosion. She was holding up a small black object.

He crouched down beside her. "You alright sprout?" he asked, giving her a hug. She snuggled into him, her confidence returning, fingering the unidentified plaything.

"I forgot. It was in my rabbit's pocket," she said, pointing to a rabbit pyjama case. "I found it in Mam's shopping bag. I used to put away the things when she came home with the shopping," she said wistfully, then dropped the object into his hand, glad to be rid of it.

He turned it around between his fingers, trying to make sense of what it was, wondering if indeed it could be the mysterious, much sought after "property", or whether it was just some innocent unknown human artefact.

"It's got a cap like a pen," Jack offered helpfully, noticing Jal's incomprehension. "You use it on a computer. My friend Colin said it might be a game but it wasn't. It was full of spy stuff. You know? What them terrorists were after," she said in disgust.

Jal smiled, imagining Jack's disappointment and swift lack of further interest when the screen of her computer filled with the boring, not very playful, work of some adult. He stuffed it into his pocket in an attempt to muffle its unsettling influence, then set about steering their conversation to a comfortable conclusion, as well as finding out what Jack knew about it.

"I see. And which terrorists are these?" he asked gently.

She heaved an impatient sigh. "The ones that were after Mam and me."

He inclined his head "Oh, those ones," he said, dismissing them with a shrug, and giving her a conspiratorial nudge.

"But didn't you show this thing to your mother? Ask her about it?"

She shrugged guiltily.

"I was going to, but she was out, so I put it away for safekeeping, and then I forgot."

Jal inclined his head again, giving her a gentle squeeze of reassurance.

"Would you mind if I asked her about it?"

She nodded, clearly relieved to be rid of the complication, and once more set upon the meagre heap of belongings in front of her.

"I'm getting too old for stuffed toys," she remarked, fondly straightening the bow on the rabbit's neck.

Jal inclined his head in wise agreement.

"Mm, you're quite a young lady now."

She cocked her head expectantly, still fondly stroking the rabbit. She looked about her den, remarking in a young lady sort of way,

"And this place needs to be kept tidy."

He looked about, making a play of studying what was missing. "Tidy, yes, but lived in, cosy."

She grinned, delighted.

"And rabbit makes the place look cosy!" she said, bounding up to carefully place Rabbit on her neat little couch.

He left Jack happily rearranging her den, her pride and rabbit intact, and the sinister little black device now forgotten.

Once out of Jack's awareness, he headed straight for his den and the laptop he'd acquired from the human world, hoping he could make enough sense of the information on the device to decipher it.

But after a quick study, he slumped in annoyance, staring sullenly at the screen. He could just about work out enough of it to know it was indeed the troublesome property, and the lead he was after. He'd spent so many months searching, only to find another problem. Plus, he was running out of time. What he needed was a human who could decipher this, find out exactly what it was to be used for. And if he found such a human, it would solve a number of problems in one.

He idly flicked through the work. He really didn't like the implications of what he could make out. He shuddered. This might be indicative of the trouble he suspected, but it wasn't definitive proof. He could have it all totally wrong, and it might be quite innocent.

Just then, he heard a familiar footfall, and he groaned inwardly, wondering how he could give himself the breathing space he craved.

"Have you got a minute or two? I'd like to have a word," Rhea said brightly, but he couldn't fail to notice her face was strained. He needed her to be in a positive mood right now. Besides, he didn't like to see his little human guest upset. He smiled a greeting, patting the cushions in invite.

Rhea perched stiffly on her cushion, her hands nervously clenched.

"Have you got any weapons?"

"Weapons?" he echoed, clearly taken aback. "You want weapons?"

She flushed, struggling to hold her nerve. After Galer's visit, she'd had a great deal to think about, to come to terms with about her hosts. She'd let it all subside into the back of her mind, allowing herself to happily slip back into an easy friendship with Jal, and the comfort of life in his household. But it had never gone away. It niggled in the quiet of the night, in those times when she wondered what would happen when she eventually had to leave, go back to her world, human world.

"I mean Aazaar, could you protect yourselves? You know, against humans?" she knew they could, they had survived unscathed for some time. That wasn't the question she wanted to ask.

Jal tipped his head, giving her a sympathetic look.

"Of course we can protect ourselves, but we don't att...."

"It must have been a shock finding we looked like your worst nightmare," she said, knowing her fear that she did, and hope that she didn't, was so obvious in her eyes

"It was, but you're not Brynewiln," he said firmly, and she couldn't help but flinch.

"I need to know why you, the Aazaar, are here." Her voice was low, with a hint of accusation.

He tipped his head, and she could see in his face that this had not been unexpected for him.

"Chance," he answered, searching her face.

"You already told me that, but why are you still here?" she asked, a look of reluctant suspicion in her eyes.

"I see," he said simply, and sat back, waiting expectantly.

"What?" she asked in confusion.

"You're afraid of me."

She gave an embarrassed laugh and flushed.

"Not you. Course not! Don't be silly. You're my friend," she protested, yet knowing he was right. And then she looked up, pleadingly more than accusingly.

"But Dreamhills is just a fragment, so what do Aazaar want with Earth?"

He tipped his head with a regretful smile, yet still pleased to be described as a friend.

"What we told you: acceptance. But right now, your world doesn't look as if she could find a place for us. We couldn't settle on Earth. It doesn't work if we're not accepted."

Rhea swallowed hard, still trying to stand firm, but that hint of wistfulness and concern in his eyes made it very difficult.

"You already told me that."

He tipped his head. "Yes, and it's still true." he said softly.

"That's why you're all into studying people," she murmured more to herself, sliding away from a confrontation she was ambivalent about anyway.

He tipped his head in agreement, and she could see relief in his eyes. "Partly, yes."

"I do understand," she said, giving him a small friendly smile, "But I would fight to protect Earth. I will..."

She stopped, looking up at Jal, her face full of anxious confusion as well as guilt. Her emotions had just ran away with her before she could think. He was her friend. Could she turn on him?

He tipped his head sympathetically, heaving a sorrowful sigh.

"You'd fight for your mother world, and that's how it should be."

"Maybe I'm not understanding you because..." She trailed off in consternation.

"There are different ways to fight," he offered.

Rhea lowered her head, hiding her face behind her hair, his sympathy causing her a physical ache of shame.

"Ohhhh you make it so hard. It would be easier if you were horrible to me. Then I'd know why I feel so frightened."

"So if it's not me, what is it?"

"But it is you," she said miserably. "What you are. I don't know anything about you."

She slumped shaking her head regretfully. "That's not really true. You've never been anything but nice to me. It's because you're making me question everything about myself, even my whole species, my world, making me realise I don't know a thing about anything."

"If we visit some of your friends, it'll help you work that out," he said briskly, leaving her stunned, and suddenly elated.

"What? Visit properly? In person?"

"In person," he echoed. "I tracked your friend Linda and

know where she'll be."

"Good choice," she agreed, and smiled bravely as another thought occurred to her. After such a show of lack of faith, he'd have no option but to send her back. But before she could question, he stood up.

"I think we could both do with a break. Get your wrap and let's go up on the high path. We'll talk there. After spending time behind this desk, I need some fresh air," he said, and she followed on miserably, feeling like she'd broken something between them.

She was glad of the change. The smell of the trees calmed her, and she settled against a boulder.

"I know I've got a cheek after what I've just said, practically accusing you and that, but I'm afraid of being left on my own," she said plaintively.

"You won't be alone. I'm coming too. Linda and her group are gathering at her caravan for a celebration. They'll be there in three days time. It's pretty isolated, so it's perfect for a first contact." he said, stretching out comfortably beside her.

"We'll only have to manage the few people in her company."

"Thanks," she started to say in relief, then the implications of the rest of his statement sank in. "What?" she stared at him dumbfounded. "You're coming with me?"

He tipped his head, holding her eyes with an amused gaze.

She burst out laughing.

"You're kidding!"

He deflected her accusation with a carefully surprised, but kindly avuncular smile

"No, not at all."

"But that's Hallowe'en," she protested, stifling a nervous laugh.

Jal inclined his head, continuing to regard her with calm interested eyes.

"I mean, me, I'm supposed to be dead!" she emphasised, unable to stop grinning at the absurdity of the thought. "Do you know about Hallowe'en?"

He tipped his head lightly.

"Isn't it an old human belief about the time when the spirits of the dead come to visit the living?" he asked innocently, leaving her speechless.

"I'd say that it's a perfect time for our visit," he added, amusement glinting in his eyes.

Rhea shook her head in wry amazement.

"Playing the innocent is a good approach to take to a situation you want to study. And why shouldn't it be fun?" he answered patiently.

"Why not?" she said, finally managing to regain her equilibrium, then a question clouded her face.

"Okay, I know you don't do such big things for frivolous reasons. So what'll you get out of this?"

He tipped his head approvingly. She was thinking clearly at last, and now he could begin to provide her with answers to the questions she had agonised over.

"Remember what your thugs were after?"

"Some sort of property. I guessed it was information," she said, somewhat bewildered by the change of tack, but gratified to hear he had taken seriously her need to find out what had been worth killing her for.

"I've got it at last, but I'd like a human scientist's opinion on it. It'll save me a great deal of time," he said, taking careful note of her reactions.

CHAPTER 6

"You've got it? And you sat there not saying anything?" She burst out in accusation before she could stop herself. She took a deep breath and just looked at him, her earlier fears rising again, and she flinched.

He cocked his head in question.

"You didn't tell me," she answered, her voice low, panicky.

He shook his head, sitting silently for a few moments, giving her time to breathe. He knew she would cope as long as he was patient.

She stiffened. She was ready for a fight, but he spoke softly, even fondly.

"What did you want with the bats in the old lorry yard?"

"The bats? Nothing. I just liked to watch them," she answered, confused by this neat circumvention of her defences.

"Yes, but why did you like to watch them?" he persisted.

The reflex to come up with an answer was too strong.

"Well, they seem full of life. I wanted to know how they managed. It's good to see other creatures going about their lives, feeling part of that," she offered.

A squirrel skittered across the dead leaves and up a tree nearby, and she saw him give a wistful smile.

"Me too," he murmured in satisfaction.

They sat quietly for a while, the yawning gap that had opened between them, quietly closing. "Right. You'd like to see a celebration." She smiled to herself. "Maybe join them."

Jal tipped his head in agreement, then took the data stick out of his pocket and held it out for Rhea to see.

"A data stick? Why have you got a data stick?" she asked confused.

"The information, the property your thugs were after," he

answered.

"Oh! What's in it?"

" What I suspected. You'd call it genetic manipulation," he said with a sigh.

"Is it about money, growing new plants or something?" she said, feeling disappointed at the banality of it all.

Jal was silent.

"So what is it about?" she prompted, now suddenly alert.

He felt her eyes on him as he idly pulled at a feathery plant stalk to chew, his face averted from her.

"I've got as far as working out it's a vaccination, for what, I don't know, and that it's only a small part of the data," he said evenly, and she wondered why she shuddered.

"Okay, but how're you going to find a scientist at a Hallowe'en party?"

He gave her a reassuring smile.

"I'm sure Linda will find a way to introduce me to one."

"Linda? She'll be terrified!" she exclaimed, then she reconsidered.

"I suppose...Linda is convinced you're a guardian spirit. When she gets over her fright, she'll be ecstatic to actually meet you."

She stopped, as realisation of what his tactics were finally dawned.

"Right."

He tipped his head.

"Good observers don't crash through the walls of our subjects of study. We knock on their doors of perception. We're less likely to scare them witless that way."

She laughed, still bemused at the thought of Linda meeting Jal. She would think she'd met a real live nature sprite, especially if he was wearing the same green, homespun tunic he was now wearing.

"But how's Linda going to find you a scientist? She's into all sorts of eco hippy stuff," she pointed out, then couldn't help adding.

"Maybe she could run up a spell to get you a Pagan one."

Jal raised an amused eyebrow.

"A Pagan scientist? Mmm" He tipped his head in theatrical approval.

"From what I know of your friend's beliefs, we'd certainly have a greater chance of understanding one another than some of the other human scientists," he noted mildly.

Rhea stared at him, her mind boggling.

"But beliefs are, you know, about emotions, feelings and morals and things. Isn't science about logic and facts?"

His eyes lit up with amusement once more. Despite the various conversations they'd had, she still hadn't thought through where those facts came from. "Yes, and I see Earth as a beautiful goddess, remember? Isn't that emotional and moral and things?" he said, gazing out across the valley from their perch on the high path.

"Oh. Like a pagan," she agreed, then frowned in bewilderment. "But what's that got to do with science?"

He looked into her expectant face, trying to think of the simplest and shortest way to explain, and in such a way as not to provoke her into intense discussions that flew everywhere at once.

"Science is a means of answering questions about your everyday life. But it's the most basic questions you ask that makes the difference. Because of your history, how you developed your scientific view, the deepest, most basic question of your dominant science is about overcoming or conquering nature, your world. Our most basic question, most basic concern, is, as you know, about integrating into a habitat. So our science is different from yours."

She nodded. "Okay, so, your science is different. How would Pagan science be different?"

"Pagans have a sense of being part of a greater whole, the Earth, of being part of their habitat, not apart from it. In short, their concern, like ours, is about being integrated."

"Ohhh wow!" she gasped, awe making her feel dizzy as she made the connections, "You and Linda have some very deep things in common then?"

And she sat for some moments, the light from this conversation giving her glimpses of the gently rocking little boat of those instinctive beliefs about living and life, that little boat which had borne her safely through the strange and dangerous currents of her recent traumatic and incredible experiences.

She took a deep breath. Those same instincts told her Jal was a true friend.

"I'm scared about going back, having to deal with the gangsters again. Could you teach me how to stay hidden?"

"It's amazing how easy staying hidden is," he said comfortingly.

"Anyway, this time, I'll be with you. You've got plenty of time to go exploring later. First, we're going to look for people who can help you work things out. Then, when we find them, you can take your time before you make any decisions."

She nodded. With every word of her proposed return to the Human world, she was exhilarated. But underneath, she couldn't suppress a slowly growing sense of sadness. She knew she would miss Jal and Dream Hills dreadfully.

CHAPTER 7

All too soon it was Hallowe'en, and a few rags of mist drifted like wistful ghosts around the treetops of Brightwood Valley, Southern England. Velvet shadows flitted silently across the dark autumn sky which sparkled with a promise of frost.

One velvet winged shadow winked into existence before disappearing again into the trees with never a sound, not even a rustle of dry, dead leaves.

Light twinkled sporadically from a large, solitary, mobile home set in a remote clearing in the woods. Two shadows advanced towards it.

Linda was in the galley of that mobile home, busy preparing the evening meal for the rest of her company, while a talkative young chap helped by hanging around entertaining her.

"You alright? You seem to be somewhere else."

Linda plastered a smile over her apprehension.

"Yes, just getting into the Samhain mood. You know? A time when the veil between worlds can be lifted, time for psychic happenings?" she said with theatrical emphasis, before concentrating on measuring in some herbs to the bubbling brew before her.

CHAPTER 7

He smiled reassuringly.

"We're bloody lucky considering. I can't believe the local police checked us out and are alright with all this," he said with a wry smirk.

She smiled

"They think we're fluffy Edenists. I knew we'd be allowed out to play," she said, then unthinkingly rubbed her forehead.

Stan groaned.

"Oh no! Incoming," he said, with a silly grin.

He knew her forehead felt hot when she got one of her premonitions.

"What?" she asked distractedly.

He flashed her a reassuring smile.

" Just ignore the idiocy."

She shrugged, looking for a pan.

"Pass me that pot please," she asked, rubbing her forehead again.

Then she looked up, her eyes distant, as if focussed on something beyond the wall of the caravan.

"We'll see Rhea tonight," she murmured, then turned to Stan. "And her guardian spirit friend."

He nodded, hoping she meant something symbolic, trying to believe it was wishful thinking, not quite knowing whether to give her a hug or not.

"You did all that was humanly possible to help her. You know what James said. You were lucky those thugs didn't come after you."

She looked up thoughtfully.

"Maybe, but she's coming all the same."

He gave her a brief hug. He knew better than to question

her assertions. Besides, he was inclined to treat her predictions with great respect. This otherwise down to earth, no nonsense woman, had demonstrated inexplicably accurate intuitions in the past, and was very sparing about who she shared them with.

"Will you be okay with that?"

She smiled reassuringly at Stan, her eyes gleaming with expectation.

"Course I will! I like being proved right."

He met her eyes briefly, trying not to show the concern that lurked in his thoughts. He looked out of the window, seeing the first flickerings of their bonfire.

"Look, I'm just going to check how everyone is getting on with the fire. Will you be alright?"

She grinned. He was so transparent, but she was glad of his kindness.

"Go on. Tell them to look after me then," she said with a wink, leaving him feeling a trifle embarrassed.

Later, in the clearing, the fire crackled high in the cold still air, forming a cosy bubble of warmth and light against the darkness and the cold that was drawing in around this small brave company of Earth's children. They were beginning their celebrations to pay their respects to this Goddess which sustained them.

Linda looked around the circle, ready to give her address. This celebration was different from previous ones. She had felt the pressure of current events, felt the urgent need to look outward, far beyond their little circle, find a means of expressing their fear for their darkening future, and need of hope to find a way through their long cold night.

"Samhain is the time when we welcome the Winter, the

celebration of the end of one cycle, a resting and reflection before the next rebirth.

"Now we all know these are troubled and dangerous times, a time of too many endings. Of course we all know that the world is always ending, for someone somewhere, but what is happening now is something much more than even war.

"We've all read exciting old tales and legends. Maybe we've even dreamed of finding some remnant, some secret knowledge. But maybe the secret was there in plain sight all along. Maybe it was a warning that we refused to see.

"In those old tales, incredible things always happened long ago in far away lands. And however fabulous these old civilisations had been, All that's left are the mysteries and the odd memorial stone, while the rest of the world toils on unheeding in its own ordinary way.

"The story of Atlantis tells a tale of a civilisation of high learning, and technology so advanced, they even tinkered with life itself, just like us, and engineered slaves of hybrid humans to work for them. And I'm sure they believed they'd go on forever. But they were lost in one dreadful night.

"We hear that Atlantis was destroyed for its cruelty, arrogance and greed, its general lack of respect for the gods, the goddess of nature.

"We've grown up with stories about pollution, global warming, shortages, and the fall of civilisation into some terrible dark age of totalitarianism that we may never survive. But even now, we can't accept that they're probabilities or even possibilities. To us, they're nothing but stories.

"Maybe what we refuse to see is that we, the people of the twenty first century, have also run headlong into trouble with the gods, the goddess of nature.

"We don't have to be intentionally cruel and arrogant like the Atlanteans. We just have to be ignorant, forgetting where we came from, forgetting our continued total dependence on the wonderful being beneath our feet, Planet Earth. We just have to be wilfully ignorant of the consequences of not respecting and protecting the rights and duties, hard won by our predecessors, that we enjoy, or the consequences of unleashing the powerful world shaking forces we have discovered and now play with.

"This time though, these events we are living through, aren't just happening on an island far away. Our civilisation is global. They are happening on every continent all over the world.

"If twenty first century civilisation were to sink beneath the waves, there would be no where left to run to, no mysteries for future generations, or memorial stones to read. There'd be no others left to toil on in their own ordinary way.

"We live in troubled times. We need to show there is a way to come through this time of endings, this Winter. We need to show there is a way to live in peace, not only with each other, but with our beautiful world, this universe, accepting what we've learned. This means not denying our discoveries, our successes, but facing up to, and learning from, their consequences, remembering where we came from, and what we are, what made us human, and what keeps us human.

"While we think of our own personal remembrances tonight, let us ask for guidance to do this. Let us ask for help to find ways to help those hurt by the troubles, and to bring about a healing for our world that will take us safely through this time of endings to a new rebirth."

There was a hush as the company absorbed and added their

silent assent to Linda's speech. They all linked hands in their circle, ready to chant. But Linda suddenly turned to look into the darkness beyond, making the rest of the group look questioningly at each other, hoping for some ghostly revelation of salvation, but fearing some thuggish attack, some end of their world.

"Rhea!" she called. Two shadowy figures emerged from the shadow of the trees, hesitating on the edge of their safe little island of light.

Everyone froze in shock, watching Linda run to a woman whom they were all certain could not be Rhea.

"I knew you were coming!" she cried out, and hugged her, so glad to find she was flesh and blood.

She stepped back to examine this rather elegant, well groomed version of Rhea more thoroughly, still shaking her head in disbelief. Having surreptitiously scanned her for signs of scars and seeing none, Linda deduced she must have somehow escaped the car before the explosion.

"Wow! You look really good! You look like you've been to a health and beauty farm and I'd swear you're taller!" she exclaimed delightedly, as if Rhea had just arrived back from a long trip, as if she'd never been declared dead, murdered with her daughter, in what the papers said was a high profile unsolved crime involving all manner of conspiracies and links with terrorism.

For now, her hurt and upset were put aside.

Rhea grinned.

"I am, thanks to Jal here."

Linda looked at her questioningly

"Jal?" she asked.

Rhea saw Linda's eyes widen as she looked up, saw her shrink back slightly, and knew she had finally seen the towering figure of Jal standing just behind her.

Linda let out a nervous laugh. For a second or two, she could have sworn she'd seen a large crow gazing back at her. Then she found herself examining a face that could have come straight out of an illustration of woodland gods and spirits. "Really not human. Very Samhain," she said, not realising she was thinking out loud, her mind boggling and her heart getting ready for running.

She gave a small nervous laugh, struggling to make sense of what she was seeing, finally coming to a certain acceptance, a decision that he wasn't too odd.

"Wings?" she murmured doing a double take. Then she shook her head, "My imagination," she muttered sheepishly. And yet she knew he had wings.

Rhea wanted to reassure her, but knew all she could do was wait, let her come to terms with their appearance in her own time.

"Come and join us," Linda said brightly, dazedly looking into Jal's face.

She was rewarded by finding something kind and warm in those golden alien eyes.

But then Jal offered her a smile of sharp white teeth that were definitely not human. She visibly cowered.

Rhea winced at Jal's gaffe, then quickly started to introduce them to each other to stop poor Linda fleeing in fright.

"Jal, this is my friend Linda who I used to work with. Linda, Jal, the man who dragged me out of the burning car."

Jal purred a hello. Linda blinked, unable to move, looking dumbly from one to another, then registered "Burning Car".

"You were hurt?" she asked incredulously, wondering why

Rhea hadn't been found in a hospital.

Rhea nodded.

"Very badly. Jal did a good job of putting me back together."

Stupefied, Linda stared up at him.

"Jal?" she queried, wondering how this hallucination could have done the job of a team of surgeons, her withdrawn mind still raking through everything she knew, to find an ordinary explanation for what she was seeing.

Then she reached out to take their hands.

"Pan," she murmured rather stupidly as she took Jal's hand. He smiled politely.

"I'm honoured, but I'm afraid I'm only flesh and blood."

She nodded, still struggling to regain her composure.

"Not human, not Earth," she managed to stutter, then blushed, realising she was holding his hand. "But what?"

"No, I'm not human. We call ourselves Aazaar Kind," he said gently, and cast a glance at the 12 mute, firelit statues who were staring at them; statues who were wondering if, even hoping, they were simply hallucinating due to one of Linda's concoctions.

"Introduce us," he urged softly, and finally she moved, leading them to join the circle.

As if in a dream, she held up their hands, grateful for the familiarity of the ritual.

"Tonight is Samhain, the night when we gather to celebrate the end of Summer and the beginning of Winter, give thanks for our harvests, the wilderness, and our place in the universe. Tonight is a time when strange things can happen."

She glanced at Rhea and smiled.

"As we have just found out. But just before their arrival, we asked for help to handle these difficult times we are living through. We were answered."

It was a moment or two before Rhea realised Linda meant that she and Jal were this answer, and felt the first prickle of panic. What strange and difficult times? What help? She couldn't help anyone. She was here because *she* needed help.

She shot a pleading glance toward Jal, but he wore his best calm, non-stick smile.

She glanced at Linda and the circle. *'They're celebrating Hallowe'en. A difficult time dedicated to the past, to ghosts,'* she reasoned and relaxed. She and Jal were the ghosts. At least she was. Her disappearance must have been hard on Linda. Of course she was only too willing to give whatever answers she could.

Linda looked around the circle.

"And it is our task to fathom what this answer means."

She gazed around her stunned and huddled company.

"This is Rhea who everyone thought was dead," she announced.

Nervously, she looked up at Jal.

"This is Jal, not human, but of the Aazaar Kind. He rescued Rhea and healed her injuries. Now we have something else to give thanks for: the safe return of Rhea and for this chance..." she paused, a little thrill of excitement tickling up her spine.

"...to welcome Jal among us, a being not of this Earth."

She gazed around the circle, letting this sink in before she continued.

"You have to admit though, their appearance amongst us tonight is more than a little scary," she said, smiling apologetically at them, then pulling herself up to her full height, she caught the eye of each of her circle. "But we are Pagans. The strange and the mysterious are what we're about; it doesn't faze us."

There was a murmur of agreement and straightening of chins and backbones, signalling to Linda that they had regained at least some of their composure, which seemed to satisfy her.

"Right then," she said briskly, "Now we've got that out of the way, we've got some very real, very dangerous considerations to deal with."

She swept her eyes around the circle to emphasise the seriousness of the situation.

"As far as the authorities are concerned, we're just a bunch of harmless weekend Edenist back-to-nature types, and for now, that cover has kept us safe from prying eyes."

There was a ripple of amused acknowledgement. "We know. We'll be good," Stan said cheekily. She grinned at him "I go on a bit I know, but this time, we've got two guests to consider, two guests who need our protection. I needn't remind you that whoever it was who hunted Rhea down, has already proved they would not hesitate at murder. So they must not find out she is alive."

"Pardon me," she said quietly to Jal then turned back to the circle. "And as for Jal, who would believe? What they'd believe was that illegal drugs were involved, which would prompt investigations, which we could certainly do without."

She paused again to allow a ripple of agreement from everyone. Then she began the formal closing of the circle.

"Rhea and Jal have been brought to the sanctuary of our circle. Let us ask that we be granted the strength to protect them with our silence. Everything that happens tonight will not be spoken of beyond this circle," she said gravely, gazing at each one of the group in turn, acknowledging their formal vow of silence on the matter, much to Jal's satisfaction.

Linda smiled, if a little nervously, raising her hands. "We've got a celebration to finish. Let's welcome our guests!" she said, now trying to raise the mood.

Rhea smiled shyly.

Jal bowed his head in respect, graciously accepting the welcome, touched by the nervous effort of Stan, the human nearest to him, who hesitantly took his hand.

"I'm Stanley Woodman. You really not human?" he asked breathlessly.

Jal smiled reassuringly.

"I'm pleased to meet you Stanley Woodman."

Stanley grinned, knowing his nerves made him flippant.

"We don't usually shake hands with the unseen ones. You alright in the circle? Not... er causing any ethereal discomfort?"

Jal's eyes twinkled with fiery sparks of amusement.

"No ethereal discomfort thank you," he murmured. Then he glanced around the still dumbfounded company.

Stan grinned impishly in his nervousness.

"We're all wondering if you'll bring your friends along to invade us."

Jal's eyes twinkled again.

"Sorry, we don't invade," he said, looking around the circle apologetically. "We're just a group of wanderers who like to do a spot of nature study."

Amusement had begun to thaw the stunned company, but Linda brought them to order. It was time to recommence the ceremony. The moon was climbing the frosty bright Samhain sky, its silvery light haunting the grasses and shrubs of the little woodland clearing. She led the whole company in a chant, soft but insistent, lifting each out of their thoughts, their isolation, until the circle moved as one. Then there was the final shout and they stood for a moment or two enjoying the flames.

Linda reminded them that there are many harvests, and the harvests of experience are just as important.

Each member of the group had made little symbols of their memories, getting ready to give thanks for successes, getting ready to let go of worn out old ways and move on, remembering and thanking those who had touched their lives, remembering those who had passed on. There was laughter over the thanking of a bad habit and wishing it a good journey. There was sympathy for those who felt the loss of loved ones.

Rhea placed her offering of pebbles and a handful of berries, recollecting her life before the burglary. She was surprised to find herself giving thanks for her little house and neighbours, her last job, and the friends it had brought. But when Linda invited her to speak, an ignored tight little button of more recent memories, of fear, began to unravel and swirl, threatening to spin her off balance. She took a deep breath, steadying herself.

"To the unknown thugs who pursued me. What you did wiped out my little world, my life. But it threw me into a fantastic world beyond my imagination. You can't know what an incredible gift you've given me."

She paused, smiling bravely, sweeping the circle with her eyes, settling her gaze on Jal.

"What got me through the shock and the injury was something simple: having faith in the care, kindness, and friendship I was offered."

She lowered her head, feeling at last, an acceptance of what had happened, feeling at peace and free enough to move on, to see her way back to her own human home.

Linda smiled warmly, carrying her chant to the next person, leaving Rhea to the privacy of her thoughts.

Rhea watched Jal, the solemn way he placed his offering of berries, touched that he should be so considerate of the feelings of this company. But then she saw a deep sadness in his eyes, and realised his offering was for those who had died. Standing there in the firelight amongst all these humans, he suddenly looked very lonely.

She took his hand and he gave a grateful sigh then he looked out wistfully across the circle.

She winced. She knew that what she had seen in that strange dream as she had fought for life, was rising behind his eyes. He'd been younger. There'd been a terrible accident.

Linda's chant eventually stopped at Jal and she asked if he wanted to share his thanks with the circle. He took a deep breath. When he'd joined this group of humans, he'd expected to keep an observer's reserve but suddenly, he'd felt as if every cell of his body was shaken by some unseen force he could not recognise. It seemed to come up from the ground beneath his feet, leaving him responding helplessly to every emotional pull.

His only option was to submit to this alien human ritual and allow it to guide him, keep him safe.

His loss and loneliness broke over him as he looked around this circle of demon-like eyes. For a split second, he felt an instinctive overwhelming terror, a certainty that these likenesses of the cruel and terrible Brynewiln were about to tear him apart. But their eyes were bright with curious kindness, a flame to thaw him. He gave an involuntary shudder and lowered his eyes.

Suddenly, an aching envy washed through him. These humans couldn't know the utter isolation he felt. Whatever misfortune befell them, they had the comfort of their mother goddess Earth, who pulsed her energy through every cell of their bodies, beating out the rhythm of their lives, making up an exuberant melody of unity through every living thing of this world. He yearned to know that same, deep, unthinking cellular certainty of belonging.

He gave Linda a regretful little smile. He'd lived so long with his numbness that the crippling lack had felt comfortably normal. Silently, he gave thanks for the lives and love of those whose graves were here on this planet before he offered what he could share with this circle.

"I give thanks that I have been granted the chance to know the beauty and the bounty of this Earth, to call it home. To know what it is to wake in the morning to the sounds of her birds and breezes, to the smell of her trees and plants. Should we find that tomorrow, we have to continue our wanderings in the empty depths of space, I am grateful that I have been allowed to share Earth's beauty with my son."

He paused, savouring this delicate feeling of gratitude before continuing.

"And I give thanks for a new friendship, with Rhea, a woman of this Earth."

There was an awed but sympathetic silence, filled only by the crackling of the fire, which was finally broken by Linda.

"Our mother Earth is here for all who reach out and come to her with respect," Linda said gently, getting a sudden glimpse of the isolation of knowing every atom of you was alien, not only to the peoples you lived amongst, but even to the very planet you called home.

Jal lowered his head, and the chanting rose again, allowing him to step back into anonymity. To this small circle of humans he was now no longer a feared stranger.

Rhea felt a tremble in his hand and just leaned a little closer. He closed his eyes, hungry as a child for comfort, swaying slightly under the effort of staying upright, as feelings he'd held at bay for years, flooded in.

He clutched her hand tighter as he allowed himself to feel the ache that had once overwhelmed him. It welled up, until it took the shape of a clear memory in his body of the utter desolation he had felt all those years ago when his wife and daughter were killed. It had been the savage end of a happy dream. Then the pain retreated as quickly as it had arrived, beginning to melt in the warmth of the moment, of the present, of a future. He would always remember but now the pain could finally fade.

The chanting of the circle ran through him, his voice soon added to the others, the effort soothing and moving the company on from their memorials to a thanksgiving for the wisdom they had now reaped.

Linda glanced over at Jal and Rhea. She smiled to think that they were dancing around this fire on a cold frosty night, as our ancestors had done for thousands of years, giving thanks for the gifts of mother Earth, but with one small difference. This circle contained a child not of our world, but one whom Linda was certain Earth would foster as her own.

Linda called for the company to reach out now. She asked them to remember the wider world and its troubles, raise their individual wisdoms, energies, into a powerful bright cone of hope which would join with every other little circle that was chanting this night, until it whirled out in a healing spiral across the land, to give inspiration to all those who wanted to find their way out of sadness, conflict and hate, and which would cheer all those who honoured the gifts of mother Earth.

"Cakes and Ale with my special soup first!" Linda said, handing around dishes to the excited company in the crowded caravan.

"You'll need it. It got really cold and frosty out there. Come on, shove up and make room for our guests." she ordered, as she bustled Jal and Rhea into the middle of the group.

Sharing a meal is that timeless way of making a stranger welcome. Sharing recipes and ideas on food is a timeless way of making friends. So Jal found himself swapping recipes and happily discussing the plants and fungi that could be collected wild in these woods, as well as his favourite recipes.

Soon, much to the company's delight, Jal was admitting that the Aazaar used lights and sounds to heal and even utilized the energy of various crystals, after a fashion. He explained, very briefly, that they used certain frequencies of energy which they focussed.

While Jal was occupied, Linda took the opportunity to have a quiet talk with Rhea.

"I'm really glad to see you," she said, drawing Rhea to the only free and relatively private space, the galley.

Rhea gave her an affectionate hug.

"Me too. Are you alright now, you know, with Jal?"

Linda looked across at him briefly.

"Woa, we'll be on all night if I start talking about him."

She looked into Rhea's eyes.

"Is Jack alright?"

Rhea nodded, her eyes shining.

"She's well and happy. Jal's son is a little older and she's with him right now. She loves it in their community."

Linda blinked. "Their community?"

Rhea grinned. "Yep. There's a whole settlement of them. They're intergalactic hippies, all peace and love. Even their name means hope. They have this beautiful place with a lake and mountains that humans don't know about and wouldn't know how to find anyway. It's sort of part of Earth but not, like a parallel existence. I don't fully understand that yet.

"They've been wandering for generations looking for a planet that will accept them. They don't have a world of their own, so to them that scrap is paradise."

Linda looked once more at the dark mahogany gargoyle crouched down at her table in happy conversation with her friends, then laughed softly. "Sounds like they found fairyland, but pretty fairy he ain't. There again, who's to say we don't look scary to them?"

Rhea's smile was a touch taut, but fortunately Linda did not notice.

"So you're safe and out of harms way?"

Rhea nodded.

"Couldn't be safer."

Linda's thoughts were racing.

"Good. Stay that way."

Rhea frowned, dismayed. "What do you mean? The characters who blew me up won't still be looking for me will they?"

Linda was, taken aback by Rhea's naïveté.

"Well they will if you suddenly appear, but we'll deal with that in a minute. You have been keeping up with the news haven't you? You know, with all the world economic problems and political unrest stuff? The police are keeping a really tight lid on things."

She gave Rhea an exasperated glance, which immediately softened as it occurred to her she probably knew nothing of the increased strife that had broken out after she had left. Maybe she'd been blind to the obvious trouble before she'd left. Linda shook her head. She'd warned her. She could go into details later.

"Just don't be in a hurry to get back here that's all."

Rhea nodded, her heart sinking.

"Okay," she said, wondering what the world looked like now. It hadn't occurred to her that it wouldn't just go on as before.

"I had hoped you might know a bit more about what happened to me," she said, feeling a little shaken.

Linda looked a little shifty.

"Not really. There was stuff in the papers about the explosion and speculation, but it was all dropped, overtaken by other events. I kept asking though."

She flushed, embarrassed. She didn't want to start talking about her feelings, she wanted to keep this tight. There would be time to talk more later, when everything was sorted and safe. But for Rhea, that time was now.

"Oh! Linda, I'm so sorry. You thought I was dead. I couldn't send any messages. I've taken such a long time to recover."

Linda shook her head.

"You were blown up." She gave a sympathetic smile and nudged Rhea playfully, hiding any concerns she had.

"Still, there was an up side for us. We've all been investigated so thoroughly that it's done us a favour. We are officially safe, non-threatening citizens, so we get to come here without a patrol car in the bushes watching us."

Rhea groaned embarrassed,

"Oh I'm so sorry. I left you with all that to deal with."

Linda gave a dismissive toss of her head.

"No, the thugs who chased you and blew you up did that," she said adamantly.

Rhea hugged her in deep gratitude for the huge effort she now knew Linda had made to put her at her ease. It was only right to accept gracefully, move on, get a start on recovering her life.

"So do you know what happened to my house?" Rhea asked, attempting cheerful, but unable to stop a minor note creeping into her voice.

Linda blinked, thrown by Rhea's sudden plaintive tone.

"It was cleared and someone else is in there now."

Rhea tried to shrug but only managed a twitch.

"Yeah, right, I suppose... but you wouldn't happen to know where my things are?"

Linda sighed and took Rhea's hands, finally realising she was still the same inoffensive frightened little woman she'd been on that fateful day when she'd seen her last.

"Rhea, it's all gone. They think you're dead," she said gently.

Rhea nodded, determined not to cry. They were just things. She'd buy new stuff.

"I know, it's silly really. I just kind of hoped some of my things got saved that's all," she said, not understanding why she had this panicky feeling.

Linda nodded.

"It must be weird."

She cast a glance at Jal.

"Jack's alright and you still have him," she said, attempting reassurance.

Rhea shook her head a little sadly.

CHAPTER 7

"If you found an injured bird, you'd nurse it back to health then let it go wouldn't you?"

Linda frowned, a prickle of apprehension about where this was going.

Rhea's eyes were bright, almost tearful. "Well, he has to do that with me. We're the wildlife to them."

Suddenly, Linda was very definitely worried.

"But he wouldn't just dump you?"

Rhea smiled serenely, automatically coming to Jal's defence.

"Course not! He said he'd help me find people who will sort out what the hell the murder attempt was all about."

Linda nodded, greatly relieved. "Whatever happens, you can't be discovered, for all our sakes, you know that, don't you?"

Rhea nodded.

"So I need someone I can trust to help me find out what went on and what's still going on if Jack and me are to have any chance of a life."

'Was it too much to ask?' she wondered.

Linda nodded, a smile slowly spreading across her face as she considered the request.

"I think I can put you in touch with just the right person. He's a policeman and you already know him. He needs to put this whole case of yours to bed for his own peace of mind. He'll be able to keep you, and us, safe. Remember my mentioning an ex tenant? Well, it just so happens that same James McCardle was one of the officers who attended your break in."

Rhea's eyes widened in amazement.

"PC James McCardle? You know him?"

She remembered the calm eyes that took in everything, and the solid, no-nonsense, patient, sympathetic manner. He'd know how to bring her and Jack back safely from her terrifying adventure, her strange fairyland sojourn, and back into her blissfully ordinary world.

Linda was scribbling something on the back of an old birthday card.

"I'm giving you his mobile number. This one's his work number. Careful with that one. He's not a PC any more, so he has people to answer his phone. He got promotion. Bright man our James. He'll understand your situation, if you take things slowly," she said, giving her a sharp meaningful look.

Rhea nodded.

"It's okay. I'm not going to tell him about Jal. Well, that he's… you know. I'm just going to avoid the issue."

Linda grinned.

"Don't forget he's a policeman. He's used to getting info out of people."

Rhea nodded.

"Okay, I'm warned. But thanks."

Linda looked thoughtfully across at Jal.

"You know all that stuff he said about energies and what have you? Is that their science?"

Rhea remembered her conversations with Jal on the nature of their science and the need to find a "pagan" life scientist. She smiled.

"I think so. They're real eco freaks. They believe in this unity of all things and respect for the life force."

Linda nodded in enthusiastic agreement.

"Yes, not genetically modified like we'll all be if things continue."

She stopped herself, knowing she'd just get into a rant, but

CHAPTER 7

also because of the alarmed looks she was getting from Rhea.

"Be careful what you say about that in front of Jal. His whole race was manufactured and they kind of find it painful. Anyway, what are you talking about?" Rhea asked, not certain she'd understood.

Linda's jaw dropped.

"They were all genetically modified?"

Rhea shook her head.

"No, created, manufactured. Oh it's a long story. I'll explain some other time. Look, I haven't seen a newspaper in a very long time. Just tell me what you mean by 'if things continue' "

Linda sighed, not wanting to upset Rhea. She had enough to deal with already, without adding to it.

"I'm sorry, it's just me. I've had to write a thanksgiving. There's the usual round of mayhem. You know? Wars in far-flung lands, corruption in politics, worry about the environment, and the rise of militant god botherers of various stripe who think they are going to bomb and beat us back to some sort of dumb paradise, with them in control of course."

Rhea laughed and relaxed, denial, and her own fervent hopes, only allowing her to hear the flippancy in Linda's remarks.

"So no change there then?" she said, remembering the newspaper headlines, and the blaring TV news bulletins of events that never touched the solid round of her mundane world.

Jal, who was surreptitiously watching them, noted with satisfaction that his first task was accomplished. Rhea now had a foothold in her own community. She could, at least secretly, visit Linda from time to time in reasonable safety.

As for himself, with an eye to his other tasks, after managing some brief interchanges with the playful but incongruously erudite Stan, he decided to enlist his help.

Stan laughed. "It seems you're what we would call an anthropologist, so maybe you can make sense of this. There's a rumour about a big project to develop and deliver a vaccine for a super contagious flu epidemic and a mass vaccination programme. Only there is no epidemic or vaccination programme. Mind you, the gossip is that it's a cover for some secret biological warfare stuff. You never know what to believe. For so called rational people, the folk who work in my field can be so outrageous sometimes, and they'll entertain themselves for weeks, even years, with silly conspiracy theories."

Jal tipped his head in polite acknowledgement. "It really does seem odd, and certainly alarming," he said thoughtfully. "So you have some skills in this field of..?"

Stan sighed. "Yes, but I'm not so keen on the orthodox view..." He hesitated then undisguised enthusiasm lit up his face. "You'll understand this. You said your science is different, based on different theories of knowledge?"

Jal smiled, this was going exactly how he wanted it to.

"Well, I'm a pagan, and not just because I want to wander around chanting in cold windy fields. I believe that it is possible to work up theories of knowledge from our basic relationship to the Earth. And that would give you a different science."

Jal tipped his head, a distinctly amused light in his eyes. "Yes, it would be integrative instead of looking to dominate nature. It would look rather like ours."

Stan beamed. "Wow! Yes, I hadn't thought of that! You did say you thought of the planet as a Goddess, as the source of, and shaper of, our very existence. I suppose I was just thinking you were some kind of intergalactic hippy, what with all the crystal

CHAPTER 7

healing and that."

"Intergalactic hippy?" Jal echoed with a soft chuckle. "I like it. But I wonder, I have a study problem that I think you could help me with. I have some notes I discovered, which your skills would help me understand. I'd also like to replicate the work. It's in the genetic manipulation area."

Stan beamed as if all his birthdays had come at once. "What? Work with someone who understands my lonely crazy way of seeing science? Wow! Oh wow! Yes! Of course! Um, settle down Stanley, Genetic manipulation? This data. Where did you get it?"

Jal smiled indulgently at the excitable Stan telling himself off, deciding he was going to enjoy working with him. "Someone had dropped it in Rhea's bag without her knowledge. So of course Rhea, and I would like to find out what was worth murdering her for," Jal said, watching Stan's face for his reaction.

"Of course! Yes. I'd be glad to help solve that little problem. It would help Linda too. Double wow! This is real scary stuff," he said, more like a breathless excitable teenager, than the seasoned professional man he was.

Jal tipped his head, amused by his exuberance. "Yes it is. I already know that there's a large organisation behind this. So I wouldn't want to put you in any kind of difficult situation."

He watched a myriad of emotions flit across Stan's face in a few seconds. Jal could see the young human was intrigued, excited, and alarmed, but he was willing.

Stan held out his hand. "I can't pass this up! What? Work with a real live alien? On some kind of big intrigue? A real live conspiracy? It's so mind boggling, it isn't even in my wildest dreams. You've got a deal. And I've got the premises."

Jal shook the proffered hand. "And as Linda has warned,

this has to be strictly secret. You will be able to stick to that?" he emphasised.

Stan grinned. "That's easy for me. My beliefs and ideas are so radical, they're considered crazy, so it's made me a bit of an outsider in my work community. Besides, I take my pagan vows, and the safety of my backside, seriously."

Jal tipped his head. "Of course, eventually I hope to find a way for you to make your work public. I understand that you, as a scientist, have a need to do that."

Stan grinned with delight. "I'd do the work anyway, but thanks. This feels like a project to get my teeth into. I'm already clearing my desk. And I get to work with an alien! What are the probabilities of that?"

At the end of the night, Linda walked out with Rhea to the clearing to say her goodbyes. Jal was on the far side, still chatting with Stan, idly stretching each wing, still boggling poor Stan's mind with this unconscious habit.

Linda watched fascinated.

"What's it like when they fly? Can they fly here?"

Rhea laughed.

"They love to fly. And yes, they can fly here. That's how I'm getting back home."

Linda raised bewildered, sceptical eyebrows.

"I may not be an expert here, but at his size he... They look quite delicate and not big enough. How do his wings keep him up?"

Rhea smiled knowingly.

"Can you imagine it?"

Linda looked puzzled, then imagined Jal soaring on the wind. "I suppose."

Rhea grinned

"So does he."

Linda chuckled.

"Mmm. I think you'll have to run that past me a few times before I get it."

Linda watched as Rhea walked over to Jal. She saw him pick Rhea up, tying her to him with his wrap, then he spread those strange black velvet wings, which for a moment, seemed to twinkle darkly in the moonlight before he leaped up into the air, and...they just weren't there any more.

It had been a very strange night. She smiled dreamily.

"Possibilities. The power of imagination. Rhea, you dreamed up one fine guardian. There's still hope for us yet."

The children were asleep and the house was quiet when Jal and Rhea arrived back in Dreamhills, but Rhea wasn't quiet. Her excitement was such that it had totally eclipsed all thought of trouble, of gangsters and genetics, plagues and police checks on innocent bonfire parties, and her thoughts tumbled out.

"Wow! What a night! Now that was amazing. I'd never have believed it! The humans with beliefs like you advanced intergalactic travellers aren't our cutting edge scientists, they're a bunch of on-the-fringe tree-huggers."

Her eyes were shining with the exhilaration of discovery, of finding a bridge between her sanctuary with Jal, and her world. On the way back, she had admitted to herself that she didn't want to let go of Dreamhills or Jal.

"Mmhm," Jal murmured in agreement, gazing out into the woods, enjoying the trees, smelling the rich damp scent of Earth.

Rhea realised Jal was caught up in his own thoughts, and remembered how unsettled, even vulnerable he'd seemed during the celebration.

"You okay?"

He inclined his head.

"It's my home too," he said softly, remembering that feeling of utter union with the circle of humans.

"Yes, it's your home too," she answered emphatically.

He looked into her sympathetic little human face.

"Thank you my friend."

CHAPTER 8

The sun slanted long wistful shadows across a strew of autumn leaves, filling the air with their decaying funereal scent. Nothing stirred, not even a blade of grass. Rhea looked up at the cloudless sky, feeling the stillness she usually enjoyed, settling on her like a heavy sigh. Her Hallowe'-en adventure had briefly filled her with excitement. But now, she realised it had left her with more questions than answers. She sighed. Poor Jal. It was obvious now he had his own problems that her presence could only be adding to. Her welcome here would soon run out and she had nowhere to go. She was farther away than ever from being able to return home. She didn't doubt, even without Linda's warning, that her would-be murderers would stop at nothing to finish the job if they got a hint of her survival. There was no escape.

Gloomily, she considered the possibility that her only alternative was a life on the run. A stab of self pity wrenched a small moan from her.

Suddenly, she felt very lonely. She yearned for the certainty, the warmth of her own little house and, the mundane little pathways of her life, which she had walked in a cosy, unthinking haze.

Jal was working on the data that was the cause of all her problems, but she needed to get her would-be murderers locked up, or else it would never be safe for Jack and her to return. She scrabbled through her thoughts to find an escape.

'The card Linda gave me!' she thought, smiling to herself in desperate relief. Jal had shown her how to use his uni communicator, so she decided to take advantage of her solitude to sound out James McCardle. He was a policeman, a senior policeman now. He'd know all about getting murderers locked up.

She hadn't planned what to say to him before she called; she had just felt he would somehow know how to pull her back to her simple little life. And now he was answering after only one ring!

"Hello."

She drew a deep breath, her pulse rate leaping. "Am I speaking to James McCardle?"

"You are," he said hurriedly, making it sound more like, "Get on with it".

"Er...um, a friend of yours asked me to call you, have you got a minute? I'm not causing you any inconvenience am I?" she stammered, flummoxed.

His tone changed, professionally neutral, but she detected a hint of warning.

"A friend?" he queried.

"Yes, she said you would be interested, I don't want to interrupt anything. I need to know you've got time and the privacy to listen to me," she babbled nervously.

There was a distinct impatient pause before he said, "Go on"

"It's about a case you worked on, a case you may still be

working on, but you must promise not to reveal who told you," she pleaded.

"Crimestoppers is anonymous," he replied all too crisply.

She hesitated, unsure what to do next, her uncertain breathing amplified by the silent room.

He prompted her.

"Why did you choose me?"

She visualised him systematically leading her through a well practised set of questions designed to surreptitiously reveal her identity. She'd seen it on TV.

"I'm in hiding. I'm believed dead. Look, it's not safe. There were some very nasty characters after me who tried to kill me and they seem to have some influential friends. Now, will you promise?"

She held her breath, listening to him shifting about as he weighed up his answer.

"Tell me who they are," he said finally, and she gave a sigh of relief.

"One is called Rod, one Tim and one Giles. They tried to kidnap me but I got away, then unfortunately, they caught up with me. They think they killed me in a car explosion. That was nearly two years ago. I don't know what it's all about. They think I had something of theirs," she gabbled, desperately scattering morsels of information she hoped he would grab.

She heard recognition in his voice, but not of her.

"Oh. Mrs Forrester? You'll be pleased to know your brown handbag and purse are safe at the station and the car hire people have been dealt with."

She knew he was playing it down, not giving her anything, even that it was a serious crime.

"Brown? Mine was black, and you'll find a few things were missing, like my purse, but you'll have my little notebook with addresses and dates of meetings of the club. Oh, and my lucky stone bird."

There was another pause. She could almost hear his brain working.

"Hello Rhea, where have you been?" he said in a very different tone.

She was relieved to be recognised, but not so much that she wasn't careful.

"I can't tell you, not yet. Someone rescued Jack and me. I promise you, we are perfectly safe. You were checking me out weren't you?"

James McCardle was finally beginning to take in the enormity of this call. This had been a big case, and weird. His copper's instincts went into overdrive.

"Yes, I was checking you out," he said gently, "But I'm a policeman, you'd expect that."

She smiled, emboldened, in the warmth of his easy consideration. "Yes, and I'm glad you did. What have you found out?"

He chuckled. "What makes you think I found anything out?"

"You're a policeman" she answered.

"I'm a policeman, and...where are you? I'd like to make sure you're safe first. Come to the station."

"No. I'm safe here. I've been hidden here these past couple of years. Couldn't be safer."

He sighed. "You're probably right."

"What's on your mind?" she asked, hopeful she'd get something to go on now.

"I'd say there's a very powerful and very shady organisation involved in your disappearance, though who and what, I don't know. I really haven't got much more," he said, his tone seeming distinctly confiding, making what he said all the more alarming. "I checked you out and as far as I know, you're not the girlfriend, sister or daughter of anyone someone might want leverage on," he reassured her.

"Nor have you worked anywhere with dubious connections," he began, becoming absorbed once more in a problem that had vexed him since she had disappeared. "You were ordinary and invisible, as far as any indicator of being involved in any crime or civil unrest of any kind was concerned. So why you? Even all of your friends and acquaintances have been thoroughly checked, and nothing's come up."

"Wow! But why? I'm sure, as far as I was concerned, it was a case of mistaken identity. Do you believe in people having doubles?" she said eagerly.

"Errm," he prevaricated.

"Are you worried about upsetting me? Cos you wouldn't. You'd be doing me a favour, and I just might come up with something."

"It's not just you. This thing is weird and just gets weirder when things do come to light," he muttered, more to himself than her.

"What do you mean?"

He cleared his throat. "To be honest, I thought it was odd from the outset, and I'm not just talking about the theft of your passport and clothes. I expected it to be taken out of my hands; I was just a humble PC then, but it was taken right out of reach of even my sharp, eavesdropping ears, and put into the hands of the serious crime squad. Then it had disappeared off my radar altogether. But I got the strong impression that investigations were never closed, just moved to more covert operations."

"So what does that mean for me?" she asked apprehensively.

He sighed. "It means that whoever tried to murder you, is not going to give up if you reappear, and that they're far better organised than your usual thugs.

"Look, things aren't exactly easy at the moment, so it makes this even more dangerous." He paused, allowing his message to sink in.

"Have you got Jack there? Can you get to the police station? Where are you? I could get someone to collect you," he said, his voice now kindly, caring.

"It's okay," she protested lightly.

"No it's not. You need to get yourself and your daughter to a police station now. You'll be safe there," he said firmly.

Rhea bit her lip, trying to suppress tears. She hadn't even had the chance to ask him to help her get back home. It wasn't safe, and it was clear he couldn't help.

"As long as they think we're dead, no one will be hurt. You must promise not to say anything to anyone. If they find out I'm alive, I don't know what they'll do to anyone who was ever connected to me to get to me," she admitted miserably.

James gave a gentle "uhuh" of agreement, remembering the panic-stricken little housewife Rhea had been when he attended the supposed burglary.

"Did you ever find the computer stick they were after?" he asked, wondering what would happen if her rescuer got his hands on it.

She sighed. "Data stick," she corrected in a flat, disappointed tone. A new, bleak appreciation of her position crept over her.

"So what's it about? Drug dealing?" he queried mechanically.

"No, it's not the usual. It's some kind of genetic processing thing, but it's what it might... what will go wrong that's the problem. I mean, they've gone to a lot of trouble to cover their tracks. Who kills over a little bit of scientific research? Who's protecting them?" she finished, wondering aloud.

James sighed. "That's something I'm wondering myself."

There was a long silence. Both of them were struggling to digest their respective unexpected platefuls of dilemmas.

James spoke first with a carefully balanced, "What do you want of me?"

A rush of emotion welled up in Rhea's throat and she struggled to choke it back. "I thought you would be able to help me to get back home," she said, hearing her own piteous voice, a faint memory that had already faded from her little house at twenty nine Poplar Close, echoing through the void.

"But I know it's not simple, nothing ever is. I'll settle for a friendly voice on the phone if that's all you can offer."

James closed his eyes in a hopeless resistance.

"Why did you take so long to contact us?" he asked indignantly.

She heard the grievance in his tone and gave a dejected sigh.

"I was badly injured. I spent a long time recovering. I suppose I'm only just getting my energy back."

He groaned guiltily.

"Which hospital were you in?" he asked in alarm.

She hesitated, trying to decide what to say for the best. He was going to think anything she said was weird, suspicious. He just had to believe her.

"I wasn't. A clever doctor found me. He didn't have time to get me to a hospital. He guessed it wasn't an accident. It makes him a target too. The less I say, the safer we all are. You'll keep me a secret won't you? Please, I don't want anyone hurt."

She held her breath, fearful that he was never going to accept he had to keep her secret, and worse, he'd start nosing around. She wished she'd never made the call. Had she caused more trouble for Jal and Linda?

James sighed. I suppose wherever you are, whoever your rescuer is, and whatever his motives, you've been kept safe all these months. Anyway, I can't offer you any real alternatives."

He groaned. "Why now? When I've got myself all set up? Nice home, nice little job," he muttered to himself. "Look, does anyone know that you've contacted me?" he asked more decisively.

"It's alright, you're safe. No one knows. Not even my rescuer," she soothed. There was no point in worrying him when there was obviously nothing he could do.

"Are you sure you're safe?" he insisted.

His concern was threatening to draw tears from her, but the absurdity of the situation broke the tension, and she let out a nervous, 'If only he knew' chuckle.

"Perfectly. No one in the whole world could find me here. Now, is it a deal?"

James paused to consider. "Hmm, I could get away with a snoop at a file or two. That's better than nothing and something might come of it. If I get caught, it could be put down to misplaced enthusiasm and my earlier involvement. So I'm happy for you to stay where you are while I get a handle on this. But call me. Don't disappear. Call in, say, a week or two. I'll have had a chance to get something by then."

"I trust you," she said, with a heart-string twanging sound like a deep sob, before he closed the call.

As Rhea heard the phone line go dead, she felt the last thin thread of hope tying her to her old life, to any sense of who and what she was, going slack.

She wandered back into Jal's garden in a fog of loss and confusion. She brushed her hand against the cool leaves of the evergreen bushes and stared up at the trees. It was beautiful. In fact, the whole of Dreamhills was as breathtaking as any of her dreams of a rural idyll. But it wasn't hers. It wasn't her own homely little yard or the old field by the railway. She didn't belong here.

"Careful what you wish for," she murmured regretfully. A fat lonely tear ran down her face and although she craved comfort, she was glad Jal would not see her like this. She knew miserable house pets weren't attractive.

She crept back indoors to bury herself and cry in Jal's heap of cushions. She stopped short as she came to his open den door. There he was, reading quietly. She wiped her face, and straightened up.

"I didn't hear you come in, not that I ever exactly hear you," she chirped too brightly.

"Oh, I've just got back," he said, looking up to smile a greeting.

Guiltily, she tried to avoid his gaze but realised he had already seen the shadows in her eyes.

He patted a cushion "Come in and sit down," he said gently.

Rhea stayed silent, still caught up in the implications of her conversation with James. It hadn't struck her yet that Jal was home much earlier than he should be.

She attempted a smile, but only succeeded in stretching her lips a little, whilst wondering how best to get away.

Jal put down his communicator to give her his full attention, and tried once more to get a response out of her

"Our outing gave us a lot to think about, didn't it?"

She fidgeted, not wanting to talk.

"Yeah, it was disturbing. I'm all over the place today," she admitted, while still avoiding his gaze.

"I understand," he murmured a touch ruefully, but she was too preoccupied to notice. She was too busy trying to put a name to the mess of emotions which were pushing and shoving her this way and that. Then it dawned on her.

"I feel lost," she said out loud, immediately regretting it.

"Lost?" he repeated with concern.

She frowned, irritated at herself. She'd given him that opening he'd clearly been angling for. Now she couldn't hold back the wash of emotions any longer. As she looked up to face him, she felt unsubstantial, as if she was fading before his eyes.

"I don't belong here. As far as my world is concerned, I died in that car explosion and there's nothing left of me. My house, my job, my things, all gone," she wailed.

Desperately, she looked about, trying to find something, anything, to hold onto, anything except his concerned gaze, too afraid she'd get swallowed up in his feelings, tangled up in his words.

He sat perfectly still, watching her struggle, and she knew he would wait until she could speak.

She straightened up, taking a deep breath.

"I've got to sort something out. I've got Jack to think of."

Jal tipped his head in agreement,

"Yes, you've got Jack. And she's got you," he said gently.

But she couldn't reach this lifeline. It only made her feel worse. Of course she had Jack. She was her mother, but what good was she to Jack like this?

Although she never meant to, she showed something pleading in her eyes, and he reached out to take her hand. She shrugged, miserable.

"I have to do this myself," she said quietly.

"Okay, but I could do with some air. Lets go and forage in the woods for supper," he suggested, much to her relief.

For a while, all difficulties were laid aside, and they rooted around looking for edible toadstools, their thoughts going no further than seeing who could find the tastiest caps. They settled under a beech tree for a reviving drink of berry juice.

Rhea sipped and savoured it, a bittersweet nostalgia bringing back memories of childhood weekend outings foraging for blackberries. Now, Jack was living that idyll, running free through these woods, learning its secrets under the watchful eyes of her self-appointed young Aazaar guardian, Marn. There were no terrorists or gangsters here, nothing to disturb the dream. But she had to wake up. Dreams always end.

She drew a long breath, now calm enough to talk without bursting into tears.

"I dreamed of living in a place like this."

Jal tipped his head in agreement.

"Me too," he said lightly.

She looked up, puzzled. "But you live here."

He looked around the wood that he loved so much.

"Yes, but I wasn't born here."

She nodded, smiling affectionately.

"I forget. The way you're sitting there, all cuddled up in the roots of that tree, you look like you just grew there."

He smiled, a touch wistfully, provoking a sigh from her.

"I miss Poplar Close. I'm not sure why. I mean, it's been a long time now."

He inclined his head sympathetically.

"It was your home."

Of course he understood. All Aazaar Kind understood about the need for 'Home'. They'd been looking for home for centuries, maybe millennia.

"I sort of knew all along. It was silly to think I could slide back into my old life," she said, aware that the din of panic in her mind had subsided, leaving her still. No, she felt numb, but at least able to consider her situation.

She looked at him, this being who didn't belong in any world of hers, this being whose very existence questioned everything her life had been built upon.

"I suppose I'm saying I don't know how to be..." she struggled to pin it down, "me. I mean, what am I? Knowing you has shown me I haven't a clue."

She gave a helpless hopeless shrug.

He tipped his head. "You know where you come from, and what you bring with you."

She sighed wondering if she really knew that.

"So what do I do with that?"

She gazed about, looking for markers and signposts in this new untried life.

"Where do I belong now?"

He studied her for a moment, and she knew he could see the

CHAPTER 8

shadows of loss and confusion that must be obvious in her eyes. He smiled.

"I like having you here. I'd miss you if you left."

'Miss me?' Rhea thought, looking up in mild surprise. Reflected there, in his warm golden eyes, she saw herself, not as a memory, or ghost, but very much alive. She gave a soft dismissive laugh at her own self pity.

"I'd miss you too," she admitted. "But I know you're not supposed to hang on to wildlife," she said, considering and rejecting the life of house pet.

Jal inclined his head.

"And this particular wildlife is welcome to stay with me as long as you like," he said affectionately.

She smiled. "Thanks."

He stood outside of everything she knew, and yet he was still drawing her back out of the limbo that she had been thrown into by the explosion. He was warming the numbness.

"But how do you see me? I mean, you're so different to anything in my world, what do you see me as?"

"You're my friend, Rhea the human," he said simply.

'Yes!' she thought bravely. Here, she was Jal's friend, Rhea the human. She let the thought sit in her mind and get comfortable. *'My friend Rhea. That's not the title of a pet,'* she reminded herself.

"It's not as if Poplar Close was the be all and end all for me. I was already trying to change. You know? All that conservation stuff I'd got into?"

He tipped his head in agreement.

"Yes, confusing isn't it? You want to change, but when it happens…" he grinned, nudging her.

"I suppose we'd all like to do it on our own terms."

She gave him a smile of heartfelt gratitude.

"If you hadn't come home early, I'd have been a soggy little heap by now," she admitted.

They sat in companionable silence for a while, Rhea just enjoying the beauty of the woods, accepting maybe that they could be her woods.

"Speaking of being early, weren't you supposed to see Stan today?" she asked lightly.

He inclined his head in agreement as he swept up the basket.

She frowned, puzzled by his avoidance.

"Jal? What's wrong?"

He tipped his head as he unfolded his wrap ready to carry her.

"I didn't feel like it. Just a bit tired."

She held up her hand to stop him, searching his face.

"And you let me just babble on like that when you were feeling rough? This is about last night isn't it? You wanted to talk, didn't you? Oh Jal I'm sorry."

He smiled tiredly, holding out his wrap ready to parcel her up.

"All is well," he said, feeling oddly dizzy and open, as if a light was searching through all his secrets. Frantically, he tried to figure out where the feeling was coming from.

She had dodged his hands as he made to wrap her up.

"Jal. Wait a minute. Come on, let me return at least a little bit of this huge favour you've done me."

"I enjoyed the forage," he said, looking distinctly dazed.

She cut him off.

"Just listen, I'm trying to say something, give you something."

She jarred him into focussing, and he gave her a forgiving smile. "I know, and I'm being ungraciously distracted. I'm sorry. You have my attention now."

She nodded. "I think I've finally got myself together enough to be able to understand. Well, not understand exactly, I did at the time. Well, in a way." She saw Jal's bewildered expression, and gave an embarrassed giggle.

"Okay, I'll stop babbling. It's just I'm trying to say I appreciate everything you've done for me. I think it's because I've stopped just taking you for granted, and started thinking about what you are as well as myself. You're not one of Linda's gods of nature. Even if you are an amazingly clever alien, you're a living being like me with thoughts and feelings. See? I've got it straight in my head. Anyway, I know what you did, and it couldn't have been easy on you," she said, gazing up at him in admiration.

As Jal met her eyes, astonishingly, he looked as vulnerable as a child. She was looking straight through him. But he seemed to be welcoming it, so she continued.

"The healing you did on me was very special. You used yourself, didn't you?" she said softly.

Bullseye! She could see her words had hit the heart of the matter, but she wondered, briefly, why he hadn't said anything, why he'd kept this amazing thing quiet.

He stood looking at her for a full moment as she puzzled over this, and yet he seemed strangely open, as if he'd wanted her to see, confess something. She wanted to hug him, tell him it was alright.

He allowed himself a twitch of a smile, then drew a steadying breath before answering.

"Yes. You were very weak, so I held you together. I did the living for both of us until you were strong enough to heal on your own. It was my first attempt."

She was surprised to see him look away, as if unsure of her.

She waited, and when he let himself look at her again, she just gave him a warm, grateful, admiring smile.

"Wow! I'm glad you tried," she said simply.

He sighed with relief.

"But I thought you were already an experienced healer," she said.

He tipped his head. "Yes, but this is different, more...I use more of myself. My people call it sirv. It means that I can not only learn to sense energies, I can learn to channel them."

He paused, and she saw him nervously checking her reaction.

"Right." she said, thinking this sounded very new age, very Linda.

"Everyone can do this, up to a point," he continued, escaping into the safety of explaining details.

Rhea cocked her head as she considered this.

"What about me? Could I? You know, sense energies?"

He smiled. "Yes, you already do. You're pretty good at knowing when the rain's coming, when there's an animal watching you from the undergrowth, you're pretty good at sensing energies."

"I hadn't thought about it," she said, realising he was right. It struck her she should find this odd, but she didn't. It was all too obvious really.

"With a sirv, it's very much stronger," he said quietly, almost nervously.

She nodded enthusiastically. It all made perfect sense, perfect Linda sense.

"It's like you had a picture of me as I should be and you held me to it until I could hold onto it myself," she said, running with this newly revealed logic.

He inclined his head, amused. "You do make things sound so simple, so acceptable." he said, an expression of blissful relief on his face.

She laughed delightedly, spurred on by this brighter reaction.

"Right! So that's how I'm growing taller. It's how you see me."

He shook his head.

"No, it doesn't work like that. I just held you together and brought you the energy you needed. Your body did the rest," he said modestly.

She nudged him. "I'm not complaining. I fancied being taller."

She considered his revelations, turning over all the implications of what he'd just told her. Then a slow realisation dawned on her.

"It's a bit weird isn't it? I mean, even for an Aazaar?"

Again, he searched her face, but she just calmly looked back at him

"It's a bit weird," he agreed softly, allowing himself a relaxed smile.

She gave a start of surprise.

"You haven't said anything to anyone have you? Not even to your best friend?"

His loneliness stood naked in his eyes for her to see, tugging at her emotions.

"Jal. What's upsetting you? Why haven't you said anything?" she asked

He nervously brushed back his hair. This wasn't the self confident man she'd known. His habitual reticence was obviously hard to overcome, even to her, even though she wasn't Aazaar.

"Because it would change things and I'm not ready to accept those changes yet," he said, almost in a whisper.

"So it'll change things. What things?" she asked innocently, then saw the conflict in his eyes.

He offered her an appeasing smile.

"It's complicated."

"Okay," she conceded, to what seemed like a demand to end the conversation. It was clearly painful for him.

Jal shook his head, not wanting to be returned to the loneliness of silence.

"No. It really is complicated. But I want to explain if you want to listen."

"Okay," she offered, but he stood there, silent, and obviously struggling.

"I know it wasn't easy on you. I suppose I was your experiment. It won't be so bad now you've tried it out," she offered, in an attempt to make it easy for him.

"I don't know," he said, his eyes dark with anxiety, deep in thought about what he faced.

"Well, just cos you can do something, doesn't mean you have to," she added brightly.

Jal sighed, "It's too late, I've tried it now. I can't stop the changes I'm going through."

She winced guiltily and he took her hand to reassure her.

"No, I'm glad I helped you. I told you I wanted to."

He smiled ruefully

"But as we discussed earlier, we might want to change, just on our own terms. The trouble is, life is not like that is it?"

They both heaved rueful sighs in unison.

"Yeah, too true," she murmured sympathetically.

"So you've always had tendencies to... what do you call it?" He tipped his head.

"Sirv." he said, as if expecting a blow, then gave a small huff as he relaxed again.

"I've always sensed I had the potential. I just wasn't ready to accept the life that goes with it."

Rhea looked puzzled.

"I don't get it. Where's the problem? I know I'm not Aazaar, but to me it sounds like a wonderful gift."

He smiled sadly.

"Maybe it is. But our custom demands that a person who shows signs of sirv must live within the protection of the Companions at the community hall."

Rhea frowned. The Companions were dedicated to the service of the community. They administered the libraries, studied, collaborated on all levels of teaching, and cared for those who were not able to safely live a free life. In short, they were a kind of public service.

"That's why I can't tell anyone, let alone ask for help. Because the moment another Aazaar knows, I will be obliged to dedicate myself to the service of the hall. And I have Marn to think of."

"You're talking as if you'd be considered dangerous," Rhea said astounded.

He tipped his head sadly.

"Yes."

He glanced at her as if expecting her to withdraw from him, now she understood. And there it was, she was appalled.

"What? Hang on. Maybe it's because I'm this dumb wild animal or something. Dangerous? Why? What'll you be charged with? Healing with intent?" She shook her head in righteous bewilderment.

He laughed softly, as much from relief as amusement, unwinding in the warmth of her understanding.

"I'm learning to use a great deal of power, so I could cause a great deal of harm."

"But how?" she demanded, now exasperated with him.

"Because I'm very much more sensitive, I can't help getting moody and self pitying. I can't help thinking that no one could understand me, or how people might be afraid of me, which makes me resentful and touchy."

He grimaced with exasperation. "I feel so useless!"

She gave a soft, affectionately mocking laugh.

"Oh. That sounds just like a teenager. Do Aazaar go through adolescence?"

"Ouch! You know just how to take the sting out of things. But yes, that's exactly what it feels like, even down to the self pity," he admitted with a rueful laugh.

"I suppose I weathered that once," he reflected, a small ray of hope playing across his face.

She sat back, smiling reassuringly. "There you are then! Sorted! You just go with the flow."

"I wish it was that simple."

He sighed, considering, maybe for the first time, some of the advantages of Hall life.

"At least the Companions can help protect me from feeling so raw."

She couldn't bear to see him looking so dejected, so defeated. It was just so unfair.

"Oh Jal, is there anything I can do?" She frantically searched through her thoughts and memories, desperate to find something, anything that would help.

He shook his head. "Right now, I don't know what anyone could do for me. But I do know I'll need help very soon."

"Will you be allowed visitors?" she asked rather plaintively. She had just begun to consider him not just a rescuer, but a friend, and she didn't want to think of losing him.

He smiled reassuringly, welcoming her show of affection.

"Of course. I just won't be free to fly where I want. I'll always have the company of the Hall Companions. It's not such a bad life."

"But you're against it. You don't want to do it," she protested, already fighting the injustice of his situation. She knew it would grieve him badly to lose his freedom.

He quickly subdued a flicker of irritation. "I think you've just made me realise I was allowing myself to simply slide into acceptance, doing what I, of all people, know better never to do. But at the same time, you know what adolescents are like. Imagine one of my age and ability suddenly sulking and crashing about," he protested with a wry grin.

But Rhea was not about to let up, not now her sense of justice had been aroused.

"You wouldn't hurt anyone. You know what's happening to you. Besides, you've been a healer for too long. And you can't do that without knowing how to avoid damage from a major sulk."

"I can't argue with that," he admitted. "I am an experienced healer, and that does take a great deal of self awareness and control," he mused, "But without a means to practise safely, I might slip up. Don't worry, I won't be going for a while yet, and anyway, whenever I do, you're still welcome to stay at my home."

Rhea didn't hear his last sentence; she was too deep in thought trying to find something that would keep him from needing to rely on the Companions.

"Practise? Okay, what would you need to do?"

Before he knew what he was doing, he'd got halfway through an explanation. He stopped. "But there's a snag. I need an anchor, a support while I practise, and only the Companions have the knowledge to do that. I know I managed to heal you, but not without a near miss."

Rhea grinned.

"I haven't a clue what you said, but I know what you mean, and it just so happens I could do that," she said, pushing out her chin in emphasis.

He smiled indulgently, touched by her determination, but clearly certain no little human could possibly help him.

"Okay, how?" he asked slowly.

She shrugged.

"Cos I trust you."

He laughed, "I'm glad about that but how would you do it?"

She smiled knowingly.

"Wow! Wake up at the back! I'm not Aazaar! It doesn't worry me, and haven't I done it before? It was just like that stuff Linda's into, you know? All that awareness and energy stuff. Your near miss? Like I said, cos I trust you."

He stared at her, reviewing her healing and that near miss. She returned his gaze. "I saw, and I was able to reach out," she said slowly.

"And you reassured me...I never gave it a thought..." he said in wonderment, then changed his mind.

"No, I can't ask you to risk it," he said, afraid that this time he might injure her.

CHAPTER 8

She huffed.

"Hey! Where's the risk? Last time I did it, you saved my life! Anyway, I'm offering! So be gracious."

"Yes. Forgive me. Even in the state you were in, you focussed my distracted attention." He gazed into her determined little face and she could see him wavering.

She grinned encouragingly.

"Oh hell! Just try something before I get all wobbly!"

"I'll try something very simple," he agreed hesitantly.

"But if you show any signs of strain, I'll stop."

She gave another impatient huff, then took a deep breath, steeling herself.

"I'm ready."

He took her hands and gazed into her eyes, leaving an image of himself with her.

Rhea felt as if he had climbed in behind her eyes, she had such a vivid picture of him in her mind. Carefully, she imagined tying a thread to his ankle, which she unwound as he moved his awareness off to the trees. As he emerged, he followed this thread.

She clapped her hands in delight.

"You did it! You did it! I saw!"

'You? You did it? A naïve minded little human? And you were here under my nose the whole time,' he thought, staring at her in utter amazement.

"Exactly. You're better off with this naïve minded little human. No highly civilised Aazaar is even going to dream what you're up to," she responded drily.

She began to blush under his gaze

"What? Oh stop it, what's wrong now?" she asked, gazing in

bewilderment at the pained expression on his face.

He was wincing with embarrassment. *'That wasn't very grateful of me was it?'*

Her eyes widened with amazement as she realised his lips didn't move. She was hearing his thoughts.

"Um no, pretty pompous really," she said grinning.

He gave a guilty laugh.

'I am willing to admit I am a proper pompous idiot. But how did you know what to do?' he telepathed.

She shrugged.

"I dunno. Just… feels right," she continued out loud.

He grinned in sheer dumbfounded delight.

"Thank you," he finally managed to say out loud.

She laughed, ready to play with this new ability, explore it like a new toy.

"You're welcome, and that sounds sincere. Wow! I heard your thoughts! No need to carry communicators now!"

She flushed guiltily, realising it would be a two way street.

"You heard me, didn't you?"

He raised an admonishing eyebrow, but then flashed her a disarming grin

"I'm afraid so. I thought we agreed we would work together."

She sighed.

"I was going to tell you about the policeman. I just wanted to think it through first."

He inclined his head.

"Understandable. It shows us we need boundaries. We could drive each other crazy very quickly if we don't learn how to guard our thoughts. We should practise. I hoped you'd agree to tomorrow?"

CHAPTER 8

She nodded "Good idea. Very good idea," she said wryly, and picked up their basket, ready to make tea at a very different home and a very different Rhea from the one who had once lived at twenty nine Poplar Close.

CHAPTER 9

James felt his mobile vibrate silently in his pocket. It was tea break time, so he allowed himself the leisure of answering. He recognised the voice immediately, and was relieved to find she gave no name to alert any eavesdroppers he now couldn't help feeling were everywhere.

"Oh hi. I was hoping you'd call. Tell you what, call me after six, and I'll know better what time I have free, okay?" he said chirpily, and rang off.

He looked gloomily out of the window, listening to the distant sound of rioting and clash of the shields of the riot police. "There'll be guns soon," he murmured to himself, as he made a move to get out of the station before the fighting blocked off his escape.

"Have you heard that lot?" a colleague remarked, "God scarers beating the shit out of each other in the name of Divine love!"

James cocked an eyebrow up towards the offices of the chief inspector. "Careful. We don't know who's got a line upstairs these days."

The sergeant sighed, lowering his voice to a whisper. "It's

CHAPTER 9

terrifying! Bloody god scarers are everywhere. I remember a time when we were here to enforce the law, without fear or favour," he said wistfully.

James nodded. "Apparently, we're defending freedom, freedom and democracy," he said in sardonic sympathy, then swept on.

Later, James McCardle sat near the door of a modest suburban café, toying with his phone as he mused on recent events. He'd been thinking about the Rhea Forrester problem when an amazing opportunity to have a sly look at some files had cropped up. He had found himself on a visit to his old station with a superior who had decided to discuss an old case with her opposite number.

He surmised that it was probably more to do with two old workmates comparing tactics and indulging in some mutual self protection, which certainly seemed the case when he saw them together.

They had soon forgotten about him, leaving him alone and unattended in a secluded office, with a suspicious laptop that was winking at him to read its secrets. True, it was in a corner, stashed under a bag, hidden by a pile of books, but wouldn't you know it? It was on standby and needed no difficult password, at least not one that wasn't glaringly obvious to the gossip aware James. "Soft intelligence," the boss had called it, though the reference had been about known crooks.

He'd been given some tedious paperwork to check out on the desktop P.C. that they'd insisted was urgent, which he'd done in double quick time. Naturally, he'd got bored and nosy while waiting. What else would you expect of a good detective?

Despite the unsettled times, and the focus on national

security and counter terrorism, when he had decided to take another look into the Forrester case, he hadn't really expected more than to confirm his suspicions that this was about some rather large, dodgy operation dealing in fertility treatments, spare part surgery or the like. Although it didn't really tell him anything about the actual case, he was shocked and outraged by what he had found.

He fiddled with his drink, feeling a touch self pitying. He had deserved his promotion. He had worked hard for it. But there, in a secret memo, he had seen that he had been fast tracked, not because of his virtuoso policing performances, but to get him out of the way, out of any link with the Rhea Forrester case. They'd concluded he was a good, honest, middle of the road copper without the imagination to be any kind of threat to the secret operation, and his promotion would be enough to put him off the scent for good. But what secret operation? He hadn't had time yet to follow up. His brain went into overdrive.

He had been glad of the promotion, even though it had meant a move to another town. He smiled grimly. He'd had a feeling he'd been watched right from the start. So he'd been checked out by some shadowy, would be, special branch set up? At least this confirmed his instincts were still intact. He took a sip of his drink.

As for Rhea, he had felt a little guilty, even crazy, for keeping her existence quiet. After reading this, he now thought he had been particularly sensible and careful. This whole thing felt very dangerous, no matter which way he looked at it. He just didn't know who he could trust, except Rhea.

He was more convinced than ever that he needed to know who was involved in the handling of this case, before he said anything to anyone official. He didn't want to find himself taking the blame for blowing some delicate operation, or worse, get blown away himself.

That meant he had to keep control of all sources of information. Apart from Rhea, there was this damned friend she mentioned. He really needed to contact Rhea and get this pinned down. He was so restless; waiting was not an option. He had to do something.

'Linda!' he suddenly thought. *'She's the one who gave her my number.'* He flushed with anxiety as he realised she too would be in the firing line if Rhea reappeared.

He had always got on well with the charming oddball Linda, and took as a given, that she was trustworthy. Indeed, they'd become firm friends over the last months, as they both came to terms with the manner of Rhea's disappearance.

He hesitated. He felt so shaken right now, he even had a moment's doubt about the safety of going to Linda's. He closed his eyes, trying to squash his mounting anxiety.

"Sod it, no harm in dropping in and checking things out," he murmured to himself, and jabbed his phone.

James settled into the comfortable little kitchen, while Linda brewed a wickedly childish hot chocolate for them to chat over.

As for Linda, she'd been only too pleased at the prospect of seeing James again, but had picked up the note of urgency in his voice, so had managed to organise the love of her life, the endlessly understanding Richard, into going out with his mates.

"Right Mr Policeman, you didn't call by to talk about the weather. Come on, tell," she briskly demanded, smiling fondly.

He stirred the creamy foam on his chocolate, still sore from what he had read earlier.

"Rhea Forrester."

Linda's smile didn't change. Indeed, she was remarkably upbeat, which eased his own nerves.

"So she called you then? I hoped she would. I gave her your phone number when she came to our Hallowe'en celebration. I thought you'd be interested and want to help."

He nodded. Linda was straight as they come, but careful. She wouldn't just give out a phone number without thinking through the consequences first.

"At Hallowe'en? Isn't that when the spirits of the departed visit?" he asked, straining to keep the smirk of disbelief off his face.

She nodded, her gaze giving him no absolution for the dig, however good humoured she appeared.

"Yes, she just turned up without warning."

He lowered his eyes deferentially, accepting he was not on top form.

"Oh don't mind me, I'm still getting used to the pagan bit."

She granted him a wry smile.

He winced.

"Truce? I am learning, aren't I? Anyway, this is serious. Where is she?"

Linda fiddled with her cup.

James took note of her reticence, mentally kicking himself for his insensitive remark. He'd have to get her on side again, so there'd be no harm in outlining the problem, and dangers.

"You know I've always been convinced from the outset that Rhea was what she appeared to be: an innocent caught up in something she knew nothing about."

"I never doubted you, or her," Linda said, raising a

questioning eyebrow that told him she was waiting for a damned good explanation from him, and not some flannel.

He smiled fondly. This was why he liked Linda. She might be one of those tree-hugger types, but she was down to earth, and sharp.

"But I am a policeman. I did check her out, and I have kept checking."

Linda's eyes definitely softened. "I'd expect nothing less. You're a just man. I know it upset you."

He looked away, clearing his throat. It had upset him badly. She'd been this bewildered, frightened, ordinary back street woman with her kid, who'd not managed to get her fears rated on anyone's radar, then, Boom! She'd been murdered, just like she'd feared. He'd felt outraged and guilty.

"She told me someone had ditched some dodgy information onto her, probably hoping to retrieve it later when things quietened down," he said, and was interested to see some recognition flicker in Linda's eyes, but only for an instant. "So did she tell you about this?" he probed.

Linda sighed. "No, she was more interested in finding out about her home, if she had any chance of getting any of her things, as you'd expect. I mean, her life's been wiped off the map, poor woman."

"Yes, she pretty much did the same with me at first. Now, she seems a whole lot more determined. She wants to find out what this thing is all about and get it sorted."

"Good for her!" Linda exclaimed. "And you've tried to help, haven't you?" she said, in that brisk, motherly way of hers.

James gave an amused smile. "Course I have! I found some circumstantial confirmation of her claims. And yes, it's very odd. But this data she had. It's about genetic engineering of all things!" He frowned, pondering this puzzle again. "Of what I don't know. I mean, genetic engineering? It seems pretty tame really. It's not like it's serious arms dealing or anything, but it still makes me feel queasy."

Linda shuddered. "Me too."

He sighed. "On the other hand, considering as how there's secret operations interest in it, perhaps it isn't quite so tame. But why? Who would use it? How?

"I mean, can you imagine one of those nutcase terrorist groups going around threatening to genetically modify your garden flowers if you don't bow to the latest sky lord?"

Linda gave an amused snort.

"It's just as well nuclear war is off the table these days. Even the craziest nutters know the risks of nuclear war are too great." He stopped, shaking his head. "But eugenic wars?" It didn't bear thinking about.

Linda had visibly blanched.

"What?" he asked.

"Eugenic wars?" she echoed appalled.

"I said genetics...oh! Oh shit! In this current political climate?"

"I know the political situation is bad, but..." she began,

"Very bad," he agreed, "with all these suddenly religious, self proclaimed, upright pillars of the community whipping up the populace at every opportunity. Bloody God scarers! I had to dodge a riot to get here!"

He sat back, considering his cup. "What'd you put in this chocolate? We're beginning to sound just like Stan with his conspiracies," he said, in an attempt to lighten the mood.

CHAPTER 9

"Maybe not," Linda murmured, then hid her feelings by busying herself, clearing up the empty cups.

"So I gather from all this, you found something worrying." She turned to face him. "For you."

"I...er..." He'd thought he was in control of things. He gave a smile of surrender. "Yes as it happens. I was shifted off the case to close down any curiosity I might have...well, I did have, as you know. It's all very shady and very worrying, for yours truly. I don't want to blunder into some big operation."

Linda nodded, her eyes now all concern.

"So you can see that I have to make sure all likely leaks of information are locked up tight," he said, throwing himself on her mercy.

"Well I wouldn't say anything."

"I know you wouldn't," he hurried on, now smelling success in getting his hoped for information. "But I've got to make sure no one will find Rhea. So where is she?"

He saw Linda's expression change, close him off.

"That is a difficult question. She is safe. No one on Earth could ever find her, not even me," she said.

He nodded. "Sounds good, so how do we contact her?"

"We don't. She contacts us."

Despite the note of finality, he noted something else in her. Was it wariness?

"And this friend of hers, the one she is staying with?"

He saw Linda's eyes become impenetrable as he asked, and had his answer. What was it about this shadowy friend?

"Who is he?"

"A trustworthy man," she said firmly.

He frowned, puzzled by the incongruence between her wary

reaction when mention of the friend was brought up, and now her certainty. "I'd like a name."

Linda sighed. James wasn't ready to discover aliens, especially not a whole settled village of them, especially not winged ones.

"For what good it'll do you. Trust me on this one, she's remained hidden all this time. No one is going to find her or her friend."

"Really? No one? What makes you so certain?" James said too sharply.

She would never lie to him, he knew that, but she sometimes strained his credulity.

"He is the ultimate in discretion. No one would ever suspect," she insisted.

He leaned forward, hoping, after their discussion of threatening events, she'd be unsettled by reason.

"In these uncertain times, everyone is watching everyone else. He couldn't get away with hiding a wounded woman and her child without being noticed."

To his surprise, Linda's eyes became hard.

"He could and he has," she pointed out reasonably.

James sighed. It was obvious Linda had met this Mr Trustworthy. Furthermore, he understood that she was not about to be easily moved to give any further information. He didn't want to antagonize her. He'd just have to be patient and alert. Still, perhaps a little warning wouldn't go amiss. She was his friend. He had to keep her safe.

"Maybe, but this was never just about Rhea. If those thugs suspect that Rhea's still alive, they could use any of us as leverage to get to her. We can't be sure who they have in their pocket. With all this public surveillance and data mining, it would be a simple thing to find her."

Much to his bewilderment and frustration, he was sure Linda nearly laughed.

"Exactly my thinking too, but as long as she stays with her rescuer, no one will ever know she is alive. And as for my crowd, we talk to ghosts don't we?" she said with a mocking grin.

He smiled fondly. "Be careful with that. As far as the rest of the world is concerned, you're an Eden Christian sect okay?"

She laughed good humouredly. "I know, Green Christians ehh?"

He nodded, then returned to his preoccupation. "I suppose I have to agree that this pagan of yours has managed to persuade even the best of us that she's dead."

Thinking of the hidden laptop computer he'd had a look at that afternoon, he mentally corrected himself from, *'The best of us'* to *'the most shadowy'*.

"Aren't you going to give me any clue about where she is?" he pleaded.

Linda sighed "Truth is, I don't know, and I don't want to know. We're all safe as long as she stays hidden."

She gave him a sorrowful, world weary glance. "Well, safer."

She looked out of the window, on their increasingly frightening and chaotic world, remembering her prayer on Samhain, and wondered just how the appearance of Rhea and Jal might help them.

CHAPTER 10

Rhea gazed entranced at the exhibition of the gorilla, chimp, and mock up of a prehistoric hominid, as they stared out into the middle distance of human evolution from their lighted glass case, in the hushed, whispering, Gothic surrounds of the Natural History Museum. Ever since the night of her first supper with Galer, she'd felt an increasing need to understand the history of her species, know what it was to be human, just like Jal knew what it was to be Aazaar. She wouldn't be victim to that feeling of being in limbo ever again.

She was waiting for James. The museum was her idea. It was not only a grand, vast hall of learning, where she could educate herself about what made her human and kept her human, it was also an anonymous public place, with lots of cameras and security guards. She'd accepted the warnings of Linda and James to be careful. She'd learned her lesson after those two thugs had caught her alone on the beach.

She'd arranged to meet James McCardle in the hope he could help get her attackers, and the organisers of their nefarious deeds, put in prison, thus getting rid of the stumbling block to her returning home. Although that wasn't exactly what she had told

CHAPTER 10

Jal.

Jal had agreed the visit was a good idea, as he thought that James would make an excellent bodyguard and guide, while Rhea visited and came to terms with the fact she may never be able to return home. Although that wasn't exactly what he'd told her.

"What did you get up to?" she murmured, staring into the glass eyes of the model chimp. "How did you get like that?"

The label explained how humans and chimps shared nearly ninety nine percent of their DNA. "That's genes" she murmured to herself, reminded fleetingly of the "property" that had caused her predicament.

She glanced at the imposing, but peaceable looking, gorilla model.

"Naa, you look too chilled to be that closely related," she muttered wryly, then found Gorillas too were very close relatives. She blinked in surprise, then looked again at the chimp, gorilla and human models.

'Well, if chimps are related, why not?' she mused, thinking of the variety of humanity she had met.

She scanned the label on a model of a curious, ape-like, upright female creature, a primate that existed just before, or during, the split between chimps and hominids. "Did chimps evolve back to a life in the trees?" it trumpeted incredulously.

'Sounds about right to me,' she thought, and drifted off into a contented reverie. "Hello Grandma. Look what happened to your kids," she murmured, as a scenario began to form in her mind of a matriarch with her squabbling brood, and problem kids.

There was the athletic, chimp-like, party animal. He was the so-called "alpha male," interested only in himself, bullying as many of his siblings as he could into serving his own self-centred ends.

There was the large, gorilla like, strong one who just wanted to be left in peace with his placid, like-minded playmates, and who would bellow now and again to chase off the irritation of number one.

Then there was the dreamy, human-like one. She was a lover of curiosities and company. She could also be found bandaging up the cuts and bruised pride of the losers of these battles, with her practical care and dreams of better things elsewhere. Of course, this loving care won her followers and undying loyalty, even when she led them off into impossible adventures.

The blurb beneath the chimp remarked that they were an endangered species. Rhea remembered a T.V documentary explaining that the ruthlessness of certain "successful" men was just like the alpha male behaviour of chimps, and therefore simply part of Human "biological" ape heritage.

It seemed odd indeed to Rhea that they used the behaviour of these poor, anything but successful, rather rare chimp creatures, to come up with excuses for why the bad, disruptive, and cruel behaviour of these human males, was really unavoidable.

Her imagination mischievously morphed one of these sleek, slick, successful men, into looking more and more chimp-like as he spoke, despite his suit.

'What you get for being an alpha male is to take you and yours to the edge of extinction,' she thought, with a satisfying flush of dark amusement.

She turned her attention back to the oddly dreamy eyed, upright hominid model. *'Such dreamers are what we are made of,'* she thought, and winked at the hominid, or as it had translated underneath, "wise man".

CHAPTER 10

"Love makes us wise. That's how she made you," she told her, remembering the strangely poetic description of human evolution she'd been given by Issn when explaining the nature of human intelligence.

"Love and a bit of hope can save the universe," she murmured.

An apprehensive James McCardle strolled up to the case, interrupting her musings, and began to study the labels in as nonchalant a manner as his tense anxious mind would allow. Rhea smiled a greeting, then realised he hadn't recognised her. He was simply admiring an attractive woman, while waiting for Rhea Forester to arrive.

"It's funny to think we descended from chimps," he offered pleasantly in return.

"We didn't. But they might well have descended from us," she answered proudly, reflecting on her recent studies.

She saw James stare in bewilderment, obviously having expected nothing more than a murmur of acknowledgement.

"I'm not a student or anything. I've just been reading up a little. It's really exciting, finding out how we got here, got to be human," she said, indicating the exhibits.

Absorbed in her inner journey she might have been, but she still watched him out of the corner of her eye. Although she could tell her voice was familiar to him, he was still sizing her up, trying to square the well turned out confident looking woman before him with the woman he had attended at the burglary.

"I thought you hadn't recognised me. That's useful," she said with a gratified smile, watching him give a start of realisation, then recover his policeman's cool almost immediately.

"It's good to see you at last. You look very well, I'm pleased to say," he said.

"Yes, I'm not the quivering wreck you might have been forgiven for imagining me to be, or anything like any pictures of me. I told you I'd be careful."

He nodded appreciatively. "Too true," he said, giving her another sweeping glance.

Rhea watched in amusement, knowing it wasn't about her attractiveness, well not all about it, he was doing that policeman's surreptitious scan of their surroundings. Then she saw him smile with genuine admiration.

"You seem taller than I remember." he said, as he checked her feet for high heels.

"I feel it," she agreed amiably.

"So let's go somewhere more comfortable and have our chat," he said briskly, making moves to leave, having noted with alarm the many CCTV cameras.

She shook her head, and beamed him a serene smile, covering her own disappointment.

"I haven't been out much. I'd like to enjoy this a bit longer if you don't mind," she said, looking at him hopefully for signs of shared interest, totally oblivious to his anxiety or the reasons for it. She was too preoccupied with resolving both her tasks of the day. She reasoned that if he could share this exploration with her, then there was a good chance he would understand her situation better.

She was met with the most neutral of expressions which she took for assent, however lukewarm, so she continued.

"Look at those bones," she remarked happily, descending once more into the depths of her musings. She did not notice that James was looking somewhat stunned by what he saw as

CHAPTER 10

her cool defiance of danger, as well as her conversation opener, or that he was more preoccupied with keeping them both below the awareness of the pitiless, all seeing, stare of the CCTV cameras and their "suspicious behaviour spotting" software. For this latter reason, he obediently stared at the exhibit of ancient primates from millions of years ago, waiting for his opportunity to get her out.

"You said you had something for me," he prompted mildly.

"Yes. We'll get on to that later. Have you got anything more for me?" she asked, now absorbed in what she saw as their companionable exploration of the exhibits.

"Not exactly, but we do need to talk," he said, eyeing up a model of a surprisingly intelligent looking prehistoric ape.

Rhea was so delighted to see him taking an interest in the exhibition, she happily set aside any discussion of attacks and crimes.

"See how that model is standing upright just about? Now look at that. It's a chimp of today. How do you think it got like that from that?"

He frowned, making a show of concentrating on the shifty looking, hunched, hairy creature with shortened, bandy legs.

"Because they live in trees," he said, his eyes covertly monitoring their environment, his mind working overtime on how to quietly lead her away from this vast panopticon of a building and its hidden eyes, which were almost certainly watching them both intently.

"Did you have anything in mind for this meeting?" he prompted, in another attempt to urge her away from the exhibit.

She gave him a curious dreamy smile, her attention still on the self centred, lazy, ancestor chimp child of her earlier reverie.

"A few things. I want to try something out on you. I just thought it might be better to talk face to face," she said, not heeding his impatience, interpreting his sharpness as simply an abrupt police manner.

He nodded.

"So why did this chimp head back to the trees all those millions of years ago?" she persisted, now watching him out of the corner of her eye, scanning his alert, rather dignified face for any signs of disapproval and disbelief.

He shrugged.

"Probably because it was the easiest way to get a good meal. I don't know. I'm a policeman not a palaeontologist," he said, hiding his irritation from her.

Rhea noted that he might have been promoted, but he hadn't lost that honest patience and understanding she remembered. He was exactly the right person to share this exploration with. If he understood this, then she knew she had a chance of him understanding her predicament, should she ever need to disclose it.

"I know but your guess seems as good as any," she agreed, meeting his eyes.

"So, do you believe me that I didn't know anything? And that the data is about genetics?" she asked, startling him by the change of subject,.

He harrumphed, covering his surprise,

"Yes," he said, prompted by her stare to justify himself. "It seems only too feasible."

She grinned, satisfied with his answer, and glanced at the bones, finding herself irresistibly drawn back to her earlier compulsion. "Why didn't they all go?" she murmured to herself.

He gave a small exasperated laugh. "Look, what's this about?"

"What made us human," she said, distinctly disappointed that he, a policeman, whose everyday work depended on understanding what the right thing to do was, didn't share her interest. "I want to know."

He relented, and decided a bit of idle culture browsing would be as good a way as any to build a working rapport.

After another surreptitious glance up revealed that the cameras were not tracking them, or even pointed in their direction, he relaxed a little, reassured that no one was likely to recognise this smart, good looking woman as Rhea Forester. What he didn't know was that they would never be able to get her true image, or his, for that matter, thanks to Jal's gadgets, which he'd insisted Rhea use for her visit.

"Yes, and right up your street if I remember rightly," he remarked with agreeable honesty. "Didn't you have a pet crow?"

She beamed, warming to him once more.

"He wasn't a pet. He was just visiting. I'd taken him in when he was injured," she said earnestly.

"Oh of course," James said politely, and Rhea smiled, gratified to find that he still had that same considerate protective manner of his that she remembered from their first encounter.

He turned to the pictures of the large clawed, lithe limbed, big toothed predators these vulnerable looking hominid creatures had to share their world with then gave a wry grunt. At least these apes had known what they were up against. The great predators of today are very hard to identify.

"I suppose they would have needed to be pretty smart and good at teamwork to avoid being lunch for that lot. They didn't have much else going for them, like big teeth or claws did they?"

he observed dryly, indicating the picture of a sabre toothed cat.

Delighted to find he was interested after all, she turned to another hominid.

"That old lad's bones have genes in them just like ours," she said with a flourish, pleased with her own understanding.

"Genes?" he queried, his policeman's senses twitching, hoping he was about to be given the scent once more.

"After all the upheavals I've been through, I want to understand what we are," she informed him solemnly, once more not noticing that she had left him off balance.

"I can understand that, but why stare at models of prehistoric apes?" he asked. "Anyway, what has it to do with your mysterious data?"

"Prehistoric hominids," she corrected.

She indicated a seat facing the exhibition of a very early female primate at the bottom of a tree diagram leading to chimps and humans.

James accepted Rhea's invitation to sit. She was relieved to find he had given up his attempts to interview her and seemed to be beginning to find her company, and even their leisurely speculations on evolution, a rather enjoyable break.

She pointed to the primate. "There's a good few million years between her and us."

He nodded, but she was so absorbed, she never noticed him studying the clear lines of her profile.

"Genes were passed down to us from those people." She pointed to the chimp. "And to him."

James raised his eyebrows in amused incredulity.

"I suppose she was just an ape then."

Rhea shrugged.

CHAPTER 10

"We don't know that. Anyway, we are just apes. Something happened and that hominid made certain choices and had a kid or kids. They had kids who made similar choices and so on, so eventually evolved into that," she said, pointing to the chimp.

"The rest of the kids made different choices, so they evolved on down the line to us."

She sat back, savouring the exhilarating feeling of intellectual exploration and the satisfaction of getting to grips with her question. But her happy contemplation was cut short by James' next pronouncement.

"I suppose humans could make choices that make them evolve backwards," he mused, shuddered, then firmly changed gear.

He'd decided that they'd been in the museum long enough. There was taking it easy so as not to attract attention, and there was hanging around long enough to tempt fate, or a bigot with a riot or a bomb in tow.

"Come on, let's find a café, I'm parched. We can continue our discussion there," he announced briskly. This time, Rhea gratefully acquiesced.

Out on the street, James strode off at a determined pace, steering her along beside him with his head down, glancing furtively from under his eyebrows from time to time, checking out CCTV s.

An unmarked police car cruised innocently towards them, and he made an abrupt turn into a small shop to avoid it, finally drawing Rhea's attention to his jumpiness.

"What's up? Do you think you're being followed?" she asked anxiously, as they headed into a side street.

He flashed her an impatient look of incredulity, before

abruptly turning into, what seemed on the outside to be, a small café. "We're fine. Just checking that's all." He then seated her in a discreet corner of the large room where they couldn't be viewed from the window.

He settled down with his large coke and sandwich, smugly gazing around, well aware this café had faulty cameras. And there was a back way out. Nor had the relevant camera on the street swung ominously in their direction as they'd entered.

She looked on puzzled.

"If you're that worried, wouldn't we have been better off in the museum café with all those cameras?"

He stared at her for a second, taken aback.

"Precisely. Cameras. We don't want you on camera. You're supposed to be dead. We don't want anyone spreading stories that it's not true do we?" he said briskly.

"But...they're run by the authorities, aren't they?" she protested.

He sighed. "I obviously didn't make things clear when we last spoke. The fewer people who know that you're alive, the better for all of us who knew you."

"Oh," she said guiltily.

He gave a friendly smile. "Besides, nobody trusts the authorities these days, not even the authorities."

She took his last remark as a joking attempt to make her feel better and sat back, sipping her fruit juice as he drained his coke.

"Needed that," he said, then fastened a business-like gaze on her.

"You look well. No scars worth mentioning."

She gave him that guileless smile of hers, and he responded in kind for a few seconds, before looking down with a soft embarrassed harrumph.

"Jal did a good job," she said.

"Uh huh, remarkable man," he answered neutrally, a questioning expression on his face, inviting her to continue.

Amusement danced in her eyes as she watched James' puzzlement and discomfort. "Oh very," she agreed and continued to sip contentedly.

"Linda seems taken by him. It's kind of him to keep you and Jack," he probed, with just a hint of query in his voice, scanning her face for any telltale signs of dissembling.

She nodded, aware he was drawing her out, but saw no harm in it, for now.

"He's like that, a really good man."

James wasn't used to hearing such an open expression of admiration in his job unless there were conditions attached. "Oh? Are you two an item then?" he asked unguardedly.

"No!" she said sharply, immediately jumping to defend Jal's honour, though she couldn't hope to expect James to guess why.

"He just puts his beliefs into practice that's all. You know? Healing? saving lives?"

James nodded in what she hoped was sympathetic understanding, but she didn't forget he was a policeman. She glanced at him warily, but rather than the cool expression she expected, he looked distinctly dismayed, crestfallen even. He had what she thought of as a nervous tic, which was to glance around furtively. Right now, in his nervousness, he tic ed, glancing at their fellow diners as well as the cameras, then quickly changed the subject.

"We need to get a few practical things out of the way first," he said, giving her a business-like smile, looking distinctly relieved when she returned it.

"We have to sort out some contingency plans. Have you got an identity card?" he asked, looking once more confident and comfortable, now he had practical details to manage.

"Why would I need one?" she asked in bewilderment.

"We don't want you picked up as a possible threat to national security do we?" he continued affably, smoothly ignoring her bewilderment as he pulled out a notebook. "I don't suppose Dr Jal could help. Could you get your hands on an old driving licence or something? It'll be better than nothing having something to flash, though it'll not do for close scrutiny. We've probably got a few months before things get really tight. In the meantime, we'll see how we can sort out something more permanent."

He sat back, obviously expecting a grateful thank you, and had rattled on for some time before acknowledging he was getting a confused disbelieving stare instead.

"But I won't need one for just walking around. I'm not opening a bank account or anything," she protested.

He nodded, clearly taken aback. "We all need one. You know? For the monitoring and random stop and searches?"

She stared at him. "Stop and searches?" she asked in alarm.

She winced under his pitying look.

"You really don't have a clue do you?"

She shook her head dumbly.

He sighed impatiently. "Terrorism."

"Oh that!" she blurted out in relief. "But the newspapers have been going on about that forever. It just means a few road blocks and checks at airports and train stations doesn't it?"

He raised his eyebrows in disbelief.

"Where have you been? Dreamland?"

She couldn't help a flash of amusement flickering in her eyes, much to his obvious irritation.

"Even you must have noticed a news item or two. Two streets away, there's a hoarding hiding a bomb site that was once a rather smart restaurant," he began irritably, but she was staring at him with a look of such total incomprehension, and a little fear, that he stopped.

She couldn't work it out. As she'd walked through the ever busy crowds to meet him, Linda's remarks about "Troubled times" had haunted her. But the city had looked just the same as it always did.

She could see James looking increasingly exasperated, and wondered just what she'd missed.

"Oh sorry. I've been in hiding. I took a long time to recover. I haven't been keeping up on the news."

"Still, you must've read about how we've got major outbreaks of flu and what-have-you, alongside all this global warming stuff," he said, shifting uncomfortably under the burden of repeating information even he clearly didn't accept. She shrugged, wondering where his argument was going. "Well yes, that was happening years ago, but what's that got to do with it?"

"Then we've got fanatics of every religion; Christian, Muslim, socialist, Ftse 100, even a bit of Buddhism, declaring how it's all retribution for mankind's bad behaviour. So they're fighting it out to bring us back to the god of their benighted choosing, and they're gaining orthodox support," he said, attempting an incredulous wry grin, but she just sat there, raising her eyebrows in dumb disbelief, giving him barely a nod.

He gave in, reverting to his own cynical take on the matter. "Alright. It's about money, globalisation, though I couldn't exactly say how. I just know this upheaval seems to be hurting millions and making big bucks for big bosses and promising more."

She'd heard this sort of thing before. Globalisation blamed for everything. It just left her cold, as she couldn't see the link. She shrugged.

James took a head clearing deep breath. "Mind you, the authorities do have a point, which they're pushing for all they're worth. There are really scary people out there who've reworked their screwed up crazed delusions into some virtual reality game version of religion. Or, to be more precise, various religions."

"Religions? Why?" she asked dumbfounded. Of course she knew there'd been terrible things done in the name of religion. But as far as she was concerned, that was walled off from real life, from here. It was in the distant past, it was history, or at least in undeveloped third world countries. What happened here were just a few mad idiots finding some new excuse for gang activities. That wasn't religion.

"They saw an easy way to get a bit of power and publicity by giving simple answers for simple people's fears. They'd be laughable if what they did wasn't so deadly. The damage and the dead they leave around aren't people to them, they're just scores. So you've got to be careful."

She shook her head, trying to fend off a growing fear. "It sounds like everything's being ripped up. But surely someone's doing something about all the trouble on the streets?" she threw out in a last ditch defence.

He nodded, a strangely resigned look on his face. "Yes. That's what I've been trying to get through to you. What they're doing is all those cameras, the stop and searches for anything the slightest bit suspicious or *different*," he said.

She slumped.

He sighed with relief. "The penny has eventually dropped. Mind you, things have happened so fast, I can see it would be hard to get your head around, even if you were briefed about it every day like me."

She gave a nervous chuckle, trying very hard not to allow the hairs on her neck to rise.

"Okay, just give me some time to digest it all won't you? Otherwise I'll be a paranoid wreck."

He nodded graciously. "Of course, but in the meantime, can we get on with the strange case of Rhea Forrester? I'd like to do something to improve your chances of staying alive."

She looked at him, the haze of unsettling thoughts he'd raised, making it harder to see the helpful, solid policeman she'd so trustingly come to meet. "Don't think I'm not grateful, I am, but I'd like to know why you're doing this."

He hesitated, marshalling his thoughts, which did nothing for her current mistrustful state.

"I felt I'd let you and Jack down. I believe in what I do. You know? Protecting people, justice? I need to do this, for my self respect if nothing else." She nodded, finding that his face was open, not guarded. James McCardle was the man of honour she had hoped he would be.

"Then there's the strangeness of the whole thing. It bugged me from the moment it was taken out of my reach. Why? Who really profits by it all?"

"You mean killing me? Well that's what I hoped to find out."

He shook his head. "I'm certain you were collateral damage. I knew it was about some kind of data. Your missing accounts stick told me that much, even before I found out it was about some kind of industrial genetic engineering information. And from what I found out later... we can discuss that tale some other time. For now, let's just say, some dangerous people will be looking for it."

She shuddered. "Yes, that's the scary thing. Jack had it all along."

"So where is it? This data on genetics? Plants is it?"

Rhea blinked in bewilderment. "Plants? No, it's not plants."

James shuddered. "That's usually what genetic engineering's about. It's got to be something that makes them money. Is it some fountain of youth remedy or something?" He ruminated, then stopped. She was staring at him incredulous. "Okay, so genetic engineering isn't my thing, so what is it?"

She sighed, a whole wash of emotions making her feel uncomfortable to find that she really knew a lot less than she thought she did, or indeed ought to know. "I just had a part of the data. It's about vaccines, something like that. Apparently, it's part of a really big experiment, so the company who's funded this will be furious after spending all that money," she said, regaining her equilibrium. That is, until she noticed that James was eyeing her anxiously.

"It's not some germ warfare stuff is it?"

"No, of course not. It's nothing like that," she smiled dismissively. "As far as I know, this is simply some corporate invention worth a lot of money. It's in safekeeping though. Anyway, I've got something else for you," she said, in an attempt to get him off this disturbing line of conversation. She had a mission to complete. She had to find a way to return safely to this world, so she was not about to entertain thoughts that would

CHAPTER 10

preclude that safe return.

"Yes but where is it?" he demanded, with a hint of repressed exasperation.

"Like I said, in safekeeping. When it's been analysed properly, I'll tell you about it," she said mulishly, clinging to the belief that since Jal and Stan were studying it, then it was under control.

"This is your Dr Jal isn't it? He's got it. That means someone else in the firing line. Whatever this thing is, I doubt it's that safe. They're not only determined to kill to get it back, it's part of some pretty heavy investigation."

It was all too much, and she was left desperately slamming down the lid on yet another terrible truth the data might reveal.

"Remember Paul the nerd?" she asked brightly, needing to find something to do to stop the terrifying helpless feeling that was sweeping over her.

James blinked, his expression a warning he thought she might be wandering off onto another crazy tangent.

"Um, yes, he was never questioned. In fact, he seemed to have disappeared into thin air some time before the attack on you. Why? What's that got to do with the data stick?"

"You want facts? I think I've got some to give you, but it'll take a bit of work. Remember the patch of scrub and trees down by the railway?" she asked briskly, ignoring his demand and the exasperation that was now clearly etched on his face. Then his warning glare softened slightly.

"You mean the conservation site?"

She nodded. "Yeah." She sat back with a satisfied grin, waiting for him to bite.

"What's the link?" he asked, frowning in confusion

She grinned, leaning forward conspiratorially, her foreboding gone, safely tucked away along with the silenced discussion on the possible terrible uses of the data, now she had something practical to do. "So you never found Paul? He knew a lot about the conservation plot for someone who said he was new to the area."

James nodded, his interest suddenly piqued.

"No, we never did find him, but go on," he said guardedly.

"Well, it's obvious really. What if the connection between me and the whole thing was the conservation site? He was the only other person who really knew anything about the place," she grinned, expecting him to get it immediately.

He looked totally baffled. "The conservation site? Okay, but why?"

She frowned, disappointed and impatient to be understood. "Because everyone in the club, and probably a few other people at the pub that me and Laura used to go to, knew I used to regularly go for walks down there. Then, of course, I was on bat watch. You know? Flittery things?" she said, waving her hands about in front of his open mouthed face. "So if I go down there, it wouldn't be suspicious," she emphasised, leaning in conspiratorially. "Supposing I was meant to carry the stick to the site. Supposing someone had dropped it off on me, knowing I always use that bag when I go to the site."

She paused to check if he had caught on yet, then gave a little smile of satisfaction that his eyebrows had come down out of his hair line and his mouth was now closed.

"Most people never bother to tip out their bags before they use them. Someone who knew me, or had watched me, would know I don't, didn't have time to go home before, and…Oh come on, don't you have hunches you can't explain?"

He sighed his admittance. "But why would anyone want to go to the conservation site? The old buildings nearby were too decrepit and too obvious to serve as hideouts." He shook his head, not entirely convinced, but curious. "Okay, I trust you. But Paul the nerd?"

She grinned. "Exactly. He was supposed to have met up with me that night, but he didn't make it."

"Okay, that tells me why Paul might be picking the thing up off you, but I don't get the connection to the site. Besides, wasn't Paul long gone before the bat watch?"

She was now caught up with the excitement of the chase, but she could see he was still more than dubious.

"Ahhh well. It was arranged while he was still with us. He did say he might go on holiday at a day's notice, but that he was sure he'd be back to do the study. Then there's how he talked about the study. It struck me that he was more interested in the site than in the bats. He even asked me where I usually sat. Anyway, no one had ever been to his flat, if he had one. Look, I can't really explain, but I just got a feeling. Where would you go if you were on the run? What I'm on about is near the old lorry yards. It won't take long Come on, take me and I'll show you."

His eyes narrowed with scepticism "Are you saying he was living there?"

She shrugged and pleaded some more.

"It's got to be worth a try. Are you doing anything else tonight?"

He gave in "Okay, I suppose it can't hurt, and it might just be possible you have noticed something relevant."

When they got there, they found the place fenced off. Otherwise, it wasn't much different from when she used to come here to sit and daydream.

"Wow! Look at those weird trees. I don't remember them," she said frowning at a group of twisted, sickly looking things.

"What are we looking for?" complained James, impatiently attempting to focus her on the matter in hand.

Reluctantly, she turned her attention away from the disturbing sight.

"I don't know. If I said, you'd think I was nuts." she said, scuffing at the low remains of a wall before sitting down. James threw up his hands in disgust. "You led me down here on a wild..."

"Just be quiet for a minute and trust me," she interrupted, then closed her eyes and let her mind go still until she could sense all those small unnoticed movements you miss in the everyday hurry. A memory of the many contented evenings she had spent here flooded through her, leaving a bittersweet ache, but she didn't have the time to reminisce.

"That's it!" she said triumphantly, getting up and tap dancing about off to the left of where they'd been sitting.

This was all too much for James, and she looked up to see his very mistrustful eyes.

She grinned.

"It's alright. I was just trying to remember where something was," she explained, continuing her queer tap dance along a path between some shrubs and down through a grass clearing, before he could stop her.

Somewhere near the old lorry yard, she found an odd depression in the undergrowth and stamped firmly. "I remember this sounded a different kind of hollow," she whispered excitedly.

James finally regained his wits enough to be horrified, and

grabbed her,

"Hey! Careful! This lot could be rotten. I don't want you disappearing down an old cellar or something." He met her eyes as realisation hit. "You can't be serious?"

"Why not? Nice cosy bomb shelter would be a perfect hideout, and there's bound to be at least one here. Let's see what we can find."

She was using a large branch as a digging stick to lever the undergrowth to one side, tapping the ground from time to time.

"I can't tell the difference, but if you can I'm willing to reconsider."

The cared-for cover she revealed, told them there would be something of interest in there. He smiled. "Whatever mother ship you're in contact with, it's coming up with some annoyingly realistic illusions," he said, smiling.

Rhea didn't notice his jibe. She was too busy attempting to heave at the cover, but just couldn't get a purchase.

James, suddenly shaken out of his bemused cynicism, rushed off to the car, coming back with a crowbar.

Rhea chuckled mischievously, indicating the offending implement. "Isn't that classed as going equipped with intent?"

James gave a grumpy grunt. "I'm into DIY" he said defensively, and heaved at the manhole cover. They were met with a whiff of decay. "Weeuph! Could do with ventilation! Now don't touch anything, and leave stuff exactly where it is," he ordered.

She held up a gloved hand. "Yessir," she grinned, already imagining laying her research before Jal.

James, finding himself caught out being a touch unnecessary, irritably muttered something about too many TV cop shows before snapping on his torch.

A narrow flight of steps led down to a sloping tunnel. There was a door off to the left which opened into a neat, tidy room, panelled with heavy, rough wooden slats at one end. It had obviously been used fairly recently, as various electrical leads lay where they'd been dropped. There was a pallet with an incongruously smart, clean, foam mattress and sleeping bag on it in one corner. In another, there was a desk with neatly stowed notebooks. "The Nerd?" he queried. Rhea grinned. "Well I said I'd find you something."

While James flicked through the notebooks, using a nail file he found in his pocket, being careful not to leave fingerprints, Rhea peered over his arm, managing to take surreptitious pictures. She then wandered off to examine the rest of the room.

He flicked the book shut. "Well, it's double Dutch to me. I think these are some sort of equations," he said.

"Uhuh," she agreed. "Looks like the stuff on the data stick."

He sniffed worriedly at the dank, evil smelling, sickly air while peering into the gaps between the wooden slats.

A shadow caught his eye as he lifted his torch. There was another room and something was in it, something he didn't want her to see. Someone had left in a hurry and not tidied up. They'd be back very soon to finish the job. It was definitely time to leave.

Rhea was too busy poking about at the other end of the room to notice. The light from her torch had glinted off something in the corner. There were the broken remains of a cup or bowl, and a nick in the wall where it had been thrown. "I'd say there's been a fight or a struggle" she said, holding up the bits of broken crockery, and pointing to the nick in the wall. He nodded, scanning the space, noticing the edge of something just under a bit of plank. He swept it up, only glancing at it before dropping it in his pocket as he took her arm to usher her out.

"This is still in use. We don't want to get caught. Come on, we need to get away from here as fast as we can," he said evenly, whilst hurrying her towards the exit and off the site. Rhea made an attempt to protest, but his urgency and distinct fear made her think better of it, and she allowed James to bundle her into the car and drive away.

When they were well on the way down the road, she dared to ask him what had spooked him.

He kept looking ahead. "Smells" he said cryptically.

"It seemed pretty clean to me. Well, alright. Definitely very pongy. Probably forgot to put out the rubbish before he went on holiday," she jested.

He grimaced.

"I smelled more than rubbish. I'd say a dead body. I didn't fancy ringing that in. Not when I was with you. And it wasn't that rotten, so it must have been fairly recent."

"Oh!" she said, shocked into silence.

"C'mon, let's see if we can persuade Linda to rustle up another hot chocolate," he said, in a more conciliatory tone while prodding his phone. "Hi Linda, I'm in the area can I drop in for a cuppa? Bringing a friend? Great, see you shortly."

Rhea sat pondering about the den they had found, wondering about the creature who had inhabited it. Was it her nerd? Was he the one who lay dead? Where? She had shone her torch right around the room. She'd seen neither body nor bloodstain. "We've got to find out who or what is in that room."

He gave her a sidelong glance. She was getting tougher.

"It's too dangerous. We don't know who the bad guys are yet, let alone where they are. I'll find a way of leaving an anonymous tip then I'll inveigle someone at the local station into innocently gossiping to me all about what they find."

Just then, there was a long, deep roar from some distance behind them.

Rhea gave a yelp. "Bloody hell! That's coming from where we've just been!"

James stared ahead into the mindless run of traffic, gripping the steering wheel grimly. He was praying no one had seen them coming from the old site.

"Nahh, it's just a plane or something," he said as lightly as he could muster.

She shook her head.

"No, I've heard explosions before. It sort of comes through the ground just like that did."

A siren sounded in the distance and his heart gave a patter of fear. He couldn't afford to be seen by any of his old colleagues, not here, not with Rhea in the car. "We'll be at Linda's soon," he said brightly, but there was obvious strain in his voice.

Rhea was frowning. "Wonder what they used?"

"If it was an explosion," he emphasised, but he wasn't convincing himself, let alone her.

Another long rumble growled towards them from some distance ahead. It was accompanied by flashes of light in the sky.

"Jeeze!" he exclaimed before he could stop himself.

Rhea craned her neck, straining to see through the muddy night air, her eyes bright with fear and shock. "That went on longer, and that definitely wasn't a plane!"

He slowed and found a place to park, to take a moment to think.

"I hope that wasn't a train crash," he said, already certain it was. He lowered his window and they both listened hard for signs to tell them where would be the safest direction to take.

"It's right in our path. In a few minutes the area will be crawling with police. Warn Linda and be discreet," he said, as he turned off the main drag.

Sirens had already begun their ominous chorus up ahead.

She flipped open his phone. "Hi, are you all unscathed in there?"

Linda groaned. "Yeah, I'm looking out of the window and the street is alright. Somebody said a train was bombed and came off the tracks. I can see smoke and smell burning."

Rhea stared out at what were once familiar and friendly streets but now they were menacingly alien. This was what Linda was talking about. This was what James had been warning her about. She swallowed back her fear and eyed the jumpy James. "We're south of it and there are blue lights everywhere, so we're going back home. Take care and I'll call you when I get back."

James nodded "Now we've got to get you out of here and somewhere safe."

She made another call. "Hi, it's me. Listen, can we drop in? Roads are busy tonight with a train crash. Okay, twenty minutes."

She turned to James. It would be a risk letting on she knew Stan, but she knew she was too great a liability for James now, and she had to get them both to safety fast. "You know the way to Stan's. We can get off this road and hole up there," she ordered.

James' eyebrows shot up in surprise.

She shrugged and smiled.

"He's Linda's mate. Like you said, he's safe."

He started up the car and flung the wheel around.

"It's as good an idea as any," he agreed.

James slowed and turned onto a side road, neatly avoiding another blue light. "We'll go the back way. I'm getting nervous," he muttered.

"So, you got talking to Stan?" she asked brightly, partly to break the tension.

James nodded, still scanning the road for trouble.

"Yeah, your inspiration, asked him about genetics. He started babbling about vaccines, just like you did. Conspiracies are his thing though. So it was hard to get him back on track to discuss genetic engineering."

Rhea raised her eyebrows in grim amusement.

"Vaccines and genetic engineering can't work together?"

A police car came past them on the other side of the road and James' face set hard like granite.

"They're too busy with other things," he muttered with relief before returning to the discussion.

"It's always about money. What better way to make money than to play on the vulnerabilities of the rich? So if it's genetic engineering, it can't just be vaccines, unless it's something to make them more beautiful or younger. I'd bet it's something to do with fertility, or growing spare parts."

"Uhuh? So it's a theory, not for certain," she said, trying not to smile at the thought of someone growing spare parts.

He answered out of the corner of his mouth. "You got any better ideas?"

Her face was grim.

"I don't know, but what about the stuff Stan was babbling about as you put it? He says there's a secret vaccination

CHAPTER 10

programme going on, but there isn't an epidemic. What do you think that's about?"

James clenched his jaw but still looked incredulous.

"And what reason would anyone have for blowing everything up?" she added.

"Destroys evidence," James answered somewhat irritably. "And that train might not have been an accident," he added grimly, "Could've been a distraction from the first explosion."

Horror and pity scattered her into a million helpless pieces. "Distraction?" she bleated piteously.

"I shouldn't have said that, I'm sorry."

Rhea felt sick. "No! All those people? All those innocent people just a distraction? How can you say that?"

All those people on their way to meet up with friends, family and lovers, as they'd always done and expected to always do, then to be wiped out so dismissively. Their harmless, seemingly solid, timeless way of life was as ephemeral and as vulnerable as that of mayflies. Linda had said something about "troubled times" and she hadn't taken it in. Then James had drilled it into her. Fear told her to run, to run to the safe haven she had in Dreamhills. But a deeper fear, a fear that was as overpowering and disorientating, and yet as difficult to apprehend, as thick fog, demanded that she had to do something, something that would save this, her seemingly solid world, or be lost in that fog.

"Just a distraction No! Why would anyone do that?"

James gave a world weary sigh. "Bury the news. With the train to deal with, who's going to look too closely at an explosion in a derelict industrial site?"

"You and me," she replied, some semblance of her sense of coherence returning, then she murmured to herself, "but what are they trying to hide, I wonder?"

"Did you see the body clearly?" she insisted, wondering how it had died.

"No, but I caught a whiff," he said tersely, underlining the finality of this conversation.

"There might have been clues on the body that could have told us how it died," she said, refusing to be intimidated into silence, refusing to stop thinking, refusing to stop and let the horror of helplessness catch up with her.

He turned down a street, backed up a drive, and pulled up in front of a seriously overgrown hedge on the side path of a large, uncared for looking house.

"Get out quick, Lift that lot to one side," he said, indicating the hedge.

She stared, her eyebrows all scepticism, but he just shooed her out. The branches were heavy, but remarkably easy to push aside. James then inched the car under the arch of the hedge and motioned her in. "The car's safely hidden here. Old Barmy Cyril will tell no one about it," he said, flashing her a sideways glance of reassurance.

"Not that anyone would want to ask him. Crafty old stick. Now, what were you saying about going to Stan's?"

She stared out from their hiding place, just in time to see a large, dark windowed limousine cruising slowly up the street. The window opened, and she swallowed a gasp as a pale face topped with cropped ginger hair was briefly illuminated by the street light.

"They're hunting someone! Come on! We've got to get inside!"

James, who'd followed her line of sight, made no argument,

only too ready to get the incriminating presence of Rhea out of the line of fire as quickly as possible. They slid like frightened ghosts, up over the single storey of the annexe, and into the rear gardens of the houses. James turned to Rhea.

"How the fuck do we get to Stan from here?"

As he looked around, he caught the faint chatter of a police radio.

"Shit! if they're looking for someone! The gardens are the first place they'll check. They'll find us. Must phone Stan," he said, hunting through his pockets.

Rhea hid a faint smile as she handed him his phone. "You dropped it," she said, then glanced towards something unseen beyond the houses. A series of crashing sounds, and yells of fury erupted from the street, followed by the various scrambling, clattering and screeching noises of hot pursuit.

Rhea grabbed James' hand and led him silently up the garden, shuddering, before ducking under some very strange saplings, then into a short alley. Indicating a closed door with a grin, she silently turned the handle and crept into a small basement room, then up through the hall, still dragging a dumbfounded James behind her. She unlatched the front door, and walked calmly down the front path. They only had a few doors to go to get to safety. She could feel the tension in James, as he gripped her hand a little too tight. "How did you know about the door?" he managed to ask, although that wasn't the biggest question on his mind.

She never stopped scanning the street as she listened for the sounds of saloon cars on the hunt. "Spent a lot of time in a garden just like that," she muttered grimly, then she swerved suddenly behind a large gatepost in the next drive, dragging

James with her, as a dark car sped up the road. As it passed, they both watched for a second or two, making sure it wasn't slowing or turning around, then fled up the steps to the shelter of the darkened porch, praying that the motion sensor light wasn't working. The door opened almost immediately as they arrived, leaving them stumbling into the hall.

"You can let go of my hand now," she said to James, as Stan closed the door behind them. James harrumphed in embarrassment on seeing the raised eyebrows of Stan.

"Come on, let's not scare the neighbours," he whispered.

Stan shrugged. "Out at work. Lucky for you, with all the noise you made. Come on, kettle's on. You'll be safe"

As Stan closed his flat door, James sighed with relief. "Whoever caused that crash saved our skins," he said pointedly to Rhea, who ducked her head to hide her grim expression. Stan, who was heading for the kitchen, grinned at James. "Yep, Jal can sure rustle up a fine racket."

Rhea continued to rummage studiously in her bag for a comb, apparently oblivious to the whole exchange. James stared after Stan, dumbfounded for a whole minute. "You've met Dr Jal?" he finally asked accusingly.

Stan returned, smiled patronisingly, and slapped down a mug of tea. "Yes, and he's just saved your skin. Now behave and drink your tea."

"I'm just praying they don't find my car."

Stan shook his head. "Nah, too busy chasing after a wild... goose," he said, grinning at Rhea.

She frowned disapprovingly.

"What 'd you tell him for?"

Stan gave her a placatory smile.

"Aww come on. He's a policeman. He'd know something was up. And he's my friend. I can't lie to friends can I?"

"Here you two! I am sitting here!" James snapped, then looked from one sheepish face to the other, and sighed.

"Under the circumstances, I suppose I forgive you, but you are going to tell me what you know about this Dr Jal," he said, sitting back, certain of the re establishment of his authority, accepting too readily the energetic nods of Stan.

"Now, can you rustle up a sandwich? All this cloak and dagger stuff is making me really hungry."

Stan and Rhea scuttled off to the kitchen together. Stan touched her arm. "You look shaken. Are you alright?"

She shook her head miserably. "But I've still got all my arms and legs. Jal is waiting."

Noises of movement from the living room made her jump. "James!" she exclaimed guiltily, and steeled herself before returning to him. She had to leave quickly, and head off any attempt by James to track or follow her.

"Look, we need to sort something out."

"Definitely!" he answered, and brought out a notebook.

"So I'm giving you a means of contacting me should you ever need my help."

It wasn't much, but it was all she had just now. She owed him, after drawing him into the intrigue that surrounded her. "You let this ring three times, then stop, let it ring again a couple of times more. It's to be used in emergencies only. And don't worry, no one could possibly trace it, not even you." She handed him the telephone number like a token of remembrance. "And thank you."

He frowned at the paper, trying to puzzle out how it related to the clearly sad tone of her voice.

He blinked in bewilderment. "What for?"

"For helping me understand," she said, and turned on her heel, leaving him puzzling over what had just happened, but only for a moment.

"Wait!" she heard him say from the other room, as he suddenly realised she was leaving, but she was already creeping out of Stan's window, her heart full, desperate to get away, desperate to protect them from her dangerous presence.

CHAPTER 11

"What are you doing out there? You'll drown, or freeze, or both!" Jal's worried voice rang out, making Rhea start, rousing her from her thoughts. Now, she really didn't want to think or talk. She'd been avoiding Jal. Indeed, she'd been avoiding all company since she'd left Stan and James. She was shocked. Some part of her mind seemed detached, busily assessing everything she'd seen the night before, the facts lining up into the narrow corridor that only allowed one terrible exit.

Jal's anxious presence scratched at her and she wheeled around with a flash of confused anger, giving him a curt nod of acknowledgement. She then finally noticed that the wind, which was whining around her ears, lashing her face with her hair, was also whipping the lake into icy, choppy grey waves that now reached around the rock she sat on. *'Even paradise had its off days,'* she thought wryly. She stepped off her rock into water, almost being blown over as she waded back to where he waited anxiously for her.

"I was just wondering if I could appreciate something, even if it turned nasty on me," she said, in an attempt at dry humour that she hoped would keep him at bay, but he had noted her unsmiling face and shadowed eyes.

"I see," he answered neutrally, whilst hurriedly wrapping her in his wrap the moment she reached him, an act she only reluctantly allowed. She was irritated, not only by him, but her own relief on seeing him.

"It is beautiful, but it's brewing up into a nasty squall. Let's get home out of this freezing wind," he said, and leaped into the air, struggling against the buffeting wind as he headed home up the hillside.

He dropped rather heavily into the garden, not freeing her from his wrap until he had hurried through the door. "Go get out of those wet clothes and I'll make a hot drink," he said briskly as he set her down.

"Will you stop treating me like some baby house pet? I have a mind of my own. I'm a grown woman!" she snapped, instantly regretting it, looking with consternation at the rain and wind battered Jal.

She made to apologise, but he just shooed her off before she could speak.

"Go on. Stop dripping there like an orphan of the storm. We'll talk in my den when you've had a hot shower and change of clothes."

She slumped, sullenly obeying, glad to get away from him, if only for a few brief minutes. Freshened up and presentable, she marched stiffly into his den, determined to stay unassailable.

"Now, we're both comfortable, and since the children are attending some meeting, we have guaranteed privacy for the next hour. So, tell me what's upset you so much?" he asked briskly, handing her a hot drink and settling beside her.

She bristled for a moment. None of her hostility had touched him, and it was so infuriating, so...Patronising. That was it! He *was* treating her like some bloody house pet. But that detached part of her mind added, with fearful treachery, that however humiliating it was, at least he wanted to keep her alive and safe. Yes, humiliated, that's how she felt.

"I was just moping," she mumbled, struggling to keep her roiling feelings under control.

He smiled sympathetically, tapping his temple. "That wasn't just moping. You yelled for me to come and get you."

That stung. She'd been caught out accepting her helpless house pet role. "Sorry. I slipped up. Okay?" she hissed, her outrage suddenly exploding.

He simply cocked an eyebrow. "This is about your visit isn't it?"

She scowled and muttered a yes, still not ready to let go of her grievance.

"Why did you just smoothly ignore me yelling at you?" she flushed in a confusion of annoyance and embarrassment.

"Because you just apologised so I was trying to let it go," he said in friendly reasonableness.

She cringed.

He smiled affectionately and nudged her "But, house pet?"

She grimaced "Well...you're always rescuing me and..." She closed her eyes. She was accusing him of caring. 'How whiny,' she thought.

He grinned. "I think I'd choose a quieter creature if I wanted a house pet." He settled back comfortably, waiting for a response, but she just picked silently at the cushion she was sitting on.

"So is it about us being different species?" he prompted.

"Yes," she said emphatically. "You're this clever advanced

being and I'm just a native of a rather backward world."

"Oh, I thought I was Jal who had a friend called Rhea, and we just happened to have different evolutionary origins," he batted back. "So what happened with James? It's obviously badly upset you."

She sighed, trying to make sense of her whirling emotions. "It's like I take you to tea to meet the relatives, and now I find that the family have behaved horribly. I feel so ashamed."

He gave her arm a comforting squeeze.

"And so angry."

"Anyone would!" She flung her hands up in exasperation, "I've just found out that my whole world is collapsing into war! People are being killed!" Her eyes prickled with tears. "People are being killed just as a distraction," she said mournfully.

"A distraction? What makes you think that?" he asked quietly, and she didn't notice the grim look in his eyes. "Oh, it was a theory that James had, but it made sense! We found a hidden bunker under the old lorry yard and shortly after we left, it was blown up. Then, just as we headed to Linda's, a train was derailed. He said it was to make sure any news about the explosion was buried. All those people killed and injured."

Jal regarded her with circumspection, and yet all she saw was his usual patient caring manner. She hadn't talked to him about her adventure since she returned. It wasn't about trust, not exactly. She trusted him implicitly and it was such a relief to actually say something.

She shook her head sadly, returning once more to why she missed all the clues of her world's slow descent into this mayhem.

"There was all that stuff in the news every night, and yet I didn't see what was happening right under my nose."

Jal raised questioning eyebrows. "You spent a long time recovering in my home. There was nothing happening here under your nose."

She shrugged. "All the same, I thought the only trouble I'd have to deal with was the trouble I got into, some criminal scam thing. But it's not is it?" she asked, reaching for the right description and failing. "It's not just a bit of protest either. It's horrible. It's scary."

"You were away from it all. It's a lot to work through." he remarked reasonably.

She shook her head sadly. "Then there's James. He only wanted to help me, and now I've put him in danger."

"No, James is safe. Stan told me he got back home without incident."

"Maybe, but he might not have. Oh why is this happening?"

"What did James say?" he asked, leading her away from her guilt.

"They're killing each other, justifying it by using religions," she felt the need to explain. "...Beliefs from our ancient history, when humans were in small tribes... when there weren't as many of us. But it's crazy! We live in a different world now! It's dangerous for all of us, including them!"

She was surprised to find he cocked a questioning eyebrow, encouraging her rant. Well she'd show him!

"We can't do that now. It's just stupid. We can't live separate little lives. Globalisation."

"Globalisation?" Jal echoed.

She gave a bashful shrug, her cheeks hot with embarrassment as her confidence faltered. "It's what they talked about in the conservation club. All countries trade with each other, though the club members saw that as bad, about money. But now, there's no separate tribes, no separate civilisations, not really, it's the whole world.

Jal smiled. "Ahh, interdependence."

Rhea shook her head against this seductively comforting thought. "Yes, interdependence, but they don't understand that they depend on each other. They're too busy making money. They need to realise they're in it with the whole planet, the ecosystem. They just don't see it."

She sadly considered her former self, her Poplar Close self, with her fairytale fantasies and her wish to explore worthy beliefs about the world. Back then, she hadn't even considered the possibility that the worthy aspirations of her little corner of the world weren't universally shared.

"I was so pleased with myself for choosing the Natural History Museum. After all that talk about Aazaar celebrating what makes you Aazaar, I wanted to know what made us human. And I found out," she said bitterly. "I thought I saw this wonderful hopefulness that brought us all the way through the millions of years to now. But then I have to find out that there's rioting on the streets and war is just around the corner!"

She gazed out of the window, into the green of the garden. She'd come to love Dream Hills, especially this hillside and the lake below. Like Jal, she thought of it as paradise, a little bit of Earth as it might have been. But right now she just felt cold, locked out, undeserving.

"You really hoped there was a chance humans might accept you," she said softly, then turned her head away. "You're better off not taking that risk."

He smiled. "You accepted me. And then there's Linda and

her friends."

"Yes, but Linda is into all that green, tree hugging stuff. She agrees with all that get -back-to-nature stuff that you like."

"They have an understanding of interdependence," he remarked.

She nodded. "True. And I suppose Linda will make sure James is safe."

Jal tipped his head. "She's monitoring him."

She heaved a sigh of relief. "Good. I don't want to make life any more difficult for him."

Jal considered her for a moment as she sat ruminating on her experience.

"It's terrible of course, and frightening, but maybe it's just the chaos before the next step. Maybe people are realising they have to let go of the worn out, but are not yet fully grasping the new possibilities."

She nodded, desperate to believe him, but as she looked up she registered, perhaps not consciously, a shadow of withheld secrets, withheld fears in his eyes.

"I hope so," she said with a grateful smile, too emotionally exhausted to think about it any more.

Jal seemed satisfied that she had tip-toed away from the shock of seeing the reality of her world.

"Jack made some soup earlier. Are you hungry?" he said as he got up, giving her a welcome break from the tension.

He returned with two bowls.

"Jack's cooking is getting better," he remarked admiringly after a couple of spoonfuls, noting with satisfaction a decidedly brighter look to her face.

She smiled her proud agreement. She would not have

dreamed of letting Jack anywhere near the kitchen back at Poplar Close, but here she was pleased to leave her happily clattering about her culinary experiments with Marn. All Aazaar Kind children took on a share of the chores of daily living from an early age. That was one of the practical elements of Aazaar's belief in being integrated with their environment. The children seemed to delight in demonstrating their skills, unlike their human counterparts who are traditionally expected to howl with indignation if merely asked to deposit dirty clothes in the linen basket. Any fears she may have had that their sojourn with the Aazaar would adversely affect Jack's development, had been swiftly allayed as they arose.

"Mm sweetleaf; Jack's favourite flavouring."

She looked over her bowl at Jal.

"I'm going to have to talk to Jack, explain things. She'll be expecting to leave sometime soon, now that I've recovered. Mind you, I don't think she's raring to go. She's really happy here," she remarked, lining up persuasive arguments for Jack's stay to be continued indefinitely.

"I know she's had problems to face, but she's never said anything."

She lowered her eyes, allowing a fleeting worry that Jack too might have shared her recent feelings of humiliating inadequacy; of feeling she is no more than a house pet.

"Still, finding out that we're staying longer might change that," she murmured.

Jal just managed a gesture of disagreement, when a bundle of energy hurtled through the door and sent everything wobbling

"Mam! I've just finished this cushion cover what do you think?" Jack yelped breathlessly, as she flung herself down beside them.

Rhea steered her teetering soup bowl to a safe harbour on a bench and laughed. "And good evening to you too!" she said, hugging her daughter.

Jack spread out the work proudly for Jal to examine. "Look, leaves like you showed me. I made them out of my old tee shirt."

Rhea watched the obvious affection between her daughter and Jal. *'You two look happy for us to stay,'* she thought, *'At least cute house pets get to live.'*

"Jack," she began, steeling herself for the difficult task ahead.

Jack looked up, alert to the warning of a serious-talking-to note in her mother's tone. "Uhu," she answered warily, her eyes bright and as attentively innocent as she could make them, though she couldn't think of anything she had broken or forgotten to do.

"What would you say if I said we might have to stay here for a very long time?"

Jack breathed a sigh of relief, wanting to get back to her projects. "Great!"

Rhea blinked, a little shocked at the brevity of the response. "You sure?"

Jack glanced surreptitiously at Jal, who gave her a smile of encouragement. She'd already asked him if she could stay. Dreamhills was her fairyland come true. She knew her mother would fret about her missing school, and might try to go back to human world too soon. But she didn't want to go back Ever. Especially while the gangsters were still on the loose. Sometimes, she found herself wanting to go see Gran and Granddad, Uncle Thomas, and her best friend. But she'd watched enough television to know that if she and Mam went back, everyone she knew would be at risk of being murdered by the gangsters. And she didn't want them to be murdered.

Jack gave her mother such an incongruously old grandmotherly smile of reassurance.

"Course. I love it here. Anyway, we can't go back now. We'll be freaks." She shuddered, imagining for a moment standing on the outside of the school playground 'in' crowd, the butt of hostile jokes and bullying because she'd been away for so long, and would never ever be allowed to tell anyone why.

And then her mind flicked back to the present. "Got to go, Marn's taking me to the music gathering at Uncle Issn's. Bye Mam. Bye Jal," she shouted over her shoulder as she bolted out of the room.

Rhea sat back. "Weeuph! Was that a whirlwind, or was that my little girl? I think we can safely say Jack won't be upset about staying here."

Jal raised amused eyebrows. "No, seems not," he said, as peace settled again.

Rhea let out a sigh of envy and fond amusement, then looked up into the golden eyes of her kindly guardian. It wasn't a bad life.

"You're right." she murmured.

Jal handed her half of his apple. "Mm" he agreed, appreciatively demolishing what was left.

She bit into her half, allowing herself a moment to recover.

"Right then! I'm staying for the foreseeable future, if not for good, so I'm ready to sort out living arrangements," she said briskly.

"I know I can't impose on your hospitality forever, but I thought maybe Jack and I might live nearby."

"What? But I want you to stay. I like you staying with me. When did I say you couldn't stay with me?" he stuttered in

CHAPTER 11

confused consternation.

She cringed in embarrassment. "No, yes, I mean, it's alright, but...you can't keep me can you? Is it alright? I mean, I know you said I was your friend and all that, but you have to set all wildlife free, and I'm wildlife. I know you won't send me back without my agreement but...I have to have my own place, don't I?"

He shook his head, deciding not to even try to disentangle this convoluted emotional thread. "But I'm satisfied this wildlife is more than capable of making her own decisions. So all I'm going to add is this: It's my home. I like you being here. I'm happy to have you stay for as long as it pleases you, and I say it's alright. Alright?" he continued, eyeing her warily in case she let loose another confusing tangle of emotions.

She groaned, "Oh hell, I've offended you."

He gave an exasperated chuckle, considering for a second or two, how simple relationships were with non-verbal wildlife. "No, at least not yet. I'll say it again. I want you to stay."

She opened her mouth to protest, then stopped. Had Vinnie fretted like this when she'd given him a safe place to stay? Course not. He was a dignified bird. She straightened up and simply smiled.

He gave a chuckle of relief and amusement. "Have a fruit bun," he said, handing her the plate.

"I never wanted to move," she admitted, mumbling contentedly into her bun.

"I'm glad," Jal said, eager to slide back into their familiar cosiness, eager to box off the coming revelations she would inevitably bring him.

"You know that conservation club thing? I'd been looking for new company, people I could share the stuff I think about without them calling me crazy." She looked up, and despite her recent maelstrom of fearful feelings, smiled fondly, shaking her head in disbelief. "And I met you."

She laughed, remembering Laura's pronouncement about her. "It's crazy alright."

"My feelings too," he said, allowing himself a secret smile of satisfaction. She would continue to be safe in his house and safely out of the reach of other inquisitive members of his community.

After this emotional conversation, she spent time contentedly working in the garden, each peaceful hour under the trees moving her farther away from the ominous growing disorder of her own world. A few days later, Rhea found a small hand-written note on her cushions. It was just a few words in her own language inviting her to join Jal on his evening promenade. Aazaar didn't have paper, so it was written on a piece of bark, albeit carefully trimmed and decorated. To Rhea, it was pure gold.

There hadn't been much time for such simple pleasures these past few days, he'd been so busy. She smiled. It was just like Jal to make it feel so special for her. Jack must have taught him how to write.

An image of him lying on the cushions with Jack, encouraging her to teach him some of her stories came to mind. No wonder Jack adored him.

When she arrived, she was glad to find him sitting gazing contentedly across the valley towards the place the sun would soon set, which he often did after the business of the day.

He gave her a peaceful smile of greeting, drawing her into the dreaminess of the moment as she slid silently down beside him, ready to enjoy this familiar ritual of their friendship.

After only a moment or two he rose, stretched out each

wing, and then drew her to her feet, his eyes now twinkling with animation.

"Come on, we're going to Bright Star clearing," he said, looping his wrap around her. And before she had a chance to ask why, she was clinging onto him as he dived into the air.

As he landed and let her loose, there was a loud squawking and cawing, a rush of feathers and wings, then a thud on her head as a large black bird attempted to settle there. The bird, sliding off her hair sideways, thought better of his attempts, and settled on a low branch beside them instead, still cawing and flicking and flipping his wings in excitement.

Vincent!" she exclaimed in delight and affection for the old bird. He preened a strand of her hair, and she gently scratched his head in return.

She beamed a glorious smile of appreciation onto Jal. Happy memories of her ordinary dreamy little life with Jack, their many contented days rambling on the abandoned, overgrown field, tip-toed gently into her thoughts. She smiled, remembering only through the golden filter of nostalgia.

"Oh that was a lovely thing to do. And I thought you were just looking for a change of place for your practice," she said, eyes shining with gratitude.

He watched them, these two friends, with warm satisfaction. It had worked. Rhea had been reminded of what she had loved about her world, what had always given her such comfort and strength.

The bird cocked its head, eyeing up Jal then Rhea, all the while churring softly.

"I think Vinnie says thank you too. Where did you find him?"

"Oh, complaining on the roof of the building you used to

live in. He came straight to me," he said, then watched them, allowing himself a wistful sigh. Rhea and this bird were so easy, so comfortable with each other, showing a gentle respect between creatures of such vastly different species, vastly different experiences. But the crow was nearer to her than he was. Somehow, instinctively, they sensed the clear inevitable lines of their shared heritage, born of this Earth, whilst he was left outside this heartening experience, contemplating what it is to have no such world of his own to claim his origins from.

She held out her arm and Vincent very delicately climbed on, his sharp talons leaving nothing more than an impression on her sleeve. "And no one saw you?" she asked, as very carefully, with a lot of sideways gazes and soft churrs of affection, Vincent walked up her arm and hopped onto her head.

"Possibly, but what they thought they were seeing wasn't a large winged alien."

Vincent then hopped onto Jal's shoulder. Rhea gave a delighted chuckle. "Looks like you've definitely won him over. So what would they see?"

The bird eyed him conspiratorially, and when Jal smiled back, gave a friendly tug of the nearest black curl. "What they wanted, expected to see. A crow, a large one I suppose."

Rhea shook her head incredulously. "I might have expected that if I'd thought about it. I think I saw you as a crow at first. How do you do that?"

"You do it to yourselves. I'm just careful not to disabuse you."

Vincent let out a soft caw of what sounded like agreement before lifting off, and returning to his perch on the branch.

Impulsively, Rhea reached up and kissed Jal on the cheek, then hugged him, taking him by surprise. Hesitantly, he returned it. It was an odd thing, but there'd been very little touching between them. True, he'd given Rhea the odd comforting hug when she was upset. And of course when he flew, he held her wrapped tightly to him but, somehow, that didn't count. It was a necessity. He was simply transport and she cargo.

She looked up into his face, her blue eyes sparkling with unreserved affection.

"Thank you. You're a lovely thoughtful man," Rhea said fondly.

Man. She said it so automatically. She saw him as a man, a fellow being, letting him glimpse what it was to feel part of her Earth. She turned back to Vincent, but Jal was glad to find she was still holding onto his arm.

"You're welcome," he purred.

Vincent, who had been gazing at her adoringly, studied them both for a moment more. Then, with a loud caw that sounded like a knowing chuckle, took off out over the lake into the golden glow of the low afternoon sun.

"I want to follow him. Would you take me?" she asked impetuously, her mind already floating out on the magical golden haze of the low afternoon sun.

Jal caught her up, and joyfully swooped down towards the lake. This time, it wasn't for any practical reason, but for the sheer pleasure of sharing the moment with her, riding the energy currents, smelling the sharp fresh tangs of the trees, and the evocative mossy scent of the lake.

At last, he caught an up draught and sailed lightly back to their hidden clearing.

As soon as he set her down, Rhea danced joyfully around, her arms spread wide like wings, replaying the memory of their skimming flight across the sun gilded lake, up the magic mountainside and above the reach of the trees. "Wonderful! That was just wonderful!" she said breathlessly. "I think I'm finally getting what it is about having wings."

Jal watched her with fond amusement, feeling that, in this moment, his heart was as light as a child's.

"Come on, let's have our snack here," she said, realising she was hungry, and he happily obeyed.

As they settled back to relax after eating, Rhea gave a shudder, noticing the growing evening chill, and huddled closer to Jal who threw his wrap around them both, just like he'd often done when they'd stopped when out foraging.

They gazed out to where the sun would soon disappear into the end of the glassy, still lake.

"It's glorious," she sighed, looking into his face with dreamy content.

Something changed, moved, flashed between them.

Jal smiled. "Yes," he murmured. "Beautiful."

Rhea only revelled in it for a moment before awkwardness took over. She drew back, afraid he might have sensed how she felt, and looked anxiously into his face for reassurance that she had not embarrassed her friend.

Again, as she met his searching amber eyes, a wild sweep of energy flashed over her, and this time, she knew he could see. She flushed, flustered. "Sorry," she said looking away.

Jal frowned; clearly puzzled, concerned and disappointed. "Sorry? For what?"

Rhea drew in a deep breath to blow cooling reason through her thoughts. "Jal, I..." Her words died in her mouth. What could she say? After he'd given her such a wonderful afternoon, she was about to spoil things. She felt miserable, lonely and guilty.

Jal took her hand in an attempt to reassure, but had a failure of nerve and just sat there, gazing at her, a silent plea for her to talk, reach out to him, in his eyes. Then he shook his head, smiling in amusement at himself.

At the same time, Rhea was trying to reason with herself. This had to be a mistake, a ridiculous embarrassing mistake on her part.

She finally noticed his smile. "Alright. What's so funny?" she asked warily.

Jal shook his head. "Oh not a lot. I'm just nervous, worried that you might think I'm some ugly old gargoyle you wouldn't give houseroom, but desperately hoping I'm just what you want."

She jumped to his defence before she fully realised what he'd said or knew what she was doing. "Well, you're my ugly old gargoyle and I like you the way you are."

He gave a happy chuckle, lifted her face and gazed into her eyes for a long minute. The shock of realisation fizzled along her every nerve. Neither one made the first move, their lips just met.

Rhea suddenly managed to free herself from his arms and sat back, shaking her head in disbelief. "You kissed me."

He smiled. "And you kissed me."

She bit her lip, a million reasons solemnly queuing up in her head to tell her why this was not a good idea, while on the other hand, her heart gave only a delighted leap. She flushed. "Too much," she murmured, glancing at him under her eyelashes,

"Maybe," he agreed reluctantly, and looked out at the fading light across the lake, still holding her hand.

"I'm frightened of losing you," she explained simply.

"We've barely started this adventure. Why would you lose

me?" he asked in dismayed bewilderment.

She swallowed hard. "Because...because...Oh hell, this changes everything. I mean, we're not even the same species. We can't..."

She flushed, trailing off into embarrassment, objections crumbling into a scramble of alphabet soup behind her eyes.

"Not the same species, but of the same heart," he murmured. He searched her face for encouragement.

He saw it, that plea in her eyes for him to reach her. "Just a little while ago, you called me a man. Not an alien or Aazaar Kind," his face crinkled into a gentle smile. "You said, "a lovely thoughtful man," to be precise, and that made me feel pretty good."

She nodded, a little smile of hope breaching the clouds of confusion in her face. He'd been her friend from the start. She smiled. Even before she understood he was real she'd trusted him with her life. Wasn't that the best basis for a romantic adventure? She gave a nervous chuckle. "Haven't you got...I don't know, rules about kissing aliens?"

He tilted her face, his eyes alight with playful affection. "Only that we do it right," he said, and kissed her very gently but very sensuously.

"It does feel right," she agreed dreamily.

He kissed her nose. "So tell me, now we've had our first kiss. How should I go about asking you to romance with me?"

"Romance?" she asked, unable to stop grinning at the oddness of the term, yet still letting the word light a deep glow of anticipation in her eyes.

"Umm. Be my girl? Date?" he continued. "Feel free to put me out of my misery when I find the most suitable human

CHAPTER 11

expression," he remarked with a wry grin.

She put a silencing finger to his lips. "I liked romance," she said hopefully.

He laid another soft kiss on her mouth. "Very well. Will you romance with me?" he asked, meeting her eyes with such hope in his.

She found it so deliciously quaint. "Yes, I'd like that very much," she murmured, having visions of many happy afternoons like this, happy afternoons that would transport her many memories away from her shattered little life.

He gazed into her strangely Brynewiln-like, blue eyes, savouring the start of this new happiness. "In that case, will you come to dinner?"

"Dinner?" she asked with a dumbfounded giggle.

"It's our custom to make a celebratory meal when we...what would you say? Start to go out? Date?" he gave a sheepish grin. "Help me out. I'm feeling very awkward now."

"Sorry. You're doing fine. It's just..." She smiled up into his face giving an embarrassed shrug. "On the one hand, it's so right. I'm asked to dinner by a man who shows every sign of actually liking me, even though he's seen me at my worst. On the other, it's unbelievable! I'm marooned here, in a beautiful place I never knew or believed could exist, living with a man from outer space, of a people I never knew, or even imagined, could exist. So excuse me for feeling more than a little overwhelmed."

She lowered her lashes, giving him a shy smile. "I'd love to come to dinner."

"Thank you. How about a den in the top woods? I have a little place I like to retreat to that I think you'd really like. It's spring festival day in four days time. It would be really lovely to have dinner there."

She nodded, noting the breathless tone of his voice. "Sounds really lovely." She flushed bright pink, wondering what to do next. "Oh, I feel so nervous here."

He laughed, breaking the tension. "Me too. So what do we do now?" he asked, hugging her close.

"I haven't a clue how to behave like a well brought up Aazaar lady. I'm bound to do the wrong thing without meaning to. You're going to have to teach me."

Jal chuckled, amused at the thought of the embarrassments that were likely to face him as Rhea found her way around Aazaar etiquette.

"True, but that should not be too much of a problem. We Aazaar keep our romancing to ourselves, at least in the early stages, so we can happily make our mistakes in peace."

She pulled a face of mock alarm, then laughed. "I'm glad you warned me before I embarrassed you. Though I suspect the good folks of Dream Hills would just think this fluffy little human was messing about, if they noticed at all."

Jal inclined his head. "Probably," he agreed teasingly. "But I'd know better," he added quickly.

They returned to the village with its familiar hum of domestic activity, and as Jal set her on her feet, he checked there was no one to see, then gave her a last surreptitious kiss before they went into the house.

While the Aazaar did not specifically disapprove of inter-species relationships, and it did happen from time to time, there were many social prohibitions on interacting with other species. These were not simply about respecting the integrity of their cultures, but to keep the Aazaar hidden and unnoticed. As he and

Galer had explained, there were others out there in space who did not accept the Aazaar's right to exist. But Rhea was part of Jal's community now, part of his world. Eventually, they would have to explain all, but not right now.

It was the day of the early spring festival. The air was clear, but cold and crisp. Beautiful haunting music echoed around the hills, as spirals of happy couples, with sprigs of green leaves in their hair and wearing animal masks and green tunics, danced in the air above the lake. Jal smiled as he saw Rhea coming to meet him.

Rhea made her way up to the high path, and her heart pattered as she caught sight of him. She was uncomplicatedly happy, here in her timeless fairyland, far away from her world's inexorable descent into war. Nothing was going to spoil this new happiness, this escape.

"Ohh, this is so lovely," she exclaimed, as he led her into a small bower built under the bushes. "Glad you like it. I've enjoyed myself this afternoon, cooking, and decorating this place, making it cosy and warm just for you."

He ushered her to a pile of cushions, their meal laid out on a low table in front. She settled blissfully by his side, their celebration meal holding no awkwardness now, only a mixture of tenderness, and the warm playfulness of people who were already friends.

Jal lay back, Rhea leaning against his shoulder, and gave a sigh of sheer joy and contentment. "Perfect," he said.

She kissed him lightly. "Mmm absolutely wonderful."

He smiled into her eyes. "From your gargoyle to my lady."

"Woodsprite," she admonished light heartedly, remembering the peace she'd felt when she'd first began to see him in the clearing. "You're my wood sprite."

"I'm your woodsprite," he agreed, and kissed her gently.

"But I've been thinking…"

Her eyes widened, "Really? You don't want to be my woodsprite?" she asked teasingly.

"For as long as you want me to be," he purred playfully, "But there's something you said that could bear repeating."

"I did? I mean what's that?" she asked, somewhat surprised.

His eyes were no longer playful but soft, thoughtful. "We might both know each other's secrets, but we have to face up to the vast differences between us. This Aazaar doesn't really know enough about your Human expectations. There are a million things I could do wrong without ever meaning to."

She lowered her eyelashes, already shaking her head in reassurance, but he stopped her.

"Hear me out. All I'm asking is that you tell me, teach me. But teach me gently."

Rhea glowed in transports of sheer delight. Once, in her other life, she'd wondered if she'd ever meet a man who understood that romance wasn't something that just happened if you bought a bunch of flowers, but something you did.

And now, with a man from out of this world, she was certain this romance would be beautiful, kind and gentle. There wouldn't be any of that feeling of being checked against a script you weren't allowed to see, knowing your sweet dreams would be suddenly smashed if you fluffed your lines or stumbled against the scenery. She realised he didn't want to be checked against an unseen script either. A little timid part of herself hesitated and asked, could she really let this alien being love her? Could she love him?

"I will, if you'll promise to do the same for me."

"I promise," he said tenderly. He wanted to give this delicate early beginning of their romance every chance to grow while they still had time.

Rhea snuggled contentedly into his arms. "Now we're officially an item, can we do all sorts of lovely romantic things? I want you to show me all your favourite playtime places. And maybe I can find ways to show you some of mine."

He stroked her face, wanting to protect her from the hurt, make it alright. "Yes," he said but she didn't see the shadows flit across his eyes.

"Okay. First heart's desire. Kiss me goodnight, each night, when we're home," she demanded with a grin.

Laughing, he sealed his agreement with a kiss.

"Discreetly of course," she added, then looked out longingly at the sky dancers. "And right now, I want to dance with you."

Jal groaned, stroking her wingless back meaningfully. "That's not fair. I can't work that one out today," he pleaded.

She grinned mischievously. "Oh yes you can."

And she stood up taking his hands. "Come on. Dance with me here, with both feet on the ground, human style."

He got to his feet, and hesitantly began to move with the music as Rhea danced within the circle of his arms.

"You're dancing to the heartbeat of the Earth," he said delightedly, as his movements finally synchronised with hers.

"The Earth has a heartbeat?" she asked, but no longer finding herself as incredulous as she once might have been.

He gave her one of his wise old faun smiles. "Ohhh she's got a heartbeat alright and it resonates through all her creatures."

Then he drew her closer.

She saw in his eyes, not only how much he wanted her, but

the yearning to belong. She understood now, that if she let him into her heart, she could bring this one lost Aazaar home.

"Can you love me for me and not simply for my planet?" she laughed.

He grinned, but his eyes glowed with tenderness. "Oh yes."

She gave a soft laugh of joy. "Then show me," she whispered.

He gave her a kiss of acknowledgement, of surrender of the ancient loneliness of his species, lost in the joyfulness of new love.

The sound of the harpists' clear tones, haunting Aazaar voices, and the buzzing thrum of the pipes swirled around and through them, as if the whole land hummed with the same happiness.

Jal felt the deep pulses of the Earth as she breathed her energy through them both. This time, in those life creating pulses, the Earth let him feel he was part of her web of life, her shimmering aura, one of her own creatures. He was too happy to ponder the meaning of this insight. His thoughts were filled only with love and Rhea.

Rhea lay in Jal's arms, now understanding so many things she'd learned over these last few years. Looking through the eyes of love, she saw, and felt, the beautiful pulsing musical rainbows of pure energy that surrounded everything, that held them together. Each of these halos, these dancing auras of love, affected those next to it. And beneath it all, subtle yet slow, steady and strong, keeping them all in time was that deep resonance, that pulse of life, the beat of the heart of the Earth. Yes! Now she could understand, with her whole being, why Jal and Linda called Earth a goddess.

"I think Aazaar science is a lot kinder than our science," she murmured dreamily.

Jal stirred from his contented drowse, lifting his head from her breast. "uhhmm?" he muttered sleepily.

She smiled, smoothing back his unruly curls, her happiness allowing her to see hope, not just for herself, but for all humans, for the whole Earth. "I mean, I know now that if we could chime the right way, you know? With the energy of love, the Earth would chime right back and we'd all be happy little fairy bells."

Jal laughed delightedly, hugging her tight. "You crazy lovely woman. Maybe that's the duty all lovers have to their goddess planet."

After they'd returned home and he was alone, he smiled in deep contentment, and murmured "Fairy bells," before drifting off to sleep.

But Rhea's optimism was far from a sign of her acceptance of reality. Since the day of the storm, she had shown no further interest in the incidents that had brought her to Dreamhills, or indeed in anything else of her world that she'd found painful. Even though she saw Jal off on his visits to Stan, she asked nothing about his work. There wasn't even a strained silence, just a blank.

Jal made no query or protest. He knew there'd be time enough for facing up to tragedy. For now, he found ways to share kinder memories of her home world.

No one took any notice of the odd couple on the all but deserted beach as they strolled contentedly hand in hand. Even when they wandered into a faded little seaside café, no eyebrows were raised among the few eccentrically dressed people who made up the clientele.

Jal did not remove his tinted glasses, or his long caped

raincoat, but that was of no note in this strange little haven.

Rhea smiled to herself. Even here, in this café among human strangers, he observed his Aazaar discretion. There'd be no hand holding and only demurely friendly glances whilst they were within view of other people.

"So you told Linda we might be dropping by? What's she doing down here?" Rhea asked puzzled.

A chair was pulled out beside them before he could reply.

"I like the outfit!" Linda said to Jal as she settled herself at their table, startling Rhea

"It's okay. No CCTV. Only people going off camera come here," Linda whispered conspiratorially to Rhea.

Unfortunately, Linda's appearance and her reference to current painful realities, were too much for Rhea's nerves, and she looked anxiously towards the cafe's owner. Jal reached under the table and took her hand, anchoring her mind to the safety of their pleasant afternoon.

"Old Rita gets plenty of warning, enough time for us to make an escape should some official or other decide to come nosing around," Linda offered in appeasement of Rhea's obvious anxiety.

"That's a relief then!" Rhea forced herself to grin and finally recovered herself. She gave Linda a heartfelt hug, looking forward to a leisurely catch up, already planning further seaside strolls with Jal.

"Yep but don't get comfortable. We're leaving in a few minutes. The festival's a few miles away and Richard's in the van. Are you two ready?" Linda asked, then noted Rhea's bewilderment. "Jal! You didn't tell her!" she admonished him with a smile.

"I was just about to," he said but Linda had already turned

CHAPTER 11

to Rhea.

"It's big, fun, with lots of bands and lots of silly singing, dancing, and it's free from any interference by our good guardians of law and order. Want to come?"

Rhea looked up questioningly at Jal.

He smiled enigmatically behind his tinted glasses, tipping his head.

"Yes," she said decisively.

Linda grinned. "Great! See you there in an hour or less," she said, and left as suddenly as she had appeared.

"A festival huh? Love it," she murmured, and planted a swift kiss on his cheek, chuckling mischievously at his embarrassed delight, then she led the way out of the café.

"Are you sure this is a good idea? I mean, won't there be police there?" Rhea fretted, hearing a distant siren as Jal readied to take off.

Jal smiled fondly. "Linda told you. No police. Here, hold my bag and stop worrying. It's safe. I checked when you first mentioned festivals. We'll have a lovely day," Jal insisted as he fastened her securely then jumped into the air.

As James had warned Rhea, everyone was checked on the perimeter roads if they so much as coughed. But, as she soon discovered, the authorities really did leave these music gatherings unmolested. In fact, Stan was to tell her, some people argued they positively encouraged them. There was nothing said officially, but the ubiquitous leaks from unnamed official sources, and the speculation of various commentators, suggested they saw the festivals as a useful means of diffusing the anger and thus the prospect of any seriously disruptive protest, against what those in authority knew was an unbearably oppressive surveillance and control of the population.

Jal landed silently among some bushes a little way off from the festival field, but within the surveillance free perimeter.

Rhea beamed up at him.

He kissed her nose. "Just enjoy."

She spotted Stan as they reached Linda and her group of companions and a little cloud of sorrow and shame briefly sailed across her sunny mood as she recollected why Jal was working with Stan. She shooed it away. Today, she would make sure Jal had a lovely day.

Jal lounged companionably with Richard in the entrance of Linda and Richard's surprisingly commodious tent, his wings sprawling untidily behind him. Shaded from the view of passers-by, he was glad to have dispensed with the cumbersome raincoat and tinted glasses, happily taking in the sights, sounds and vibrations of the festival as Rhea chatted with Linda and Stan.

Richard studied his strange guest for a moment, glad he was finally getting the opportunity to find out for himself what this curious being was all about. It wasn't that he didn't trust his adored wife's judgement, just Jal was such a monumental concept to grasp, and he was well aware it was too easy to allow hope to overwhelm reason and common understanding.

"Something out there interests you?" he asked affably.

Jal gave a slow contented smile. "A number of things," he said, indicating a grubby looking ruffian who went to help a rather awkward, well dressed character who was struggling with an expensive looking tent. "I'm glad to see that."

Richard smiled, also pleased by this little display of spontaneous kindness.

Jal inclined his head. "Very human," he observed pleasantly.

Richard nodded thoughtfully. "Yes I suppose it is."

He looked at Jal, determined to be certain just where he, and maybe all humans, stood with this rather alarming looking being. "So, is it very Aazaar?"

Jal smiled, well aware of Richard's concerns, revealing his now famously sharp looking, white fang-like teeth. This caused Richard just a moment of unthinking primeval alarm, despite his determination to remain reasonable.

"The urge to help? Cooperate? Yes. As a matter of fact, it pops up all over the universe," Jal said, the fleeting glance of agreement between them a handshake on their common understanding.

Richard visibly relaxed, then looked out at a group of would-be strolling players in crazy make up and bright trailing clothes. "Must be vastly different from your festivals," he observed.

Jal watched a child happily stringing daisies together. "Not really. We do the same, dress up, act, play music, celebrate what it is to be Aazaar, what it is to share the joy of life with other living things in our surroundings."

Richard scanned the milling crowds. From across the field, the sound of drums, didgeridoos, guitars, the odd flute and other miscellaneous instruments, had finally reached a happy consensus, underscoring the joyful rhythms of this vast crowd of humanity at such innocent, life affirming play.

"I never thought of it like that," Richard said, deciding he liked this man, even if he wasn't human.

"Want a beer?"

Linda saw her beloved clipping the caps off two bottles and laughed. "So, already got him on the beer I see? Don't forget, we're showing him the stones later," she warned her adored husband.

"Is this one of those energy sites?" Jal asked, diverting Linda's attention from the problematic beer, thus earning a knowing, all-boys-together, smile from Richard. He also diverted Richard's attention from his bottle, which he discreetly tipped, though he did have a small taste.

"Yes. It's a sacred site. There are legends, old stories that go back thousands of years," she said, warming to one of her favourite topics.

Rhea caught his eye, believing this was what must have inspired his curiosity. He inclined his head. "Old stories," he murmured thoughtfully, looking towards Rhea.

"Yes, but important ones, folk wisdom if you like," Linda explained.

"I see," he said, watching Rhea register exactly what he was doing. "Does everyone believe in these stories?"

Linda gave a contented little huff. She was in her element explaining the spirituality of the land. "No of course not, but it's still part of them, part of their history."

Stan nodded "Yeah, it's sort of comforting to come together with like-minded people when everything goes crazy."

Jal caught Rhea's eye as he tipped his head in agreement with Linda.

"Why do people want to live by ancient fairy stories? The politics of long gone savage tribes?" Rhea murmured to herself, remembering their previous conversation.

Jal smiled. "Mmmhm"

Rhea nodded apologetically. "Yeah, but this is different. It's about celebrating life," she said with a defiant smile.

"Lot of it about," agreed Stan absent mindedly, delighted to

CHAPTER 11

find the chocolate bar he'd been rooting around for in his bag.

Jal, wishing he were near enough to give Rhea a comforting touch, gave a head bob of agreement to Stan. "Yes, it is different," he murmured.

The fluting of pipes suddenly became clear above the waves of sound and Jal was relieved to see Rhea's attention diverted by the music.

Her face broke into a wistful smile. "Fairy bells, like the Aazaar spring festival."

Jal gave a puzzled, slightly disgruntled blink. "These drums don't sound anything like…oh!" His irritation left him as he too became aware of the effect of the music.

"They're talking with the Earth," Rhea said delightedly, glad to find that same innocence she had witnessed in the Aazaar festivals.

Linda laughed. "Course they are! It's the Talking to the Earth festival."

Richard rolled his eyes, murmuring mutinously, sharing Jal's ambivalence about the drumming. "And the sky, trees and anything else that can't get away."

"Ignore him. He prefers guitars and fiddles," Linda said, nudging her husband affectionately. "Go on then, get your guitar out. I know you want to," she continued.

Richard began what soon became a happy jam session, with various members of the company joining in on assorted stringed instruments, whistles, and even with wordless singing. Even Rhea joined in, singing along with the rest, her shining eyes on Jal, willing him to join in.

Jal simply listened. Unnoticed by the others, he moved out of the way of the musicians to contentedly lounge beside Rhea.

But his contented obscurity was short lived. "I think we've been excluding our guest," Stan said. "Didn't you just tell me you have music celebrations in that Aazaar township of yours? How about giving us a tune?"

Jal began to make declining gestures, overcome with shyness at the thought of doing something so revealing in front of non Aazaar, but Rhea pounced. "Ooh yes! The whole community sings or plays something." She flashed Jal a mischievous grin. "And Jal plays really well," she added brightly, sealing his fate.

Richard nodded his encouragement. "But no drums," he said dryly

"No drums," Jal answered. "Just crystal harps and some stringed and wind instruments, none of which I have with me," he said, in a last ditch attempt to get out of performing.

Rhea laughed, she liked the drums, but before she could say anything more the whole company had started to chant "We want a song."

Jal turned to Linda for help, but she just motioned him to begin. He gave in and revealed he did indeed have a small crystal harp. He'd intended to play it, but just for Rhea. "I hope, after putting me on the spot, you're going to sing with me," he murmured hopefully to Rhea. "After you," he said, then suddenly donned his coat and glasses and shuffled deeper into the shadow of the tent. A spatter of rain had herded three passers by under a neighbouring tree.

Rhea followed him in. "Come on. Let's sing an Earth song," she whispered, before taking a few steadying breaths then made a liquid birdlike call of sheer delight. He stroked his harp in response and, hesitantly at first, they began call and answer of her voice and his harp. Then Rhea let the music take her and Jal's purring voice answered, resonant and sensuous, the whole effect of voices and harp perfectly blending.

Their performance had a spellbinding effect on the company and even the strangers under the tree.

Once they had finished their song, the passers by left, all except one individual in a green hooded robe.

"Wow! You two had us rocking!" Linda said admiringly.

Jal tipped his head. He was even beginning to overcome his resistance to the drumming.

Stan stared in amazement, Richard raised his beer bottle in salute. "To one crazy old hippy star man."

Robby, who usually said very little, raised his fifth bottle of rather alcoholic home made lemonade. "Yeah, respect to the Earth. No more man made germs, no more man made men. The reaping is coming!" he pronounced theatrically, and everyone laughed, everyone except Rhea and Jal that is.

Rhea exchanged a perplexed glance with Jal, who couldn't help a hint of irritation for the abrupt interruption of their glorious mood.

The stranger settled beside them. "I loved your piece. Who wrote it? Are there words?"

Rhea flushed. "We just made it up, you know? Like a prayer to the Earth," she said, feeling a little shy.

"Would you mind if I sang it?" Jal watched from behind his tinted glasses, recognising the stranger's voice as that of a singer he'd heard earlier that day. Rhea looked to him for agreement and got it. "Be our guest," she said delightedly.

The stranger smiled her gratitude before taking her leave.

Rhea turned back to the now comical scene amongst her company.

Robby continued his monologue, oblivious to the discomfort he had caused. "Everyone's a government spy these days."

The drowsy voice of the recently woken Gerry demurred. "They're different this time. They don't work for the government, but the government might be working for them or with them… Don't care. I've found myself a nice cosy nuclear bomb shelter."

He blinked at the bewildered faces around him, which spurred him on to further pronouncements. "What? You don't believe me? There's loads of them and they've just been abandoned. Mind you, you've got to know where to look. They're really strong and big enough to live in comfortably with my bike thank you very much."

Everyone fell about laughing at Gerry's monologue, everyone except Rhea. Richard tactfully struck up a traditional summer song, and the company enthusiastically joined in.

Jal had seen a curious expression flash across Rhea's face, but she wasn't sharing it and he couldn't work it out. All he sensed was a sudden restlessness that grabbed at his heart.

As Rhea and Jal left the festival for Dreamhills, somewhere among the throngs, another group of particularly accomplished musicians were attempting a musical prayer to the Earth, improvising around the sound of an experienced voice.

Jal looked out towards the hills and heard a rumble of distant thunder. It seemed to him as if the music rose from the ground, from the rocks and trees and grass, as much as from the humans, as if the very Earth was crying out to them. He prayed inwardly that enough of the humans would hear and understand.

Later, when they were home, Rhea looked up from her perch by the window and smiled pensively. "It wasn't just the festival, the whole place seemed…" She pondered for a moment.

"Mysterious."

She glanced fondly at Jal.

"Thanks," she said, as she got up to settle down beside him, "I did have a good time."

He kissed her nose. "So why those sad looks?"

She sighed. "Fairy bells," she murmured. "I can't help feeling that if enough of the opposite happens, then what causes the earth to resonate is bad."

She gave a melancholy little sigh, making him shiver and he gave a soft groan, gathering her close, tucking her in until he enveloped her in a protective ball. He smoothed her hair and spoke so softly, he almost seemed to be talking to himself.

"All the more reason to send out great beams of love while we can."

CHAPTER 12

Rhea felt her communicator buzz twice then stop. Her heart rate rose and the hair on her neck prickled. It was James.

She tried to focus on the task in hand, tuning into James' phone, admitting to herself he'd called at an opportune moment. She'd made a decision. It was time to stop hiding from disturbing realities. It was time to stop being a liability, allowing Jal to do her investigations, and do something. She knew, vaguely, what the attack on her had been about, but she didn't know who was behind it, or what they wanted to do with it. There were so many unknowns. What she did know was it was big. The explosions at the lorry yard and the train wreck told her that much. Still, she found it hard to allow herself to contemplate the full implications of what she did know. She was all too ready to rush back into denial.

Her com buzzed again. She swallowed hard, straightened up and took a deep breath. James had traced the number she had given him to the call box he now stood in.

Rhea smiled, imagining his irritation at not tracking her down. "Hello James," she trilled, "I was just thinking of you."

He answered with a bit of a surprised gargle. "Where are

CHAPTER 12

you?"

She gave a wry chuckle. "Did you want to talk to me or were you just trying to find me out?"

James gave a resigned snort. "I think, after you skipped out on me the way you did, you owe me, but I'll settle for talking to you," he said warily.

There was an irregularity about his breathing that warned her something was wrong. She could hear his feet scuffing as he fidgeted uncharacteristically. Her foreboding deepened as she imagined him nervously checking the street. Poor James was definitely in trouble.

"Okay," she said, trying to balance concern and interest in her voice. "What can I do for you?"

He shuffled again, annoyed at himself for his nervousness. In a happier time of innocence, one of his gadget-mad acquaintances had made him a present of an electronic sweeper as more of a joke than anything else. But now, he found himself routinely using it in earnest to check he wasn't bugged.

"Oh nothing, I just want to meet up for a chat," he said, leaving a meaningful silence.

A slight ripple of alarm made her heart patter, and her recent training to be alert to unspoken hints kicked in. "Aww, it's all right. I'll come over. See you in about an hour. Go order me a hot chocolate," she said soothingly.

Despite his annoyance and anxiety, he smiled. She was good. He hoped, after that coded hot chocolate direction, that Linda was in. He knew a few discreet little cafés if she wasn't. Anyway, the prospect of having Rhea's company cheered him. That, and the fact she was the only one whom he dared to talk to about his present predicament.

ENDSONG

Jal was working with Stan when Rhea called to say she was going to meet James.

"Can't you wait until tomorrow? I'll be free to take you then," he protested.

"Silly man, I'm not asking you to. I'm just telling you where I'm going. I can use a transporter quite well now. See you later," she chirruped, not giving him any more chance to protest, or pick up any hint of her alarm.

Rhea slid gently along the energy currents towards Linda's building, her foreboding suspended by the excitement of her solo journey.

Silently, she dropped into the tree outside Linda's home and looked about. James' car was a little way down the road and she could see him fussing about in the driver's seat. Linda was obviously out.

She scribbled a quick note to Linda to say she hoped to drop by later, then she eased herself unseen to the ground.

She strode purposefully down this familiar city street with its incongruous blanket of everyday ordinariness that Rhea Forrester of Poplar Close would have taken for granted.

James jumped as she appeared at his window "Oh! Where did you leap out from?" he asked, as he anxiously hurried her into the car.

"Hello," she soothed, settling elegantly beside him. "Let's go to a café, then you can tell me all about your news."

"It's six o'clock. I'll see what we can find open. I think I've got something for you," he said as he started up the engine, glad to get moving, the act of driving soothing his jittery nerves.

"Oh?" she asked hopefully, but he was distracted by a car that had just overtaken him.

"They're always at least in pairs. Pray they don't recognise me!" he muttered.

"Who?" she asked carefully, trying to look around without appearing to.

"They're police. It's not just dangerous for you," he hissed, throwing an exasperated glance her way, so she thought it better to stay quiet.

She stared out at the endless, seemingly timeless, traffic stream. Nothing looked that different, that dangerous. That's what made it all so scary.

They drove in silence for a while. "Safe now," he finally said, breaking the tension.

"Safe enough to talk to me?" she asked lightly, once her heart rate normalised.

He gave her a wry, sidelong look, annoyed at his own discomfort. "Sorry. Yes, I've swept it for bugs. I'm just jumpy," he admitted in contrition. "After considering the situation, I've come to a decision."

"Good," she said as neutrally as she could manage.

He kept his face impassive, but Rhea spotted the slight raise of his eyebrows and anxious glance. "Okay, just to recap; after you first called me, I had to do some checking up on you as well as the case, and it seems you were caught up in something far greater than a bit of gang crime."

Rhea felt the hairs on her neck standing up. "I gathered that after the explosion...sorry. Are you saying you've got some proof?"

He nodded.

"And whatever it is, it was big enough to get rid of me quietly, so no one would notice, and I wouldn't continue to dig."

She swallowed hard, "Wow! What do you mean get rid of you? Are they going to..."

"Nahhh," he interrupted. "More subtle than that. It's already been done. I was transferred, given a promotion. And it would have worked. Just I'm a nosy c... er sort, and the opportunity availed itself. I found some records in a surprising place."

He watched the traffic in silence for a few moments as Rhea absorbed this.

"I suppose I'm feeling a little bit isolated. I could do with a friend," he said finally.

"Ah. And since I'm in this mess too, I'm safe to talk to and we can help each other?"

"You got it," he said.

"It seems to have given you a bit of a shake," she probed.

"You could say that," he said and she saw his grip on the wheel tighten.

"I believe in my work." He sounded almost wistful, even regretful.

She suppressed a shudder as she wondered what could have shaken the confidence of this rock solid policeman. "Yes, I get that impression. You're a fair man," she said, drawn to repair that rock of confidence.

"So this surprising place?"

He sighed. "Yes, it made me reassess everything."

She nodded; he was taking his time to tell her. Was this deliberate? Was he trying to shake her? Was the "everything" that he'd reassessed her innocence? Was he compromised? She looked about for an excuse to stop, a place with a loo, anything to be not locked up with a policeman who might suddenly reveal he was handing her in to the authorities as a suspect in a serious crime.

CHAPTER 12

"It's just, there's the proper thing to do, the thing that keeps your bosses smiling, keeps your job, your promotion,and your mortgage paid, and then there's the right thing to do, the thing that stops your head from exploding, the thing that lets you sleep at night," he continued, his voice now soft, distant, clearly talking to himself.

"Yes and you would always do the right thing," she said, as evenly as she could manage.

She saw his hands relax, saw him smile.

"Thanks, for the vote of confidence. It's just hard, you know, to risk everything when you're just getting used to looking forward to the promotions. You can't help wondering if you *are* doing the right thing."

"But you're a policeman *because* you believe in doing the right thing. You believe in justice. Well, that's what Linda says."

"Oh well then, if Linda says," he said, with a relieved laugh and smiled into her face. "Oh! You look terrified."

She'd tried, and failed, to look calm.

He shook his head. "Believe it or not, I was trying to reassure you. What I found suggests you were caught up in something very odd and very big."

She eyed him, beginning to relax a little. "Erm, okay. So, are you going to tell me about this proof?."

"Yes, but it's where I found the plans to get rid of me that made me think. They were in my boss's office."

"What?" she gasped in fearful bewilderment, no longer afraid of him, more afraid for him.

"I was moved, promoted, to get me away from even thinking about your case."

She blinked, dumbfounded; it would take some digesting to

understand the full implications of this. "But...who? Why? You found nothing."

He gave a dejected sigh. "Well I did establish it was a bit more sinister than a simple burglary if you remember. That doesn't matter now. There're all sorts of possible motives but it's left me with a problem. Who can I trust?"

"Me for a start!" she said quickly.

He smiled a rather worn, but nonetheless grateful, smile. "Yes, you. I've got no choice. I'm doing the right thing, not the proper thing."

For the rest of the journey, Rhea sat in stunned silence trying to make sense of what he'd just told her. Her emotions had told her he could be trusted, and that, like her, he was being thrown out of his old unthinking life, thrown onto relying on his own solid character, his own conscience and humanity. But the implications of the rest of what he'd said; the who, the what, and the how, that was a dark shadowy threat that had now grown larger.

"Right, I've got something for you. I want to make a stop off at a pub I used to frequent and pick it up. I won't be long," he said, interrupting her ruminations, and turning off the main road into dark, quiet, side streets.

He drew up on a street of houses, by a footpath that meandered through shrubs across a small green. "I'll be 15 minutes tops. I just want to leave a message. I have a friend who's going to give us some information. You'll be safe. Just keep your head down."

She nodded as she settled down to wait. He'd stopped well away from the pub. He was careful, she had to give him that. She switched on her com and tracked his phone, keeping half an eye

CHAPTER 12

and ear on her surroundings.

After a while, she stirred. He'd been ages, much longer than 15 minutes, and he'd used his phone. Something wasn't right and her nerves tingled. She checked her com and saw he was in a Chinese takeaway close by.

She opened the door and sniffed the air, then looked around, took the car keys, and headed towards the smell. The place was crowded. She slipped into the shop behind a big bald bloke, and hid behind him.

She spotted James, then her blood froze. Rod the thug again. She watched him eyeing up the oblivious James, wanting to scream for him to get out. She looked about for a way out, a way to distract Rod.

She had just decided on causing a fight when James was given his order. She saw him taking a taxi card and getting out his phone then Rod, who'd watched him do this, shrugged, turned on his heel and left.

She slid out into the night, in step with a couple of young lads who were busily munching on spring rolls. Checking for Rod and any possible associates, she hurried away across the darkened street and around the corner, back to the car.

She sat, a bundle of anxiety, wondering where he'd got to, when he suddenly yanked open the door, filling the air with Chinese spices. "Get down and don't get up until I tell you!" he hissed, and threw the car into gear, nonetheless driving off very smoothly and quietly. They drove for five minutes or so like this. All she could see from her vantage point was that his fingers were gripping the wheel very hard.

"What happened?" she muttered anxiously.

"I found a dead chimp on the road, then things got crazy."

"A dead chimp isn't crazy? And you stopped to get a Chinese?"

He snorted. "I had to. As a cover. I was followed. He left."

She shifted uncomfortably in the foot well. "I'd like to get up now."

He scanned the road. "Okay, clear now."

She settled herself in the seat, adrenaline still pumping through her system. "Did you see that ginger thug? That was Rod," she hissed.

"Yeah. What? How do you know?" James flashed her a worried glance, then checked his mirror.

She stretched out her cramped back. "I came to get you. I saw him in the shop watching you."

He set his jaw in exasperation and not a little fear. "I warned you to stay out of sight!"

"I did," she retorted.

He couldn't help a wry grin. "Suppose…I spotted the ginger thug but not you."

She gave him a cheeky smirk, glancing in the rear mirror. "We don't appear to have a tail."

He too glanced in his rear view mirror. "Seems so."

She nodded. "Yeah, clever that, picking up a taxi card and getting your phone out."

He gave her a startled glance of admiration. "Wow! You are observant."

"And now I'm all ears. So tell me. What happened?"

He glanced back at the rapidly cooling package on the back seat. "I'll take you to my cousin's flat. It's okay, they're away. I promised to keep a check on the post. We can sit down and eat and I'll tell you all about it."

CHAPTER 12

Once James had fussed with the microwave, settled the now piping hot supper on the little table and Rhea had organised the heating, she insisted on details. "So, you came across a dead chimp. I'm hoping you never touched it."

He gave her a withering look.

"I had to ask. I'm nervous."

"You and me both. I'm still clenching! I'd just got out of the pub. The last thing I wanted was complications."

She nodded, thinking, rather guiltily, he was referring to her.

"It had died of some kind of poisoning by the look of it. Anyway, I rang it in, got out smartish, and hid around the corner to see who would come first. The first car on the scene was your favourite thugs, then an unmarked police car. They certainly looked pretty pally," he said with distaste. "I heard them say that I'd rung it in like the good little woodentop I was! I'm plain clothes!" he protested rather pathetically.

"Yeah and smart enough to fool them, eh?" she reminded him in an attempt to smooth his obviously ruffled feathers. It was clear that he'd taken quite a battering to his ego tonight.

"I saw a couple of biohazard suits carefully shovel up the chimp and that in itself gave me pause for thought. They weren't part of our crew. They had the look of some private get up," he mused to himself, then came back to his tale. " I realised that they were checking out the area, so I nipped down the shortcut to Willy Wong's as fast as I could. Fortunately, the place was packed out. Willy saw me and was sorting out my chicken and cashew order before I got a chance to draw breath. I hope you like chicken and cashew with black bean sauce."

She smiled, nodding enthusiastically. "Lovely. Anyway," she prompted.

"Seconds later, your favourite ginger thug came through the door, clocked me getting my order, so it looked like I'd been there for ages. Fortunately, my flimsy ruse worked. He spotted me waving that taxi card around, then left. I checked when I came out. There was no one following me, but I took no chances. I actually called a cab with a couple of lads."

She nodded encouragingly, despite his account leaving her with an increasing sense of disquiet.

"So you called it in about something that's pretty weird and sounding nastier every minute. Then the ginger ones turn up and senior staff are pally with them? Is this your proof? "

He shook his head. "No, it's just one more reason for me keeping this back."

He handed Rhea a data stick. "It's from the bomb shelter. I've got all the originals in safe places. I want this to go to your Dr Jal and Stan for checking."

She coolly regarded this man beside her. James, the straight up copper was now, not so much stepping over the line, as motoring off into the boundary-less sunset. "You sure you're alright with this?" she said, considering the little thing in her hand.

"Yes, after what I've seen tonight it's the only way I can make sure it doesn't get into the wrong hands. There's something very disturbing going on here."

She nodded.

"I don't know who those goons are but from what I can gather, they've got contacts in very high places...very high places indeed. I'm inclined to think maybe Stan is right about some government conspiracy for once." He pondered for a moment. "And that stuff they're after. I really don't get it. I know there's genetic engineering involved. This is something to do with a vaccine which won't surprise you. And, this is really weird. It's about gear to send out some kind of silent broadcast. It's an odd collection of bits and pieces, yet somehow it's linked. But hell, I haven't a clue how and I can't help feeling I don't want to know."

Rhea shuddered. "You should let this go. It's really sounding dangerous for you now."

He gave a short harsh laugh. "Not on your life. I'd not be me if I did that. Now, let's enjoy our meal and then I suggest you call your Dr Jal and arrange a pick up. I can't chance meeting up with Stan tonight. In fact, I think I'm going to have to cut direct ties for all our sakes. You never know with surveillance. They definitely have me in their sights."

"Maybe they're just monitoring you. You know? After your contact with me. Just to make sure you continue to be the "woodentop" they expect, which, of course, you've played expertly to your advantage up to now. I mean, if this thing really is so big that they went to all the effort of moving you on and out, they would wouldn't they?"

James nodded. "You're good. I ever tell you that?"

"Thanks."

He sighed, deep in thought, turning over everything he'd found out. "I'm not kidding," he said softly. "This is looking like some official operation, some very nasty dark opp."

He scuffed his feet, looking away, then rubbed his face.

"Let's get on with it!" he said briskly. "You go catch your lift. You'll be safer with Dr Jal."

Rhea reached out a hand, then gave him a hug. "You stay safe. I'll be in touch with the translation. Call me, you know it's untraceable. And you can call for emergencies too. I can pass messages to Stan and Linda and they will never be intercepted, I promise."

He nodded, smiling sadly. "And you stay safe Rhea Forrester, now get out of here."

CHAPTER 13

"So the chimp thing was a bit random, but after Rod turned up...what do you make of it?"

Rhea had been talking for some time, before she'd noticed that Jal had gone very quiet

She frowned, taking a long worried look at him.

"Jal?"

He was standing eerily still, just staring at the read-out of the data James had handed to her the night before.

"What's wrong?" she pleaded, feeling suddenly alone.

She stared helplessly at the screen, unable to decipher whatever horror had frozen Jal to the spot.

"It was probably a test subject from the experiments I was looking for. We have very little time," he said suddenly.

She blinked in bewilderment, unable to stop her fear rising.

"What? Jal? Test subjects?"

"The chimp," he answered flatly, still staring at the screen. She stood up, tentatively reaching out a hand to him.

"What I hoped I'd never find," he murmured.

"You can read it now? Without Stan?"

He stirred out of his dazed state and looked down at her hand as if surprised to see it there. Avoiding her eyes, he suddenly drew her close, pressing his face to the top of her head, squeezing his eyes shut against the menacing data on the screen.

She thought he was about to speak, but all that came out was a faint sigh as if he was struggling for words. Finally, he shuddered, then stiffened into a strained calm.

"We're safe here," he murmured distantly.

She stayed still in his arms, glad of the comfort of contact, but frightened by the shock she could feel in his rigid, rock-like muscles. She'd found the key to the mystery that had made the destruction of her life collateral damage, the mystery that had caught the interest of this naturalist from the stars. She thought that, for this at least, he would be relieved for her. Why was he not relieved?

She reviewed everything that had happened since she had got back in a desperate effort to work out what could possibly have disturbed Jal to this extent. After all, he would have seen the bad behaviour of humans previously.

His fingers dug into her flesh painfully, and she could feel a bruise developing beneath them. She had to move before she winced, before her fear and sense of foreboding became unbearable for both of them.

"Nobody saw us. James has kept this hidden, and I'm fine," she said soothingly, wriggling to free herself.

He was slow to respond and let go. "Jal?" she asked gently, hoping to reach him, not wanting this, her sanctuary, to be tainted by the shameful troubles of her world.

"I'd have coped better if I hadn't begun to go through my change," he murmured to himself.

"Change? Is that it? You're afraid of your change? Cos I'm

not," she said, desperate for this to be the explanation, yet knowing, somewhere in her mind, it wasn't.

He gazed sorrowfully at the data image again, watching the current projected damages of what, many months ago, Rhea had unknowingly called the plague of the Brynewiln.

"It's not just me and my escapades that's got you worried is it?" she said softly, glancing at his screen where her newly discovered data was displayed.

"No," he said distractedly.

Rhea shuddered. "Oh come on, leave that alone and take a breather," she said, desperate to break the tension, hoping that whatever she'd just shown him might not look so terrible if he rested.

Jal gratefully curled up among the cushions as if in a nest. "I wasn't unprepared, I had contingency plans," he protested to the air. "I knew I'd feel shocked, but not like this."

"Jal? What's upset you so badly? You're talking in half sentences. Help me out," she begged, stunned to realise that her strong steady Jal was in shock.

He shook his head at his own thoughts.

"You had so much to cope with, it should have broken you into little pieces, but it didn't. You can do it now, if I hold onto you. If I don't fall apart. I can't. I don't have that luxury."

"Jal. What are you talking about?" she pleaded, now really frightened, now knowing for certain that something so terrible had happened, something even more terrible than the revelations she had just experienced, and it had shaken him to the core.

He nuzzled her face. "I do love you," he said softly.

Rhea smiled back hesitantly. His words had seemed to echo over a chasm from a happier time. "I love you too," she answered, still waiting for his revelations.

She touched his lips with hers, waiting, but the hoped for kiss never came.

His eyes were dark. "It's time for the hard work now," he said briskly.

She smiled. "Phew! For a minute I thought you were going to say we had some hard work ahead!" But the expected smile from him didn't come.

She sighed resignedly. "Sorry love, you're not in a joking mood are you?"

He touched her cheek, his expression softening, and gave her a light kiss.

"That's better," she said, stroking his face. "Now you feel like you're at least on the same planet as me."

It raised a smile but the shadows stayed and he continued his speech as if she hadn't spoken. "And I need you to remember I love you when things get rocky."

He searched her face, silently demanding an acknowledgement.

She nodded. "That's when I'll need you most," she answered with a sad little smile, repeating the declaration he'd made in a happier time. "So we've got some talking to do," she urged, now desperate for an explanation, an end to this terrible suspense.

His eyes darkened further. "What you called the plague, it's started. The weapon, or tool, was, is, in two parts. There's the primer, that's carried by a vector, that's what you and Stan suspected, and I hoped, was merely a vaccine. It lies dormant until it is triggered. This, this is the plan of the trigger," he said, pointing to his screen. "That's what the data you've just found is about."

She nodded, alarm making her heart patter for a moment,

then she burrowed into his arms for comfort. It had always been there, this threat, waiting. She'd banished it to the back of her mind but it was bound to find a way out. Now, wondering what the hell was going on, was over. The battle could finally commence.

"I knew James had found something in that underground shelter. He had held on to it while he decided what to do. I guessed it would be something pretty terrible," she said resignedly. "I couldn't tell you about it straight away because, after the underground shelter was blown up right after James and I had been there, I couldn't bring myself to even think about it. I'm sorry."

Jal sighed. "Yes, I can understand that," he admitted, and a sad little silence stretched out between them for some minutes as they just held each other.

"Aazaar are vulnerable to it," he said quietly, then waited for her reaction.

Her immediate fear had now subsided into a curious daze that allowed her to talk, ask questions, as if she was at some distance from herself, her fear. "Does it affect your people badly?" she asked, hoping it might have no more effect than a flu epidemic.

He sighed, "Yes. It will kill Aazaar."

He stroked her face. "It's a dreadful weapon. It's a means of social control." She stared at him uncomprehending. "What? Social control? How?"

He gave her such a sorrowful look, she shrunk back, but he held onto her, clung onto her. "Mass killing, and...mass biological changes..."

His words stung, left her unable to speak for some minutes. So her world would not end with a nuclear flash after all. It would be much worse.

"You must hate me," she said in a small voice, now knowing the pain that Jal must be feeling, the fear and shock, and the humiliation. Humans were acting like the Brynewiln. She tried to curl away from him in her shame, seeing in her mind's eye sick and dying Aazaar.

He pulled her to him, holding her so tightly, he was almost suffocating her. "No. No, I don't hate you. You're not responsible for this," he said desperately.

"How can you not?" she shivered miserably.

"Because you gave me a taste of what it's like to be part of your beautiful Earth."

"But I'm human."

"And Stan, Linda, Gerrard, Richard, they welcomed me. How could I hate them? And all those like them, who would welcome me and my kind if they could. You all know what made you human."

She managed to reach up and stroked his face, knowing no words would help. He suddenly relaxed his grip.

I've got to talk to the council."

Rhea nodded her agreement. She knew he'd have to help make arrangements for some kind of illness prevention, but she couldn't help her own sense of growing dread.

"When are you telling them? she asked mechanically, struggling to keep any anxiety out of her voice.

He looked towards his communicator which immediately sported an image of the meeting hall and meeting times. "I suppose I'll have to tell them this evening."

She nodded dumbly, stirring his impatience, his fear.

He took her face in his hands, an urgent pleading expression in his eyes. "I wish I'd had the time to be gentler about this, but I can't risk you hearing this without me. When the community leaves, we go together."

Rhea stared at him for some moments in utter incomprehension.

A flood of horror and terror finally broke through.

"Leave? What do you mean? Go where? We live here. The community, it's their home. What's happening?"

Jal just closed his eyes against her panic, against his mistake. He let out a soft groan. "Dreamhills won't be safe any more. We can't protect ourselves for long. The triggering mechanism will go online very soon."

"But you're more advanced than humans, you must know how to find a way to stop it," she said, still unable to accept the danger could reach even here, in their beautiful scrap of paradise

"It can't just be stopped. You know that already," he said quietly but firmly.

She spluttered in shock. "I already know? What? I don't understand. What do I know?"

Jal was shaking his head. "You know the story of the Brynewyln. You called it their plague."

She stared in incredulity.

"It's just a …a story, a legend. It's about a war, genetic engineering, not a plague," she protested desperately.

"It's not just a story, you know that. We, the Aazaar, were created using that Brynewiln technology."

"But you are a good thing." she protested.

He gave a faint pained smile, shaking his head. "Are we? We don't belong anywhere. We have no connection, no natural kinship with any life. Cells in the body that grow without such kinship are a cancer. It is our beliefs, our spiritual life, that keeps us within the web of life, prevents us from becoming that danger."

The Aazaar a cancer? Rhea winced, stared at him, all sorts of primeval fears roiling around her head, colliding and fighting with equally deep urges to run to his aid, protect him and his kind from such a terrible condemnation. "But...you, the Aazaar don't... you..." she looked around at the living, organic room they stood in, trying desperately to find the right words. "Even your science is...green..."

Jal gave a faint, sad, fond smile of acknowledgement. "No, we don't. Our science flows from our spiritual beliefs," he said softly, then continued, quietly, precisely. "This plague is a process that will sever, is severing, humanity's physical kinship with your world, with life. The pathological beliefs, ideologies of those who have set this in motion, are the plague that has made this engineering possible. It is also what makes this weapon, them, such a terrible threat. Anything that goes against their beliefs will be eliminated, wiped out. Everything else will be made to conform. They, what humanity will become, will be a cancer that will destroy its host, its goddess."

Did she know that? She wasn't sure, wasn't sure what it meant, but she did feel afraid. For a moment, she wavered, thought of nothing else but running for safety with Jal and Jack. Then she imagined herself leaving Earth as it crumbled behind them, the cries of millions of bewildered sick people screaming in her ears.

"Jal. We can't... Not just like that. This is your Earth too, you said so."

He closed his eyes against her onslaught. "Yes I did. You know I don't want to leave, none of us do, but I'm only one man.

CHAPTER 13

All I can save is Jack and you."

"But we can't just leave," she pleaded, not heeding his distress, only desperate to get him to agree. "Jack won't understand, and what about your son? He was born here, born of Earth."

"The community must leave. We'll prepare to leave the moment I tell them. I've stayed silent for as long as I can. Now I have no choice. I must tell them." The words just came out of his mouth, flat, sharp, and she flinched, shocked and dismayed.

'He's not of this Earth, not a creature of any world!' echoed through her thoughts and she was sure he could hear. He seemed to pale, diminish, as if that bright energy of Earth were draining from him as she looked at him. A cold flash of realisation juddered through her heart. "You stayed silent? You knew?"

He met her accusing eyes with anxious remorse.

"You didn't come upon me by chance did you?" she said, her voice cracking with dismay.

"No, it wasn't like that," he managed hoarsely, stunned and struggling not to hurt her more, but he was too late.

"I told you my fears about you, but you kept yours from me! You kept silent, kept it all from this poor pathetic human!" she spat out, feeling utterly betrayed. She looked up into his face, so hurt and suspicious.

"No, it was, it..."

Jal was desperately trying to galvanize his shocked woozy brain into action, but he was too slow to catch Rhea. She was running away from him with every word, and the path behind her was disappearing.

"I didn't know anything for sure, nothing I could speak of."

"You knew." she said miserably.

"I came across you by accident, sitting there on your log," he said in sorrowful nostalgia.

She stiffened, her eyes cold blue grey pebbles. "Yeah, I was sitting dreaming of a kindly wood sprite, like a right fluff head, while you were gathering evidence of how terrible we were. Those thugs were honest. They threatened me for their information. You…you used me!" she said in an accusing voice that chilled him.

"No, I didn't use you…" he began, then adrenaline finally cleared his thoughts. "Yes I knew. Before I found you I had suspicions and a few alarming observations, the implications of which I couldn't bear to consider, but I had nothing I could burden anyone else with. I needed to understand more about your civilisations. I needed something solid first. You helped me get that. Don't condemn me for what I learned."

He looked into her eyes, his soft with regret. "Yes, I was following a trail when I first found you. But you knew that from the outset. Seeing you sitting there, so full of joy, love for your fellow creatures, seeing that deep connection you had with your world, gave me hope. It was more than that. You could see beyond your immediate little world. You saw me. I couldn't ignore you, your plea for hope, for help. I had to try to keep you safe."

He shook his head sadly. "I'm sorry. I can see now it looks bad but I only ever wanted to spare you," he admitted.

"But you didn't say anything, didn't give me a chance, didn't trust me!" she protested, struggling to reach him, hold on, as the solid ground of her faith in him shook.

"Oh I did, but in such a way you weren't likely to heed what I'd said. It was definitely a case of what you'd call being too clever for my own good," he said ruefully, hoping to arouse her sympathy, but she was building defences with every word he spoke.

She nodded.

"Yes," she agreed coolly.

Rhea looked up into this sharp, dark, alien face, those strange tawny eyes that flickered with sparks of who knows what kind of consuming fire. So he'd been ready to save her. As what? Some specimen? She was angry, not just annoyed, deeply angry, betrayed. Did she really know him? Did he really accept her as she was? She loved him. She knew him as a good man, a gallant man. He'd risked his life to rescue her and he had always been so kind. Hadn't he? But leaving Earth, just leaving like that, was all wrong, it didn't fit. True, he wasn't human, but this Earth was now as much his as hers. He wasn't human. Was that it? Could she live with that?

"We can't just leave them to die. We have to at least warn them," she said quietly.

He looked at her sorrowfully, desperately. "Rhea, that's what I've been doing, with Stan, with James. I wasn't just getting information; I was helping them understand the implications, helping them understand that they had grounds for their fears. I've done all I can and far more than I should. And I was glad to do so," he said in a softer, gentler tone.

"Should? What do you mean? More than you should?" she asked accusingly, her eyes sparkling dangerously.

"Rhea," he pleaded, realising his mistake, but she backed away. He dropped his hands, shaking his head as he tried to get it right. "You know it's not just our code, our law. It's fundamental to everything we believe in. We aren't supposed to interfere."

She stared at him incredulously, struggling with what to her was a huge contradiction. "Not interfere? You're part of my world now. You can't just decide it's nothing to do with you if it gets a bit dodgy. Anyway, you interfered when you helped me. I'm human," she said, her voice ominously soft, desperately fighting to salvage her image of her kind and loving Jal.

He spoke gently, but he was hopelessly floundering now, and feeling quite odd. "You helped Vincent when he was hurt. But you wouldn't dream of interfering in his crow society. You know you could cause more harm than good," he pleaded, knowing the moment he'd spoken, it was a crass thing to say.

Her anger exploded, and she finally faced him across the vast chasm of their differences. "Crow society? Is that how you see me? Us? Just another interesting topic of study?" She shook her head, accusing tears in her eyes. "Jal! What about us? You and me? All those things you said?"

He took her hands, and she focussed on their paleness against the dark rust red of his, not wanting to look at him, wanting to be anywhere but here in this pain. "I meant all those things I said, just as you meant it when you promised me understanding. And right now, I've never needed your understanding more."

She looked up under her lashes, seeing his hopeful expression, but she couldn't let him in and shook her head.

"You said I brought you home."

She searched his stricken face in the hope of finding their lovely dream still alive, the hope that she would still find all his joyful brave promises to live here under the protection of this wonderful goddess Earth. It was easy when the planet was shining with gentle beauty, but the real trial of his promises, his heart, was surely to have faith in the beauty he knew was there, even when Earth was dark and dangerous.

CHAPTER 13

"I know I've handled this badly for you. I should have told you, but I was in turmoil. The danger of this plague isn't just about one discrete process like some illness. So if you only saw bits at a time, it was easy to miss, especially when you'd rather not see it. I knew your people don't just look like the Brynewiln, some of them were acting like them. But some of them weren't. There was hope. Can't you see my love? It was hard for me to face what I was seeing. I kept hoping, for your sake and mine, I was wrong. I kept hoping I'd made a mistake. I even managed to stop any formal discussion of the problem within the council, even though some people were clearly concerned. I thought I was sparing you, everyone, my unfounded fears. It sounds so stupid now, but..." he babbled desperately.

She didn't hear any more. She was furious, and just wanted to rage. Her lovely Earth, which he himself had opened her eyes to. Her lovely Earth, who had welcomed him in as if he was a child of her own, given him the most precious gift an Aazaar could wish for, couldn't just be left to be torn apart while he calmly packed up and left. She wanted to shake him and scream at him. She wanted to make him realise just how betrayed, alone, bereft, and absolutely terrified she felt. What would she be without Earth? How could she be human without Earth? If she didn't know what she was, how could she be anything with him? All she could see of their future was a huge hunched beast waiting to tear out an essential part of her, leaving her not living, but existing in some terrible limbo. There had to be something they could do.

She suddenly realised her nails had drawn blood but he wasn't moving, hadn't even flinched; he was just waiting for her to speak. She accepted his tiny blood sacrifice and it soothed her enough to reflect. However angry his words had made her, she could see he was struggling and just as shocked as she was, but she couldn't help him, not now. "I need time. I'm too upset to talk or take in anything you say," she muttered miserably.

He looked anxiously into her eyes, not wanting to hide anything from her, but at the same time, not wanting to inflame matters any more. "I have to tell them," he said gently.

His quiet insistence on the community's right, *his* community's right to know, angered her afresh, and she hissed at him, her eyes flashing with self righteous fury, "And I have to tell them! Doesn't my world deserve to know?" She looked at him across the divide of their differences. He had no right to be so demandingly sorrowful. It wasn't his world that was about to be devastated. He didn't have a world. He could just fly away and find another one.

"Oh tell the council!" she spat out angrily. But even in the midst of her fury, she was unable to tug her heart away from him entirely. "But do you have to make plans? Can't you say you'll talk, I don't know, in a couple of days?" She tightened her lips, staring defiantly at him.

He inclined his head in agreement. "Yes, that sounds sensible. They won't have the device ready to fire for a while yet. A day or two won't make any difference. I think we'll all need a little time to gather our wits, prepare."

She nodded. "Good. Well don't follow me or contact me. I'll contact you when I'm ready," she said tersely, looking directly at him but not seeing, not wanting to see, for fear of collapsing into tears.

Giving her fingers a sad squeeze of affection, he reluctantly let go. "I'll be waiting. Wherever I am, call me, I'll come to you," he said as she stood up and headed out of the door.

CHAPTER 13

She kept walking, off into the peace of the trees, feeling him watching her, feeling the weight of his sorrows pressing on her, and wanting to be out of reach of his needs, to rage and grieve in peace.

CHAPTER 14

Rhea kept going, not really heeding where, until she reached the only sanctuary she could think of. Linda's flat. She needed to do something, tell people. She needed to talk, find comfort for her breaking heart. She looked around at the unusually quiet street as she waited on Linda's doorstep, blocking out any ominous implications that stillness contained, focussed only on speaking to Linda and finding some hope.

"Oh Linda, I'm so glad I've caught you in. Are you alone? Are you free for a chat?" she said, the anxiety that had frozen her, disappearing in a rapid melt water of words.

Linda hurried her in, her face tense as she led her into the kitchen, the sinister sound of sirens blaring through the walls as police cars passed by. But although Rhea's ears heard them, her mind simply filtered it out as the usual background noise of the city.

"This is about you and James's adventure isn't it? Is Jal coming?" Linda asked over her shoulder.

Rhea hesitated, suppressing her dismay and a little prickle of anger at the mention of Jal's name. "No, he's got things he has to do," she said, but only the tightness of her mouth gave any indication anything was amiss, and Linda wasn't looking.

"Sit down and get comfy," Linda said, marching across the kitchen to fill the kettle so as to give herself a breathing space, pointing to the window as she went. "It's open if you need to make an escape. If you hear a knock, don't wait. Just get out quick. It'll be the police."

"Police? What's happened?" a startled Rhea asked, looking nervously about.

Linda's head whipped around, and she looked at her askance. "What's happened? It's been happening for long enough. Haven't you noticed the barricades, and armed police on the streets?"

Rhea stared, stunned and uncomprehending. Barricades? Armed police? No she hadn't noticed. But what did that matter now?

Linda sighed ruefully. Fighting with Rhea was the last thing she wanted to do.

"The police are looking for a terrorist who's gone to ground in this area. They're not letting anyone in or out, and they're going from door to door. But don't worry, they've already been here."

Linda's words were calm, but her quick fidgety movements gave away her anxious thoughts. "Tea and cake?" she said vacantly, rinsing a teapot in a distracted play of her usual hospitality, the radio tinkling cheerfully to itself in the background.

"Yes please," Rhea answered in automatic politeness.

"Terrorists?" Despite her own desperate preoccupation, Rhea finally managed to register the more immediate possibility of desperate, determined men on the run, hiding in gardens, or even bursting into houses.

"I think we should get out of here," she heard her fear suggest in an absurdly polite voice.

"It's okay. I don't think anyone will come back here," Linda said, giving Rhea a weakly, helpless bunny of a smile that didn't convince either woman. "I know it's pretty wild out there, but it's cosy here. Besides, Richard is stuck outside the perimeter. He'd really worry if he got back and I wasn't here. I've got plenty of food in. We could make a bite to eat."

Her eyes were pleading for agreement.

Rhea tried not to grimace at the thought of food, her outrage still rumbling away inside. "Maybe later. Let's just have some tea and cake for now."

A grateful Linda cut a great big slice of her home made carrot cake.

"I made it just before you came. I bake when I'm nervous," she explained, as Rhea raised astonished eyebrows at the neat rows of cakes cooling on trays.

"So, this stuff Stan's looking at, what do you make of it? You know he's into his conspiracies don't you? As if the current situation weren't bad enough," Linda said briskly, changing the subject from her wobbly nerves, dropping that promised great slice of cake on Rhea's plate.

Rhea stared at the slice, and the tears she'd suppressed in front of Jal, now pricked her eyes, as she heard her own voice deliver the terrible news. "He's right this time. It's a weapon. Once started, it'll quickly get out of control."

She looked up, steeling herself for questions, explanations. The look of horror in Linda's eyes told her that now she'd said it, there was no where left to hide.

"No! That can't be right. Are you sure? I mean Stan is brilliant, but he can get carried away. Who would be so blind

CHAPTER 14

and stupid enough to want to do this?" Linda blurted out, unable to accept Rhea's news.

"This came from Jal, not Stan. And as for who would be so blind, James doesn't get carried away, and he's convinced it's coming from some secret organisation that's got government support with promises of social control," Rhea heard herself answering. She raised steady sorrowful eyes on Linda, wanting nothing better than to run back to the apparent safety of her unheeding past.

A shocked Linda huffed on the starting blocks of an outraged devastated rant, but a bedroom door creaked faintly, and a startled Rhea jumped, waving Linda to silence, her self pity ending with her immediate need to protect her distraught friend.

"It's just a draught," Linda whispered in desperate hope, whilst staring anxiously towards the door. "Isn't it?" But it was all too much for her already reeling mind, and she froze.

Rhea shook her head, her Aazaar trained senses now in overdrive. They both knew there was someone in the other room, and it wasn't a friendly neighbour or the police dropping in for tea and cake.

Within milliseconds, Rhea's fear-fuelled brain had assessed various scenarios and escape options, which she'd then discarded.

"Listen, I don't think our guest can make out what we're saying over the music," she whispered, "I think our best option is to pretend we're expecting them, like it's the most normal thing in the world, and just keep them talking."

Linda nodded obediently. From within her childlike state of shock, she was glad to let Rhea weave spells to protect them both. She obligingly moved her chair, so that they both faced the door.

"Oo, I'm rather pleased with this. It's turned out okay

hasn't it?" Linda said out loud as she took a bite of cake, all the while fearfully watching Rhea's eyes trace the path of inaudible footsteps.

"I haven't had cake like this for years," Rhea prattled theatrically as she eyed the door.

A gaunt figure, more boy than man, swaggered into the kitchen.

"What are you doing? Lazing about eating cakes! Where are your husbands?" he announced, in a well-rehearsed, haughty, somewhat mediaeval manner, designed, he thought, to give him the upper hand.

Rhea and Linda met his attempted arrogant stare with sympathetic smiles, then passed each other a conspiratorial look as ancient as that of fairy-tale witches.

"Aah there you are. Come and sit down and I'll get you something to eat. You look worn out. Look at him. He's so thin. Here, have some cake while you're waiting. I've got a nice crusty baguette to go with your soup, I'll just butter it," Linda said, the taking of her cue allowing her to recover somewhat.

The young chap blinked, his mouth open in stunned, half relieved surprise at the lack of the fear and aggression he had expected. Rhea pulled the other chair back, inviting him into their circle, her eyes never leaving his face, her smile imprisoning him in a fairy glamour of homeliness.

"It's my own vegetable soup. Won't take a minute to warm up," Linda continued, not letting up on the impression he was an expected and welcome guest, neither of them allowing him the prerogative of asserting his impression of powerful intruder.

He stared at the kind smile of Rhea, his face softening, showing his terrified boy's heart and his desperate yearning to

CHAPTER 14

just let go and slide into the motherly comfort these two women were offering

Rhea saw a hesitation, a last ditch attempt to cling onto his hostility.

"Come on. Take the weight off your feet. You do look tired and hungry, and she really does make wonderful soup," she said, patting the chair beside her.

He sat down in a relieved daze, delighted to find a hot mug of tea appear in front of him, soon followed by the promised large steaming bowl of soup and the well buttered bread.

Rhea and Linda settled back to their own tea and cake, making small talk about cooking, all the while making reassuring faces towards the lad between them, every time he looked up.

The hot soup worked its magic, melting his fear enough to allow him to take an interest in his hosts.

"Erm, you must be wondering what I was doing in your house," he ventured nervously.

"I assumed you were doing the same thing she was doing," Linda said hospitably, indicating Rhea.

Rhea leaned over in a mock of conspiracy.

"I'm dodging in out of the way of that mess outside too."

He blushed, looking confused as he was reminded of why he was there.

Rhea sat back, sharing a knowing smile with Linda. "It's going to be some time before they go, so we might as well settle down and pass the time together. You don't mind do you? Being stuck with two housewives?"

He blushed again, only this time due to shyness, all signs of his comical mediaeval manner gone.

"Er…er no, thanks…"

Rhea nodded.

"Yeah, well we're all in the same boat aren't we? You can't even walk down the street without being stopped by the police."

He nodded enthusiastically, trying to finish another comforting mouthful of soup and bread.

"We do. We get stopped just for being on the street!" he agreed excitedly.

Rhea rolled her eyes grinning, and as he took a sip of tea, she shared a surreptitious glance of triumph with Linda. They had won his confidence.

He beamed, eager to impart his great knowledge. "People don't live moral lives any more, even me once. My life was an empty struggle. I was educated, I worked hard on my career, but however hard I struggled, it didn't help. My birthright, the bright future my father and mother had worked so hard for me to have, turned to dust in front of my eyes, and I began to lose everything. I watched as the world grew increasingly sinful around me, and I could do nothing. I was lost until I realised that all things come to those who submit to God." he said beatifically. "Heaven will be mine."

Linda choked down a shudder of fear, keeping up her kindly smile, and they all nodded wisely. "Mmm, how's that?"

He grinned. "Our world is changing so fast, it has forgotten what God can do. It is written, that in the past, God gave the richest lands to righteous nations of proud warriors, who had lived in righteous hardship and walked in his peaceful ways. He is coming to do it again. He is coming now to do this for us, the righteous."

Rhea blinked, as she tried to disentangle the breathtaking twisted logic of his speech, then suppressed a shudder

CHAPTER 14

"Coming to do it again? Now?" she asked in confusion.

He smiled benevolently, mistaking her confusion for fear. "I and my brothers and sisters are compassionate. We must spread the word, save those who submit and repent of their sins, of their corruption, their fornication before we bring in the end to this world. And when we sweep away the sinful, we shall reap the riches of this land."

Rhea struggled to stop a shocked whimper, as her shell of innocence was battered.

The pressure to fill the ensuing ominous silence became too much for Linda, and she found herself questioning his certainty. "Okay, so these great warrior peaceful nations you mentioned, who lived their simple, harsh lives. How did they get their lands in the first place?"

He smiled benignly. "God had a plan for them. First he tested them for their faithfulness. There was a great famine in their lands, their flocks starved, and they went hungry, almost starved to death, until God saved them, showed them these lands, flowing with all manner of wealth.

"And did he hand over these lands, you know, unoccupied? Or were there people already living there?" she asked politely.

He was enjoying himself too much to notice anything disingenuous or challenging in her questions. Besides, his belief in his superior knowledge and intelligence, blinded him to that possibility. "No, the lands were full of wicked people, who traded all manner of wondrous foods, and who made all manner of fine goods, but they didn't honour god. They sang and danced, they drank alcohol, they fornicated, the women painted their faces, they questioned everything, so God told the warriors to put the fighting men to the sword, and the rest, to put them in chains to work."

Rhea sat in silent horror, listening, donning a suitably impressed expression, nodding enthusiastically and smiling from time to time, when his gaze turned her way.

Linda shook her head.

"It just sounds like very ancient tribal politics to me. You're saying these warriors went into other people's lands who were minding their own business, made war on them, massacred them, made slaves of what was left, so that they could take their land and property? And you see that as righteous?" she asked in wonderment.

"I know what it looks like, but it's not politics. It's the word of God. This country will once again be great. All will bow at our feet," he patiently explained. "Those who wear tight revealing clothes, make exhibitions of immodest dancing and singing, even homosexuality, those who don't listen to the word of God's representatives, are decadent, corrupt, immoral, don't deserve to live."

He smiled, looking from face to face, encouraged by their silence. "You see? the West has walked away from God and must be punished, must be brought under the heel of the righteous."

Rhea nodded, unable to speak. She understood, but not as he did. He wanted to see the culture that had nurtured him, gave him his well-fed strong body and educated mind, as well as the centuries-long, hard-won freedom of speech and thought, wiped off the face of the Earth. And why? Because it too did not follow the long ago discredited and defeated, forbidding ways, his idea of God had prescribed. Apparently, "The West" and even "The East" was now morally bankrupt, and his God was about to destroy its people. And of course, he believed his God would bestow the most precious fruits of said destroyed culture, on him and his ilk, though he hadn't considered the fact that said precious fruits depended on said corrupt culture for their continued existence. *'Talk about crazy nasties!'* she thought.

It struck Rhea as so familiar, if you peeled back the heavy religious bits. She could see that his well heeled-lines of argument, his well-educated tones of guilt about the speed of change and the moral state of the world, sounded very like the conversations of those bright, knowledgeable, well connected creatures she had been so in awe of at the conservation club.

But she wasn't that ignorant any more. She knew now his self-righteous horror, his guilt, was the sound of fear, outrage about not being able to keep his standing in a world that was changing so fast, he couldn't prepare for it, let alone hope to inherit the comfy life his parents had tried to carve out for him. He wanted to run back to some mythical golden age, a place of unthinking innocence. She almost pitied him.

"Swept away?" said Linda, unable to keep a hint of alarm out of her voice.

He gave her an avuncular smile. "You have nothing to fear, you are good, genetically pure women."

It was that word "genetically" that froze the hearts of Linda and Rhea, as they struggled not to show their shock or fear.

"You, and your children and children's children, will live in peace, in the world perfected by His word, which He has granted to our scientists. Our ancestors were children, and God guided them as children. Now, He has decided we are grown enough to handle greater, compassionate ways to do his work. God has given our scientists a gift to eliminate all that is evil, corrupt and deformed, all that are against his laws. All the abominations will go, and will never be seen again."

He looked about the cosy productive kitchen, and smiled, as Rhea contemplated in horror, the implication of his "compassion", the implications of the safety of his regimented, unchanging unchangeable prison of a paradise, which she now understood, his terrified child soul desperately craved.

He beamed benignly at them.

Bang! Bang! Bang!

"Open up! This is the police!"

They all jumped, startled, staring towards the hall, then Linda silently pointed to the slightly open window which led to a flat roof from which their visitor could make his escape.

"On my way," she shouted down the hall, and motioned to Rhea to clear the plates.

The policeman strode into Linda's hallway, as Rhea, now trapped, stood hidden in the kitchen, her escape route blocked by the crazy kid who'd scrambled out, and was now making an unnerving, attention-drawing clatter across a shed roof. She took a deep breath, working out a scenario that was plausible, but vague enough not to drop Linda in it should the police insist on speaking to her.

"They just came to tell me it's all clear and give me a warning," Linda announced as she returned. And with that, they both slumped down into their chairs, both exhausted by fear and contemplation of recent events. Then the sound of a scuffle and yelps of pain from a backyard a few houses up, made them both exchange glances and sigh with pity, before sliding back into their own thoughts.

"At least we know he won't come back," Linda remarked with a shudder, addressing her own train of thought. "He might have been a pathetic little idiot, but he was a dangerous little idiot."

Rhea nodded, thinking of all the other dangerous little idiots out there, all blindly following some fantasy dead cert fix for all the world's supposed ills, no matter what pain it cost them and their own. "James was right," she murmured into the numbed forlorn silence that had settled around them.

"What? James?" Linda exclaimed, unable to make the connection.

"Religion. He said that cynical sorts are using religion to control the likes of that little idiot. Jal tried to tell me I was right when I said there was a plague. That's the plague," Rhea mused.

Linda frowned, giving a small mirthless laugh, "Plague? I suppose you could call it that," Linda said, referring to the intruder's appalling world view, still reeling from the shock of having come face to face with it, still reeling from the shock of having had her neighbourhood in lock down with armed police everywhere, despite being well aware of the deteriorating political situation of the last couple of years.

"But you heard what he said, he was talking of genetically engineering the whole bloody population! You don't think that's what you found do you?"

Rhea shrugged. "Probably."

Linda gave a smile of relief. "Then that's it! That's what you and everything's been about! They've caught them before..."

Rhea was shaking her head. "He wasn't talking of bringing down the government. Neither was James."

Rhea's emotions were in an even worse confused mess than before she'd left Dream Hills, ricocheting between disbelief and horror, still leaving her trying to grasp what had happened to her world. "It's out of control," she murmured, remembering her last terrible conversation with Jal.

She let out a quivering sigh and looked over at Linda. "I just wanted to see you."

"Out of control? Stan's big bug conspiracy? Really? out of control?" Linda's voice was thin, needy, as she struggled with their interrupted conversation.

Rhea started, had she really said that out loud?

"It couldn't be anything else but out of control with ideas like that kid's driving it. Jal knew. He took till now to tell me. He knew," Rhea muttered, still caught, still held helpless by the disabling betrayal she'd felt upon his announcement.

"Jal knew?" Linda echoed in disbelief, her confusion of pained emotions looking for a focus, a person to blame.

Rhea looked up, startled into a defence of Jal by the sudden accusatory tone of Linda's question.

"He knew they were looking into a particular kind of bio engineering. He knew it wasn't just a bunch of terrorists when he found me, said it was some shadowy group, about money, but he was trying to concentrate on pinning down the technology first," she reviewed sorrowfully, feeling a surge of selfish anger at the terrible events that were now steadily carving such a vast chasm between them.

"I knew about the bio-engineering bit from Stan, sort of, enough to know it was pretty frightening. But... that kid? Ohhhh! He's made it hit home hasn't he? Genetic warfare?" Linda gasped, lost in her own horror.

Rhea slumped deeper into her own morass of self-pity and guilt.

"We had a fight..." she started, only to find that her conscience, her heart, wouldn't allow that to stand. "I got angry at Jal," she admitted.

"Because he knew? About this mess?"

Linda's tone took her by surprise, making her all the more defensive.

"Yes, I mean, how could he know? How could he know and not tell me?"

She looked at Rhea for a moment, considering her question, realising she too had felt somewhat betrayed by him "Well, how do you tell somebody something like that? Especially when they're seriously injured. I mean, you didn't listen to me either, when I tried to warn you how bad things had got. I suppose I was so worried about you, I wasn't going to push it."

Rhea winced guiltily.

"It's just, I felt so betrayed. Straight after telling me, he announces he wants me to leave with him!" she moaned with a flourish of self righteousness that failed to even convince herself. "It was all too much, that"s why I came here, " she murmured, in a final attempt to justify herself, but getting a creeping feeling of unworthiness instead.

"Oh! He's leaving?" Linda looked stricken.

"They're all leaving. They have to. They were doing nobody any harm in that little scrap of paradise of theirs. Now they have to leave, or they'll get ill and die," she said, her own words bringing back images of an innocent, devastated Jal, which now pained her.

"I just thought, maybe the Aazaar would, might, do something," a dejected Linda moaned.

Rhea rolled her eyes, a darkness, a conflicting urge to disparage any utterance of hope, overcoming her, as she began to struggle with her own failure.

"Do what? Turn up on the world's stage and knock a few heads together like a bunch of stern nannas?"

Linda shrugged, childlike in her shock that even these technologically advanced beings saw little hope for her world, her whole planet.

"Well, it might work, you know? show them they're not the centre of the universe, they're not all knowing and all powerful," she began desperately.

Rhea shook her head. "They'd have to see the Aazaar as people first, and that's not likely with their beliefs is it? They'd be delighted to condemn them as evil demons, and probably blame them for their own disasters."

She sighed.

"Anyway, even if they could, and they really can't, why should we expect them to wade in like some divine babysitters to clear up the mess we've made?"

"But you wish they could," Linda said quietly, understanding and sharing Rhea's shame and outraged helplessness.

"Yes," she admitted sadly.

For a long moment, they just hugged each other. Both women were giving up the struggle, and slowly turning towards the peace of resignation. They sighed in unison, looking up as if they were in the bottom of a very deep well.

Rhea stared in numbed silence, the long line of hopeful human evolution, all those little acts of kindness and support of one another that made us human, replaying in her head like some crazy cartoon, only to fall in dying shreds as it reached the present.

"So Jal didn't discuss it until the last minute? No doubt he told you he was only trying to avoid upsetting you. Bloody men the universe over!" Linda remarked, breaking the silence.

Rhea smiled, momentarily comforted by Linda's gossipy tone. "True, but he was all caught up too. He didn't want to believe what he'd found out. And I was so caught up with my own things, I couldn't see that, couldn't be there for him. I probably never could. I mean, we've just buggered up our world and we're wiping out his too. With all the things his beliefs, his whole way of life is opposed to, he must really hate me," she said, wondering with deep shame, just how much like the Brynewiln humans were.

Linda smiled. So, they really were an item? It was an amazing little light in this gathering darkness.

"He never looked like he hated any of us. I mean, you tried. I'm sure that's what he saw and tried to protect in you, and why you saw him." She cocked her head. "Your heart saw something in him." Linda said softly.

Rhea nodded. *'But I didn't try hard enough,'* she thought ruefully, as she fell to contemplating their fate.

Linda patted her hand thoughtfully. She wasn't finished. "Remember that Hallowe'en? I had just finished asking the universe for a sign. Then you both appeared like some miracle. Of course Jal and his people aren't here to babysit, But it's changed everything, and I've been trying to work out the lesson ever since."

Rhea gave her an admiring wistful smile as she remembered that night.

"It's amazing how like you they are, even their science. He sees Earth as a Mother Goddess, I mean, we were all born from her, and we, and every living thing on the planet, all depend on her."

Linda shook her head sadly, and hugged her, now able to see

what Rhea faced, aware of what she must do. Love, real love, was never that easy, even in the quietest of times. But these two had to reach across vast expanses of space, and in the worst of troubled times. "And that's what the lesson was, is. That's our hope. It's our only hope."

"What? What lesson?" Rhea said, blinking into her face in confusion.

Linda gazed into her face. "He's not human." Rhea nodded. "Right..."

"But you are. And yet, you share the same way of looking at... well... everything, looking at life."

Rhea frowned. "What? How? You can tell that?"

Linda nodded. "When you said 'he sees Earth as a Mother Goddess' you glowed. It's obviously what's in your heart."

Rhea smiled wistfully. "True. And I have him to thank for helping me know that. You know? It is true. We're closer than we look."

Linda's face changed. "You've got to go," she said urgently.

Rhea didn't want this finality, this acceptance.

"You could survive. He, we, might find a way yet; maybe I could ask him to take you too..."

Linda just gazed at her with sorrowful eyes, shaking her head. "Don't you see? I've got to stay. I've got Stan, and James, and the others to look out for. Jal's put a lot of hard work into getting Stan and James to understand what's at stake; so have you. Jal and you have given us this opportunity to find a way through, make our peace. Humans have got to remember what made us human, what makes us human. If it doesn't work, then..." She smiled sadly. "You two have given us the chance to have someone to tell our story, remember us."

CHAPTER 14

Rhea shook her head, heaving a deep breath, trying to clear the ache in her chest.

"How can I be human without Earth?" she whispered despairingly, but Linda gave her a grandmotherly smile.

"You have Jal. It's cycles of life. You left all this life behind a long time ago. You've been studying it ever since, not living it. You'll carry Earth in your heart forever, but you belong to another world now, Jal's world." She shook her head in protest, but Linda stood firm.

"You've got to go, for our sake as well as your own. If we won't change, we die. Everything dies sometime. We have to give thanks for what we had. You must sing our story, our End song, to whoever you find who will listen, for whatever comes after us, because what comes after, certainly won't be human any more."

Rhea gave Linda a sorrowful smile, her heart aching at the sadness, the grief of loss and defeat she could see in her face. It was time to be strong, be brave. She knew Jal would never abandon her, knew now that the chasm that had seemingly opened up between them, was an illusion. She could leave, she had to, for Linda's sake, for all those like her, and all those she had ever cared for, to take their story with her. She would live. She couldn't bear to even think what would happen to Linda.

"They won't be going straight away. I'll call."

Linda nodded, then got up and opened the window.

"Endings and new beginnings," Linda said softly, as she watched Rhea climb out adjusting her transporter belt. "Endings and new beginnings."

CHAPTER 15

After Rhea left, Jal did what he had to do. He had played the council like a musical instrument and felt no shame in doing so. In fact, he felt little of anything, which would normally have concerned him. Now, he was glad he was numb, closed down, focussed only on the tasks he had in hand.

The meeting had been full, with many people urgently wanting to air their news and local concerns. So it had been easy for him to stay quiet without it appearing to be strategic.

He had waited for that point in the proceedings when everyone had enough time for their concentration to be focussed. His presentation was a perfect performance. He had paused in all the right places, allowing them just enough time to wonder but not enough time to come up with questions or suggestions. Instead, he smoothly suggested they think it through for a couple of days before anything was discussed or planned. It was then easy to get agreement from them not to mention anything of his announcements outside the hall.

He noted, with relief, that even Galer had indicated his agreement and didn't appear to be about to question him.

As he'd gazed around the hall, he'd seen that, despite the

CHAPTER 15

dismay, there was little surprise. In each pair of eyes he'd met, what he'd seen was a heart wrenching resignation. He had paused in sorrow, but only for a second. He knew he could offer nothing. He shared the same despair.

He took the opportunity to slide unnoticed out of the hall only to find Galer waiting for him. He had considered trying to quietly track Rhea, give himself the reassurance she was safe, to sustain him before he saw Stan. He knew he had no chance to do that now. Galer would want to talk, question him. So all he could hope for was that Galer would be satisfied with taking up only the rest of his evening, leaving him time to deliver his terrible message to Stan and get Rhea back before his time, and what little energy he had left, was swallowed up by his extra duties for the great departure.

"I need to unwind. Will you join me?" he said as he reached Galer's perch. Galer smiled and fell in beside Jal, accepting almost instantly that it was not a time for words.

They searched out Issn who was so engrossed in his musical journey he took some time to become aware of them.

Just before the meeting, Jal had visited his brother and briefly explained all he'd found. But long before this briefing Issn had picked up hints, odd jarring vibrations, cries on the streams of Earth's energies, that something was wrong.

Jal settled beside him, picked up a crystal harp and began to play, with never a word between them.

Issn smiled a welcome, then regarded his brother with otherworldly eyes, seeing tension and turmoil sucking on, and dulling Jal's recently brilliant, clear aura. He would lead him above their crabbed influence, all the better to find his way. He knew how. That was why he was a musician.

Soon, Galer, Issn and Jal were sending rivers of music cascading through the night.

Issn's magic worked, and a calmer Jal played a prayer of gratitude to Earth for his life here and a prayer that humanity would find the strength to face, with dignity, the terrible crisis they had stumbled into. Tomorrow, he would go to see Stan.

Next morning in his den, Jack studied Jal for a moment, watching him gathering up the human world computer. Increasingly these days, she didn't like him leaving the safety of Dreamhills, though she hadn't thought out why.

"Why is everyone all serious this morning?" she asked querulously.

He turned with a ready smile. "Are we? What are you doing today?"

She cocked her head on one side, gazing at his bag questioningly, but when he said no more, she gave him a hug. "Marn's going to help me with my transporter flying, and we're going to have a rehearsal of what it's like on the big space ship."

Jal smiled. "Sounds like a full day," he said as brightly as he could manage, his heart heavy.

She looked about. "Yeah, it is great. Where's Mam? She's not come back yet."

"Your mother needed to go see some friends she was worried about," he said, as he continued his busy morning routine. But Jack wasn't so easily satisfied.

"Have you had a row?" she asked with that startling accuracy of innocence, then shook her head, certain she knew what had happened.

"She's gone off without waiting for you again hasn't she?"

Jal gave a chuckle, noting once more that Jack never missed

a thing, and stopped what he was doing. "No, I knew she was going, she told me. She just wanted to go see some friends without me."

She nodded, but he hadn't time to see if she was satisfied, because Marn appeared.

"Wow! Everyone's leaving today! Will you be long? Do you want us to go over to Uncle Issn until you get back?" Marn asked as he eyed the computer and wrap beside Jal. He liked Issn's music and his cooking.

"Yes, good idea. I'll be away overnight, so will you look after everything for me?" Marn grinned mischievously, rolling his eyes. "I thought I'd have a few friends around, say thirty or forty, for a bit of a get together, take my chances while I have the house to myself," he said, cocking his head to judge Jal's reaction.

Jal's eyebrow raised infinitesimally and his mouth twitched in an amused warning. "I see, so any damage will be made good before I get back?" he asked mildly, fondly acknowledging Marn's teasing.

"I'll take care of it all," he said, giving Jal a hug before leaving with Jack.

"They're hiding something from us aren't they?" Jack asked when they were out of earshot.

Marn shrugged. "Think so. The assembly was all stirred up after the meeting last night but nobody's telling," he said, frowning. "Yes, they were all serious and tense. And you're right. Something's going on with Father and Rhea. It's got to be something about that data stick and the people who blew up your car."

"Oh, you mean the eco terrorists?" Jack sighed, briefly recalling their escape. But it was so long ago, and she lived here now. She didn't want to think about it any more, and wondered why their elders had to keep on poking at things for so long, especially when they were sad things.

"Yeah I suppose so. I wonder if that's why we're leaving now? I never got to say goodbye," she said, wondering, with a little pang of sadness, where Colin, Vincent and Gran were now and if they'd still remember her.

Marn laughed, "No silly! How could those eco whatevers cause any trouble for us here? They can't get across the disjunction, nothing can."

All the same, he felt uncomfortable. He hadn't questioned why they were preparing for a journey. He'd just assumed, since it was due, it was the Great Gathering. They'd have a big party, then come home. He didn't like the thought of not returning to Dream Hills.

"Vincent found a way through, and you brought me and Mam through, and other animals did," Jack pointed out in irritation.

"We could look," he said thoughtfully, now only too ready to reassure her and himself. So he and Jack set off for the council hall to sneak a scan of the closed council coms.

"What are you doing here child?" an imperious voice rang out. Marn may have felt a thrill of alarm as well as dismay, but he didn't show it.

"I'm just picking up my father's bag. He left it after the meeting," Marn said pulling the sweetest expression he could, promptly producing a bag he'd had with him. Of all people, it was the stone faced, eternally suspicious, Cenna who'd caught them.

Jack didn't like the sour disapproving face glaring at Marn, and looked up at her with mulish resentment. Cenna regarded her coolly. "Ah, the little human child. I wonder how you'll cope with

CHAPTER 15

leaving your home world?" she murmured, her eyes glittering with icy disdain. Jack recoiled, and Cenna returned her attention to Marn. "Well? Off you go now."

Marn, more troubled by Cenna's remark to Jack, than her nearly catching him out, lowered his eyes in a semblance of respect, and protectively reached for Jack's hand, leading her swiftly towards the exit.

"That's that. She'll watch us until we go," he muttered querulously to Jack. She nodded, puzzling over Cenna's remark about leaving. To get to the gathering, surely they had to leave Earth. But she knew that, and looked forward to it. Would they go forever? Not come back? "I suppose we could sneak a look at the computer when Jal gets back."

Marn gave an amused snort. "You've never tried to sneak anything past my father have you?"

Jack shrugged sheepishly, beginning to wish she'd never started this venture, trying not to think about what Cenna had meant. "Well you think of something. Oh come on, show me how to do that loop dive."

Marn stared at her. "But you're scared when I do that!"

She grinned "Yeah but it's good scared," she said, delighted to have found something to take her mind off what was really scary, and they both flew off laughing.

Jal tried hard not to think about his last conversation with Rhea as he made his way to Stan's flat. Once there, he struggled to keep focussed on what he had to do, just wanting to slide into comforting, companionable chatter.

He looked at Stan, the bright, young, nervy human he was about to give the cruellest burden and he hesitated, wondering for the umpteenth time if there was any point. Might it be kinder to say nothing?

"Have you got my electronic projects at hand?"

Stan reached inside a cupboard and fished out a box. He smiled indulgently. "Here's your fidget box big fella."

Jal pulled out the articles and sat them on the coffee table in front of him.

"You look pretty grim. Something happened?" Stan queried as he watched Jal arranging his playthings

"Rhea gave me some more data yesterday. Do you know how to work this?" Jal asked, pointing to the box at the end of the line.

Stan nodded. He always appreciated Jal's gadgets, but he was eager to get onto more pressing matters. "I know how to switch it on. It's a pretty neat job." He glanced around expectantly. "More data?" he prompted.

Jal picked up the object and turned it around. "It'll do," he said, "I'll just check."

"Jal, you can play later. What about the data?" Stan said impatiently eyeing the com where the promised new data was.

Jal glanced up and Stan shuddered at the darkness in his face. "Woa. I gather I said something wrong."

"No, you didn't say or do anything. You've just seen me at a bad moment." He turned the little box around. "I hoped you'd never need it," he murmured sadly.

Stan frowned and cocked his head. "I know it's a kind of monitor. I helped you put it together remember? What's going on?"

Jal rubbed his face, trying to wipe away the creeping exhaustion he was feeling.

"Just give me a minute. I could do with a drink first, maybe tea," he said, then sat back closing his eyes, thinking to just give in for a few moments to clear his head. Even Issn's magic of the night before had been drained from him.

Stan slid a steaming mug of tea in front of Jal, and surveyed the neat row of objects in front of him with a new interest. "What're you monitoring? You think I'm being bugged?" Jal gave a small mirthless chuckle. "No. I took care of that some time ago. Remember?"

Stan nodded. "Oh yeah, you said you'd set something up. So what's up with the new data?"

Jal offered him the box. "It means that you will need this. I need to finish off the calibration," he muttered to himself.

Stan studied Jal for a moment. "You look done in."

He smiled at Jal's puzzlement.

"Tired," he explained.

Jal tipped his head in acknowledgement. "Yes. Very tired."

He patted the boxes insistently.

"We'll need my electronics because the data Rhea and James found, confirms my suspicions."

"That sounds bad," Stan said, finally taking the com from beside Jal, scanning the information quickly.

Jal just sighed wearily, making no attempt to stop him.

Although he hadn't read it all, Stan quickly saw enough to understand. He flung himself down in his armchair in shocked outrage.

"Well! This has called time on the party. If this is activated, it's the end of the world as we know it! The end of humanity at the very least!"

"Yes," Jal murmured in agreement, so absorbed with his own turmoil he hadn't fully registered Stan's distress.

Stan snorted, rounding on Jal to vent his fear and anger. "Thanks for the faint concern!"

Jal started, then attempted to rouse himself into reasonable working action.

"I'm sorry. Your world will be devastated and I know nothing I do or say can make it any easier to bear."

He cast a sorrowful glance at his little human friend, angry at his own helplessness. Energies whose sources he couldn't pinpoint, let alone identify, were swirling around him, battering his emotions this way and that like a butterfly in a gale. And Stan, he could see him struggling, casting about in impotent fury for someone to blame.

"You'd think whoever's letting this loose would have had a little thought first."

Jal sighed.

"No, they can't. It's part of their inevitable pattern, the culmination of a long series of choices. It's an historical process."

"I can get depressed without any help from you thank you. What's the matter with you?" Stan interrupted, glaring at Jal. The moment he'd spoken, his irritation dissipated.

"It must have been hard to come tell me about this," he said taking a good look at his friend. He could see the big Aazaar's usual air of quiet confidence was gone, and he now sat slumped dejectedly on his sofa.

Jal smiled weakly. "I meant to make a better job of it."

"Yeah, it is a bit of a shocker," Stan agreed in a conciliatory tone. He cocked his head, thoughtful for a moment.

"You've seen this sort of thing before haven't you?"

"I know of it, yes," Jal agreed ruefully.

Stan sat back as realisation dawned. "Okay, so why take so

long over this, if you had an idea already? You're not going to tell me it was my sparkling conversation are you?"

Jal smiled affectionately "And you're not going to admit to having anything other than sparkling conversation are you?"

Stan couldn't help a smile of acknowledgement of their friendship, then leaned over the work. "All the same, why so hesitant?"

Jal tipped his head. "Hesitant? Yes, that's true. Because of our laws. They protect us both."

Stan rolled his eyes. "Your laws? But didn't you stretch things just showing yourself?"

Jal eyed him warily, not in the mood for a discussion, wishing he'd let it go but accepting he was owed an explanation. "Your personal beliefs reduced that risk. And since I was merely presenting you with Human information…"

Stan interrupted with a snort of derision. "Yeah, sailed close to the wind on that one. But you still dragged your heels."

Jal gave Stan a rueful look. "I set out to…Understanding something so very different and contentious is as much about developing the confidence to let go of…current paradigms." He stumbled through the sentence, feeling worse by the word.

Stan gave a short ironic laugh. "Right, tutoring me by pretending you didn't understand."

"I was talking about you, but that's not the point. I really didn't want to face what I was seeing," Jal finally admitted.

Stan nodded as he tried once more to come to terms with what he had just read. "I'm with you on that," he commiserated.

"So, with an updated transmissions risk rate, we have to factor in the range of this triggering mechanism."

Jal merely flinched. He knew Stan was trying to hold it

together by getting on with the work in hand, and he'd already roughed out a plan of action himself, but he could not answer, his mind was blank, nothing came.

Stan looked up, puzzling over Jal's incongruous diffidence and distinct despondency.

"Oh," he said quietly. "This is going to affect your people too."

Jal sighed his agreement.

"But how? Can't you protect yourselves? Won't you be protected in that anomaly you live in?" Stan protested.

Jal looked away, dodging a wave of sadness. "No, not from this, not permanently. Anyway, the anomaly was only ever there because it shared the possibility of your world's brighter future. So, as that possibility fades, it'll disappear."

"Shit! So we don't just take ourselves down?"

Jal sighed, now too exhausted to summon up any matching emotions.

"It was the end of a dream, a hope for acceptance."

"Do the rest of your people know?" Stan asked.

"Yes, I told them last night. They're preparing to leave Earth soon."

'*Leave Earth? You'd leave Earth just like that?*' He heard Rhea's sad accusing cry in his thoughts, leaving him with a deep haunting ache in his heart and chills that ran up and down his body as more energy leaked from him.

Stan whistled.

"I wouldn't have liked to be in your shoes," he said, and then Jal's pitying eyes met his.

"It's my turn now isn't it?" he muttered, suddenly feeling very cold and decidedly weak.

"What will you do now?" he finally managed to croak.

Jal shook his woozy, hopeless, overloaded head. What could he do? He'd run out of time. He'd failed. "It's not just a technical problem. My insistence on keeping everything under wraps until we had incontrovertible proof has meant delays in getting and setting up tracking equipment for the activating frequency," he said then shook his head remorsefully.

Stan blinked. "We have to try," he said softly

Jal gave a sad smile. "You have to try," he murmured

"What am I up against?" Stan asked the air.

"Getting the perpetrators to see the error of their ways and then to stop. Especially since the process appears to offer them such a seemingly simple method of social control, of keeping their advantages," Jal said drily.

"The perpetrators? What do I know about the perpetrators? Who the hell are they?" Stan huffed in exasperation.

"You told me remember? And from the little this outsider has to offer, I'd say you're right."

"So what do I do?" Stan asked the air

"I really don't know," Jal began, then he cast a sympathetic glance at Stan and smiled ruefully. "I just need to stop, just for a little while, stop thinking, just do anything but think, even if just for half an hour."

"Me too," Stan agreed dazedly, "But I think we need a little longer than half an hour."

He stumbled out into the kitchen to root in the fridge.

"Old human tradition. When everything looks bad. A spot of oblivion. Ahh, there's two here!" he called from the kitchen, regaining some of his normal bounce, and dumped a cold bottle of beer in front of Jal.

"We are going to get drunk and shout at something mind numbingly silly on the telly," he announced.

"And we'll need more than one each for that!" he said, phoning for a party delivery of beer.

Jal fingered the bottle hesitantly, then lifted it up to Stan in salute. He normally would never consider this human ritual of getting drunk but in his present state a touch of oblivion sounded very attractive indeed.

"Here's to you Stan Woodsman, to friendship and understanding."

"Here's to you Batman, friendship and love," Stan chirped with bright camaraderie, before murmuring sadly to himself, "May the coming reaping be mercifully swift."

Then he took a long draught and the two of them settled back to enjoy their companionable escape.

A while later, the phone rang. Stan winced, tipsily putting his finger to his lips for silence. A woman's voice chattered invitingly from the answer machine. "That's the lovely Sophia," Jal whispered, recognising the voice of the latest focus of Stan's romantic attentions, and like an over-eager aunt, did an energetic, comic mime, urging Stan to answer. Stan shrugged a diffident schoolboy refusal. "Yees…it's complicated."

Jal raised mocking disbelieving eyebrows.

"I know, end of the world and all that. Should take my chances while we still have them, but Sophia? Oh, women can be difficult," Stan explained, grinning lopsidedly.

Jal raised his bottle in salute and agreement, giving a heartfelt, "Ohhh yes."

Stan homed in on this admission, giggling delightedly. "Oh? So even the super cool Jal can have troubles of the heart?"

CHAPTER 15

Jal winced, throwing Stan a sheepish glance of discomfort.

"It's not just you humans who have that inconvenience," he protested beerily. "I have even heard of it happening among higher intelligent robots."

"Ahh, stop trying to lead me off the scent! Tell me who it is!" Stan crowed.

"We Aazaar don't tell," Jal said, attempting to appear dignified, but only succeeding in sliding off into clownish alcoholic primness.

"I live in a watchful community. Think of the privacy issues," he pleaded, hoping it would be enough to shut Stan up.

"Okay, I'll ask Rhea, she's not Aazaar. She'll tell me who this mystery woman is," Stan said, enjoying his friend's discomfort.

'No, she's not Aazaar,' Jal thought, feeling a stab of guilt for his failure to help her fellow humans.

Stan frowned, puzzling over Jal's squirming.

"It's Rhea? It's not Rhea!" he said incredulously, searching for proof of his contention and finding it.

Jal flashed Stan a sheepish look. "Um..." he muttered in drunken sorrow.

Stan grinned, half in delight and half, but not total, surprise now that he'd had a chance to reflect on when he'd seen them together or when Jal had spoken of her.

"Ho ho ho? Our Rhea. And look at your miserable face. Had an argument then? No time like the present to go and make it up and we might only have the present."

He paused, in a clown like attempt at consideration, holding up a warning finger.

"Oh oh. Beery fumes. Not good. Best wait until tomorrow," he said, laughing to find the once scary Jal was as helpless as the next man when it came to love.

Jal sat back, the alcoholic haze that had numbed his anxiety over Rhea, now priming his nerves.

"Can't. She's insisted I don't try to follow her or call until she's ready and calls me," he mumbled pathetically, slumping even more into the sofa.

Stan whistled through his teeth.

"Sheesh! That's been some argument! You're in real trouble mate," he teased companionably. "What the hell did you say?"

Jal winced. "It's what I didn't say. I couldn't."

He sighed, a fresh wave of fretting hitting him.

"She's out there somewhere, I know that much, and with all this going on! It's my stupid fault," Jal moaned guiltily, suddenly knowing a drunk's self-pity. He agreed that of course she needed time to think things over, but she knew he'd worry. She had to know it was piling more onto him with all the other troubles and worries he had. At least she could tell him where she was and when she'd be back, he thought, as he put his drained bottle down next to his row of empties.

Stan finally registered Jal's anxiety. "She'sh here? Thiss sside?" he said, gazing at him from shiny drunken eyes.

Jal tipped his head.

"Oh man!" Stan exclaimed in sympathetic alarm, before wincing guiltily.

"She'll be shafe," he slurred in an attempt to reassure Jal and himself.

"She'shh probly investigating with James. Call him."

Jal shook his head morosely. *'James? Of course she would be. No doubt the lovely James, whom she was so anxious about, would be oh so attentive,'* he mused in a jealous haze.

"If I try to find out where she is, she'll know. And that will only make matters worse."

Stan nodded his understanding.

"She knows how dodgy things are. She wants you to sweat it out. They do that. But our James is discreet. He won't tell on you."

Jal sighed, "It was my fault. I avoided talking. You've been working with me and yet you still freaked on me when I brought you the results. I landed all of this on her all at once. I can't blame her for being angry."

Stan shook his head. "Poor Rhea," he mumbled sympathetically, then took another swig of beer. A boozy heroic plan began to form in his mind. He might not be able to save the world, but he could, and would, help Jal save a tiny bit of it.

"Tomorrow. I'll go look for her. I'll bring her back. Can't drive like this though. Tomorrow. Hic!"

He tried to focus well-meaning beery eyes on Jal.

"This mess is… this mess is our fault. Not you. Our fault. You've got to take her and little Jack."

Stan flung his hands up, looking toward somewhere beyond the ceiling.

"Two who'll escape. We've got to have someone escape."

He leaned into Jal's face, swaying unnervingly, wagging his finger emphatically and pinning Jal's arm to the chair with his other hand.

"You take her with you mate. Get her away from thiss. thiss mess. We've got to know someone makes it. You, you take her with you right?"

Jal tipped his head, wrapped up in his own drunken self pity.

"Sorry, so sorry. There's nothing I can do. I wish there were.

I would if I could. The Aazaar must leave. I've got to go. You understand that. Nothing I can do."

Stan patted his arm.

"I know, I know, jus make sure you take her. Make sure mind. You take her. You done all you can...You done all you can, it's our mess....Jus...you be good to her right? You take her ..."

He threw up his arms again in a pantomime of flying up to the sky.

"I knew. I knew all along. I knew! Just. No proof. Couldn't tell her! Couldn't say anything with no proof could I? Cause unnecessary panic...couldn't say...Community wouldn't want to believe me without proof...Couldn't even tell you. Would you say without proof? Had to keep it quiet till I knew. I couldn't tell her," Jal continued, pleading his case from the dock of his alcoholic guilt to the severe judge of his own conscience.

Stan spread his hands in drunken magnanimity

"Hey, you did your best, got the evi...the evidensh to me.... Let me see for myself. Not to blame. Ush shtupid humans..."

Jal tried to focus earnest yellow eyes on Stan, murmuring sorrowfully as he slid further down the sofa.

"I told you. I did, I showed you everything. You know I told you everything."

Stan nodded, and sensing the onset of imminent drunken collapse, he suddenly sat upright, his last shred of rationality sparking into action.

"You're too big for that sofa, get the cushions on the floor and I'll throw a duvet over you."

He scrabbled in the innards of a footstool, dragging out a duvet, and turned, just as Jal stood up, holding cushions, dropping open his wings to steady himself, swaying disturbingly.

CHAPTER 15

Stan giggled "Woah with the wings! Small breakable space. Small breakable human. Ow!" He got slapped by an unruly wing as Jal tottered and they both fell into their respective heaps.

"Well, that was an exclusive end of the world party," Stan muttered into the carpet before alcoholic oblivion took over.

Stan woke with a fright, to a series of crashes, thumps and mutterings, thinking his flat had been broken into, before he remembered Jal laid out on the floor like a giant dead butterfly.

"Put the kettle on when you've finished smashing the place up," he mumbled from under his cushion, to be answered by a distinctly inhuman, half moan half growl, then another series of thumps, as Jal stumbled into the shower.

Stan hauled himself off the floor onto a chair

"Did you break much?" he asked, eyes still closed, holding his delicate head in his hands.

Jal slapped a mug of tea down beside him, giving an ill tempered grunt of denial.

Stan nodded his thanks, glancing up at Jal.

"You even shaved." he said, surprised to see, through his own grubby, hungover haze, a neatly turned out Jal

Jal growled back irritably, "Don't shave. Our creator liked her men smooth."

Stan gave a mischievous giggle then gingerly looked around, half expecting his little sitting room to be strewn with wreckage. "And you tidied up," he said in amazed admiration. "Did she give you a house proud gene as well?"

Jal glowered at him over the top of his mug, narrowing his eyes against the thumping of his sore head.

Stan grinned knowingly.

"Was it worth it?" he taunted breezily, then winced as Jal

retaliated by savagely yanking back the curtain, letting a sudden blaze of sunlight hit his eyes.

"I welcome the pain. It salves the guilt," Jal's normally purring voice gravelled out sardonically, his amber eyes glowing warningly.

Stan shuddered nervously, deciding not to provoke Jal any more, then hauled himself off to the kitchen and began to noisily clatter pans and plates around.

"Eat," he ordered as he thumped a plate of pancakes down rather too heavily for Jal's delicate head.

They ate in silence, their companionable taunting long dissipated, once more both silently contemplating the terrible realities they faced.

"I'll talk to James, explain the situation, make sure his hardware and technology is up to the job and keeps him invisible. He's the last one. The rest of the network is ready, and will be safe," Jal offered. And he couldn't help thinking that if he found Rhea with James, it would actually be a coincidence he would be glad of.

"I'll ask him to help find out where Rhea is after we've eaten," Stan said into his plate, as if he'd just read Jal's mind.

Jal tipped his head.

"You are taking Rhea with you aren't you?" Stan asked, already resigned to the inevitable.

"Of course," Jal said, admitting to himself that he would move mountains to find her and keep her safe with him.

"James will take the lead in the investigation of who's involved in promoting this sad scheme," Jal remarked.

Stan nodded.

"He'll help you find a way to make some headway with your

warnings and stay out of trouble."

Stan eyed Jal.

"Do me a favour. Explain to me how I have a chance of doing this."

Jal met his eyes. "Because you are a child of goddess Earth."

"What? Oh, the pagan thing...What?" Stan said in bewilderment.

"Yes, the pagan thing, and your position. Because of your world view, I hoped you'd find a chance...be that chance."

"Be that chance?"

Jal sighed. "Your ethics."

"Oh!" He flushed with embarrassment. "That makes me a chance?"

Jal raised a tired eyebrow. "Stan, you are being annoyingly dense. Just think it through."

Stan groaned. "I'm used to keeping that under wraps and being called crazy."

Jal fixed him with his gaze. "Remember when you first encountered me? All those things you talked about?"

Stan frowned, studying the remains on his plate. "Can't remember discussing saving the world."

"Oh? You came upon a man who wasn't from your world, and you talked about how your society, indeed your world, was seriously threatened by all manner of wrong thinking, and the blind ignorance and greed of powerful people. 'Children playing with matches' was one of the milder phrases you used. Then you proceeded to work with me to resolve what you thought was a major threat to said world."

"I know...but this is...what can I do now?"

"We have discussed your strengths, your ethics, now look to

your advantages, and use them."

"But I'm an outsider."

Jal tipped his head. "Maybe, but because of that, you are seriously underestimated, seen as harmless, easily managed. Your obvious efficiency in your current post, coupled with an assumed gratitude for any promotion given you, makes you an excellent candidate. It would be very easy for you to allow yourself to be moved into a more authoritative position. Especially now, in this climate of upheaval and growing disruption. Besides, your current position doesn't make you that much of an outsider."

Stan laughed. "Damn me with faint praise won't you? But you're right."

He took a swig of his cooling tea. "Yeuck! Anyway, how did you know about the enquiries about me? I said nothing."

Jal raised amused eyebrows.

"Okay, plan. I get myself more power. That'll have to be leading a bigger research unit. But that'll take time we haven't got. I suppose there are those enquiries from that rather shady government thing that came up, which you mysteriously know about which I could have almost instantly, and which I was avoiding like the plague," Stan prattled on sarcastically before reconsidering.

Jal just watched, his face composed into an expression of mild interest, waiting for Stan to come to his inevitably suitable conclusions in an inevitably circuitous way.

"Plague? Hah! Oh! When it's raining, it's best to be indoors," Stan said as inevitable conclusions were reached.

"And you have your secure network, Linda's secret army. Anything you send out will never be traced back to you," Jal added, once Stan stopped talking.

CHAPTER 15

Stan nodded, pleased with the solidifying of an actual workable proposal.

"Provided you leave no clues in the actual data that is," Jal said wryly, falling back into the habitual pattern of friendly teasing that had characterised their friendship.

"And there it is again. A demonstration of your unshakeable faith in me," Stan huffed mockingly, his good humour a cover for his anxiety.

Jal watched, with sorrowful satisfaction, as Stan began to mentally organise his next plans of action.

"Yes! Sounds doable. But. Time. Where will I find the time?"

"I'll cover you. The monitor is all but running now. I could run interference on any early frequencies before..." Jal began, but Stan stopped him.

"No," he said quietly but firmly, and with as much dignity as he could muster. "They won't be starting yet. I could be in that job by tomorrow. It's time for you to go. You've risked enough and done more than anyone could expect of you. Leave this up to us now."

Jal tipped his head in respectful acknowledgement. He patted Stan's shoulder in a silent, final leave taking, then headed towards the window. Stan did not move or turn, but as Jal threw open the window he called, "Been great knowing you, Bat man."

CHAPTER 16

The city beneath him bustled greyly under a blanket of sodden clouds as Jal began to make his heavy-hearted way home. He hoped he'd bought some time for Stan and his little band of friends, time that might give them a chance, if not for survival, then to make their peace.

As he gazed down, it seemed that the incessant wail of sirens, rushing towards yet more disturbances and disasters in the streets below, was temporarily hushed.

Suddenly, a series of malign energy emissions silently sliced their way through the unheeding leaden day of those unsuspecting bustling millions and slammed through Jal. He shuddered and, semi-conscious, struggled to stop his fall.

He managed to make it to a high rise rooftop which was rather too exposed for his liking. He hunched up, panting and shaken, desperately trying to stay hidden from the street below and from the skies above, in the menacingly stooped shadow of a ventilator housing. He noted the dot of a helicopter on the horizon, thrumming its way towards him. He wouldn't have long.

After taking a few minutes to regain his composure, he opened a com channel to Stan, desperate to give him as much of a chance of survival as he could provide.

"I've just flown through a whole volley of different activating frequencies as I was leaving the city. There's no time to finish your setting up. The monitor's ready. You must get it online now. A few pulse scans is all I'll need and I'll work on pinpointing the source for you. Then you can fire up that neutraliser I left you. I'll call you once I'm back at my den."

He heard Stan groan his dismay and shocked disbelief. "It's not set up. You said we had time!"

"I'm sorry. I felt a sustained volley in your flat last night and didn't realise what it was till now. Someone has brought the attacks forward. I thought you'd have a week or two more to prepare it and finish off setting up the back tracer. At least you had your dose of protection before it started."

"Not your fault. Not your business now," Stan muttered.

"I need those scans Stan. Just do it," Jal insisted.

There was a reluctant pause before Stan answered. "Okay, I'll try. Maybe James and me can do something with the results," he said, attempting to hide his true feelings, but it didn't work. Stan's huffs of panic and fear had rattled out of Jal's com, and he steeled himself against it. He knew Stan would surely die soon, as would countless millions, but not yet. He wasn't ready to let him die yet.

Jal sucked in a head-clearing lungful of air. "I'm going to get onto James now."

The echo of raised voices alerted Jal to a roof door he hadn't noticed, forcing him to make a swift getaway. He finally settled, like an extra gargoyle, in the protective labyrinth of turrets and towers on the roof of an old Victorian building.

He had to find James and fast. James was the only one of

Linda's little band of humans who had not received his dose of protection. He'd estimated that, with James's contribution, this little band had a considerable set of skills for navigating this catastrophe.

After her visit to the museum, Rhea had told him how humanity had almost been wiped out before they'd started. They'd dwindled down to a very small group, and yet they'd overcome whatever deadly challenge had faced them. And now, they had spread over the whole planet. It was certainly a very slight possibility, but maybe they could do so again, if they found a way through.

He gave a wry smile as he made his call, wondering what future generations might make of James as one of their founding ancestors.

"Ahh Dr Jal. I'm alone in my car out west here and have a long drive across the city ahead of me. That's plenty of time to listen to long stories," James said in answer.

"Have you had any vaccinations lately?" Jal asked, knocking James off balance. "No. What? Why?"

Jal sighed with relief. At least James had taken that warning of Stan's seriously. "You must not try to cross the city. You're in imminent danger. The information you found was details of a control. Someone is firing it at the city. It's a virus activating control and you have no immunity. I will provide you with the necessary protection once you've reached a place of safety. So drive immediately to a village called Foxton Topp. Come alone, do not contact anyone, keep off camera as best you can, and do not stop for anyone. They might already have activated infections. And I'm sure I don't need to remind you not to leave other electronic traces of your whereabouts. So take the battery out of your phone, scramble your sat nav. Do it now."

"What? Firing? But...viruses are spread by coughs and sneezes?" James sputtered in alarm, which Jal interrupted.

"Too late. It's already been spread. The damage is caused when it's activated. As I said, this one has remote controls that someone is firing as we speak. Just get to safety and let me help you."

He heard the sounds of alarm, and then a measured consideration from James.

"I gather the attack is a massive one."

Jal sighed. "Yes I'm afraid so."

"Then I should stay and help," James protested in the calm dutiful voice of the policeman he was.

"That sounds honourable, but you will be far more use if you can avoid becoming a casualty yourself. Now, should you by some misfortune have become infected, the full effects of the attack will not show up for a day or two, so you have time to let me give you this protection."

Jal waited for his message to sink in then he heard the sounds of the car speeding up, the sounds of James' acceptance of immediate danger.

"I'm on my way. I know Foxton, I should be there in a couple of hours," James said smartly, before closing his phone.

Jal smiled into the face of the stone gargoyle his arm was draped around.

Rhea wasn't with him after all,' he thought with momentary relief, then sighed anxiously, just hoping she was home by now, safe and sound. He took one last pitying look at the stricken city, then he dived into the fading light.

James drew into the roadside and picked up Rhea, telling

her what had just happened. She said nothing, only nodded her assent. He flashed a querying glance Rhea's way. Her face was dark, closed, leaving James feeling like there was something about Dr Jal that Rhea was not happy about.

"I'll take any protection I can get," he said, giving a shudder. "So, you're coming with me to meet him?"

This time she definitely looked grim. "I'm coming, but not to meet him," she said, "Just drop me off in the village, we'll meet later."

He nodded, feeling a little thrill of triumph.

"So, the shine has come off our Dr Jal?" he asked, but Rhea gave him such a steely look of contempt, he backed off.

"We're in serious danger of being killed, and you want to snipe at the man who's trying to protect you?" she hissed.

He nodded. "Point taken," he said contritely. "So, I bring him down to meet you later?"

She sighed. "No, Jal has things he needs to do, so don't tell him about me."

James gave her a swift, sidelong glance of appraisal, but kept his counsel.

"First thought right thought," he murmured to himself. Now certain there was something between them, but what, he wasn't sure.

"Getting practical, it's unsafe to drive through the night without checking the situation. We need a plan and somewhere to stay."

She nodded. "Already thought about it. I'm sorting somewhere for both of us,"

she said in a curiously flat voice.

"We'll be alright," he reassured her, but Rhea never answered.

CHAPTER 16

He glanced her way again, and was certain he saw a tear.

"We'll be alright," he repeated gently. All he'd been told by Linda was that she wanted him to pick Rhea up and get her out of the city. He'd made an attempt to ask her what was up, but could only surmise that some more evidence had turned up, and that it was pretty scary. Now, after Jal's urgent call, even if he didn't know the full details, he knew for certain it was very scary. "Radio controlled viruses?" he asked incredulously.

She sighed. "Sort of. Remember that data we found? In the bunker? Anyway, it's a set of frequencies which activate the different types at different times, in particular patterns. So someone is sitting there, with their controller and can of caffeine, playing the last computer game of our lives."

She gritted her teeth, and he could feel anger radiating off her

"It's so hard for me too," she said after a pause, with such a softly pitiful voice, he shuddered involuntarily and didn't want to ask what she meant. He was now officially scared, very scared. He reached out and patted her arm, as much for his own need for comfort as hers. Things had just gone beyond crazy, and his mind screamed to reject what she and Dr Jal had just told him. In fact, he wanted to reject the whole terrifyingly unbelievable nightmare, but he couldn't. There was proof. He'd seen it, gathered it and built it up bit by bit whether he liked it or not. He set his jaw. A pattern, proof, a case. That is what he could hold onto. But there had to be a motive. He'd been the one to suggest motives. He silently groaned at the thought that he'd given Stan grounds for a full blown conspiracy theory. All he needed now to complete this bad B-movie of an experience, was some creature not of this world to appear to say it was a conspiracy for them to take over the world. He flushed. He had to get a grip and keep a tight focus. They drove in uneasy silence for the rest of the journey.

"I'll catch you in an hour," he said, as he let her out.

She turned to him. "Jal's done his best. He's taken huge risks to help you," she said quietly, her eyes so sorrowful, he felt a lump rise in his throat, then she disappeared into the night.

James parked up in the tiny car park meant for visitors to the curious conical hill that was the Topp. It was hidden from the road by hedges, and enough distance from the houses for privacy.

He gave a thin little smile of approval of Jal's venue, then he got out to stretch his legs and check the place out. When he was satisfied he'd got there before the mysterious Dr Jal, he took the opportunity for a piss against a tree.

"You're a good friendly old tree," he murmured, looking up through the branches to the dark still sky, comforted by its many-armed abiding solidity in his increasingly chaotic world.

It suddenly rustled alarmingly in the still air, as if something large had just landed among its vast ancient branches, so he hurriedly retreated towards his car, whilst fearfully looking every which way at once for someone with a ray-gun ready to activate his viruses.

All was silent again. He sighed, embarrassed about his alarm, and was about to get back into the car, when he felt something stab his hand causing him to take a sharp intake of breath and a mouthful of what he hoped were bits of leaf drifting down off the tree. He looked down to find a spiny twig that had snagged on his sleeve, then saw a slight movement from the corner of his eye.

"Hello James. No, don't look round. It's better if you can't identify me."

Recognising the voice as Dr Jal, James nodded, deciding he was probably right, but not before catching a glimpse of an

CHAPTER 16

alarmingly tall shadow against the trees.

"Okay, so you've got my attention. Are you going to tell me what this is about? You don't just want to look after my health do you?" he asked, keeping his back to the shadow, but listening out for any threatening movement

Jal smiled. This was going to be easier than he thought.

"True, though I would have helped you anyway. Have you got a co... a laptop with you?"

James grunted

"As it happens yes, why?"

Jal gave a satisfied smile.

"Good. I'll sort out some cover, make it invisible online. You'll use satellite, and I'll give you a mobile power source."

James coughed his surprise.

"You'll what? How? I mean, why?"

"How do you propose to continue your investigations when you're holed up in a small village?" Jal asked.

James gave a small, slightly nervous, laugh.

"Holed up? Why should I do that?

He heard an impatient rustle.

"So that you can give yourself the chance of surviving long enough to do something useful. Stan and I have been working on what the threats are and how it's done, while you have been investigating who is responsible."

Jal watched James weighing up his response.

Despite the terrible situation, which was finally dawning on him, and the imminent danger to himself, James was forced, by the emotional puzzle of his journey with Rhea, to question this Dr Jal.

"Right, but before we go any further, it's just you and me

and the trees, so we can speak freely. Just tell me. What's your motive for this? I mean, first you rescue Rhea and her kid, you do all that big doctor act and even give her a place to lie low, then you do all this stuff with Stan. You must be very rich, which, given current revelations about shady organisations causing this mayhem, makes you a suspect in my eyes. What do you get out of it?"

"Fair question. You require reassurance. I get a chance to help find a way to salvage something from this mess and protect some people I happen to admire, you, Rhea and Jack included. We have only a small window of opportunity. After that, it will eventually devastate the rest of Earth. So, what is your motive?" Jal said briskly.

James coughed in polite disbelief, still wanting to run and hide in whatever shreds of out of date reasonableness he could find.

"Now it's my turn to say that sounds… honourable," James said sarcastically, only to be met with a silence that made him wonder whether he'd pushed his luck too far. He peered into the darkness, but the shadows were so deep he could see nothing.

"Look, I know it's pretty bad, some idiot thinks they could use bugs as weapons, and I understand it has got out of control and could kill thousands, maybe a million or two. But the whole planet?" he reasoned, hoping to re-engage Dr Jal, hoping he was still within earshot.

Jal waited for a moment or two more, letting James consider the possibility of his own terrible suggestion, allowing his imagination time to shout down his disbelief. He needed James motivated to a high enough level to stay steadfast through what would be extremely testing situations for this cynical human.

CHAPTER 16

"You already suspected as much," Jal said, a hint of menace in his even tone.

"So maybe it could, but how?" James eventually conceded, grumbling defensively, still trying to slip a glance at Jal, but all he could make out were shadows without definition.

"I know viruses can spread around the world, but epidemics usually stop," James said.

"True, when those with immunity are left, or all possible hosts are dead. But as you already know, this isn't about a disease. The virus is only a tool. This was designed as a means of bioengineering a whole population, namely all human beings, at will in whatever way they choose. It's an attempt by one group to subjugate the world's population to their will, using a bio bomb," Jal said in his calm presentation voice.

James let out a gasp of exasperation. "A bio bomb? This is way out of my league. I'm into bog- -standard crime, maybe a bit of smuggling or something, but not international bio warfare!" he protested, fear making his skin crawl, as well as causing him to wonder just how effective this protection was that Dr Jal had promised him. His mind was racing. He needed more information. He was good at information. Information was what he did. A self-powered shielded computer would indeed be very useful. If he couldn't move about, at least he could get in contact with some very useful people. And it gave him a stronger chance to keep Rhea and him safe.

"You haven't told me what your motivation is," Jal prompted.

"Er, I don't like what is going on. It's just plain evil, against my sense of justice and honour if you like. The more I've seen, the blacker it looks. Those with power owe a duty of care to the rest of us, to the world. But this sounds like the ultimate exploitation, the ultimate control."

He hesitated.

"And I can't trust my own organisation. I don't know who I can trust," he said, realising he was putting his trust in a man he had never set eyes on.

Jal smiled. James was hooked. "It offends your sense of justice? Mine too," he said in a more relaxed tone.

James gave a wry smile into the darkness, realising he was definitely warming to the strange Dr Jal. "Seems we are on the same team. Feels wrong not facing you," he probed hopefully.

"I understand," Jal said non-committally.

"But what do I look for? I don't even know how to recognise when there is an attack," James protested.

Jal gave a small smile of satisfaction. James was listening now.

"Keep in close contact with Stan. He's got the technical knowledge and facilities. He'll tell you."

"And the perpetrators?" James asked. "Any ideas?"

He heard Jal heave a sorrowful sigh.

"I can only surmise from the fragments of what we have, and the weapon itself. Whoever commissioned this weapon appears to have a plan of what humanity should be, for their own benefit of course. They aim to manipulate the physical structure of an elite few, themselves and their families, to make them fit this ideal blueprint. The rest? It looks like those they don't aim to kill are to be re-engineered into biddable labour to tend their new Garden of Eden."

Jal watched James go to work, nosing what he'd just been told, in the hope of finding a scent to follow.

"I've had similar thoughts though maybe not as far fetched. But from what you've just told me, I'd say my suspects would know exactly what the plan is."

He shook his head, murmuring to himself. "I don't like political explanations. Our government wouldn't just sacrifice its citizens like that. I mean, we fought world wars against such things."

"Yes, but the ideology of perfectibility and independence from your fellow creatures, your planet, as opposed to adaptability and interdependence, was never seriously addressed. The powerless and marginalised are always sacrificed. It's the victims, the ones left destitute who were and are scapegoated or used as cannon fodder."

James sighed "Yeah...suppose so... but I'm looking for good solid motives I can demonstrate and prove. How can that be sold to anyone?" he asked, musing over Jal's dry academic explanation.

" 'Glorious martyrdom in this world, and pie in the sky when you die,' or, in less religious terms, 'after the revolution', or perhaps more pertinently, 'the market rewards hard work' I suppose," James said, answering his own questions. "And that fits with this extremist turn of events. But if I believe you, the damage you're talking about will bring the perpetrators down too."

"Yes, that's my point. They don't see it. They only seem to have considered the changes they want, not the changes that will happen," Jal insisted.

"I know I'm going to regret this, but explain the logic behind the science, and remember, in plain simple English, with the emphasis on the simple!"

James pleaded.

He heard a soft chuckle of agreement from Jal. "Every living thing on the planet is, however distantly, related, born of the earth and made up of combinations of the same basic structures. You share some with that massive old tree for instance. And those basic structures became what they are, through responding to their surroundings."

James couldn't help but wince at the thought he might have pissed on a cousin, however distant.

"You are what your choices have made you. Unfortunately, our mystery would-be rulers of the world, just don't seem to be able, or want, to take that into account," Jal continued.

James gave a chuckle. "So Linda's idea of Mother Earth does have a scientific basis?"

"More to the point, her and Stan's science is informed by their emotional and spiritual relationship with Mother Earth," Jal said crisply. "Rather than the case of your prevailing science, which is informed by the opposite, a rejection of that relationship. In other words, the subjection of life and the planet at the whim of whoever has the power to do so. "

James shuddered and looked up to the skies, and Jal could see his colour drain, even in the dim light in the car park. After a minute, he seemed to gather his wits again

"It really is out of control isn't it?" he said softly.

Jal sighed.

"Yes. A few more activations and the changes will reach a critical level."

He paused.

"It's not just humans who will die in their millions. And without those plants and animals, the Earth will die and become as barren as Mars," he said quietly

"They've got to be mad." James spat out in fearful outrage.

"We might consider them seriously misguided, but I doubt

they are mad," Jal insisted, hoping James would not be tempted to underestimate any of them, or the power of their ideals.

"It's bloody religious fundamentalism! Sorry Linda, it's monotheistic fundamentalism!" James proclaimed.

"I prefer the term ideological despotism. But that is a speculation we must keep for any leisure we may have later," Jal said reasonably.

"Okay, fascist, national socialist, FTSE 100, Dow Jones...what did you say? Ideological despot fundies of any stripe." James growled viciously.

"For now, let's concentrate on what we do have. We've found no evidence they tried to produce an antidote vaccine, which suggests whoever commissioned this weapon, has, or at least believes, they have protection against it without a vaccine. That heavily suggests they are most probably living in an insulated, or at least isolated, environment for now, which they believe keeps them safe from any activating frequency," Jal explained. "It also suggests they won't be firing for long. They're clearing the land to make it their playground."

"No vaccine? So what about my shot?" James spluttered anxiously

"It's done. But it is limited, so don't take any risks."

Jal smiled as James automatically looked at his punctured hand. The device James had swallowed was crude, but serviceable, and he'd broken no Aazaar codes or laws by producing it. Stan could have produced it, if he'd had the time, which meant it was within the capabilities of current human science, and thus untraceable.

"So if you two made a vaccine, why couldn't they?" James asked.

"Their ideology, their view of the world, just can't fully accommodate what they have discovered."

" Ahh, now you're about to get way too technical."

Jal sighed a little impatiently. "If you don't know about aeroplanes, you don't build parachutes."

"Okay, so I'm no philosopher," James huffed, finally getting the gist of Jal's comment.

"Sorry, I didn't mean to offend," Jal said, feeling more than a touch of sympathy for this beleaguered little human.

"Stan and I will have something for you to work on within a few hours. He'll contact you. You'll find the hardware you need in your car. It'll keep you online and hidden. In the meantime, I suggest you find a bed for the night, away from the city, while we all try to find you some more permanent arrangement. Even with your new immunity, you're not likely to survive a mob of the infected who've been activated."

"Chee! I thought it was like flu, not something that makes them rage like mad dogs."

"Like I said, a disease with controls," Jal said sadly.

James opened his car door. "And Rhea and her kid? Are they safe with you?" he asked worriedly.

Jal involuntarily clenched his jaw. "Rhea is my guest and free to come and go as she pleases," he said coolly, realising too late how defensive he'd sounded

James nodded, giving an enigmatic smile to hide his triumph at finally realising he'd guessed something right about Dr Jal.

"It wasn't a dig. I'm still a policeman. This all started for me as a case of burglary, then her supposed murder. I just wondered if she needed help."

"I'll keep Rhea and Jack safe," Jal said, and James smiled at his softer tone.

"You're a really strange man. Very hard to read."

He measured his words with a calm policeman's control, before turning to gaze meaningfully at Dr Jal. "Normally..." he continued pointedly, but the edge was lost as he anxiously cast his gaze about for his missing target.

"I'll be waiting for that call," he said with a resigned smile and he contemplated his not so little disappointment that Rhea and the strange Dr Jal really could be an item.

"Good luck James. Be well and stay safe," Jal said in regretful farewell as he watched James climb back into his car, knowing the brave little human faced a war he barely understood, and may well not survive.

CHAPTER 17

Shaken by his encounter with Jal, James had found himself obediently heading for the little town when he was stopped by a call from Rhea. She had arranged for him to stay in a cottage nearby. Apparently it belonged to Rowena, a friend of Linda's he had never met. He accepted without demur, glad to find he had a place of safety with people he could have faith in. He trusted Linda's judgement. Rhea excitedly informed him that the cottage was rigged with enough sustainable power and food sources to see him through a century or so, but this only succeeded in dispersing his recently gained morsel of comfort.

He looked around the deserted road, almost expecting a road block and a crazy, virus-stricken mob, but it was bereft of any sign of humanity. A tiny flash of horror of being the last man standing had made him shudder. He speeded up through the dark, winding, woodland road, prompted by an urgent need to get into the presence of another human being.

Rhea opened the door and it was all he could do not to throw himself into her arms. "Am I glad to see you!"

"Kettle's on and we have some soup. Tinned I'm afraid, but at least it's hot," she said, bustling him into the kitchen where a fire burned smugly in a small wood burning stove. She settled him at the table in front of the steaming bowl. She watched him as he ate, deciding to give him time to get a grip after his disturbing meeting with Jal before questioning him. After a few spoonfuls, he let out a sigh of relief, and Rhea gave a satisfied smile.

It hadn't taken her long to wake the house from its chilly, uninviting slumbers, transforming it into a cosy, comforting hideaway, the surprising virtues of which, she explained as he ate, in an attempt to keep him anchored to some comforting semblance of familiarity and everyday rationality.

"...and of course, with all this independent power, you'll be able to use your computer as much as you like," she said with a delighted flourish.

"Right but what about internet visibility? I can't get a connection without attracting attention." His tone was gentle, like that he might use on an over enthusiastic child, which immediately irked Rhea.

"Hmph! Have you never heard of satellite connection?" she responded, nevertheless, noting how his tension had uncoiled a little.

"Yeah, that's what your Dr Jal said, and that he'd sorted my laptop and phone, though how the hell he did that, I'm not sure. I didn't see him, let alone hand the things over."

"So now you've met Jal?" She noted the ordinariness, the lack of shock in his remark.

"I heard him, but I never clapped eyes on him. Funnily enough, I do trust him, got to I suppose," he mused, considering the situation he was in.

She gave a curious shadowed smile. "Yeah, you can trust him. So, he's given you something to help protect you. Did you talk about the stuff you gave me?" James sighed heavily. "Yeah." He paused, looking down into his bowl.

"I'm still trying to take it all in," he murmured, then looked up.

"A threat to civilisation as we know it? To the whole world?"

Rhea gazed at him dark eyed and nodded gravely.

"Yes, I know. It's ..." she looked away, feeling a surge of inexplicable guilt.

He rubbed his face, still contemplating what he had been told and exhaled an exasperated helpless "Chee!" then looked up. "Your good Dr has had similar suspicions to me about official involvement," he said, suddenly catching her eye and becoming a policeman again.

"Yes," she agreed.

"Any idea how he knows that?"

She sighed "He's observant. He listens."

He nodded. "And, he's not involved with, anyone other than the tree huggers, nothing...more...radical?"

Rhea's eyes glittered like hard impenetrable jewels as she struggled with a surge of defensiveness on behalf of Jal, but she smiled. "You're questioning him now James?" She looked at him askance then shrugged. "What can I say? He's the original outsider. He has no vested interests, no connections to anything, except your favourite tree huggers. His idea of heaven would be to live peacefully amongst said trees. And before you ask, his idea of fighting is to survive, hide in the shadows, let the idiots get on with it and exhaust themselves. Didn't he tell you that?"

James winced. "Not exactly, no. He was more concerned with describing the oncoming Ragnorok and making sure I didn't just dismiss it. I did say I trusted him," he protested, and took

CHAPTER 17

another bite of bread.

"He appeared to be inducting me into the group, as if I was being appointed investigating officer." He caught her eye. "But you don't sound exactly approving of this guy."

Rhea gave an exasperated snort at his last remark before continuing.

"Well you are our investigating officer, aren't you?"

She sighed and slumped, tired from supporting everyone else, tired from being strong.

James reached out a hand in comfort. "Hey, I'm sorry. You've gone to a lot of trouble to get me out of that mess in the city and keep me safe. I did listen to some radio before I picked you up. We got out by the skin of our teeth. And that's down to you and Dr Jal."

Rhea heard, but didn't show any response, she just watched him flinch, get the message that he should stop.

"Okay, this computer and phone modding? Before I get into my new post flying this desk, maybe I could contact my sister and our dad," he said hopefully

Rhea regarded him with intense pity in her eyes. "Stan is waiting for your call. You two have a lot to catch up on," she said, firmly steering him towards urgent matters, steering him towards his fate.

He sighed. "Maybe not a good idea then?" he asked in an uncharacteristically pleading tone.

She could see, despite his best efforts, he was in shock, so he would need time to think things through and come to terms. It was a small enough comfort, and she knew she could trust him not to freak out and go inviting people to stay. He was trained to be wary. "So where are they? Have you got anywhere to hide them?"

He nodded.

"And you won't be sending anyone who's had vaccinations to an innocent village?"

He smiled sadly. "I'll be very careful, I promise."

"Go on then, but be careful. No matter what, absolutely no one can know about this place. What about your girlfriend?"

She winced, remembering as she said it, why he had been Linda's tenant

"No girlfriend. It didn't work out," he said flatly, before turning toward the computer.

She slapped his outstretched hand before it reached the keys, and handed him his phone. "It's alright, Jal doctored it, remember? It'll give you a chance to chat comfortably."

He gave her an amused grateful smile as he prodded in numbers. She was doing a good job of looking after him, he thought, as he waited for the call to connect.

She tactfully retreated, busying herself connecting up generators and batteries. She was ticking off her tasks, building a dam of virtue to block out thoughts of the oncoming disaster, but she couldn't stop her growing feeling of helplessness and anger.

"I just wasn't looking that's why! And I couldn't take it in even when Jal was telling me! So how could I expect anyone else to take it in?" she moaned to herself guiltily. *'I can't do this. How can I sing an End song when even thinking about it wipes me out? But I promised.'*

A sudden yearning to be back with Jal overtook her. She sighed, memories of their night, the night of the spring festival, suddenly washing through her. "Fairy bells, if we could chime with the energy of love, the Earth would chime right back," she

CHAPTER 17

murmured sadly, *'And Linda would definitely agree with that, with all her chanting.'* She sighed, her thoughts wandering into memories of the Talking to the Earth festival. She'd sang so hopefully with Jal. "All that music. All those prayers. You heard us. I know you heard us." she muttered resentfully under her breath. Now, Linda had said she must leave Earth with Jal, survive and tell the tale of this threatened world.

An Endsong has to be the right kind, the kind of song that could sustain a raggle taggle of survivors across the world. "Oh Jal, help me," she whispered into the dark. *'Chanting?'* she sat up. *'Linda likes chanting. She shall have chanting, and the world will ring with its sound,'* she thought

She settled at the computer and began to draft out a message. She might not know how to do this, but she did know someone who could.

James peered around the door.

"Are they okay? None of them jabbed or anything? Did you get them set up?"

He nodded. "I persuaded them to go to my cousin Gilly's farm for a family celebration. By the time they get there and realise I'm not coming, they won't be able to leave. They'll be okay. Thanks for that." he said, cocking his head in curiosity at the computer. She smiled fondly then looked back at the computer.

"It's just something I have to do."

"To a friend?" he asked.

She shook her head. "Not exactly. It's for Frankie, that singer who does the Earth festivals. Here, have a look; it's only a draft."

"It's more or less what Dr Jal told me, only in arty talk," he said tactfully.

She sighed. There was no point in arguing with him. "She'll be another source of information for you. Keep an eye out for her, won't you?"

She smiled. Musicians. They were the specialists in that arty talk. They were good at reaching the spirit in people. Everyone heeded what they said, even without realising it.

James settled back in the armchair by the stove.

"You're not just a pretty face are you? You've set up quite a neat little centre of operations here."

She grinned. "That was the intention."

"So it's just you and me now," he said, with a hopeful question in his tone.

She dropped her eyes. "You'll be fine. Rowena and a couple of her friends will be here soon."

"Will I see you again?" he asked, his eyes showing a hint of pleading.

She sighed.

"You're going back to Dr Jal," he said, never taking his eyes off her face.

She nodded.

"You could stay, you'll be safe with me," he said hopefully.

"I have to go James. I have to think of Jack. We'll be safe with Jal. Anyway, I have things I must do," she said gently.

He nodded, his eyes more than kindly. "Well, you know how to find me."

She gave him a hug and he hugged her back, then pushed her away. "Go on, just drop me a line, let me know you're okay."

It was the early hours of the morning when Rhea got back to Dream Hills. She made straight for Issn's home. Sure enough, she spotted him lounging at his window.

CHAPTER 17

He invited her in, seeming unsurprised by her visit.

"I need your help," she began as he settled back into his cushions.

He tipped his head in acknowledgement, studying her face with a hint of concern.

"A while ago, I was at a human gathering called "Talking to the Earth"."

She gazed at the peaceable, dreamy Issn and gave a wistful smile. "It's your sort of thing, you know? Folk of all abilities improvising and conversing in music."

"Yes, and the Earth answered," he said, idly picking up a crystal harp.

"You were there?" she gasped.

Issn met her eyes with a hint of a mischievous smile that clouded into concern before giving the harp a very delicate touch.

She brushed off the effect of that soft, haunting note, determined not to be sidetracked.

"Then you've known for a while that something pretty dire is happening in my world."

He tipped his head, his eyes sorrowfully downcast.

"I know music can help. But I'm not a musician. I don't know how to talk to a musician," she said all in a rush.

He gave a soft chuckle. "You're talking to me."

She shrugged her confusion, struggling to put together what she'd learnt, what she now knew, so she could persuade him to help. "Yes, but... Issn, things are really bad. In my world, people are cut off, they can't feel. No, that's not right, they just don't know how to feel, you know? Connected, to their world? They need a way to realise... speak to each other. You know they need it."

He tipped his head, gazing at her with compassionate eyes.

"I want a composition, some music I can hand on, a kind of prayer, to help them face the challenge. I sang at the festival... but it won't be any good."

"May I hear it?" he asked.

She flushed dropping her eyes.

"Please," he insisted gently, turning brilliant, dreamy green eyes on her.

She took a steadying breath and tried a note or two then coughed. "I'll begin in a moment," she said, flustered.

Issn cast his eyes down again, beginning to play. "What do you know?"

She sighed. "What I told you."

He shook his head. "Listen."

She let the music wash through her, play on her emotions, echo with wildness and haunting poignancy, the majestic beauty of her Earth, and the heart rending yearning of the Aazaar to belong, be accepted. Tears of loss ran down her face, tears that she'd held back for so long.

Issn respectfully left her to her grief as he played on.

She heaved a deep sigh, and dried her face. "Yes, that says it. Will you let me share it?" she asked, knowing that this music would get through to Frankie.

Issn considered her pleading eyes.

He finally tipped his head in agreement. "If it will help. Sing, sing what you feel."

This time, she didn't hesitate. Issn drew out of Rhea, the sounds, the story he knew were there until the music became hers.

Later, when she sat at her com, Rhea noted with satisfaction,

CHAPTER 17

the "read" indicator that told her that Frankie, having listened to her music, was now reading her carefully crafted e-mail, which welcomed them to the safety of their network. Jenny would have reassured them Rhea was to be trusted. She wondered how long it would take Frankie to answer.

On first checking out whether this conversation was feasible, she had been relieved to find that Frankie and her little group were safe, miles away from any town or city. Apparently, they'd fled in fear of impending civil breakdown when massive power outages brought troops and rioters onto city streets. She was all too relieved to think, that of all the places for them to end up, they'd found Jenny's bolt hole, another of Linda's Samhain circle. But it made sense. At the festival, Jenny had been so enamoured of Frankie and the band, she'd determinedly found a way to get to speak to them. And Jenny was a self-sufficiency fan of the first order who owned a fine array of green technology, which would have lured the most tech-addicted musician to her hideout, let alone ones who espoused such a green earth ideology as Frankie and her bandmates. Most importantly for Rhea's purposes, Jenny was adept at keeping her computers invisible online, as well as having the capability of keeping them fired up through massive power collapses. She also had the ever alert and gallant Gerrard keeping watch over her small holding.

Rhea waited rather nervously, but it didn't take too long before she received a wary reply.

"The rioting on the streets is terrible, but do you really think we're in this for the long haul?"

Rhea sighed, and sent a question. *"Did you notice anything odd about the rioters?"*

She waited anxiously. The band was in shock. They'd need

careful handling to get them to acknowledge what they had seen, but she didn't have a lot of time.

"*Like what? Apart from the fact they were burning down and wrecking everything they could get their hands on.*"

Rhea hesitated before asking, "*Anything else?*" After about 10 minutes or so, an answer finally came through. She gave a sigh of relief. They'd obviously discussed it, which meant that they were considering the matter. "*Didn't get that close, but they moved strangely, awkwardly. Some of them just started to fall down.*"

Rhea nodded. "Good," she murmured. "*Did you get the emergency inoculations?*" she typed, trying to be as neutral as possible. There was another long pause, during which she sat biting on her lip with tension.

"*No, we haven't been called yet,*" came the answer.

"*The rioters had the inoculations,*" she typed, relieved to find there was a possibility of keeping Frankie and her band safe, for the time being at least. "*That's how this thing is being spread. Now stay as far away as possible from anyone who has had the jabs, preferably at least 10 miles! As for vaccination records, that will be sorted out for you, and a card you'll need to carry. See the example I'm sending you. It'll keep any jobsworths at bay.*"

The promise of official records had solidified her credibility, and the next line of text was far more favourable, even collusive.

"*Wow! Very scary! We're staying in our wilderness hidey hole. We've all avoided vaccines for years. Now you've given us a good reason for our fears. If you can arrange some papers, that'd be great.*"

Rhea bit her lip, tears springing to her eyes again, as she read their next message.

"*Okay, so we're convinced. What do you suggest we do? We'd prefer to do anything rather than just sit here waiting our turn to die or worse.*"

CHAPTER 17

It was clear that she'd propelled the already severely shaken Frankie and her bandmates into a state of such shock they were in danger of sliding into a gloomy helplessness. What could she offer them? Not certain survival, but it was a lifeline of sorts.

"You know how music heals? You can sing from that hidey hole of yours and never be found. Sing, play music. Sing to the Earth, pray to her. Sing and play for all of the people left abandoned out there, those running from this terrible reaping, and those who unleashed it. Sing and play for the animals. Tell their story. But most of all, sing and play about what it is to be part of this Earth, what it is to be human."

"You really have a lot of faith in our abilities!" came the wry reply.

"Extraordinary people for extraordinary situations. And situations don't come any more extraordinary than this." Rhea now felt oddly at peace.

"But it's useless. We're all going to die," Frankie added.

Then, when Rhea began to think she'd never hear from them again, the message alarm chimed.

"But we're not dead yet! Here goes for the biggest farewell performance of all! BTW, that was beautiful. I've heard that instrument before, being played by someone in the tent village at the Talking to the Earth festival. I only heard a snatch, but it has a similar vibe, similar wistfulness. Good call. We should have something ready by tomorrow. Have we got until tomorrow?"

Rhea took a deep breath, tears pricking her eyes, before typing again. *"You're safe for now, as long as you stay away from the cities and mobs. You couldn't do better than Jenny and Gerrard."*

"One more thing. Who are you?" Frankie asked.

Rhea sighed. Who was she to expect Frankie to take heed of her? She hadn't thought of that. Who was she indeed? An insignificant single mother from a council estate on the outskirts of the city? A survivor of a murder attempt who, to the world, was dead? She shook her head. She was the woman who had lost her place on earth allowing her to see and escape, the giant wave that would drown this current unheeding Atlantis. Tears of loss pricked her eyes, and threatened to engulf her.

But just as the first sob escaped her throat and the first fat tear coursed down her cheek, a peaceful vision of a dreamy eyed ape, one of a severely diminished species, gazing bravely into the unknown, crept softly into her mind. She smiled wistfully. "Hello Grandma," she said, letting the image soothe and strengthen her, and she raised her head to consider the unknown that lay ahead of her.

"Oh Jal," she murmured, her heart aching from a different kind of loss.

'2ust Rhea. Rhea of Earth," she finally typed. She mouthed the name, the name Jal had given her, now knowing what she was, seeing into a future when she would tell of a mysterious lost civilisation that had been wiped from history, tell their tale to beings who weren't human, on worlds where her green Earth was nothing more than her wistful tale of what paradise could be.

CHAPTER 18

Jal sighed, sorrowfully looking around the ruined copse that had been Rhea's woodland retreat. Debris had been scattered everywhere, and the shattered trunks of trees lay around at crazy angles. No one would look for him here.

He shuddered as a wave of loss rolled over him, knowing he wouldn't see family or friends again. He had worked side by side with them to keep his little community and his family safe. Now he had to let go, trust he'd done enough. A memory of the tiny chubby Marn, fretting and crying for him when he had been too helpless, too deep in grief to be of use, flashed through his mind. He shook his head sadly at his own present helplessness.

Issn, his dreamy affectionate brother, would always be there for Marn and Jack. They in turn would love him. He smiled, wondering what the curious, lively Jack would make of her first journey into space. Marn would gladly and sensitively care for the little human. He felt a wave of parental admiration and love for his son. He was growing into a strong, compassionate man. He'd seen the beauty in this chaotic, frightening world. He'd also seen enough in the battered Rhea to become fond of her, as well as her daughter, even before she'd recovered, despite him thinking her a member of a frighteningly destructive species.

He looked around and smiled. Rhea's log had survived, and the tree he'd watched her from was miraculously still whole. It was an oddly peaceful spot, considering it was in this now wartorn human city.

He made toward the log, staggered with exhaustion, then managed to catch himself before he fell over. As he sat down, a crow settled in the tree beside him and cawed companionably. "Do you know Vincent?" he asked wistfully as a soft comforting blanket of memories began to wrap around him. The day he'd taken Vincent to visit Rhea, the day he'd first kissed her, and an echo of that first thrill warmed him.

The crow gave an amiable flip of his wings and looked up, cawing to its companions who had begun to settle noisily in the tree, his tree. He was glad of them. He didn't want to be alone.

He fretted that Rhea may not have forgiven him. He admonished himself. Of course she would. How could he doubt her now? She'd just needed time to think, take it all in. A lump formed in his throat. "I'm sorry our time was so short my love," he murmured, and wondered if he could chance contacting her. He shook his head, dismissing his self-pity, feeling so tired, so very dizzy, and slowly slid to the ground. *'I have to do this, protect you,'* he protested. *'I'm sure you know by now I really did try.'*

Finding himself face down, a memory of her gazing happily up at the flittering bats soothed him, and he relaxed, letting go. Giving himself up to the Earth, he breathed in the tang of dead leaves.

"What was it you said my love?" He gave a soft chuckle of affection. "You said that it's easy to love the Earth when she's bright and green with spring. But the real trial is loving her when she's wild, dark and deadly."

CHAPTER 18

Something landed on him and began tugging at his clothes, his hair. He opened an eye, and came face to face with an excited crow.

"Vincent," he murmured, and attempted to raise his hand in salute, but it just flopped.

"I can't come with you. I can't throw off this illness. I'll be dangerous," he murmured, "I've got to go. Let me sleep." He wondered if there was any way the bird could take a message to Galer. What would he say? You were always my good friend? There was nothing greater he could say.

The bird stayed on his shoulder, cawing softly to him. A curious feeling of serenity took him over. Soon, he would give back to the Earth what his body had borrowed. But he'd been granted something precious, drawn in by his love, to feel through the heart of a child of this Earth. Trees, birds, stones, he could feel them, feel the scamper of little creatures in the undergrowth, feel the trees and weeds, feel in his very cells, a deep, primeval connection. He belonged. His slowing heart gave one last little patter of bittersweet joy. He belonged! He heard a rustling, felt something very light land on him, then a shower of light rustlings, as the crows took turns to drop leaves over him. He tried to smile.

Vincent cocked his head as if he'd understood, then let out a single caw before flying up onto a low branch. The other crows continued their task, and soon, all there was to see, was a heap of dead leaves. He gave silent thanks to these crows, these creatures of Earth who had come to accept him into their planet's circle of being.

"You brought me home, Rhea. Your Earth is taking me as one of her own."

Printed in Great Britain
by Amazon